I Love You,
Sunday Sunset

I LOVE YOU, SUNDAY SUNSET

Paperback ISBN: 979-8-9883810-9-9
Ebook ISBN: 979-8-9883810-8-2

Printed in 2025

Published in the United States of America

By Brandbureau Consulting LLC
Cheyenne, WY 82001

Cover design by Aina Robeniol

For Carlos, Luis and Julia

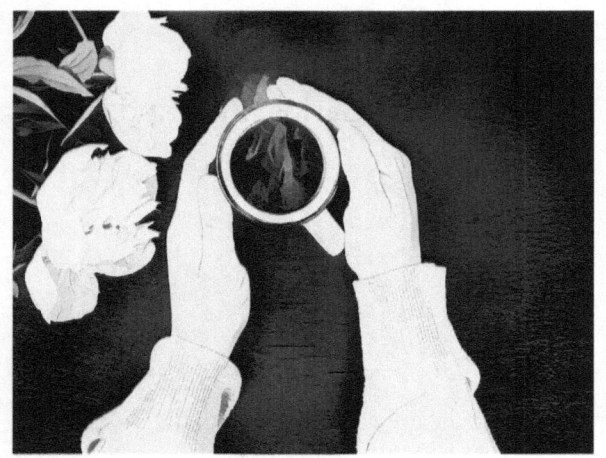

Spotify Reading Playlist

PART ONE

*"You've been my light in every darkness, Sara.
Every moment with you has been worth more than
a thousand lifetimes anywhere else."*

- HECK

1

I Love You, Sunday Sunset.

I typed the words onto the manuscript's blank page, each keystroke breaking the silence like a measured heartbeat. They felt inevitable, as though they were always meant to find their way here—not just to the story, but to a part of me. The title wasn't just formed words; it was a promise, a fragment of a memory, or maybe something hoped for. It had taken months to reveal itself, and now that it had, it felt as though the entire piece had been waiting for this moment to breathe. From my seat by the frosted glass window, I caught sight of the world outside.

New York City glittered like a snow globe come to life. Twinkling fairy lights draped the leafless trees lining the streets, their glow reflected on wet pavement kissed by a light snowfall. A chorus of holiday cheer filled the air, with vendors hawking roasted chestnuts from steaming carts and carolers singing in perfect harmony on the sidewalk. The city was alive at night with the magic of Christmas—dazzling store displays, bustling crowds bundled in knit scarves and woolen coats, and the scent of pine mingling with the crisp winter air.

But inside this cozy haven, the world felt smaller, quieter. I slipped my hands into the roomy pockets of my worn-out gray NYU varsity hoodie, letting its soft fabric warm my chilled fingers. I drew a deep, steadying breath.

"Here's your latte, Sara. Decaf, as you requested," Lily's cheerful lilt interrupted my thoughts as she placed the steaming mug in front of me alongside two chocolate chip mint cookies arranged on a Santa hat plate. The scent of espresso mingled with the sweetness of melted chocolate, wrapping around me like a warm hug. She cocked her head toward my laptop screen, curiosity sparking in her brown eyes. "I Love You, Sunday Sunset, huh?"

"Thank you," I replied, offering her a small smile. "Yep, that's the title for my manuscript. Finally found the one that feels right."

"Well, it sounds dreamy," Lily replied with an approving nod. "I'll leave you to it, then. Just holler if you need anything." She winked before spinning off toward the hum and bustle of the café.

I watched her go, her curly hair neatly braided and topped with a green bandana that matched the coffee cup stamped on her black apron. She glanced back once more and flashed me a wide smile that could brighten any room. Lily was woven into the fabric of our story— Heck's and mine.

Oh, Heck, the man who somehow turned my very ordinary life upside down. To the world, Hector Archibald IV was New York royalty, the twenty-eight-year-old heir to a sprawling banking empire. The tabloids called him Manhattan's most eligible bachelor and a socialite's best catch, plastering his glossy photos in headlines about gala dinners and sleek, black cars. But to me, he was something else entirely. He was an old soul with a deep dive for music and poetry, a contrast to the flashy narratives of the tabloids. The man who made me laugh at ridiculous things. The man who remembered café orders after our very first meeting. The man who made choosing me—a nobody in Manhattan's grand design—feel like the easiest, most natural decision in the world.

Except, I wasn't sure I believed it. I caught my reflection in the fogged café window, the glass distorting my features into vague shapes. Even on good days, I found it hard to see the beauty others insisted I possessed. My hazel eyes, large and doe-like, were my saving grace. The rest? Unremarkable. Brown hair that never did what I wanted, brushing against shoulders crowned by messy bangs that defied every attempt to style them. At five foot seven, I was tall enough to stand out, yet I never felt like I did, especially not next to the leggy, magazine-cover blondes who seemed to belong in Heck's world.

And yet, he chose me—Sara Emily Miller, a twenty-five-year-old copywriter and nobody extraordinaire. How? How does a guy like Heck, with his perfectly untouchable charisma, fall for someone like me? It didn't make sense. This wasn't supposed to be my story.

But it was.

And today, in this little café filled with the low buzz of conversation, the soothing hiss of milk steaming in pitchers, and Lily's bright voice calling out orders, I attempted to piece together the next chapter of my half-written manuscript. My life with Heck already felt like a story I wasn't entirely sure I believed. Living it thrilled me, terrified me, and left me endlessly wondering what came next.

I glanced around. Tribeca Trickle was still the same as when Heck and I first met. This hidden gem was tucked away in the heart of New York City, between East 76th and 2nd Avenue. The interior was a harmonious blend of rustic and modern aesthetics. Exposed brick walls, painted a soft cream, contrasted beautifully with the green and red Christmas decorations and dark mahogany tables scattered throughout the room. A long, cushioned bench lined one wall, filled with an assortment of Santa throw pillows. The opposite wall featured a large chalkboard menu adorned in whimsical, looping cursive.

The atmosphere inside was welcoming and warm, a stark contrast to the white snow and gray skies just beyond the windows. The usual soft indie music had given way to classical melodies, punctuated by the occasional clink of coffee cups and the low murmur of patrons. This café wasn't just a place to grab coffee; it was a sanctuary for those seeking refuge from the chill outside.

This place, our cherished haunt, overflowed with memories. Sometimes, those memories were painful, yet they offered a peculiar comfort. It was the closest I could come to feeling Heck's presence.

A month had passed since I returned to the hollow shell of what used to be our home. Heck was gone—just as I had asked him to be. Ours was always a tangled, messy love, born in the shadow of his unraveling marriage. It was wrong, undeniably so, and I had no moral foundation to excuse what we had become. When the news broke that Sophie, his wife, was pregnant, reality collapsed in on itself. I couldn't ignore it. I wanted Heck to make the right decision, even if it meant losing him. Asking him to leave felt like my only act of grace—if that's even what it could be called.

I told him to work things out without me. I knew, with me there, he couldn't think clearly. And I couldn't live with the weight of him making a mistake he might regret forever. The night he left, I cried until my body felt hollow, until my tear-streaked face burned, and my eyes turned raw. The heartbreak didn't feel poetic or noble; it felt brutal, like something had clawed its way out of me, leaving behind a deep, pulsing ache.

Every corner of the house pulsed with his absence, mocking me with its silence. I still caught the vague, lingering notes of his aftershave hanging in the bathroom air—sharp and clean, like a ghost clinging to the edges of reality. His fingerprints remained smudged on the mirror, remnants of a presence that felt both impossibly close and infinitely far away. I missed him in ways I couldn't articulate, a loss so visceral it was like a phantom limb reaching for something no longer there. The ache tore deeper than I thought my heart could bear, settling into a grief that refused to fade no matter how much I willed it to.

This café—our place—was the only solace I could find when missing him became unbearable. It was where it had all begun, on a night that felt both accidental and fated.

I closed my eyes, letting the memory spill over me, trying to relive that night, and trace its details. Some of it blurred at the edges, but the feeling stayed sharp, and vivid. It was as though I was trying to map my dreams against the fragile outline of reality, a bittersweet dance between what was and what I desperately wished could still be. The café's low hum surrounded me, a familiar lullaby grounding me even as my thoughts drifted back to him.

"Is this extra seat taken?"

The voice came smoothly, a serene ripple breaking through the soundscape of the café. I looked up, my gaze meeting a striking

5

silhouette framed against the warm glow of the lights. He gestured toward the empty chair opposite me with a casual ease, exuding a natural confidence, as though he inherently belonged wherever he chose to be.

He was tall–six feet two inches, at least. His presence filled the space effortlessly. Tousled hair fell across his forehead, and a soft shadow of stubble graced his jaw, giving him the air of someone who lived by his own rules, unfettered by society's constraints. His worn jeans and gray T-shirt clung to him with the familiarity of an old friend, less an outfit and more an extension of the man himself, every thread narrating its own story of comfort and authenticity.

"Go ahead," I murmured, my voice soft, yet somehow clear amidst the café's gentle din.

He took the seat opposite me with practiced charm, an easy warmth radiating from his smile. "Just so we're not strangers—I'm Heck," he offered, extending a hand with the same openness reflected in his grin.

A simple exchange of names turned into something more—a spark that transformed the ordinary into the extraordinary.

And as the weeks passed, we found ourselves meeting here again and again, whether by chance or through some unspoken design. Over *brinner*— a word coined by Heck, which meant breakfast food for dinner—we shared our favorite films, TV series, music, and the half-formed dreams we clung to. He had a fiancée, Sophie, one of New York's reigning socialites. I had Matt, the boyfriend I'd been slowly growing apart from. For months, we were simply Sara and Heck. No full names, no numbers exchanged, no glimpses into worlds beyond the café. We just appeared at the same table, as though guided by some invisible clockwork of destiny.

Heck and I talked about our lives over stacks of pancakes, strawberries, and bacon—exchanging dreams as if they were secrets no one else could understand. Heck spoke of expanding his art gallery, and, to my surprise, he shyly mentioned dabbling in poetry. I shared my own secret yearning—to leave behind the comfortable monotony of copywriting and write a novel, an enduring story I could call my own. Each dream shared between us felt like a secret, made sacred in the quiet warmth of our conversations. His encouragement was boundless, urging me to chase what mattered. Go to Paris, he'd said more than once. *Walk where Hemingway walked. Find your own Gertrude Stein. Be bold.*

This café became more than a meeting place. It was a world of its own, a sanctuary for our ambitions, and a quiet witness to the fragile, unspoken pull growing between us. I began to notice how his presence started filling spaces in my life in ways I couldn't name, a connection that felt both impossible and inevitable.

And then Matt and I broke apart. Our love had long been a frayed thread, unraveling even before Heck entered the frame. Packing my life into suitcases, I left New York behind, along with the café, and Heck. I told myself Paris was a chance to start over, a blank page for my untold story. But if I were honest, I wasn't just running toward a dream; I was running away from something too terrifying to face.

Living in Paris was beautiful, if uneven. I swapped my relentless office job for the steady rhythm of a worn espresso machine at Café Boheme, a small café nestled in Edgar Quinet, just a short distance from my rented one-bedroom apartment. The café became my world, a quiet job carried out with French phrases that felt uncomfortable on my tongue, but with a humility I began to cherish. My evenings were spent in my tiny apartment, learning to live simply. I fell briefly into the affections of a charming man named Gabriel and made unexpected friendships with my much older neighbors—it was my version of 'Juliet-Dawsey-Isola-Amelia-Eben' from my favorite novel, *The Guernsey Literary and Potato Peel Society*. I struggled to learn French and perfected the delicate art of making lattes. It was a patchwork life, far removed from Manhattan's skyscraper enormities, but perhaps richer for its simplicity.

The best part, though, was the unhurried rhythm of it all—so far removed from the relentless corporate rat race I had left behind in New York City. Paris felt like stepping into a living painting, a canvas awash with color, texture, and light. Each day, the city shifted effortlessly—from cozy outdoor cafés basking in daylight to lively, buzzing pubs as night fell. Slowly, I allowed myself to forget New York and the life I had left behind. That was, until one afternoon, when I wandered into Shakespeare and Company to shop for books—and there he was. Heck. Standing outside the café beside the bookstore, looking at me with that grin that drove me crazy.

If my life were a romantic drama, my time with Heck in Paris would have been the chapters I pressed flowers into, the ones I'd reread until the pages wore thin. It felt like the perfect love story. I spent my days writing while he sketched the world as he saw it, and together, we made love in the most unexpected corners of the city. I knew he was still married, but in those moments, I didn't care. I was in love. We were in love. And for a time, we were happy—lost in the illusion that this could last forever.

But like any good story, ours had to end. Heck stood at a crossroads, torn between the life he yearned for and the one he had been born into. That was when I learned the truth—I hadn't just fallen for an artist with a troubled heart. Heck was rich. Not just wealthy, but the heir to New York's largest banking empire—a world far removed from the life we had created in Paris.

He didn't want the gilded cage that came with his legacy. He tried to chase a different dream, to grow in the arts. But duty called, and he couldn't ignore it forever.

His life was never as simple as mine. For Heck, it wasn't a matter of choice—his path had been set in stone from the moment he was born. And yet, somehow, we found a way to make it work for a while. What unfolded between Paris and our inevitable return to New York was a dream I didn't want to wake from—a story I thought we could write together. It was everything I had hoped for, until it wasn't.

Now, here I am again, back where it all started. Sitting alone in this café, caught between daydreams and reality. The endless dance of 'what if' and 'what should be.' This time, though, the scales tip more toward the latter. I've been piecing my life back together bit by bit, trying to create something whole again.

Returning to work at Milliford & Associates as a copywriter felt like slipping into an old but familiar coat. Kelly, my boss—dubbed the 'Ice

Queen' for good reason—welcomed me back with her usual frosty poker face. Still, I could tell she was glad to see me. My friends, Andi from accounts and Alexi from the art department (the self-proclaimed heartthrob who somehow balanced flamboyance with charm) were overjoyed. The trio we once were, bonded by endless laughter and overdramatic mornings, began rekindling our coffee ritual: gossip, caffeine, and inevitable complaints about office dramas.

But something had shifted. Those first few days, I couldn't bring myself to care the way I used to. Paris had altered me. Heck had transformed me. I wasn't the same perpetually disgruntled Sara who railed against the universe for its injustices. Somewhere along the way, I realized the truth: the world doesn't revolve around us or our grievances. It spins on, consumed by crises far greater than our discontent.

The thought brought both relief and a quiet sadness. Perhaps that's what growing feels like—not abandoning the past, but learning how to carry it differently.

Now, I found myself relating more than ever to Kelly's approach— prioritizing tasks and ensuring they were completed by the day's end. The world wasn't idly waiting for us; we needed to keep pace or risk being left behind. So, I poured my heart and soul into my nine-to-five job. Then, I spent my evenings writing. Occasionally, I wrote here at my favorite spot, particularly when the memories of Heck within our apartment became too overwhelming. But wasn't this place just as haunted? It reminded me of him. Yet, where else could I go?

I made a point to abstain from attending meetings with Gold Standard Bank, owned by Heck's family and Milliford's top client. The last I heard from Alexi, Heck was attending those meetings. Before we parted ways, Heck and I had made a pact to meet once he had sorted out his complications. There were moments when I was tempted to call him, to ask him to return. But I knew Heck would abandon everything to rush back to me, compromising his ability to make an unbiased decision. Yet, every single day, every minute, every second, my thoughts invariably drifted back to him.

And this morning, the unexpected happened. I wasn't ready. How could anyone be prepared for something that would change their life irreversibly? Yet, in the middle of the shock, it gave me something—a thread to hold onto, anchor myself, and move forward.

When I woke, something felt... off. The air seemed heavier, clinging to my skin like a damp sheet, and a strange nausea churned low in my stomach. The familiar scent of bagels baking from Betty's Baked Goods, the bakery down the street, drifted through the air. Once, it had been a comfort, warm and inviting. Now, it clawed at me, sharp and cloying, turning my stomach as if the world itself had soured.

A quiet unease crept through me, crawling just beneath the surface, nibbling at the fragile edges of my awareness. It wasn't missing Heck —not this time. I knew that grief well; its weight was an old companion by now. But this... this was different. I felt unmoored, as if something crucial had shifted while I wasn't looking, leaving me out of balance and out of tune with myself. My body, my senses, my very being seemed to exist just enough to remind me of what didn't feel right. A ripple of disorientation passed through me, faint but unsettling, and I couldn't shake the uneasiness it left behind. It lingered, unwelcome and unrelenting, whispering that something had changed, though I couldn't yet name what.

I reached into my vanity drawer for paracetamol, assuming it might just be a headache. But as I shuffled through the contents, my eyes fixed on something that made the room tilt and my breath hitch. My Tampax box was untouched. Weeks had passed.

Two weeks.

A cold wave of realization surged through me, prickling my skin as nausea tightened its grip on my stomach. My legs carried me to the bathroom before I had time to think. I yanked open the cabinet, my hands frantically searching until I found it—the pregnancy test I'd shoved in the back months ago, as if denying its existence could somehow spare me this moment.

My hands trembled as I unboxed the test, the plastic stick cold and alien in my grip.

The bathroom blurred around me, shrinking to just this tiny, impossible object lying across my palm. My chest tightened, each breath shallow, my mind racing with everything this could mean.

I meticulously followed the instructions, setting the test down on the sink afterward. The wait for the result was torturous, each second dragging by at an agonizingly slow pace. I paced the confined space, a tempest of emotions raging within me—fear, hope, desperation.

Finally, I dared to glance at the test. Two red lines stared back at me.

Positive.

Pregnant.

The revelation rooted me to the spot. The shock froze me in place, and then a tidal wave of emotions swept over me—joy, anxiety, confusion, relief. I was going to have a baby. Heck's baby. A piece of him would always be with me. Should I tell him? Or should I withhold the news until he returned—if he ever returned? The prospect of single-handedly raising our child loomed dauntingly large.

I collapsed onto the floor, the positive test clenched tightly in my trembling hand. Tears and laughter tumbled out in chaotic harmony. My life had veered onto an uncharted path, one that felt equal parts terrifying, exhilarating, and impossible. But one thing was certain: I was not alone. I carried a piece of Heck within me, and that made everything seem a little less terrifying.

Steadying myself, I rose and splashed cold water on my face, letting its sharp edge pull me back to the present. "You can do this, Sara," I murmured, meeting my own gaze in the mirror. The woman staring back looked different—stronger, more resolute than I'd ever seen her. There was clarity in her eyes, the kind of boldness that comes when someone decides to stand and face their fears.

I grabbed a white towel from the rack and blotted my face. A fresh determination settled deep into my bones as I fixed my hair and added a swipe of lip gloss. "I'm ready," I said, the words a quiet promise to the reflection watching me.

Without hesitation, I stepped out of the bathroom, my heart pounding with each step as I made my way toward the place where everything had begun. Tribeca Trickle.

And so, here I am, doing the one thing I know best—writing. *I Love You Sunday Sunset* was a poem by Heck, one I'd had the privilege of helping him publish in *The New York Times*. It had been a parting gift, timed just before my departure to Paris. Now, I've adopted both its title and concept for my novel, a personal tribute to Heck and me. I labored over this untitled work for months, only to halt abruptly when Heck left my life.

Today, however, marked a change. I reopened my manuscript, intending to pick up where I'd left off. Yet, the words proved elusive— slippery and distant, as if they had grown cautious of me in my absence. Even forming a single coherent sentence felt like an insurmountable task. I remembered how Heck once curated playlists to pull me out of these creative ruts. Fishing my AirPods from my bag, I slipped them in and scrolled through the collection of melodies we had once carefully assembled. The familiar chords of Remy Zero's *Fair* poured into my ears like an old companion. Closing my eyes, I rested one hand on my stomach, warm with the knowledge of the life quietly growing within me. "We're going to be okay, sweetheart," I murmured, and with a steadying breath, I began to write again.

The pain still lingered. It was always there, coiled tightly in the edges of my heart whenever I thought of him. But so, too, was the joy—those radiant, fleeting moments we had shared. They swirled together, bittersweet, with every sip of my cooling latte. This corner of the café, once ours, now belonged to my solitude. Yet here, surrounded by the echoes of our laughter and the ghosts of our whispered dreams, I felt something I hadn't expected—tranquility. Each word I typed became more than just a fragment of a sentence in a novel; it was a piece of us, a testament to the love we had created and the loss that had remade me.

I wrote until the foam in my latte had long dissolved and the cookies were cleared from my plate. Time blurred, unnoticed, as the café began to hum with the rise of chatter and the clinking of cups. Voices melded with the shuffle of baristas fulfilling orders, but I stayed firmly planted in my own little world, protected by the stories spilling out of me, sentence by sentence.

Then, out of nowhere, a shadow fell across my space. I looked up, momentarily startled. And there he was. Those cerulean eyes met mine.

His hair was an unruly tumble of waves, as if he'd only just rolled out of bed. The shadow of stubble on his jawline hinted at days without a razor. But it wasn't his usual worn jeans or his snug, lived-in T-shirts I saw this time. Instead, he stood draped in a charcoal grey suit, the tailoring impeccable, a crisp white shirt beneath it accentuating his frame. The transformation was startling. It sharpened every detail.

And then, he smiled. That smile—devastating and magnetic, the kind that could shatter darkness with light. It hooked me by the heart, pulling everything I had meticulously put back together into chaos. It had been a while, yet it felt like no time had passed. That smile held the power to make me forget the aching bruises I thought had healed.

He stood there, utterly composed, as my entire world shook.

2

"Hello, Pender. Is this seat taken?" His voice—so achingly familiar—cut through the ambient noise of the café, threading itself directly into my thoughts. For a moment, everything else faded. I looked up, and there he was. Heck. That disarming smile. Those cerulean eyes, restless and unrestrained, like the sea under stormy skies. My breath hitched. My words tangled in a knot of emotions, refusing to surface.

He chuckled, a sound as warm as sunlight breaking through clouds. "This is where you're supposed to say, 'Go ahead.'"

"Heck..." I stammered, tugging the AirPods from my ears as the weight of reality crashed in. He was here. Right in front of me. "What are you doing here?" My voice splintered on the question, as if saying it out loud might make him vanish. But he didn't. He was still here. Real. And real was dangerous. Real meant unraveling.

I realized he was still standing. Forcing myself to focus, I grounded my thoughts as his presence loomed. "I'm sorry," I murmured, catching myself. My hand gestured weakly toward the chair across from me. "Please, sit."

The invitation felt small, almost meaningless, against the tempest swirling in his eyes. Those eyes. They hollowed me out, laying bare everything I wasn't ready to face. My hands curled into fists under the table, nails pressing crescents into my palms. I had to keep them there, fighting the aching urge to reach out and bridge the gap between us.

He smirked faintly, though the edges of it didn't quite reach his eyes. "Clearing my head," he said, his gaze holding mine with startling intensity. "I drove here, hoping... hoping to find you."

I froze, caught in the quiet plea that hung between us. "We're not supposed to meet, Heck," I murmured, the words more for myself than for him. They were a futile reminder of the boundaries we had drawn—boundaries now dissolved by his presence.

"I know." His voice softened, cracking at the edges. "But I had to see you. I needed to. You have no idea how much." Vulnerability bled through his tone, his practiced smile faltering to reveal the raw ache he rarely showed. It pulled at something deep within me—a part I was so sure someone had sewn shut.

He sat down across from me, the motion slow, almost reverent, as though afraid his presence might shatter the fragile calm I'd created in this corner of the café. A silence stretched between us, heavy with the ghosts of unsaid words and unhealed wounds. I resisted the urge to reach out, to bridge the physical distance between us. The ache was almost unbearable—the longing to press my head against his shoulder, to breathe in the familiar scent of him, and pretend, for just a heartbeat, that we hadn't broken apart. That everything could still be undone.

Instead, I stayed locked in place, my fingertips brushing the thin edge of reality, resisting the relentless pull of what we used to be. The ghosts of our past pressed in, heavy and suffocating, stealing the air from my lungs. He was here. I was here. And in this brittle sliver of time, our worlds collided once more, trembling under the weight of all we had tried to leave behind.

Heck leaned forward, his elbows resting on the table, his gaze steady and intent. "I've missed you, Pender," he confessed softly, the weight of his words hanging in the air between us. Some called each other 'babe,' 'darling,' or 'love.' Heck and I were always 'Pender' to each other—the name of the character Gil Pender from our favorite film, *Midnight in Paris*.

I swallowed hard, feeling my heart race. "I've missed you too," I admitted, my voice a whisper of vulnerability. "But we can't go back to what we were. Not yet. You need to figure things out with Sophie... and you're having a child, Heck." The last word felt heavy, almost choking me. I resisted the urge to touch my belly—a secret I held close.

A shadow of pain flickered across his face, and I saw the sorrow in his eyes. "I know," he said, his voice barely holding together. "But I can't help but hope... hope that, somehow, we can find a way to be together again. That we'll figure this out together."

I looked away, out the window where life continued, oblivious to our silent storm. "There's something you should know," I ventured, my heart pounding louder than my voice.

Heck's eyes widened with a mix of anticipation and fear. "What is it?"

I froze, my hand reflexively moving toward my stomach before I caught myself and clasped it tightly in my lap. I wanted to tell him. The words were on the tip of my tongue, yet I feared the consequences. If I told him, would it shatter whatever fragile balance he'd found? He might use it as a reason to walk away from his obligations, and Sophie would fight for him fiercely. The thought stopped me cold. Drawing in a steadying breath, I forced myself to take another path, steering the conversation elsewhere.

"I went back to my old job," I said, my voice low but firm. "I'm working on your bank's communications now. Part of the team managing your advertising and PR."

His hand reached across the table, warm and steady as it covered mine. "I know," he murmured, his thumb brushing against my knuckles. "Alexi mentioned it. He also said you asked not to be in any meetings if I would be there." His voice dipped at those last words, strained.

I pulled my hand back, the loss of his touch almost unbearable, but necessary. "I can't, Heck. We can't keep doing this," I said, the weight of the truth pressing down on me like an unending tide. My voice didn't waver, even as my chest tightened with its ache.

He looked at me, his gaze stripped bare, raw in a way that left me defenseless. "Can we at least try to work together?" he asked, his voice laced with desperation that cut straight through me. "I need someone I can trust. I'm barely keeping my head above water here."

Then his hand closed over mine again—not timid, not hesitant, but with a weighted grip that spoke of someone clinging to the edge, terrified of slipping. "Please," he whispered, the word trembling in the space between us. It wasn't just a request; it was an anchor, thrown out in one last bid for stability.

The plea hung in the air, heavy with unspoken layers I wasn't ready to unfold. I nodded—more reflex than decision—my heart pounding an uneven rhythm against the stillness that followed. It was an agreement, but a fragile one. Beneath it, the truth waited, unbroken and unrelenting, biding its time until we could finally bear to face it.

"I've moved back in with my parents. Temporary, of course. Never thought I'd do that again," he said with a dry chuckle, clearly trying to lighten the mood.

"Your mother must be thrilled to have you home," I replied, a small smile tugging at the corners of my lips.

"Yeah, she is," he said, flashing that boyish grin—the one that always had a way of unraveling me. "She likes you, you know." Almost without thought, our hands found each other, slipping into the familiar rhythm of thumb-wrestling, just like we used to.

"I like her too," I said, my smile softening. "She's so elegant and kind. I love the way she talks about you and all those stories she tells. She truly loves you, Heck."

His laugh came quieter this time, touched by something deeper. "I appreciate her now more than I used to." He paused, the faintest shadow tipping the edge of his smile. "Ahhh! She's doting on Zaldy now. They really hit it off at the gallery."

I laughed, shaking my head. "Of course, they did. How are you managing everything, though? The new role? The weight of it all?"

17

"It's a lot," he admitted, running a hand through his hair, ruffling it the way I remembered he did when he felt overwhelmed. "I'm going through management training for bank operations. At the same time, I'm leading Advertising and Communications." His face split into a sheepish grin, and he added with a wink, "Which is exactly why I need you."

"Well, you're in good hands then. Kelly and the team are amazing," I said, a note of pride in my voice.

"I've heard my supposed copywriter is top-notch," he teased.

"Obviously!" I shot back, feigning offense. Playful banter drifted between us, light and easy, slipping into place like a long-forgotten habit.

Then his voice softened. "Sara..." The way he said my name, so quiet and measured, reached out and pulled me from the whirlpool of my mind. His hand stopped thumb-wrestling with mine, instead holding it steady, as if tethering us both to something fragile but real. "Things will work out soon. The lawyers are handling the child support... if the child is mine. Sophie can keep the apartment. We could always look for something closer to my parents. Mom's been saying she wants us nearby."

His words hung heavy with restless hope, a glimmer of possibility lighting up the uncertain void between us. I managed a smile, though it felt like a fragile mask over the storm inside me. Joy flickered at the thought of what could be, but it was undercut by the raw tension of everything left unresolved. My voice wavered, quiet but firm enough to steady the moment. "Until then... can we just be friends?"

For a moment, he said nothing; he just studied me with a kind of painful sincerity that made my heart ache. Then he nodded, his grip on my hand tightening briefly before releasing. "I'll take whatever I can, Sara. Even if all I can do is love you from a distance. It's better than not having you at all."

I swallowed hard, but my voice steadied as I asked, "So, friends?"

"Yeah," he said, his lips pressing into a thin but tender smile. "Friends." It was a promise, though we both knew it might not be one we could keep.

3

I stepped into my apartment, the soft click of the door shutting behind me, slicing through the quiet night. The cold lingered like a shadow, clinging to the edges of my scarf and coat, trailing me inside. Heck had offered to give me a ride home, but I'd declined with a small smile, leaving him where we always parted—outside the café, beneath the golden glow of the street lamps.

Snow fell in gentle whispers, tiny fragments of stardust drifting down from the heavens. Each flake caught the light, flashing briefly before melting into the growing blanket on the ground. The world seemed hushed, wrapped in the intimacy of winter's lull, as if even time itself held its breath.

"Gnight, Sara," Heck had said softly, his voice warm enough to push back the edges of the cold. His hands were tucked into the pockets of his dark overcoat, a line of warmth against the frozen backdrop.

"'Night, Heck," I replied, my breath forming faint clouds in the frosty air. My trusty winter jacket layered over my hoodie did little against the chill, which seeped through the fabric to nip at my skin.

We used to say goodbye like that, lingering just a moment longer outside the café—our spot. It had been so long since we'd done it. The ritual felt like a memory almost forgotten.

We turned then, moving silently in our separate directions. The crunch of my boots on the snow-packed sidewalk filled the space where words wouldn't. A part of me wanted to glance back, just once. But I didn't. Instead, I kept walking, my eyes fixed on the path ahead.

Still, I felt it—that presence. The weight of his gaze lingered, as if it had a warmth of its own. I could almost see it behind me without looking —a tall silhouette framed by the glow of the lamp posts, his breath visible in the icy air, standing still, watching. For a fleeting moment, the world felt suspended, like some unspoken connection tethered us under the falling stars.

I flagged down a yellow cab, hurriedly sank into the backseat, and instructed the driver to head to my apartment building at 89th Street. I closed my eyes, drawing in a deep breath, trying to steady myself and push the weight of the evening to the edges of my mind. But the effort was futile. The memories crept in regardless, unraveling like a reel of old film I had no power to halt. The drive passed in a blur, and before long, we pulled up in front of my apartment building. This place... it carried too much of my past.

There was a time when I lived on the seventh floor, crammed into a rundown one-bedroom apartment with my ex-boyfriend, Matt. Thinking back, it's hard to understand how we even ended up together. Matt was the polar opposite of me in so many ways. Every corner of his life was measured, precise, like the ticking of a Swiss clock. He woke at 5 A.M. without fail, followed by a punishing workout and an elaborate skincare regimen I could never hope to rival. His world was anchored in schedules and plans, every detail preordained and polished.

And then there was me, far more invested in the unpredictable realm of words than in routines. Writing was my passion, my lifeline, but Matt never saw it that way. To him, it was a pipe dream, a whimsical notion that had no place in a "proper" life. What I really needed, he'd say, was a decent, dependable job. Passion, in his eyes, was nothing more than a corporate fairytale spun to distract people like me from sensible ambitions.

I tried to ignore it, to shrug off the sting of his dismissiveness, but his words lingered, pressing on the edges of my dreams like a weight I couldn't shake. For Matt, life was about stability, structure, and playing it safe. For me, life was about chasing stories and finding meaning somewhere between reality and imagination. Looking back, I suppose we were bound to falter, as mismatched as stray puzzle pieces from two entirely different sets.

I remember the walls—cracked and crumbling, with paint peeling in uneven, jagged patches. During winters, the heating barely sputtered to life, leaving us bundled in layers to fight off the biting cold. The charm was there, somewhere—in the grit, perhaps, or the defiant spirit of its tenants. Still, it had its downsides, like the inevitable encounters with rats and cockroaches that felt almost obligatory for New York City living.

Everything shifted in an instant. Hope Williams, a neighbor and dear friend to both Veronica and me, unearthed a family secret no one could have predicted. She discovered she was the unexpected heir to a vast real estate empire. The revelation didn't just upend her life; it reshaped ours as well. Newly empowered by her inheritance, Hope bought the building, pouring fresh life into a place that had once seemed irreparably broken.

What followed was nothing short of extraordinary. The renovations were stunning, reimagining the dilapidated structure into a sleek, modern sanctuary. The cracked walls gave way to smooth finishes; reliable heating replaced the old, clunky pipes. The place became unrecognizable in the best way possible. Suddenly, this shabby corner of the city turned into a coveted residence, a beacon along 80th Street. And as much as the change felt surreal, it was hard to forget what it had been before—how we had survived in its imperfection. That memory lingered, wrapped in the echoes of what once was.

It was through Hope's generosity that I found the courage to move to Paris when I desperately needed to escape—from Matt, from the chaos, and eventually, even from Heck. She gave me an out when I couldn't find one on my own, and somehow, in helping me run, she also gave me the space to begin finding my way back.

When Heck and I returned from Paris, he bought this two-bedroom flat for us. It was his way of giving us a fresh start, a place to rebuild while grounding me in the familiar city that had shaped me. This building, these neighbors… they were the closest thing I had to family. The Sungs—Charlie and his daughter, Veronica—were my Asian neighbors who owned the charming floral shop on the ground floor. They always looked out for Hope and me during the days when we struggled to scrape together rent. Charlie had a knack for knowing when we were running on fumes, both financially and nutritionally. He'd show up with food, often without a word, because he knew our dinners usually came from a hotdog cart or the donut shop on the corner.

When I told Heck we needed to separate so he could focus on working through his issues with Sophie, he didn't hesitate to leave the flat to me. He knew I couldn't afford to start over somewhere new, and this was his way of making sure I had a sense of stability, even as everything between us was falling apart.

Heck moved out and settled into his gallery, *Entre Nous*—a name that forever lingered in my mind. It meant "between the two of us" in French, a fitting name for the space where he'd poured so much of himself.

The gallery sat at the heart of the Lower East Side, a lively corner of the city where art and grit came alive in an unpredictable dance. From there, Heck settled into his own apartment just a short walk away, carving out his own pocket of the world while leaving this one for me. He had moved back to the Archibald Mansion, a decision I hadn't anticipated, but one I was relieved he made.

And so, this place became mine. Our nest, once alive with shared laughter and whispered dreams, now held quieter echoes. The memories lived within the warm, earthy tones of the walls, offering a strange comfort. Even in its silence, it felt like a steady anchor in the drift of change. It cradled both the bittersweet weight of what was and the quiet hope of what could still be.

The living room remained much the same—a comfortably worn yellow sofa facing the fireplace where photographs once filled the mantel. Now, only one photo remained: a candid snapshot of Heck and me taken during a sunlit afternoon at the Alexander Pope Bridge in Paris. When I took down all the framed photographs, I couldn't bring myself to remove it, so it stayed. I paused there for a moment, tracing the edges of that memory before drifting into the kitchen, where the faint aroma of morning coffee still lingered. Though he was gone, his presence lingered here—in the walls of this apartment, in the echoes of laughter we once shared, and in the silence that had come to fill its place.

As I replayed the day's events in my mind, a wave of relief swept over me for having held back the truth about my pregnancy from Heck. I had been so close to revealing it, knowing he wouldn't let me handle this alone. Part of me longed to have Heck on my side—so desperately. But this time, I wanted a real happy ending—the kind where we could truly say, *and we lived happily ever after.* If Sophie were to find out, she'd fight fiercely for her child's place in Heck's succession, leaving no room for fairness. I didn't want that for anyone involved. If the child were Heck's, I wanted him or her to have their rightful place in the Archibald family. Being the other woman was already a difficult weight to carry; being pregnant with his child while he was still married felt like an entirely new burden... one this society would never forgive.

"Little Hemingway, we'll have to wait for Daddy to fix the mess," I said aloud, gently cradling my still-flat tummy, hoping somehow he could hear me.

Tonight, I was grateful for the fragile thread of friendship we had managed to reweave. For now, being friends was something I could hold onto. In fact, it was something I needed.

I hung my winter jacket on the hook and tossed my bag onto the couch. The keys landed with a soft clink on the glass coffee table as I crossed the living room. The day felt heavy, clinging to me, but I didn't pause. Instead, I walked straight to the bathroom, the familiar solace of routine guiding me.

I turned on the faucet, letting warm water gush into the tub, returned to the living room, and bent down to collect the scattered mail from the floor. Bills, flyers, a letter for Heck... I set them aside without opening any. Slowly, I began to undress, peeling away my clothes like shedding a tired shell. Each piece dropped to the floor, and with it, the weight of the day seemed to lighten.

The tub filled steadily as I reached for the small vial of lavender oil perched on the edge of the sink. A few drops rippled into the water, the fragrant steam rising to meet me like a gentle embrace. I slid in, the warmth wrapping around me, easing the knots tangled deep in my chest. Closing my eyes, I sank further, letting the quiet hum of the water mute the world outside.

Bit by bit, the tension dissolved, giving way to wandering thoughts. I allowed myself to daydream, to picture the future I cautiously yearned for. Images came unbidden but vivid, tugging at my heart. I imagined telling Heck my secret, here in this very tub where we once shared stolen moments of intimacy, laughter, and quiet. I could see his face lighting up the way it always did when I revealed something silly or unexpected. And I dared to imagine more—to picture us building a life together again, one not haunted by the shadows of the past. A life where we were bound not just by love, but by the tiny life we'd created. I lingered in that vision, holding onto its fragile hope as the warmth of the water cradled me, soft and forgiving.

Steam curled around me, soft and languid, as I sank deeper into the bath. The warm water cradled me, lapping gently at my skin, its soothing rhythm lulling me into a dream. My mind drifted, untethered, into a vision so vivid it felt real.

I saw us—our little family—together on lazy Sunday mornings. Sunlight poured through gauzy curtains, painting the room in golden tones. I could almost hear the soft strum of laughter shared over mismatched plates. The scent of pancakes wafted through the air, rich and sweet, mingling with the earthy aroma of fresh coffee brewing in the kitchen. A record spun somewhere in the background, crackling with the warm, nostalgic tones of an old favorite tune.

I pictured him there, flipping pancakes with a rare, easy smile, his sleeves pushed up carelessly while I stood at his side, teasing him for burning the edges. A giggle—a child's—danced through the spaces between us as tiny feet pattered across the floor. Later, we'd collapse into a heap of blankets on the couch, the three of us cocooned in the kind of comfort that only comes with feeling truly at home.

That life felt achingly close, just one step beyond my grasp. But then, there was Sophie—pregnant and still tethered to the life Heck was unraveling. Her presence loomed like a shadow at the edge of these sunlit dreams. How I longed for it to be over, for that chapter to close so we could truly begin.

The water rippled around me, pulling me back slowly. I opened my eyes, the steam swirling like wisps of my daydream, just out of reach. *Someday*, I thought, sinking back into the warmth, *we'll make those Sundays real.* And in my heart, I refused to believe otherwise.

With a soft smile, I placed a hand on my stomach, a silent promise to the life growing within me. I would wait patiently to tell Heck, knowing our journey was only just beginning. For now, my daydreams were enough to sustain me, filling each moment of waiting with hope and love.

————

As I blow-dried my hair, dressed in my go-to dark gray yoga pants and an oversized white shirt boldly emblazoned with *FVCK IT!*, the doorbell rang. Oh, right—movie night with Veronica! I quickly switched off the dryer, placed it back in the cradle attached to the bathroom mirror, and hurried to the door.

When I opened it, I was greeted by Veronica, my lively Asian neighbor who owned the charming floral shop on the ground floor with her father, Charlie Sung. She was balancing a pack of beers in one arm, a box of pizza in the other, and holding a DVD case between her teeth. The sight of her juggling everything made me burst into laughter.

"Ronnie! Need a hand?" I asked, reaching out to relieve her of her cargo.

"Please!" she mumbled through the DVD case before spitting it into my hands.

As we shuffled indoors, the wafting scent of pepperoni teased my stomach. I glanced at the DVD cover. *"The Holiday?"* I said, holding it up, my voice bursting with excitement. "Oh my God! What a classic. You know, the one where Cameron Diaz and Kate Winslet swap homes and their lives magically transform." I paused, then quickly added, "That cute English cottage! What was its name again?"

"Rosehill Cottage," Veronica replied with a grin, dropping the beers onto the coffee table with a satisfying clink. "Who needs Netflix when we can relive a masterclass in rom-com perfection?"

"Yeah, that's it! I can't wait," I said, practically giddy as I turned the DVD over to admire the cover. "Can we talk about Jude Law's smile in this movie? It's like... illegal."

"Criminal levels of charm," Veronica agreed, collapsing onto the couch and flipping open the pizza box. "Forget Netflix and chill—this is *The Holiday* and swoon." She popped open a can of beer and handed it to me. Instinctively, I almost reached for it, but then I remembered—I was pregnant.

"I'll pass on the beer tonight, but I can't wait to dive into that pizza," I said, trying to sound casual.

Veronica raised an eyebrow, her expression curious. "Are you okay?" she asked, her tone a mix of concern and teasing.

"Of course I am!" I replied, brushing off her concern with a wave of my hand. "Let's dig into that pizza and get the movie started. I've been craving this all day."

I cozied up beside her, sans beer this time, but with a hefty slice of pizza in hand. The title screen glowed on the TV, and with a theatrical flourish, Veronica pressed play.

The evening unfurled as a perfect cinematic escape. We giggled at Cameron Diaz's over-the-top meltdown in her Hollywood mansion, but when she arrived at Rosehill Cottage, Veronica sighed dreamily. "I would live there in a heartbeat—squeaky floors, icy bathrooms, and all."

"Same," I said, already imagining tea by the fire with snow blanketing the countryside outside. "But we both know the selling point of this movie comes later. You know what I mean."

Veronica smirked knowingly, inching the pizza out of my hands so I wouldn't drop it when the moment arrived. The scene we were waiting for—the turning point. And there he was: Jude Law as Graham, leaning against the doorframe, his face practically carved by the gods.

"*Hello*," he said, his voice smooth, each syllable dripping with charm.

Veronica clutched her heart. "Seriously?! What gives him the right?"

I laughed, though I was equally captivated. "The dimples. The accent. The way he says 'hello' like it's a spell? I need a minute."

Then came the line. The scene where he said, with subtle vulnerability, "*It's Christmas, and we're all in misery.*"

"He's misery?! I will volunteer as tribute to fix that," Veronica declared, faking outrage before dissolving into laughter.

We quieted down slightly when the iconic tent scene came on—Graham tucking his daughters into their adorable fairy-lit fort, his gentle warmth spilling into every word. We were both a mess of "aww"s and wistful sighs by the time he said, "*I'm a total Bridget-Jones-ing wreck,*" his honesty surface-level vulnerable but heavy with unspoken depth.

"At this point," I said, setting my pizza plate aside, "any girl not falling hopelessly in love with him must be legally required to watch this movie on repeat."

"Or have their pulse checked," Veronica added, reaching for another beer. "I mean, come on—hemmed shirts, endless charm, good with kids, AND he cries while drunk? Perfect doesn't even begin to cover it."

"And that kiss," I said as the infamous snow-drenched kiss scene began playing. We both leaned forward instinctively as Graham and Amanda stood under the sparkling snowfall. When their lips finally met, Veronica fake-swooned dramatically, causing me to burst into giggles.

"Men have their action movies. This," Veronica declared, gesturing at the screen, "is our blockbuster."

By the time the credits rolled, our pizza was gone, the beers (hers, at least) were empty, and our cheeks hurt from grinning. The glow of *The Holiday* lingered in the room, wrapping us in its warm, cozy magic.

"Jude Law," Veronica said reverently, breaking the comfortable silence.

"Jude Law," I echoed with a laugh, hugging a pillow to my chest.

If there was one thing a girls' night with a rom-com like this did, it was leave us swooning and dreaming of English accents, fairy-lit cottages, and the kind of romance that only exists on a Sunday night screen.

4

Seated in the sleek, glass-walled meeting room, I couldn't stop fidgeting. My palms were damp, and my eyes kept darting to the panoramic view beyond the transparent walls. The bustling office outside felt like an aquarium of organized chaos—a blur of faces moving between their little glass boxes. Archibald Tower wasn't new to me; I'd been here before, pitching ideas as part of a team. But today felt different. More personal. It was as if the air itself carried the weight of what was about to happen. And the person who was about to walk through those doors? That made it all the more nerve-wracking.

Kelly had pulled me into this at the very last minute, insisting I was the one who could bring the new tagline and messaging to life since I'd created it. The problem? Public speaking was my personal kryptonite. I thrived behind the scenes, orchestrating ideas from a comfortable distance. Meetings like this—with all eyes on me—turned my stomach into knots. Kelly knew that about me, but here I was anyway, planted between her and Alexi, completely out of my depth.

I felt underdressed. Everyone else looked flawless in tailored suits and polished shoes, while I sat there in my snug denim pants, black knee-high boots, and an oversized white turtleneck. It wasn't like me to feel this self-conscious, but something about the moment magnified every small imperfection. Although my pregnancy wasn't showing yet, I couldn't shake the feeling that my wardrobe was already betraying me. None of my decent clothes seemed to fit quite right anymore.

I glanced around the room, surrounded by people who looked

effortlessly professional, and an overwhelming urge crept in—to appear like I truly belonged here. But today, I didn't. That belief settled deep, convincing me I wasn't just unprepared, but also falling short in something as seemingly insignificant as the 'outfit of the day.'

Our presentation was already on the big screen, ready to go. Kelly was set to lead, while my role was to step in when it came time to explain the thinking behind our tagline: *Your Trust. Our Priority. Banking Made Simple.* It was a straightforward line, yet one we'd painstakingly shaped to reflect the bank's brand values.

Then I saw them through the glass. Him. Heck, flanked by two impeccably dressed women and an older man in a pinstripe suit who exuded authority. At first, I barely recognized him. The charcoal gray suit, crisp white shirt, and pink tie transformed him into someone polished and corporate—worlds away from the laid-back artist I once knew. His hair was neatly trimmed, not a strand out of place. Yet there it was: the familiar light blue-faced 1978 Rolex on his wrist. The same watch I'd noticed the first time we met at Tribeca Trickle, standing out even more back then against his worn gray T-shirt and ripped jeans. That watch had sparked a funny and unforgettable banter between us. Seeing it now, amid all this formality, tugged at something deep inside me.

When his gaze found mine, his smile spread—warm and disarming. It was still the same Heck underneath it all. That small moment eased a bit of the tension swirling inside me.

We stood as the group entered.

"Please, everyone, take your seats," Raul Clifford, the head of communications at Gold Standard Bank, said, gesturing toward us. In his early sixties, Raul carried himself with the kind of polished confidence that came from decades in the corporate world. His salt-and-pepper hair was always neatly combed, and his tailored suits hinted at a man who valued precision and professionalism. "No need for formalities. Welcome back, Sara. It's been a while. We're pleased to have you here today."

I met Raul's gaze with a polite smile, determined to keep my nerves in check. "It's nice to be back, Raul."

Raul and I went way back, having worked together on past campaigns long before Heck became part of the picture. Back then, Raul and I had collaborated seamlessly, while the Heck of that time was likely busy cultivating his playboy persona or pouring his energy into art.

Raul's voice cut through my wandering thoughts. "Shall we get started?"

Kelly kicked off the presentation, expertly covering the campaign's background and target audience. She painted a vivid picture of what made our demographic tick and how the bank aimed to capture their interest.

Next, Alexi took over, showcasing the fresh layouts and imagery before wrapping up with the new tagline. "The imagery and colors are vibrant, resonating with our target audience," he concluded. "I'll let our copywriter explain the tagline," he said, nodding toward me.

I cleared my throat, forcing myself to steady the flutter of nerves building in my chest. With my hand firm on the laser pointer, I aimed it at the screen where the tagline glowed in bold letters: *Your Trust. Our Priority. Banking Made Simple.*

"This tagline communicates several essential ideas," I began, ensuring my voice was steady and deliberate. I wanted the room's focus to be on the words, giving them the space to absorb their weight and significance. It wasn't just a slogan; it encapsulated what we stood for. My goal was to help everyone in the room not just understand the message—but feel it.

"Trust," I stated, pausing for effect. "This word underscores the bank's commitment to valuing and prioritizing customer trust, suggesting reliability and security in its services." I noticed the women beside Heck taking notes diligently, while Raul's eyes remained glued to the screen. However, Heck was focused entirely on me, making me even more self-conscious. This was the first time we were in a business setting together.

"'Our Priority' highlights the bank's dedication to addressing customer needs and satisfaction," I continued. "Customer-centricity means putting the customer first." I paused, letting the message sink in.

"And simplicity," I added, "suggests that the bank offers straightforward, user-friendly services, making financial management accessible and hassle-free for everyone." I looked directly at Heck, knowing he would have the final say. Kelly had brought me in as a strategic move, hoping my presence would seal the deal.

I met Heck's eyes and offered a small, measured smile. "The core message is about building a genuine, trustworthy connection with customers while providing banking solutions that are straightforward and accessible."

I paused, the words hanging in the air. And then it hit me—I had no idea how to neatly wrap up the presentation. My mind raced. Should I say, *Thank you*? Does that sound polished enough? My gaze dropped to my hands, fidgeting with the edge of my notebook. The silence stretched just a little too long, and I could feel the awkwardness creeping in.

Heck, reading me like an open book, stepped in without missing a beat. "Thank you, Sara," he said smoothly, redirecting the room's attention with practiced ease before turning toward Raul. "What's your take?"

Raul leaned back in his chair, nodding thoughtfully. "It's solid. I like it. Jen?"

Jen Barrows, the bank's marketing associate, tapped her *Le Petit Prince* Montblanc pen against her notebook, the motion deliberate and almost rhythmic. Her perfectly French-manicured fingers wrapped around it carefully, as if even her smallest gestures were curated. "It's promising," she said, her voice smooth and measured, "but I'd like to explore other options before we commit."

Her words landed like a thud in my chest. I flinched inwardly, trying to steady my thoughts. The image of her immaculate blonde bun, every strand obediently in place, paired with her pale green suit that looked like it was tailored just for her, made me feel instantly out of place. Sitting there in my shabby outfit, I couldn't help but feel like a forgotten rag doll tucked into a display case full of flawless porcelain figures.

The thought of starting this process over again felt like nails screeching across a chalkboard. My unease must have been written all over my face, because from across the room, Heck's eyes found mine. It was as though he could see right through me, reading the words I hadn't dared to say out loud.

"I believe we've already explored a range of options," Heck said, his tone measured but firm. "This one is concise, memorable, and effective."

Alexi quickly jumped in to support the momentum. "It's important we finalize the direction now so we can focus on activating the campaign across platforms. While we have some runway, tying up loose ends early is always better."

Raul leaned forward, addressing Kelly. "How soon can we roll this out?"

Kelly answered smoothly, confidence lining her voice. "If everyone's aligned, we can start working on final formats for approval immediately. Once the budget is approved, we're looking at a six-week rollout timeline. Does that work on your end?"

"That should be fine," Heck said with a slight nod of approval. Then, to my surprise, he added, "Well done, Sara."

The unexpected praise caught me off guard. Suddenly, all eyes turned to me. I felt heat rise to my cheeks, but managed a sincere smile, even letting out a light laugh as Heck chuckled softly. Somehow, the weight in the room seemed to lift at that moment, letting me breathe a little easier.

————

The best part of any pitch meeting was always the casual chatter over refreshments. Feeling famished, I trailed Alexi to the refreshments table, which was nearly overflowing with assorted canapés and petite sandwiches sliced into dainty squares. Flutes of champagne glinted under the soft lighting, the bubbles rising like tiny celebratory fireworks. No wonder Alexi and Andi never missed a meeting with the bank. This wasn't just business; this was indulgence.

I reached for a smoked salmon and cream cheese canapé, its delicate garnish almost too pretty to eat. But hunger won over hesitation, and as I savored the first bite, I caught a glimpse of Heck at the other end of the room. He stood near Kelly and Andi, his head tilted back in laughter, his smile brimming with a kind of easy charm that both enchanted and annoyed me. God, he looked good. Too good. And, much as I hated to admit it, I missed him.

"You're staring," Alexi's voice snapped me out of my unintentional daydream, and I quickly turned my attention back to the table. He was meticulously piling canapés onto his plate, his grin teasing.

"I think we nailed it. Sealed it, Sara," he said, his tone laced with satisfaction.

"You think so?" I asked, trying to focus, though my heart was still tethered to the other side of the room.

"Oh, no question," Alexi replied, giving me a sidelong glance. "You just looked like you were about to keel over out there."

"Seriously?" I groaned, rolling my eyes. "Was it that obvious? God, why do you guys always throw me into the fire?"

"Well, we're trying to bring this deal home," he said with a shrug and a mischievous smirk. "A little pressure doesn't hurt."

"Right, using me as the sacrificial lamb," I huffed with dramatic flair, pouting as I grabbed another canapé.

Alexi chuckled, but his eyes darted behind me. "Oh, the handsome big boss couldn't take his eyes off you." His voice was sing-song and dripping with insinuation.

"Oh, come on. That's not true!" I protested, feeling my cheeks heat.

"Speaking of the devil..." Alexi nodded over my shoulder. "Here he comes. I'll leave you two to it." And, like the sly escape artist he was, Alexi was gone in an instant.

I barely had time to register his disappearance before I felt a shift in the atmosphere. I didn't even need to turn; I could sense Heck's presence behind me—the warmth of it, the way it made everything around us seem quieter somehow.

"That was impressive, Sara," Heck's voice broke the silence, smooth and warm, as he extended a flute of champagne toward me. I took it instinctively before halting.

"Oh, thanks, Heck, but I should stick to water," I said, offering a polite smile. "Still have a mountain of work waiting for me after this."

He arched a brow, his look equal parts curious and amused. "Your job's done," he said simply. "I've already signed off on it."

I hesitated, caught somewhere between relief and disbelief. My gaze flickered up to meet his, and before I could stop myself, I reached out to brush my fingers through his neatly trimmed hair. "You look... different," I murmured, aware of how close we were but unwilling to back away.

"Different good or different bad?" he asked, his low, teasing tone drawing a small laugh from me.

"Definitely good." I pulled my hand back, suddenly aware of how bold I'd been. "It's just—not what I'm used to. I liked your messy artist look."

He stepped closer, a playful glint in his eyes. "Want me to grow it out again?"

I shook my head quickly and laughed. "No, no. You look… decent," I teased, popping a sandwich into my mouth to hide my growing grin. But then, as if on cue, a strand of my hair fell loose and into my face. My hands were full, but Heck leaned in, brushing it back behind my ear with a touch so light it sent sparks along my skin.

The simple gesture drew my breath up short. His hand lingered near my face, and as I met his gaze, the world seemed to shrink until it was just the two of us. His fingers tilted my chin gently, his eyes searching mine, a quiet storm between us.

"Sara," he murmured, his voice featherlight but brimming with something unspoken.

"Heck, please…" I whispered, though I wasn't even sure what I was asking for. My heartbeat thundered in my ears as the moment stretched between us, fragile and electric, charged with an intimacy I couldn't ignore. Everything else faded, leaving only the quiet hum of what might happen next.

5

The inviting hum of laughter and clinking glasses greeted us as we stepped into Pearl & Pine, one of Manhattan's finest bars. It was the kind of place where chandeliers cast buttery, golden light across gleaming mahogany tables, and everything—from the faint scent of citrus and oak to the soft chime of ice swirling in crystal glasses—seemed designed to seduce its patrons. The crowd was polished, their conversations like carefully choreographed dances. Sharp suits and flowing dresses filled the room, a mix of well-heeled professionals—Wall Street types—and creatives who all looked like they had somewhere far more exclusive to be.

The Milliford and Gold Standard Bank teams sprawled across a semi-private corner, commandeering the space with giddy post-meeting relief. After weeks of deck edits, late nights, and moments when the deal seemed doomed, Heck decided it called for a celebration. Tonight had every excuse to end with champagne and raised glasses.

The room hummed with lively energy—the kind that bubbles when hard work meets hard liquor. Champagne flutes clinked softly as they passed from hand to hand, their sparkling contents glittering under the warm light. Some team members indulged in more spirited choices, the familiar aroma of whiskey and citrus wafting through the air. Jen was already on her second Moscow Mule, the copper mug as much a prop as a drink, spinning idly in her well-manicured hand. Her dark pink strapless dress hugged her figure perfectly, and her laughter rang out occasionally—loud and just on the edge of too much, like a punctuation mark in the din of conversations.

I perched on a high stool. My black spaghetti-strap dress clung softly to my frame, its low back brushing coolly against the air. I'd chosen it carefully—not too flashy, not too demure. Just enough to blend in while still feeling flattering. I crossed one leg over the other, tugging the hem slightly to fall just right, thankful that my body still felt like my own, at least for now. My beer bottle rested against my palm, its cool condensation dampening my fingers as I absently traced patterns over the glass.

I hadn't taken more than a polite sip, and even that felt like too much. The bottle was merely an accessory. Every untouched drop felt like both a deception and a quiet act of defiance. A protective instinct hummed beneath my skin, an unspoken resolve to shield the delicate, quiet truth of what I carried. For now, this secret was mine alone, and it felt like the only safe thing in a room full of clinking glasses and polished smiles.

I glanced at Jen, now tossing her hair back as she leaned into a joke, her voice rising just a touch too high, her copper mug raised like a trophy. Around her, the laughter swelled, bouncing off the warmly lit walls. I stayed in the margins of it all, wearing a tight smile that no one stopped to question. They didn't know, and that made it easier. For now, I could just listen. Just watch. Keep this small spark burning quietly while the rest of the world spun on, oblivious.

"You're just gonna stare at it all night?" Heck's voice broke through the chatter, his warm New York accent laced with playful amusement as he slid onto the bar stool next to me. He leaned in slightly, brow arched, cerulean blue eyes glinting under the dim light.

I shrugged, hoping my nonchalant smile would distract from the heat creeping up my neck. "What can I say? Beer just makes a better decoration than a drink tonight."

"Oh, come on, now," he teased, tilting his glass of bourbon toward me. "You don't wanna miss out on the best way to celebrate."

"I'm fine. Really." I laughed lightly, tucking my hair behind my ear as I avoided his gaze, afraid that his scrutiny might uncover more than I was ready to share.

Jen seized the moment, sliding her chair closer to Heck's. Her coral-painted nails rested on his forearm like they belonged there, and she angled her body toward him just enough to catch his attention. Or try to, anyway.

"So, Heck," she purred, her tone too sweet for my liking. "How'd you find spearheading one of the busiest departments in your company?"

Heck's lips quirked into the kind of polite smile he wore when humoring someone. "Don't know exactly, Jen. Just a lot of work and, well… a good team."

His gaze flicked to me as he said the last part, and my stomach fluttered despite my best efforts to remain composed.

"Oh, sure," Jen replied, her laughter bright but misplaced. Her hand lingered on his forearm. "But I bet there's something more. You've gotta have a trick up your sleeve."

I swirled the beer bottle on the table, suppressing the low thrum of annoyance building in my chest. This was ridiculous. She wasn't doing anything wrong—not really. And yet I found myself gripping my bottle tighter, forcing a smile through the tingling heat on my cheeks.

"Jen." Heck's voice was soft yet firm, laced with just a trace of amusement. He shifted slightly, his movements fluid as he eased himself out of her reach. His arm slipped away from her touch as he turned, angling his body toward me instead. "If there's a trick to it, I'd bet Sara's the one who knows. She did most of the heavy lifting."

The pivot was seamless, like watching water shift over stone. My shoulders stiffened under the sudden weight of his focus, but somewhere beneath the simmering irritation, pride sparked. His words carried an undeniable warmth, a quiet acknowledgment that shouldn't have made my heart skip the way it did. But it did.

And then I felt it. Heck's hand settled against the small of my back, his fingers brushing gently against my bare skin. A thumb traced slow, deliberate circles, the heat of his touch radiating outward like ripples through still water. The sensation seized me, scattering my thoughts until they dissolved entirely. I struggled to concentrate, but everything narrowed to the point of contact—sharp and electric.

I heard the lazy clink of ice against the glass and looked up just in time to catch the flicker of disappointment crossing Jen's face. Her expression wavered briefly before she buried it behind a long sip of her cocktail. Her eyes flicked between us, unreadable now, though the tension in her grip on the glass betrayed her. She smiled faintly, but it didn't reach her eyes.

If Heck noticed, he didn't react. His hand lingered on my back, steady and warm, anchoring me even as everything else felt as though it might come untethered. I forced my lips into a composed smile, all the while hoping no one noticed the slight tremor in my breathing.

The hours slipped past in a slow haze of chatter and drinks, laughter rising and falling like the pulse of the crowded bar. But eventually, the tide turned toward goodbyes and practicalities—the logistical aftermath of projection screens and late nights replaced by Uber rides and wave-offs to yellow cabs.

"I'll drive you," Jen declared, her words cutting sharply through the growing quiet. She waved her empty mug as she looked at Heck. "You know you've had too much to drive yourself, and I'm fine."

Heck shook his head, a lazy grin softening the rejection. "Appreciate it, but I think you've had one too many Moscow Mules to be convincing anyone to get in a car with you. Call an Uber, alright?"

Jen pouted but didn't argue, tossing her hair over her shoulder as she tugged her phone from her bag.

Heck turned to me, his smile softening into something warmer. "Come on. I'll take you home."

I raised an eyebrow but didn't protest. "You don't have to, Heck. I can get a ride myself."

"Sara," he said, his voice dipping into that quieter, familiar register that always managed to undo me. "I'm taking you home. It's settled."

The drive to my apartment was cloaked in silence, but it wasn't uncomfortable. It was heavy—charged. The city blurred by in streaks of gold and crimson, the hum of the engine filling the space between us. I tapped lightly on my knee, trying to ignore the electricity humming under my skin every time his hand brushed the gear shift too close to mine.

When we pulled up in front of my building, I hesitated. My fingers curled around the door handle, but the words slipped out before I gave them permission to form. "Do you want to come in?"

He turned to me, his sharp blue gaze locking onto mine. For a moment, I thought he might say no, that some unspoken line we'd danced around for months would finally pull taut and snap us back into place. But then, the corner of his mouth lifted—a slight, knowing smile.

"Yeah," he said simply. "I'd like that."

The elevator ride to my floor was quiet but charged, the space between us simultaneously shrinking and expanding with every drawn breath. My heart thundered in my chest, anticipation pooling low in my belly as I keyed the door open.

Inside, the world seemed to shrink. It was just the two of us now, alone in the warm cocoon of my apartment. The air felt electric, the tension between us shifting from the lingering whispers of professionalism to something raw, unfiltered, and undeniable.

He took a step toward me, his movements measured but deliberate. His hand brushed the side of my face, his thumb grazing my cheekbone like he was memorizing the feel of me. "Sara..." he murmured, his voice low and gravelly, the sound sending shivers racing down my spine.

Then his lips found mine.

The kiss started soft, tentative, but quickly unraveled when I responded, pulling him closer. His hands slipped down to my waist, his fingers digging into the fabric of my dress as though desperate to bring me nearer. The rest of the world dissolved—the city, the clock, and the doubts that clawed at the edges of my conscience. All that mattered was him.

He kissed me like the city outside had vanished, like the only thing real was the space between us. Every touch of his lips on my skin felt heightened, my senses sharper, my body more alive than it had been in months. He kissed me until I was breathless—until my knees felt like they might buckle. His lips burned a trail down my neck, lingering just below my ear, and when he growled softly against my skin, a desperate sound escaped my throat.

"Jesus, Sara," he groaned, his hands moving lower, sliding beneath the hem of my dress. "Do you even know what you do to me?"

"I think I'm starting to get the picture," I whispered, unable to keep the teasing lilt from my voice, though it trembled under the weight of my own need.

He chuckled—a low, restrained sound that sent heat pooling beneath my skin. His hands gripped my thighs, and before I could process it, he lifted me effortlessly, carrying me toward the bedroom.

"Fuck, Heck!" I moaned as I grabbed his hair. I wrapped my arms around his neck, and when I bit lightly on his earlobe, his response came in a deep, primal growl I felt more than heard.

"Fuccckkkk! You're driving me off the edge when you talk like that," he nibbled my neck, which I'm pretty sure will leave marks by tomorrow. But I don't care. All I wanted was for Heck to consume me.

We moved through the quiet hum of the apartment like a rhythm, shedding tension and barriers in equal measure. His hands left no doubt of their destination, his fingertips memorizing the curve of my back as he lifted me effortlessly into his arms.

When the back of my shoulders met the softness of my bed, I gasped at the cool sheets against my heated skin. He hovered over me, his eyes hooded with unbridled desire, but beneath it, there was something tender. His eyes never left mine. They're on fire, with hunger. He pinned both my hands on top of my head with his left hand while he slowly rubbed his hands on my thigh, pushing the hem of my dress to my waist. I was so eager to meet his hands, but he took his time. It wasn't rushed, wasn't frantic. It was unhurried and deliberate, as though every movement was as much about remembering as it was about experiencing.

"You're beautiful," he said softly, almost reverently.

His lips met mine again, but this time, it was unhurried. His hands explored the curve of my hips and the sharp lines of my collarbone as though savoring every inch of me. When his fingers lightly brushed the edge of my black lace panties, my breath hitched, and he paused to look at me—a silent request.

"Yes," I whispered. "Please."

He slipped the fabric down with agonizing slowness, his fingertips leaving trails of fire on my skin. I gasped when his hands gripped my thighs, his lips following the path his hands had mapped moments prior.

"God, Sara," he murmured, the sound muffled against my skin but no less potent. "You're perfect."

Every touch sent my nerves alight, every kiss drawing me further into a haze of desire. His name spilled from my lips again and again, becoming a prayer, a plea.

"Heck, please…" I begged.

His lips left that part between my thigh… wanting. Instead, his tongue brushed my parted lips as his finger touched the pleasure nub between my legs. My movements were so erratic that he chuckled. He knew this was driving me mad. The tip of his nose traveled from my neck to the hollow of my breast. His tongue dipped inside my dress, seeking my right nipple.

"Heck, take me now… "I begged again.

"No, I want to see you wanting it. Begging for it," then, without warning, he dipped two fingers inside me.

"Oh, God," I cried.

"Sara, you look so hot right now, even with your clothes on, " he said as he pushed his fingers deeper until he reached the part that drove me even more crazy. I was losing it as I moved my hips, meeting his fingers. When I couldn't stand it any longer, he withdrew them and dipped them in my mouth. "Taste yourself for me," he moaned.

I knew Heck was great in bed, but this is the other side of him I haven't encountered. I sucked his fingers and tasted myself for the first time. It was wild. When he took out his fingers from my mouth, he kissed me like he was trying to suck everything from me. Without warning, he flipped me on my knees and spanked my buttocks. And when he finally entered me, the connection was overwhelming—borderline shattering. He moved with deliberate care. Each thrust was deep. Each pulled slowly. It wasn't hurried, but it wasn't hesitant either. It was raw. Powerful. A rhythm we hadn't needed words to create, one that seemed inevitable from the moment we'd met.

His name escaped me in broken syllables as I clung to him, his fingers digging into my hips, desperate to anchor himself to something more. He pushed me closer and closer to the edge, and when I fell, it was with a force that left me gasping and trembling beneath him.

He followed soon after, his breath heavy in my ear as he buried his face in the crook of my neck. "Sara," he whispered hoarsely, like the word itself held a thousand meanings.

We stayed like that for a moment—caught in the quiet aftermath, in the space where nothing else mattered but the sound of our breathing and the warmth of his body against mine.

Eventually, he rolled to the side, pulling me with him, his arm wrapped protectively around my waist. He placed a soft kiss on my neck, and I swore I felt him smile against my skin. His touch burned away every ounce of doubt I'd carried that night, leaving only this—this quiet, breathtaking union.

The bed felt impossibly soft beneath us, the sheets and the city's distant hum fading into the background as he held me close. His lips found mine over and over, the sound of my name escaping him in a whisper that left no room for anything else.

When sleep finally took me, it offered no dreams—only the heavy stillness of exhaustion. But with morning came reality, creeping in along the soft light threading through the blinds. I stretched under the warmth of my blankets, momentarily cocooned in its comfort, until my palm met the other side of the bed. It was empty. The faint trace of warmth lingered where his body had been, but Heck was gone. My stomach tightened—not with regret, but with the weight of all the words that had gone unspoken.

I drew the blankets closer to my naked body, as if they could shield me from the questions unfurling in my mind. There was excitement in the memory of last night, a connection I couldn't deny. But beneath it lay confusion, an unease I couldn't quite place, and something dangerously close to fear. What did this mean for us? Was it a fleeting moment, born of late hours and blurred lines? Or was it something tangible, something real?

And then, the dreaded thought rose unbidden in my mind. *Professionalism.* Heck wasn't just someone I'd shared a vulnerable moment with—he was a client. Last night had obliterated that boundary, leaving it in irreparable shards around us. The ramifications loomed large, impossible to ignore.

It wasn't just about what had happened. It was about what it meant, what it had irrevocably changed.

I sat up slowly, raking a hand through my hair, my gaze settling on his jacket draped over the back of my chair. Its presence carried the invisible rope that tied us, something delicate, impossible to define, pulling at me with relentless weight. Staring at the jacket and then at the empty space beside me, it was clear—this wasn't just about work anymore.

For a long while, I stayed like that, frozen between unexplained emotions, staring blankly at the ceiling. Overthinking every second of last night, every word, every touch. The clock on the wall might as well have stopped moving. Time felt like it had gone still alongside me.

Eventually, the buttery glow of morning filtered further into the room, but I'd already been lying there, wide awake. The sheets still clung faintly to his warmth, a grounding reminder that the night wasn't some hazy dream.

I released a long sigh, sitting up and knotting my fingers through my hair once more. It still smelled faintly of him, and the ghost of it sent a new wave of anxiety rushing through my body. My eyes drifted once again to his jacket, to the evidence of his presence hanging in my space, as if daring me to confront what had happened.

Finally, I swung my legs over the side of the bed, shaking my head as if I could scatter the thoughts crowding it. "Coffee first," I murmured into the quiet of the room. "Freak out later."

6

The usual office buzz greeted me as I stepped in, but today, it felt sharper, almost stifling. Or perhaps it was just me—overly conscious of every glance that lingered too long, every smile that felt just a little too knowing. I forced myself into my usual rhythm: head down, coffee in hand, bags under my eyes that I'd tried—and failed—to conceal with concealer.

"Sara, if I didn't know better, I'd say you've got our biggest client wrapped around your finger again," Alexi chimed, his voice teasing yet sharp enough to make me freeze mid-step.

"What?" I stopped in my tracks, my chest tightening. My mind leaped to the worst possible conclusion. *Did they…? Oh, God, had they guessed what happened last night?*

Alexi's smirk widened, his eyes gleaming with the kind of mischief that made my pulse race for all the wrong reasons. "Oh, don't play coy," he drawled. "Mr. Goldstar himself? You know what I'm talking about."

"So that's what you call him now?" I giggled, hoping to deflect.

Without missing a beat, he grinned. "Yeah, Gold Standard Bank is too much of a mouthful—too exhausting to say every time. So I've decided to shorten it. Goldstar… has a nice ring to it, don't you think?" He paused, his grin turning sly. "And about last night? Especially considering how he dropped you off."

I managed a weak laugh and shook my head, trying to shake off the tension. "What are you even talking about, Alexi?" My stomach flipped, and I scrambled to keep my expression neutral. "We're just friends. That's all," I said, my tone deliberately nonchalant. I tucked a strand of hair behind my ear, avoiding his gaze. "Anyway, he's a client of the agency, not exactly someone I can ignore," I added with a quick smile for good measure. "Someone's got to make them feel special, right? Clients aren't going to woo themselves."

Alexi arched a perfectly manicured brow, his smirk refusing to budge. "Right. Because that's what 'just friends' say when they're bending over backward to justify whatever *this* is." His sarcasm was sharp, his dramatic eye-roll even sharper. "You think no one noticed the way he was hovering around you last night? Please. Even Jen couldn't push her way through."

I barely had time to scowl before I reached my cubicle. But any response I planned dried up the instant I saw what was waiting for me. Sitting squarely in the middle of my desk was a massive bouquet of pink roses, their petals soft and full as they spilled over the vase's edge. Their scent was overwhelming, wrapping around me in a floral cocoon. My heart stumbled in my chest.

I didn't move. Not for a long moment. My fingers clutched the strap of my bag, unwilling to set it down just yet, as if holding onto it might keep me grounded. Naturally, Alexi's footsteps followed soon behind.

He leaned in with impeccable timing, his heels clicking just enough to announce his arrival. "Ohhh, my God," he squealed, barely containing his glee. "Sara. Roses?! Yeah, sure. 'Friends.' Totally convincing."

"Alexi…" I glared at him in warning, but he was already reaching for the card nestled within the blooms. I swatted at his hand, snatching it first, my fingers trembling slightly as I slid the envelope open.

Inside, the note was simple and direct. It wasn't signed, but I didn't need the crisp, no-nonsense handwriting to know who had written it.

Pender,

Sorry, I had to rush this morning. Didn't want to wake you.

My breath caught in my throat. A flicker of something unnameable lit behind my ribs, threatening to blossom into a smile. Heat rushed to my cheeks, and I swallowed hard, tucking the note back before Alexi could pounce.

"Well?" he demanded, practically bouncing on the balls of his feet. "What does it say? Don't even think about playing coy."

"Alexi," I said sharply, turning toward my computer and praying the redness on my face wasn't as obvious as it felt. "Don't you have something else to do? Where's Andi?"

"She's on the 30th floor, meeting with a client," he said with a dismissive wave of his hand. "But trust me, when she sees this, both of us will be waiting for all the juicy details at lunch." He leaned in again, lowering his voice conspiratorially. "It *is* from Heck, isn't it? I mean, come on. Pink roses. The note. The way he kept hovering all night? Even I'm swooning a little."

I sighed firmly, sitting down in the hopes that planting myself behind my desk might end the discussion. "Heck and I are friends. That's all there is to it."

"Fine, fine," he said, straightening up and brushing imaginary dust off his blazer. "But the three of us are having lunch. Don't think you're off the hook just yet." Alexi rolled his eyes, the picture of skepticism. "Right. Friends with roses. And cryptic notes. Sure," he muttered under his breath, loud enough for me to hear.

Without waiting for permission, he swept off toward his own desk, leaving me with nothing to do but stare at the roses in front of me. I traced the edge of one perfect petal, its softness startling, out of place against the cold, utilitarian gray of my desk.

They were beautiful, yes—but they were also dangerous. They carried last night into today, something tangible I couldn't push away or pretend hadn't happened. Despite myself, a warmth lingered in my chest, sparked by the simple gesture, by the way, his words lingered on the page like a whisper only I could hear.

Heck had a way of throwing me off balance. As I turned my focus back to the blinking cursor on my screen, I realized I didn't know if I wanted to find that balance again.

7

Weekends had always felt like a gift. No alarms, no pressing deadlines —just uninterrupted hours to pour into my writing. It had been far too long since I'd penned a proper scene for my manuscript, and my creative well was running frustratingly dry. But this morning, the café was my sanctuary. The early hours meant near silence, save for the soft strains of indie music playing in the background and the occasional hiss of the espresso machine.

For the first time in days, my phone was off—a silent rebellion against the constant work demands. It was just me, my laptop, my notebook, and the quiet hope that inspiration might strike.

"Chamomile tea for my favorite writer," Lily's voice broke through my thoughts, warm and familiar. I looked up to see her balancing a tray, her trademark radiant smile brightening the dimly lit space.

"Lily, you're an angel. Truly," I said, watching as she placed the teapot on the table with practiced grace, followed by a plate piled high with pancakes, syrup-drizzled strawberries, eggs, and crispy bacon.

"I took the liberty of prepping your breakfast," she said with a cheeky shrug. "You looked famished."

Laughing, I shook my head. "What would I do without you?"

"You'd starve," Lily teased, her eyes twinkling. She tucked a stray strand of dark hair behind her ear as she lingered momentarily.

"How's the writing coming along?"

With a sigh, I leaned back in my seat. "It's not. I haven't written a single word this week. Work's been… relentless."

"Figures," she said, rolling her eyes dramatically. "Corporate life—the ultimate creativity killer."

I smirked at her. "At least you're not juggling cereal campaigns and client decks."

"Work always gets in the way," she said, rolling her eyes again in exaggerated frustration.

"How's your review? Are you ready for college?" I asked, pouring the hot tea into my cup.

"I'm taking the test next week."

"Oh, don't worry about it. It's standard procedure. You're smart and capable. You're getting in—I'm sure of it," I said, offering her a reassuring smile.

"Thanks, Sara. Anyway, enjoy your breakfast while it's hot. And don't worry—your muse always shows up eventually."

I smiled as she walked away, leaving me alone with the feast in front of me. The buttery scent of the pancakes mingled with the sharp aroma of the tea, making my mouth water. I hadn't been hungry when I sat down, but the first bite of syrup-soaked pancake melted any remaining resistance. Warm, fluffy perfection—tiny reminders of comfort, of simple pleasures that didn't demand anything from me. Between bites of sweet strawberries and salty bacon, my thoughts started to drift—to Heck.

Brinner. That's what he'd called it. Breakfast for dinner. It had been our thing on late nights when work bled into every other hour of the day, when takeout became a staple and exhaustion weighed heavy. The memory tugged at something deep in me. It had been days since I'd last seen him, though we'd maintained a steady exchange of emoji-filled texts. Even in silence, he had a way of staying present in my life.

"Figured I'd find you here," a familiar voice said, cutting through my wandering thoughts.

I looked up sharply, my fork pausing midair. Heck stood towering over me, dressed in his usual jeans and that gray hoodie he seemed to wear incessantly beneath his black winter jacket. His hair was slightly tousled, and his cheeks were flushed from what I assumed was his morning run.

"Heck," I said, startled but not entirely surprised. Somehow, I'd known he'd show up sooner or later.

"Your phone goes straight to voicemail," he scolded lightly, his hands resting on the back of the chair opposite me. "Figured that meant you'd gone off the grid. Again."

I gestured to the notebook and laptop in front of me. "Off the grid for work reasons. Had to turn it off—too many distractions." I hesitated, then added, "You're a pretty big distraction, too."

That earned me one of his trademark grins. "Mind if I join you?"

I nodded, watching as he removed his jacket before slumping into the chair with the kind of ease that spoke to how comfortable we'd become around each other. He glanced toward the counter, catching Lily's eye, and gave a small nod. She returned it, wordlessly preparing his order. Those two always seemed to have an unspoken system.

"So," I started, raising a brow playfully, "what's with the no-goodbye notes?"

He leaned back, his grin softening. "I didn't want to wake you. You were out cold. And... well, self-preservation. You aren't exactly the type who loves post-morning walk-ins."

I folded my arms, feigning offense. "Did I snore again?"

"Oh, you bet," he teased. "Like a freight train."

"Ugh, I knew it!" I groaned, covering my face with my hands.

He laughed, the sound deep and free, and I couldn't help but roll my eyes. "But you're cute when you snore, so I couldn't complain too much," he smirked.

Before I could reply to his jab, his tone shifted, turning serious in an instant. "The paternity test results came in."

I froze, my fork suddenly heavy in my hand. "What? Already?"

He nodded, his eyes meeting mine. "Yeah. Sophie's kid… isn't mine."

The words flipped my world on its axis, even though I wasn't sure why they hit me so hard. Relief, surprise, guilt—it all warred in my chest, leaving me stunned and speechless.

"I knew it," he continued, his voice steady but quieter now. "I was careful, Sara. I wasn't ready, and I knew better than to risk it. But still…" He trailed off, his gaze falling to the table.

I swallowed, unsure how to respond. Words felt inadequate. "I'm so sorry, Heck," I said finally, reaching across the table to place my hand over his.

He looked down at where our hands met, then turned his palm upward to clasp mine. "It's for the best. I mean, I'm relieved, in a way. But it still stings, you know? Knowing she thought I'd believe a lie like that."

I nodded, squeezing his hand gently. "You didn't deserve that."

His lips curved into a small, bittersweet smile. "Thanks, Pender."

And yet, as I looked at him—his quiet strength, his unspoken hurt—I felt the secret I'd been carrying swell inside me like a storm threatening to break. How could I tell him now? After everything he'd just said about not being ready, about being careful? How could I tell him… I was pregnant with his child?

Heck's voice pulled me from my spiraling thoughts, heavy with guilt. "Somehow, I feel sorry for her. Guilty. Did I make her like this? Was it my fault, for turning our marriage into an open relationship?"

I turned to him, his words echoing doubts I'd buried myself. "Don't say that, Heck. It always takes two to tango."

"But any decent guy wouldn't agree to something like that, right?" His question cut through the air like a blade, sharp with self-loathing.

I faltered, unable to respond right away. Because, deep down, I agreed. I had thought the same—marriage, love, connection—they weren't things you could spread thin across others. The certainty of my belief felt heavy, but so did his pain.

After a long silence, I finally said, "No." My voice was quiet but firm. The truth hung between us, raw and unflinching. His eyes clouded, and I could see my words had hurt him, but he deserved honesty.

"Ours is different," he said softly, his voice trembling with unspoken feelings. "I don't want to share you. I can't... I can't even stand the thought of anyone else looking at you. I just want to be with you—all the time."

The vulnerability in his words sent a wave of emotion through me. I felt the weight of what we were, what we had both tried to ignore for so long. "Then why did you marry her, Heck?" The question escaped me before I could stop it. It had been clawing at the back of my mind since the day I left for Paris.

He sighed, his shoulders slumping slightly as if the mere act of answering would break him. "Because I hadn't met you yet," he admitted, his voice hushed. "I didn't know what love was. Sophie... she was beautiful, and we were good together in bed, and I thought that was enough. I thought maybe those things were the formula."

He laughed bitterly, his lips twisting in a broken smile. His boyish shrug might've been charming once, but now it cut me. "What a lie that turned out to be."

"I wanted to ask you to call it off before I decided to leave for Paris." My confession was barely above a whisper, almost swallowed by the quiet air between us.

He leaned forward, his eyes piercing mine. "Why didn't you? I would have. I would've stopped the wedding... everything... for you."

"Because I thought you loved her," I admitted, my throat tightening. "How could I compete with someone like Sophie? She was perfect, and we... we were just strangers who met in a café. I didn't even know your name back then, not really. You were just a boy named Heck to me."

His gaze softened, carrying a tenderness that made my breath hitch. "You know we were more than that, Sara," he said, his voice thick with emotion. "You made me see the world differently. You made me feel things I didn't even know were possible. I couldn't name them then, but I knew... I knew it was real."

His hand reached for mine, and before I could stop him, he brought it to his lips. He kissed my knuckles gently, the touch so fragile it felt like it might shatter if either of us moved. It wasn't the bold, confident Heck I'd met months ago. This was someone who had been broken, rebuilt, and softened by storms that left invisible scars.

I stared at him—at his blue eyes, weary but so full of yearning. Deep down, I knew this moment, this quiet corner of the café where we'd created something uniquely ours, would one day fade into memory. But sitting here now, with him trembling beside me, it felt so achingly real. And I wasn't ready to outgrow it. Not yet.

8

Clothes were strewn across my bed in a chaotic tumble of fabrics, as if my wardrobe had exploded in a frenzy of indecision. This felt absurd. It wasn't a first date. Heck wasn't even involved—this was dinner with his mother. And yet, the desperate hunt for the perfect dress felt no less weighty.

Yesterday, my phone buzzed, the sharp sound shattering the stillness of my afternoon. I frowned, glancing at the glowing screen. It wasn't an unknown number, but it was someone I hadn't expected to hear from. The name blinking back at me stirred a prickling unease.

My thumb hovered over the green icon, my mind sparking with indecision. I was caught in the tug-of-war between curiosity and avoidance, my breath hitching as the phone continued to ring. The fourth chime echoed in the quiet, stretching the moment thin. The fifth ring tipped the balance, curiosity breaking through as I pressed to answer.

"Sara here," I said, aiming for calmness but stumbling straight into awkwardness.

"Hello, Sara! It's Helen. How are you, dear?" The voice on the other end brimmed with poise, a soft lilt wrapped in warmth and control, like it belonged to royalty. It made me sit straighter, instinctively smoothing a wrinkle from my shirt. Her tone carried that Julie-Andrews-as-Queen kind of grace, a detail that somehow sharpened the edges of my surprise. This was Helen Sylvia Archibald. Heck's mother.

Elegant, composed, and the kind of fifty-something who turned every head in the room without even trying. Her presence had always been both impressive and a little bit terrifying.

"Oh! Helen!" My voice shot up an octave, betraying the surprise that had taken root in my chest. "Hi! I wasn't expecting…"

"It's been far too long," she continued, effortlessly brushing past the awkward crease in my words. "I thought it might be nice to catch up over dinner tomorrow at Daniel's. I've already made a reservation."

She spoke with such ease, as though we'd been in regular touch all this time. But that wasn't far from the truth. Helen and I had crossed paths several times when Heck and I lived together. Our first meeting was a dinner at the Archibald home, a night I'd expected to be stiff and overly formal. Instead, Helen swept away my apprehension with an ease that surprised me. She had a way of making you feel like the most important person in the room without even trying. When her arm slipped around my shoulders, guiding me on a tour of their sprawling home, I felt myself relax.

She talked about Heck endlessly, her stories weaving between his mischievous childhood antics and the rebellious tumbles of his teenage years. There was a warmth in the way she spoke, an obvious adoration that made it impossible not to smile. That first dinner unfolded like something out of a storybook, setting the tone for the others that followed.

For a while, the dinners became a quiet, cherished rhythm. But when Heck and I went our separate ways, those evenings abruptly ended.

And now, this call.

"You don't have to say yes, of course," she added, though her words brimmed with her unique quality—graceful insistence. "Heck is off at that cigar lounge with his father. I don't much enjoy those places, so I thought… why not us?"

I stopped for half a second, the hesitation hanging awkwardly in the air, before jolting myself into action. "Of course! I'd love to," I said too brightly, the cheerful edge of my tone feeling slightly overdone, like a vase polished past its natural shine.

"Wonderful. I'll pick you up at 6:45. Our reservation is at seven," she said, her voice smooth as silk but edged with a quiet finality, something that left no room for refusal.

"Oh, that's alright; I can Uber!" I offered hastily, not wanting her to think I expected to be chauffeured.

"Certainly. Seven o'clock, then," she replied with the ease of someone accustomed to handling every detail perfectly.

"Thank you! It's the one on 65th, right?" I asked, instantly regretting the question. Surely, I should've known this.

"Yes, that's correct. I'll see you soon, my dear." And with that, the line clicked off, leaving me standing there, phone in hand, feeling both nervous and slightly out of my depth.

And just like that, I was back in Helen Archibald's perfectly restrained orbit.

Now, standing in front of my closet, that feeling hadn't diminished. *What am I supposed to wear?* Next to Helen's elegance, I would probably look like a piece of rag. *What do you wear to match the effortless sophistication of Helen Archibald?* I sifted through hanger after hanger, the pressure to make a good impression tightening around me like an invisible corset. This wasn't our first meeting, but it was our first without Heck buffering the space between us.

After what felt like a lifetime of waffling, I pulled the black dress from the depths of my closet. I'd worn it to my NYU graduation, and miraculously, it still fit as if it had been tailored yesterday. The short sleeves whispered at the edges of my shoulders, and the neckline dipped just enough to hint at allure without being overplayed. The fabric hugged my frame, skimming the curve of my waist and gently cinching my silhouette before falling gracefully to a hem just above my knees. It was classic, understated, and just daring enough.

I paired it with my Aquazzura bow-tie pumps, their black suede and delicate bow details lending a touch of playful sophistication. The ensemble struck the balance I'd hoped for—elegant but not trying too hard.

Leaning closer to the vanity mirror, I added a dusting of powder to my cheeks, a faint blush to bring life to my complexion, and finished with a swipe of natural pink lipstick. My hazel eyes gazed back at me, framed by naturally thick lashes I decided not to tamper with tonight. A pair of pearl drop earrings gleamed softly under the glow of my lamp, completing the look with a touch of timeless class. For someone who rarely fussed over appearances, the transformation felt significant.

I stepped back, surveying my reflection. At 5'7", my swimmer's build gave me almost straight lines where I sometimes wished for more curves, but tonight, the dress seemed to soften those edges, adding a touch of grace that made me stand a little taller. My long brown hair was swept into a messy bun, with a few wisps allowed to frame my face, softening its sharper angles. I barely recognized myself for a moment—the polished woman staring back seemed miles apart from the girl lounging in yoga pants and oversized shirts just hours earlier.

I took a deep breath, nerves bubbling to the surface. This wasn't supposed to feel like a test, but it did. Helen's grace, her quiet authority—it was intimidating. I squared my shoulders, smoothing the fabric of my dress one last time. "You've got this," I murmured to myself.

Grabbing my Ralph Lauren silver wallet on chain from the dresser, I threw on my beige winter coat, its length brushing just above my knees, its tailored silhouette adding an extra layer of polish. The moment I opened the main door to leave, the chilled evening air rushed in, bracing but invigorating. I stepped out into the night, the muted glow of streetlights casting elongated shadows on the pavement. I didn't allow myself a moment to second-guess.

―――――

The moment I stepped inside Daniel's, the air seemed to shift. It was a study in understated luxury—a sanctuary of amber lighting, the soft hum of conversation, and the faint clinking of crystal stemware. Chandeliers hung like halos above the patrons, casting a warm glow over polished mahogany tables dressed in crisp white linens. Every detail, from the subtle gleam of the silverware to the precise angles of the folded napkins, whispered elegance.

A man in a sleek black suit approached me, moving with quiet authority. He exuded a professionalism that perfectly matched the venue's ambiance. "Good evening," he greeted, his tone refined yet approachable. "May I have your reservation, please?"

"Helen Archibald," I said, my voice betraying a flicker of nerves.

His eyes barely skimmed the screen of his tablet. The name alone seemed to suffice. With a polite nod, he gestured for me to follow.

"Right this way," he said smoothly, relieving me of my coat with practiced ease.

I trailed him through the labyrinthine seating area, weaving past tables illuminated by candlelight. The crystalline glasses shimmered like tiny stars under the chandeliers' glow, and the murmurs of intimate conversations hung in the air. My heartbeat thudded in my chest, anticipation mingling with gnawing nervous energy as we neared our destination.

And there she was. Helen Archibald sat poised, regal as a monarch on her throne. She radiated an effortless sophistication I could never hope to replicate. Dressed in a burgundy sheath dress that skimmed her slender frame with precision, she looked like a portrait come to life. Her golden-brown hair, softly waved, framed a face seemingly untouched by time. Her striking blue eyes held a calm intensity, exuding a timeless beauty that commanded attention without a single word.

As I approached, she rose gracefully, her smile warm enough to melt the edges of my anxiety. We exchanged a polite kiss on the cheek, her skin smooth and cool against mine. "Sara, darling," she said, her voice as mellifluous as I remembered. "It's truly wonderful to see you."

"The pleasure's all mine," I replied, the words feeling both sincere and overly formal as they left my lips.

The waiter pulled out my chair, and I eased into it, straightening the hem of my dress. Though nerves still danced beneath my composed exterior, I reminded myself to relax and simply enjoy the evening.

"You look stunning, dear," Helen said, her gaze appraising yet warm.

"Thank you, Helen. Though standing next to you, I feel like a flawed extra in a Vogue spread." I laughed softly, trying to mask my awkwardness.

She responded with a gentle laugh, her eyes twinkling. "Oh, you do know how to make one feel special," she teased, amusement lighting her expression. "Heck has always had a way with words, just like you."

"I wish I could dress like you and look flawless," I said, my words laced with honesty rather than flattery.

"I'll take that as a compliment—gracefully," she replied, her eyes meeting mine with a knowing look. "Being Hector's wife is no simple task; there's a lot expected of you." Her gaze seemed to suggest, *This could be your challenge one day as well.*

As we perused our menus, a sommelier appeared, cradling a bottle of deep red wine. With expert care, he poured a measure into Helen's glass before turning to address me. "For you, Miss Miller?"

The use of my name caught me off guard. Perhaps Helen had mentioned it when making the reservation. I offered a polite smile, gently covering my glass with my hand. "No, thank you. I'm fine for now."

His practiced expression didn't falter as he inclined his head. "Perhaps some sparkling water, ma'am?"

"Yes, that would be lovely," I replied, finding his professional formality oddly reassuring.

Helen glanced up, a flicker of curiosity in her eyes. Her gaze lingered on me for a beat longer than usual, but with the poise of someone well-versed in discretion, she said nothing. She simply nodded as her glass was topped off and returned her attention to the menu.

Once the waiter retreated, Helen's focus shifted fully to me. She closed her menu with a confident snap, the gesture suggesting she'd already decided on the perfect order. "Shall I handle the menu selection for us?"

The offer was a lifeline, and I grabbed it. "Please, Helen, yes." The thought of navigating the sophisticated menu felt too daunting tonight.

Helen turned to the waiter, who had been lingering just behind the sommelier, waiting for his cue. She spoke with a natural grace, the kind that hinted she could recite the menu from memory. Her poise was enviable—almost intimidating. Once we were alone again, her expression softened, and she leaned slightly closer, resting her hand lightly atop mine.

"How are you, dear?" she asked, her voice a quiet anchor in the lively hum of the restaurant.

I exhaled a shaky breath, the simple kindness in her touch melting a layer of my unease. "I'm managing," I said honestly. "Went back to Milliford."

She nodded, her hand remaining as a steady reassurance. "Heck mentioned as much—that you're back working on the bank campaign. And that you both crossed paths at the Tower," she said, referring to the office building as though it were a castle.

"We actually saw each other first at the café we used to frequent," I explained, keeping my eyes on our intertwined fingers.

"How's our company treating you so far?" she asked.

I laughed lightly. "It's... been an adjustment. Gold Standard is so different. The Milliford team can be chaotic, loud, and overly creative. Your people are direct, no-nonsense."

Helen's laughter was like the soft chime of a bell. "I can only imagine. But that's the brilliance of collaborations, isn't it? They meet in the middle somewhere."

"Yes, somewhere," I agreed, though I felt I was still searching for that elusive intersection.
    Her voice softened as she added, "How are you and Heck working closely again?"

"I feel very lucky to be part of that team," I said, a smile tugging at my lips. "The people on Heck's team are so cooperative, and they really know what they're doing. And... well, he's completely different from what I'm used to." I hesitated, realizing I was rambling. "But in a good way," I added quickly. "He's still so creative and hands-on with both the designs and the content. It's impressive, really."

Helen's expression softened further as she nodded. "He's learning quickly. Raul even mentioned it the other day, and Hector is quite impressed, too."

Her words sparked a flicker of pride for Heck, but then she leaned closer, her tone shifting slightly. "How are you and Heck managing to work together?"

I paused before answering. "The first few weeks, I avoided the meetings," I admitted with a wry smile. "But eventually... well, we had to talk. There were things that needed sorting out—things we couldn't ignore forever."

"And now?" Helen asked, her eyes watchful, her patience unwavering.

"We're friends," I said quietly, meeting her gaze. "That's where things stand for now."

"And is that where you'd like it to stand?" Helen's voice was gentle, her curiosity light yet probing, as though she already knew the answer but wanted me to say it aloud.

I held her gaze, my heart stuttering for a moment under the weight of her perceptiveness. "I want him to have the space to... resolve things," I said carefully, each word measured, my emotions hovering just beneath the surface.

She nodded slowly, her fingers brushing over mine in a gesture of reassurance. "I understand, Sara. But listen to me—he won't resolve those things without you. Being friends is better than keeping your distance."

Her eyes searched mine, her expression unconsciously maternal. "He loves you, Sara. I know that because he brought you to our home. Do you realize you're the first woman he's ever brought home to meet us?"

"Apart from Sophie, you mean," I said quietly, assuming the obvious.

Helen shook her head gently, her voice carrying an edge of knowing. "No, not even Sophie. We met her outside after the wedding for dinner. When I invited them to the house, Heck refused."

I stared at her, startled by the revelation. "I don't understand what he sees in me," I admitted, the thought slipping out unbidden. "I'm so... ordinary. I can't compete with the women in his life."

Helen's lips curved into a faint smile, and her thumb traced a soothing line over my knuckles. "I'm going to stop you right there, Sara. Never sell yourself short," she said, her voice firm and steady. "You are beautiful—naturally, effortlessly beautiful—and incredibly smart. Heck doesn't care about expensive clothes or social posturing. What he loves about you is your authenticity, your intelligence. You're what he craves most—a woman who challenges him and makes him better."

Her fingertips tapped my hand gently, guiding my gaze back to hers. "And you are anything but ordinary, Sara. Believe me, you're everything to him—even if he hasn't yet found the words to tell you."

I swallowed hard, warmth blooming in my chest at her words, though doubt still lingered at the edges. "That's very kind of you, Helen. But… I just don't see myself that way."

"That," she said, her smile softening, "is exactly what makes you so attractive. You don't assume. You don't force yourself into the spotlight. You don't even realize the light you bring into the room."

Her reassurance pulled a small, sincere smile to my lips. It wasn't much, but it was genuine.

"Give him time to sort out his divorce and whatever arrangements need to be made with Sophie," she continued, her voice calm yet unwavering. "He will run to you the moment it's done. And when he does, you have no reason to hold him back. He knows that as surely as he knows you're the one."

I couldn't bring myself to meet her eyes. Instead, I fixated on how her hand rested on mine—steady and warm. I feared that if I looked up, even for a second, the flood of emotions I'd been holding back for weeks would rush forward, unspoken truths spilling over to the woman who had raised the man I was beginning to admit I couldn't stop loving.

Helen's voice was soft, a delicate thread of warmth. "Sara, darling, is something troubling you?"

And just like that, the dam broke. The emotions I'd been suppressing for weeks surged out all at once. Without warning, tears spilled down my cheeks, unbidden and unstoppable.

"Oh, my dear," Helen said gently, reaching for my hand again as her other hand offered me a pristine white handkerchief. She didn't release her hold, grounding me with her quiet presence.

"I'm sorry," I murmured, dabbing at the corners of my eyes. My voice trembled, betraying the storm inside me. "I'm just... so overwhelmed. I don't know what to do."

Helen's eyes softened, her gaze full of understanding. "How far along are you?" Her question was tender, free of judgment. She wasn't prying—she was opening a door.

My breath caught as I stared at her. "How... how did you know?"

She smiled knowingly, her expression so graceful it brought fresh tears to my eyes. "Sara, I'm a woman. The moment you walked through that door, I felt it. There's a glow about you—something special. And," she added with a light laugh, "you turned down the wine."

I exhaled shakily, caught between relief and disbelief. "Maybe ten weeks," I admitted, my voice barely a whisper. "I haven't seen a doctor yet. Everything feels... unreal."

Helen's hand tightened over mine, her grip as steady as her voice. "Does Heck know?"

I shook my head quickly, my free hand instinctively brushing over my abdomen. "No, not yet. Please, Helen, don't tell him. I need time to figure this out."

Without hesitation, Helen nodded. "Of course, my dear. This is your choice to make. But," she added, her voice taking on a tone of gentle insistence, "we need to get you to a doctor. You and the little one deserve the very best care, starting now."

Her words cracked something open inside me, and my aching chest finally eased. The relief that came with being understood and held in this moment was overwhelming. "I've been so emotional," I confessed, trying for a weak smile through my tears. "I cry over everything— things that wouldn't have fazed me before."

Helen chuckled softly, her laughter tinged with a tenderness that wrapped around me like a warm blanket. "Oh, my dear, there's plenty more of that to come. Trust me."

"Thank you," I managed, the words thick with gratitude. "I mean it... thank you for understanding. No judgment. I'm so scared to tell anyone."

"There's no need to thank me," Helen said, her smile radiant yet kind. "You're carrying my grandchild."

Her eyes glistened, and for a moment, I saw her composed demeanor flicker as emotion swept over her. She hesitated, as if weighing her next words carefully. "Sara... would you mind if I got involved, even just a little?"

"Of course," I said immediately, my heart lifting at the thought. "I'd love that, Helen. Really."

Placing my left hand gently over my abdomen, I rested my right hand in Helen's. Her palm was warm and steady against mine. It felt as though something vague but profound had bound us together—a silent thread weaving through our newly formed bond and all the words we hadn't needed to say. The thought of her being there for me, for us, sent a quiet wave of comfort rolling through me, one I hadn't realized I needed so deeply until now.

A faint smile touched my lips. I whispered, soft enough for only her and one other to hear, "Hear that, Little Hemingway? That's Grandma talking."

Helen's laughter bubbled up, light and musical, cutting through the thickening emotions between us like sunlight-piercing mist. "Oh, yes," she said with a playful lilt, leaning in close. "Tell Mommy to listen carefully to Grandma and trust that we'll visit your doctor very soon." Her teasing tone was tinged with a deep care that tightened my chest. Her eyes glistened, their warmth flowing like an unbroken current, and I saw my feelings reflected in them. It was strange—magical, even —how this baby, not yet known by the world, had already bound us together.

We lingered in that delicate moment a while longer, sharing no words but everything that couldn't be spoken aloud. Then the waiter approached, his presence expertly timed, his footsteps nearly silent, carrying two dishes that looked like works of art.

Before us, he placed plates of seared scallops gently nestled on a bed of golden saffron risotto. A delicate drizzle of truffle oil glistened like liquid sunlight under the warm chandelier glow. The scent rose immediately—heady and rich, teasing the air between us, breaking the spell of stillness in the most graceful way.

"Ah," Helen said, her tone lighter now. "Daniel's scallops. They're divine, Sara. You must savor every bite."

And so I did. The scallops were tender and butter-soft, their edges kissed by caramelization. The risotto? Creamy and indulgent, with just a hint of saffron that teased the palate rather than overwhelming it. The truffle oil wove everything together, its aroma lingering like the last notes of a favorite song. My nerves, once tightly wound, began to unravel in this atmosphere of good food and soft laughter.

The main course followed seamlessly—a plate of herb-crusted lamb chops, their surfaces a mosaic of green flecked with rosemary and thyme. Beside them, roasted asparagus spears glistened, their tender crispness a colorful counterpart to the lamb. The dish was dressed with a luminous red wine reduction, each bite bursting with flavor—fresh, earthy, and utterly indulgent.

Helen shared stories between bites, recounting with great humor and fondness her experiences being pregnant with Hector. "I craved nothing but marmalade and cucumber sandwiches for three months, can you imagine?" she said, laughter sparkling in her words. Her anecdotes flowed with a warmth that pulled gentle laughter from me. I, in turn, found myself sharing fragments of my plans, my worries, and the uncertainties I rarely voiced aloud. To my surprise, Helen listened with the same attentiveness she might reserve for a gala speech—her demeanor disarmingly kind, as if we were secluded inside a sanctuary of our own making.

I nearly sighed at the sight when dessert arrived—a decadent chocolate soufflé with its delicate, cracked crust and molten center. Each spoonful was indulgence embodied, so rich it melted the moment it touched my tongue. Helen's eyes lit up with delight at her first bite, mirroring my unspoken awe.

By the time we reached the final lingering moments of the meal, our laughter had softened, the conversation turning to lighter topics. A calm harmony settled between us, warmed by the pleasure of good food and each other's presence. The air seemed to hum with a quiet contentment, and the thought of facing the future together—especially for the child I was carrying—felt less daunting, even hopeful.

I gazed across the table at Helen, then, truly seeing her. There was a beauty to her that went far beyond the elegance etched into her features or the poise in her posture. Her beauty was rooted in something deeper—in the compassion she carried, the strength woven into the fabric of her grace. Her love for her son, for the tiny life whose heartbeat felt like a shared prayer, was unmistakable. Helen was the sheltering oak in a storm, her presence steady, her words soothing. She held her family together with decorum and an overwhelming capacity for genuine, selfless care.

For now, at least, the worries of the future felt temporarily shelved, resting somewhere on a distant horizon. Tonight, there was only this— a meal shared between two women, a delicate but deepening bond, and the tiny, growing life that promised to shape tomorrow. And for the first time in weeks, I no longer felt like I had to face it all alone.

9

The doorbell rang far too early, jarring me from the morning haze. My first thought was confusion—who could it be? Heck was still overseas with his father, so it couldn't be him. Rubbing the sleep from my eyes, I shuffled to the door and opened it to find Veronica standing there, her arms filled with an enormous bouquet of pink roses. Their petals were impossibly soft, blushing as if they carried the warmth of sunrise.

"Special delivery. Your Valentine's flowers," she announced, her smile bright as she handed me the bouquet, already beautifully arranged in a clear glass jar. The delicate blooms seemed to shimmer with life, their sweet fragrance unfolding like a story I'd forgotten I was living.

"Oh, fuck." The realization struck me like a bolt. "It's Valentine's Day!" I blurted, my voice a mix of horror and disbelief.

Veronica smirked, her eyes glinting with mischief. "Did you forget?" she teased, tilting her head like a cat eyeing its prey.

"Not about Valentine's Day itself," I muttered, taking in the exquisite arrangement as their perfume curled into my senses. "Just... everything else. My plate's so full I completely lost track of the date."

She grinned knowingly. "Well, they're beautiful, aren't they? Only the best for you. I picked them myself. Heck told me to make sure they were perfect."

I couldn't help but smile as I leaned in to inhale deeply. The intoxicating scent soothed something unspoken inside me. "You nailed it, Ronnie. They're stunning."

"Wanna come in?" I offered, though I knew the likelihood of her accepting was slim.

Veronica shook her head with a theatrical sigh. "I wish, but the shop's a madhouse today. We're drowning in orders, and we're short-staffed. Gotta run!" She started down the steps, then called back over her shoulder, "Catch you later! Oh, and Happy Valentine's Day!"

"You too! Thanks again!" I called back as she hurried off, then closed the door behind me.

I carried the bouquet into the kitchen and set it gently on the counter. Up close, the roses were breathtaking—blushed petals unfurling in perfect spirals, each velvet-soft edge glowing in the morning light streaming through the window. There was an elegance to them, a quiet beauty that felt impossibly tender yet alive with promise. They weren't just flowers; they were a message across the distance, a piece of him reaching me from halfway around the world.

My eyes caught on the small white envelope nestled between the stems. I pulled it free and flipped it open, my heart leaping at the simple, handwritten note.

You always had me at hello, Pender.

A quiet laugh slipped from my lips, a fondness settling over me like a warm blanket. It was one of our favorite movie quotes, from *Jerry Maguire*—a line we'd repeated too many times, always with that same playful smile. I snapped a picture of the roses with the note in the frame, typing a quick caption—*I miss you*. Pressing the 'send' button, I felt the weight of the distance between us lighten, if only a little.

Still holding the note, my hand instinctively drifted to rest on my stomach. It was slight but unmistakable—a small bump pressing against my palm. A new reality was taking shape, one that would soon be impossible to hide, especially from Heck. He knew my body's every nuance too well. For now, though, it was a secret I carried alone—or almost alone. The roses and the note reminded me of him, and in that moment, I didn't feel entirely alone this Valentine's Day. A part of him was here with me. He'd made sure of that.

The stillness of the moment dissolved, giving way to the weight of the day ahead. My first doctor's appointment loomed, arranged by Helen, who had encouraged me to take this step. This appointment offered a slender thread of certainty in a web of endless doubts about how I would manage the unknowns of this pregnancy.

There was no denying it—I was pregnant. My body had made it impossible to ignore, betraying me with relentless signs. Morning sickness hit like waves, triggered by the faintest whiff of certain smells. Fatigue made a home in my bones, pulling me under. Nausea followed me everywhere, weaving itself into the fabric of my days. Yet knowing wasn't the same as confirming. Helen had insisted that I see a gynecologist to determine how far along I was and to ensure I received the best care from the very start. It wasn't just a practical step; it was the first tangible move toward understanding something much bigger.

The thought of it buzzed in my chest, a strange mix of anticipation and apprehension. I'd spent the previous night tossing and turning, my mind a whirl of excitement and fear. This first prenatal checkup would take what had already felt surreal and transform it into something undeniably real.

True to her word, Helen's chauffeured car arrived right on time. I stood waiting at the curb, clutching my tote bag as I fidgeted with the hem of my dress. The uniformed driver stepped out with practiced efficiency, opening the back door for me. Inside, Helen greeted me with her signature poise, radiating elegance in a fitted, salmon-colored sleeveless dress that hugged her figure and ended just at her knees. Her sun-kissed skin and perfectly styled hair only added to the effortless glamor she always seemed to exude.

I slid onto the seat, suddenly hyper-aware of my own understated outfit—a simple sky-blue dress paired with ballet flats. My ponytail felt almost childish next to Helen's polished waves.

"Good morning, Sara," she said warmly, leaning in to exchange a light peck on the cheek. "You look radiant."

"Thank you," I replied, though I couldn't help but glance self-consciously at my reflection in the car's glossy window. "I wish I looked half as put-together as you."

Helen laughed, a soft, melodic sound. "Nonsense. You're glowing. But you're sweet to flatter an old lady."

"Old lady?" I snorted. "You look barely older than me. If this is what aging looks like, sign me up."

She tilted her head, giving me a playful wink. "Skincare, darling. Never take it for granted."

The car hummed down familiar streets as Helen reached into the seat pocket and handed me a stack of glossy catalogs. Pages of pastel-colored cribs, plush rocking chairs, and every imaginable baby essential filled the booklets.

"I thought we could start preparing," she said, her tone casual but laced with excitement. "I'd like to set up a nursery at home. Somewhere the baby can stay when they visit their grandparents." She said it as if it were the most natural thing in the world.

I blinked, my cheeks warming at the thought. "Helen, that's so thoughtful. But..." I hesitated, chewing on my lip. "Heck's not ready yet. I mean, he..." I trailed off and shared with her what Heck and I had discussed about the paternity test with Sophie.

Helen gently patted my hands with both of hers, her voice calm but resolute. "Heck always says he isn't ready. But trust me, my dear, he always rises to the occasion when it matters. Don't carry his worries on top of your own. Right now, you focus on yourself and the baby."

Her reassurance soothed my nerves a little, though not entirely. The truth was, I still hadn't figured out how I would tell Heck. For now, I held onto Helen's steady presence like a lifeline.

The car slowed in front of an old but meticulously maintained building on the Upper East Side. Always one step ahead, the driver opened my door before I could even move. Helen guided me inside, her hand resting lightly on my arm as though she could sense my nervous energy.

The private elevator whisked us directly to the clinic's reception area, which was serene and soothing, more like a luxury spa than a doctor's office. The faint scent of lavender lingered in the air. A blond receptionist greeted us with a bright smile, her attention firmly fixed on Helen.

"Good morning, Mrs. Archibald."

"Good morning," Helen replied effortlessly. "Is Dr. Michaels ready for us?"

Before the receptionist could respond, a nearby door opened. A woman in her forties stepped into view, her sharp, discerning eyes softening as a warm smile lit up her face. She was my height, her presence exuding elegance and ease. Loose waves of auburn hair framed her face, cascading just past her shoulders, and her flawless makeup was balanced to perfection, as though she'd just walked off the set of a medical drama. She could have been a real-life Addison Montgomery from *Grey's Anatomy*.

I couldn't help but marvel, my internal monologue dripping with dry humor. What was it about women on the Upper East Side? Did they all just wake up polished and fabulous?

"Hello, Helen," she said, exchanging cheek kisses before turning to me. "And this must be Sara! I'm Dr. Evelyn Michaels. Come on in." She firmly shook my hand, then glanced at the receptionist. "Can you bring Sara's file?"

The examination room was far from the cold, clinical environment I had dreaded. Soft lighting, plush chairs, and warm neutral tones replaced the usual sterile white walls. A nurse handed me a fresh gown and gestured toward a private bathroom.

After changing, I returned to find Dr. Michaels seated with a tablet in hand. She smiled and gestured for me to sit on the examination bed. "All right, Sara. Based on your records, you're about eleven weeks along. Today, we'll confirm that and check on the baby's progress."

I climbed onto the bed, my heart pounding in my chest. "Is Helen... still outside?"

"She wanted to give you privacy," Dr. Michaels replied with a knowing smile. "But if you'd like her to join, just say the word."

"Please. I'd rather she be here."

Dr. Michaels nodded and left briefly. Moments later, Helen reappeared, her face bright with anticipation. She beamed and took my hand, squeezing it gently. "Of course, darling. I wouldn't miss this for the world."

Dr. Michaels adjusted the bed, propping me up slightly before draping a blanket over my legs. Her voice was calm, soothing as she explained the process.

"We'll be doing a transvaginal ultrasound since it's still early in your pregnancy. You might feel some pressure, but it shouldn't last long."

I nodded, gripping Helen's hand tightly as a wave of anxiety rose within me.

Dr. Michaels moved with a calm precision that should have eased my nerves, but the sound of the machines and the quiet of the room only made my heart pound harder. Lying on the examination table, the blanket over my lower half felt far too thin. My palms were damp, and Helen's hand, warm and steady, was the only thing grounding me. Still, my thoughts churned with nervous energy.

"This might feel a bit strange, but I'll be gentle," Dr. Michaels said. She held up the transducer, a long, slender device fitted with a protective sheath and slick with gel.

I gave a faint nod, my chest tightening as a flicker of vulnerability surfaced. The room seemed to close in around me, quieter except for the hum of the machines.

"Take a deep breath for me," Dr. Michaels instructed. I obeyed, inhaling slowly as she carefully guided the device into place.

The sensation wasn't painful, but it was foreign, an odd pressure that made me hyperaware of every inch of my body. My muscles tensed, and Helen squeezed my hand, her grasp firm.

"You're doing so well, Sara," Helen whispered. Her voice was soothing, maternal in a way that made my chest tighten with gratitude.

I focused on her, on the warmth of her hand and the quiet reassurance in her gaze. Bit by bit, my tension eased, though my heartbeat stayed quick and uneven.

"There," Dr. Michaels said softly, her tone almost reverent as she adjusted the device's angle. "We're picking up the image now."

I turned to the monitor, my breath catching in my throat. At first, it was just a swirl of black and white, a strange, pulsing blur that didn't look like much of anything. But then Dr. Michaels moved the device again, and the screen shifted.

"There's your little one," she said, her lips curving into a gentle smile.

I stared at the screen, my world narrowing to that single fuzzy image. The shape was so small, so delicate, so surreal—but there was no mistaking it. Tears welled in my eyes, and my throat tightened painfully.

"That... that's my baby?" I croaked, my voice breaking as I instinctively reached toward the monitor, even though I couldn't touch what I was seeing.

"Your baby," Dr. Michaels confirmed with a nod. "And everything looks just as it should at this stage."

"Do you see it, Sara?" Helen's voice was thick with emotion beside me. She leaned closer to the screen, her free hand pressed to her chest as if she could steady her own racing heart.

I nodded, unable to form words. The tears that had been threatening spilled over, streaking down my cheeks as I took in the tiny, miraculous reality in front of me.

And then, the sound came. A rhythmic thumping, steady and strong, filled the room. It was almost too much, more overwhelming than I could have imagined.

"That's your baby's heartbeat," Dr. Michaels said softly, but her words barely registered.

The sound roared in my ears, louder than anything I had expected. I gasped, overwhelmed. It was real. All of it. This tiny, growing life inside of me, the insistent rhythmic proof that I wasn't alone anymore.

"Oh, Sara," Helen murmured, her voice trembling. Tears shimmered in her eyes as she tightened her grip on my hand. She was crying, too, her joy as raw and unguarded as mine.

I couldn't speak. My free hand pressed against my chest, as if I could calm the storm raging inside me. Joy, fear, awe—it all tangled together in a knot so tight it hurt, but in the best way.

Dr. Michaels moved the transducer slightly, pointing at the screen. "See that flicker right there? That's the heartbeat. Strong and steady."

I stared at the flicker, mesmerized. It was so tiny, no bigger than the tip of a pencil, yet it carried the weight of the universe. My universe.

Helen leaned closer, her tears falling freely as she smiled at me. "Isn't it the most beautiful thing you've ever seen?"

I nodded, unable to tear my eyes away from the screen. I couldn't fathom how something so small could feel so monumental. My baby. My own.

Overwhelmed by the moment, I whispered, "It's real. I mean, I knew, but... this makes it real."

Helen cupped my hand in both of hers. "Of course, it's real, darling. And you're already doing such a wonderful job."

A laugh broke free from me, shaky and wet with emotion. "I haven't done anything yet."

"You've done everything," Helen said, her voice firm and full of conviction. She brushed a stray tear from my cheek. "And you're going to be an incredible mother."

The words hit me square in the chest. I didn't feel ready—not even close. But at that moment, as I listened to the steady thump of my baby's heartbeat and felt Helen's unwavering support, I started to believe her.

Dr. Michaels worked with quiet precision, moving the transducer to bring the image into sharper focus. Each adjustment made the connection between me and this tiny life more vivid. I could no longer see the boundaries of where I ended and this new existence began. We were intertwined in a way I couldn't explain.

When the examination ended, and the screen went dark, I felt an ache, a sudden loss of the immediate connection to my baby. But as Dr. Michaels stepped back and helped me sit up, her warm smile reassured me.

"Everything looks perfect so far, Sara. Keep taking care of yourself, and we'll check on the little one again in a few weeks."

I nodded, dazed, as Helen helped me off the table and back into my clothes. The moment lingered in the air, etched into my soul like a permanent mark. Despite all my fear and uncertainty, one thing was undeniable—my heart and this tiny, growing life were forever bound.

10

Monday.

The Uber pulled away just as I stepped onto the sidewalk in front of my apartment building. The crisp night air nipped at my cheeks, but before I could take a single step toward the entrance, I spotted Veronica bounding toward me, her straight hair bouncing with each enthusiastic stride. She held a massive bouquet of vibrant flowers in her arms.

"This is for you!" she declared, grinning from ear to ear. "It'll brighten up whatever new surprises are waiting in your apartment."

I took the bouquet, burying my nose in the delicate mix of roses and wildflowers. Their soft, sweet fragrance washed over me like a calming wave. "Gorgeous," I murmured, holding them up to admire the hues. "Wait—you said surprises? What are you talking about, Ronnie? What new things?"

Veronica trailed behind me as I marched into the building, jabbing the elevator button with unnecessary vigor. "Oh, didn't Dad call you? A remarkably elegant woman arrived earlier, accompanied by a small army of uniformed maids. She asked him about your key—to move in some boxes, loads of them."

Her words brought me to a screeching mental halt, anxiety clawing at my insides. "Boxes? From who?"

She shrugged, completely unfazed. "How should I know? I thought you might recognize her. She was very, you know, Chanel chic." Then, with a dramatic pause, she added, "Oh, and by the way, that fancy flower arrangement? It wasn't free. Total bribe. Dad was dumb enough to hand your keys over to some stranger! Those boxes could be anything. Drugs, guns, who knows?"

My stomach sank. "Holy shit, Ronnie! You're freaking me out," I snapped, though her paranoia was starting to get to me. The thought of someone invading my apartment sent a chill coursing down my spine.

She raised her eyebrows in mock seriousness. "I'm just saying, Sara. Dad's not equipped for jail. And don't even think about calling the police yet. God, how could he be so stupid?"

The elevator dinged, and I darted inside, Veronica hot on my heels, her overly dramatic energy buzzing around me like static. When we reached my apartment, my keys trembled in my hand, clinking audibly against the lock as I fumbled to open the door. Finally, I managed to get it unlocked, my heart pounding in my chest.

"Oh my God..." I whispered as I stepped inside.

The transformation was immediate. The dining table now hosted a neatly arranged vase of lilies, fresh and perfectly placed as though they were part of a meticulously planned theme. On the small kitchen island I'd barely used in months sat a high-powered food processor, pristine and expensive-looking. Beside it were carefully labeled containers of prenatal vitamins arranged in a sleek, clear box.

My gaze wandered further. The counter was covered with baskets of fresh fruit. Plump strawberries, shiny apples, bananas, and pears that looked straight out of a glossy ad filled the baskets to bursting. Artisanal loaves of bread, muffins, and pastries wrapped in paper were added to the display. Veronica, of course, had already made a beeline for the fridge.

She swung it open with the enthusiasm of a curious child on a treasure hunt. "Sara!" she exclaimed. "Your fridge looks like it belongs on a cooking show. This is insane! Look at this! Bottled juices, meal prep containers, and not a single week-old pizza box in sight. What happened to you?"

I peered over her shoulder. The fridge's interior practically sparkled, its shelves now stocked with freshly prepared meals arranged neatly alongside handwritten note cards detailing reheating instructions. There were vibrant leafy greens, crisp vegetables, yogurt parfaits, and rows of cold-pressed juice bottles labeled 'Green Glow' and 'Morning Boost.'

"Wow," Veronica declared, her eyes wide with delight. "Your fridge looks like Martha Stewart just blessed it. Wait… I've got it. You're not poor after all, are you? You're a runaway princess. Confess—you're secretly royalty. Is she your long-lost mother? Holy fuck! You're the next Hope Williams!"

I couldn't stop laughing at her over-the-top theory. "Ridiculous! No, she's not my mom. And I'm still very much not a princess. She's just… the kindest, most generous person I've ever met. And for the record, I'm no Hope Williams."

Pulling my phone from my bag to distract myself, I scrolled through my contacts as Veronica rattled off more jokes about castles and tiaras. Helen's number was already on my top speed-dial list, and I pressed the call button instinctively, suddenly needing answers.

She answered on the third ring, her soothing voice greeting me. "Sara, darling! How are you feeling today?"

"Helen, thank you—for the food, the vitamins, all of it. It's incredible," I said, lowering my voice to avoid catching Veronica's attention. She was fully engrossed in a bottle of juice, reading the label aloud with theatrical exaggeration. My fingers were crossed tightly, hoping she wouldn't notice the prenatal vitamins sitting so obviously on the counter.

Helen's soft laugh traveled through the line. "Dr. Michaels was very clear about the importance of the first trimester. You and the baby need proper nutrition, and leaving weeks-old leftovers in your fridge definitely isn't the answer."

I couldn't help but laugh. "These could feed the entire building! It's... overwhelming."

"I know how busy you are, so I had everything prepared by my dietitian. There are instructions marked on the packages—you can take them to work, too."

"You're spoiling me, Helen," I said, my words tinged with gratitude, though part of me felt uncomfortably out of place with all this attention.

"Of course I am! You're carrying the next Archibald heir," she replied casually, yet the statement landed heavily on my chest. That reminder. Those words should have made me feel special, even honored, but instead, they settled like lead. This wasn't just my child anymore. It was an Archibald legacy, a role steeped in expectations. Sophie's treasured dream was now, unexpectedly, mine to bear. A swirl of emotions spun inside me, leaving me momentarily speechless.

"Thank you again, Helen," I said softly, managing to find my voice.

"You're welcome, my dear. Take good care of yourself, and call me anytime you need anything."

When I ended the call, I realized Veronica was watching me, her brows raised in curiosity. "Okay, who is she? She's gotta be someone big to make your fridge look like that."

I sighed, debating how much to reveal. Honesty seemed like my best bet. "Helen. Heck's mom."

Veronica's jaw hit the floor. "Whoa. She likes you that much? Sara, I'm telling you, this is like next-level respect. I've seen movies where the rich family pampers the daughter-in-law carrying their grandchild. But in your case, you're her son's not-exactly-pregnant girlfriend... or something. This is wild!"

"She's nice," I mumbled with a shrug, nervously rubbing the back of my neck. "We just… clicked."

Grinning, Veronica grabbed a container of strawberries. "Since you're stocked for an army, you wanna share? I'll trade you for Dad's pho tonight. You know he's making his special noodle soup today."

"Who'd say no to Charlie's pho?" I replied with a grin. The thought of warm, savory broth and perfectly cooked noodles lit a spark of excitement in me. "Deal. I can't wait!"

Veronica wandered back to the fridge, gushing over my so-called "glow-up" as she inspected every shelf with childlike excitement. Meanwhile, I found myself caught in a quiet tug-of-war of emotions. Helen's gestures, undeniably thoughtful, had lifted weights I hadn't even realized I was carrying. For that, I felt a deep sense of gratitude. But beneath the gratitude was sadness. The reality of what my child would represent crept in again. It wasn't just my baby. This was an Archibald heir, and that meant expectations and responsibilities would shadow him from the moment he was born—so much like the burdens Heck carried himself.

And yet, as I looked around at the tangible support forming around me—from Helen to Veronica and her father—I felt my worries soften just a little. Maybe, just maybe, I thought, I was overthinking it all.

11

As I stepped into the conference room at Archibald Tower, the weight of numerous eyes fell on me, a collective judgment for my tardiness. My morning had been chaos, a blur of nausea and nerves. Morning sickness had hit like a sucker punch, leaving me unable to keep anything down—not even breakfast. The frustrating dance of booking an Uber only added to my already frazzled state.

"I'm so sorry for being late. Something came up," I said, my voice steady despite the turmoil churning inside me. The warmth of the room offered a welcome reprieve from the lingering winter chill outside. I had opted for a practical but polished outfit: fitted black-and-white checkered pants and a crisp white turtleneck. The tail end of winter still held its grip, but spring was just around the corner. Unwrapping the red wool scarf from around my neck provided a small sense of relief.

Heck caught my eye, his smile breaking through the tension like sunlight cutting through clouds. It was reassuring, though tinged with awkwardness. "Hey there. We just got started," he said, standing to pull out a chair for me. The gesture was kind, though marked by a hint of hesitation, as though he wasn't sure whether to welcome me or scold me.

I slid into the seat he offered, my heart still racing from the rush to get here. Now settled, I found myself seated across from the bank's team, flanked by my own.

Kelly, my boss, shot me a look that spoke volumes—disapproval wrapped in thinly veiled impatience. I mouthed a quick "I'm sorry," hoping it would suffice for the moment.

Jen's voice cut through the room, sharp with irritation. "As I was saying before we were interrupted, we need to place those out-of-home digital billboards at bus stops. This is about retail banking; our target is the working class."

Kelly responded, her tone calm but authoritative. "We sent the spot details to your email last week, Jen. We also included the frequencies we should buy for the placements."

The discussion felt tangential to my role. My focus was on campaign development—not on advertising placement or budgeting. Still, Kelly had insisted on our team's presence, likely to bolster Heck's confidence in the proposed budget.

The room bustled with activity, a chaotic symphony of clattering keyboards, animated voices, and shuffling papers. The table was a battlefield of laptops, mobile phones, and iPads, each demanding attention. On one side sat my team from Milliford Marketing: Alexis, endlessly enthusiastic; Kelly, composed and commanding; Andi, sporting her new purple hair; and Dennis, the wide-eyed intern, eagerly absorbing every detail. Opposite them was the Gold Standard Bank team (and me), led by Heck in a sharp navy suit and light blue shirt, exuding charisma and authority. Flanking him were Jen, Raul, and Stephanie, all deeply engrossed in the dialogue.

Heck's glance met mine briefly, his smile steadying me for a fleeting moment in the whirlwind of the room. Though we were keenly aware of maintaining professionalism, the underlying dynamic between us lingered, unspoken, in the background of the lively energy.

"We should leverage social media trends more aggressively," Alexis proposed, his fingers flying over his laptop as he pulled up supporting data.

Kelly gave a small nod, her gaze darting between the budget details and the screen. "Absolutely, but we need to ensure our budget can sustain that shift. Compromising other key elements isn't an option."

Heck leaned forward, his voice confident and persuasive. "We're prepared to allocate additional resources for this adjustment. The engagement metrics we're aiming for will make this a worthwhile investment."

The conversation flowed like a carefully orchestrated dance, blending intensity with collaboration. The snow-blanketed city outside provided a serene contrast to the electric atmosphere inside the glass-walled conference room.

Slowly, I settled into the discussion's rhythm. The usual tension between Heck and me felt muted, replaced by a shared focus on the campaign planning. For now, personal matters receded into the background, overshadowed by our professional objectives.

Just as I began to feel a modicum of calm, a familiar wave of nausea surged through me. My body tensed, torn between darting to the restroom or grabbing a bottle of water from the refreshment station. Opting for the latter, I rose carefully, silently willing my body to cooperate. But as I stepped forward, my vision blurred at the edges, a cold sweat breaking out across my skin. The room, once sharp and vivid, wavered like a mirage. Each step grew heavier, the air thick, pressing down on me.

My breath hitched, my heart pounding in my chest. Then, my legs gave out. Unable to keep me upright, they buckled, and I sank to the floor.

"Sara?" Alexis's voice pierced through the growing haze, his concern cutting sharply through the dull roar in my head.

The hum of casual conversation turned to panicked commands.

"Someone grab water!" Kelly's voice rang out, firm and urgent, directing action.

I barely registered the hands steadying me, but among them was a presence that anchored me. Heck. His hands cradled my head with care, his voice calm yet tinged with urgency. "Call for medical assistance," he instructed, the command cutting through the confusion in a tone that left no room for delay.

I wanted to respond, to tell him I was okay, but the words dissolved on my tongue. The vibrancy of the room faded, the frantic noise dimming to a muffled hum. And then, the world went dark, the collapse of my senses complete as I plunged into silence.

———

As I stirred back to consciousness, the fragmented murmurs around me began to take shape, threading themselves into coherent voices. I blinked against the murky fog clouding my vision, slowly pulling the room into focus. The air carried a faint, sterile scent that tugged at a distant memory of childhood hospital visits. My gaze wandered, catching sight of the white walls and the rhythmic beeping that enveloped me in an odd, steady calm. Beyond the glass window, snow drifted lazily from the sky, its soft light filtering through the blinds and painting intricate patterns across the tiled floor. Despite the haze, a warm sense of relief washed over me—I was safe.

My attention shifted to the corner of the room, where my clothes and bag had been neatly folded—a small act of care that made the space feel less clinical. Then I saw him. Heck sat close, his chair pulled right up to the bed. His hand was wrapped gently around mine, his fingers warm and grounding against my skin. There was something raw in his expression, a tangle of relief and worry etched into his face. His restless eyes searched mine, as though needing to confirm I was truly awake.

"Sara," he said, his voice low and careful as he leaned closer. "How are you feeling?"

I summoned a weak, half-hearted smile, my lips barely curving. "Like

I got hit by a truck," I murmured, my voice scratchy but laced with a flicker of humor. "But... otherwise, I guess I'm okay. What happened?"

His brows drew together, the lines of concern deepening even as he tried to muster a reassuring smile. His grip on my hand tightened just enough to tell me that, whatever had happened, he had no intention of letting me face it alone.

Kelly, who had been pacing anxiously, spun around at the sound of my voice. Her eyes, once clouded with worry, softened with relief as she hurried to my side. Andi and Alexis, who had been sitting quietly on a couch nearby, followed close behind.

"You fainted during the meeting," Kelly explained, her voice still carrying a trace of tension. "It was a real scare. You've been unconscious for a couple of hours, but the doctors say you're okay."

"I'm sorry, Kelly," I murmured, guilt creeping in for disrupting the meeting.

"No need to apologize," Heck interjected before Kelly could respond. "You scared the shit out of me."

Panic fluttered in my chest—what about my baby? I searched their faces for signs of distress but found only concern for me. "What did the doctor say?" I directed the question primarily at Heck.

"You're fine," he reassured me. "They mentioned it might have been stress-related. That's all they could disclose."

Andi nodded in agreement. "They couldn't tell us much, though. Said they needed the family to discuss the medical details."

As if on cue, Helen entered the room, her elegance undiminished by the urgency of the situation. Her presence filled the space with a comforting warmth. Heck looked momentarily puzzled by her arrival.

"Mom? How...?"

Helen approached me directly, positioning herself opposite Heck. She offered a reassuring smile, ignoring her son's surprise. "How are you feeling?" she asked softly. "You're going to be just fine. Dr. Michaels is on her way to make sure everything's alright."

She then turned to Heck, her tone calm and matter-of-fact. "I'm listed as Sara's emergency contact."

Heck nodded, absorbing this information while keeping his focus on me.

"Thank you, Helen," I said, my gratitude genuine.

Sensing the need for privacy, Kelly gestured to Andi and Alexis. "We should give you some space," she suggested gently. "Sara, take your time. There's no rush to get back to work. Just focus on getting better."

"Thank you, everyone. I'll be up and about soon. And I'm really sorry," I added, the apology slipping out instinctively.

Kelly nodded reassuringly. "Just promise you'll get better." It was a rare glimpse of her softer side, a maternal instinct peeking through her usual stern demeanor.

"Thank you," I repeated as Alexis and Andi waved their awkward goodbyes and exited the room. Their presence left me feeling deeply appreciative.

Once they were gone, the room sank into a calm, soothing quiet. Helen took my hand, her warmth easing my frayed nerves, while Heck shifted his attention back to his mother.

"Mom, tell me—why are you Sara's emergency contact?"

Heck's question hung in the air, the weight of curiosity and a need for answers etched across his face. Helen shifted slightly, her usually steady composure wavering as she considered how to navigate the delicate situation without revealing too much. Before she could respond, the door swung open—a welcome interruption that gave her a moment's respite.

Dr. Michaels entered, flanked by two interns in pink scrubs who skillfully wheeled an ultrasound machine to my bedside. The quiet whir of its wheels provided an unexpected comfort, grounding the room with its gentle hum.

A steady presence throughout my prenatal care, Dr. Michaels greeted us with warmth. "Sara, Helen, it's good to see you both," she said, her voice infused with reassurance. She nodded politely to Heck, acknowledging him without breaking her professional tone.

Heck stood beside the bed, his expression a mixture of interest and concern. His eyes darted between the machine and me, searching for answers.

Dr. Michaels turned her full attention to me. "How have you been feeling, Sara? Any changes or concerns since your last visit? And, of course, with today's incident."

I shook my head, though my heart raced. I tried to project calm as I answered. "Overall, it's been manageable. But I've been more tired than usual," I admitted. I paused, adding, "This morning was rough—I threw up most of the food I ate last night."

Dr. Michaels nodded, taking in my words with her characteristic empathy. "And how's your sleep?" she asked, gently helping me sit up to check my vitals with her stethoscope. "Take a deep breath for me," she instructed, her voice steady and calming.

"I've been staying up late the last few nights," I confessed, feeling the weight of the admission. "We're in the thick of campaign development at work."

Dr. Michaels leaned in, her stethoscope pressed gently against my chest, her expression calm and focused. "Your vitals are stable," she said reassuringly, her pen scratching quick, deliberate notes across the clipboard. "Now, let's check on the little one," she added, her hands adjusting the ultrasound machine with quiet confidence.

She stepped closer, carefully folding the blanket to keep me covered while exposing my abdomen. The cool gel spread across my skin, a sensation I had grown accustomed to. Its chill was a small trade-off for the comfort of what came next. The transducer moved smoothly over my belly, and the room settled into a peaceful hush, the only sound the steady hum of the machine.

Then it came—a tiny heart's rhythmic, steady beating, filling the space with its reassuring thrum. A sound so pure it seemed to drown out every worry. My breath caught as the screen flickered to life, revealing the unmistakable form of my baby—small, delicate, and miraculous. The fragile gift that had endured so much already was there, alive and strong, its heartbeat filling the quiet with hope.

Helen moved closer to Heck's side, both of them staring at the screen in awe. My eyes were glued to the image. My baby's safe! I glanced at Heck, watching his expression transform from confusion to amazement as the reality of the moment unfolded before his eyes. I could see the shift in his demeanor, the surprise mingling with a dawning joy.

Tears streamed down my face as I watched Heck grasp the significance. "That's... our... baby?" he asked, his voice a blend of disbelief and wonder.

I nodded, my voice choked with emotion. "Yes," I whispered, my heart swelling with joy. "Little Hemingway." As we watched the screen, I felt a deep connection to both Heck and the life we had created.

Heck's hand had never left mine since I opened my eyes, his grip firm yet tender. "Sara, I had no idea," he confessed, his eyes shining as he gazed at the screen. "This is incredible."

A deep sense of relief and joy enveloped me as the weight of secrecy lifted with our shared moment. I squeezed his hand, feeling the warmth of his excitement.

Dr. Michaels, observing our exchange, offered a gentle smile. "Everything looks perfect. You're doing great," she affirmed. Then, turning to Heck, she added with a playful wink, "I can send you a copy of this."

Heck chuckled. "I'd kill for that copy."

Dr. Michaels lingered with the transducer, allowing us a longer glimpse. Heck, eager for more information, asked, "Can you tell how strong the heartbeat is? Or the gender yet?"

"It's too early for gender," Dr. Michaels replied. "But the heartbeat is strong. The baby's healthy." She carefully removed the transducer, cleaned the gel, and adjusted my gown. "So much excitement for the new mother."

"Will Sara need to stay in the hospital?" Helen inquired, her voice tinged with concern.

"No, she's quite alright," Dr. Michaels replied, her tone reassuring. "I want her out of here as soon as possible. She needs to rest somewhere comfortable."

"You're coming home with us," Heck declared, his voice firm with determination.

"Heck, you're being overly dramatic. My place is perfectly fine," I countered, trying to assert some independence.

"I understand, but after what happened, you shouldn't be alone," Heck insisted, his gaze unwavering.

"Hey, I'm fine. Ronnie is just a few doors down. Plus, I have work," I argued, hoping to sway him.

Heck shook his head. "That's not happening. You're not going back to work anytime soon," he stated firmly. I noticed Helen and Dr. Michaels exchanging amused glances, as if wondering who would win this verbal tug-of-war.

"I'm needed at work. We're in the middle of a campaign," I reminded him, emphasizing my sense of responsibility.

"Sara, forget about the campaign! Your part is done. Don't make me pull the contract," he warned, though his voice carried a hint of jest.

"Come on, that's an overreaction," I said, trying to lighten the mood.

"I'm serious. It's you and our child who matter right now. Don't challenge me on this," he replied, his eyes resolute.

Turning to Helen for support, I found her smiling sympathetically. "Heck, I'm really okay at home," I pleaded one last time.

"Darling," Helen interjected gently, "why don't we agree to stay with us until the weekend is over? Knowing you're safe and cared for will give us peace of mind."

Heck looked at Dr. Michaels for backing. "What do you think, Doctor?"

Dr. Michaels nodded thoughtfully. "Sara, as your doctor, I advise you to rest completely. Having someone with you would be beneficial," she recommended, glancing at Helen for emphasis.

With three against one, I sighed in resignation. "Are all the men in your family this overbearing?" I asked, glancing at Helen.

Helen laughed warmly. "They certainly are, especially when we're carrying their child," she admitted with a knowing smile.

"Let me handle your discharge," Dr. Michaels offered, heading toward the door. "You should be out of here shortly."

As Helen accompanied Dr. Michaels out, Heck leaned in, tilting my chin gently to meet his gaze. In that instant, the world around us faded, leaving us suspended in a bubble of shared joy and newfound hope. His lips descended onto mine with a passion that ignited every part of my being. It wasn't just a kiss; it was an unspoken promise, a binding of our souls.

The warmth of his touch melted away the lingering traces of worry and fatigue, replacing them with an overwhelming sense of love and belonging. In that kiss, I felt the depth of his emotions—a tidal wave of devotion and gratitude that swept through me, leaving no corner of my heart untouched. It was as though every fear and every doubt we had carried was washed away, leaving only the pure essence of what we had created together.

As we pulled apart, I looked into his eyes, seeing a reflection of my own feelings mirrored back at me. There was an undeniable clarity at that moment, an understanding that this was the beginning of something beautiful yet overwhelming.

Heck whispered softly, his voice laced with emotion, "I love you, Sara. More than words can say."

A fresh wave of tears sprang to my eyes, but they were tears of joy, relief, and a love that had deepened in ways I never thought possible. "I love you too," I replied, my voice barely more than a breath, carrying the weight of a thousand unspoken sentiments.

We stayed there in that precious cocoon of intimacy, the outside world temporarily forgotten.

12

As we stepped into the grand entrance of the Archibald home, Eugene, the ever-dutiful butler who had served the family since Heck was a child, greeted us with a polite nod.

"Good evening, Madam Helen," he said warmly, assisting her with her coat.

"Thank you, Eugene," Helen replied with a gracious smile as she handed it over.

Eugene's eyes twinkled with familiarity as he turned to us. "Sir, may I take your coat?" he offered to Heck before extending the same courtesy to me.

Heck shrugged off his coat, handed it to Eugene, and then turned to help me with mine. His hands worked with quiet care, and though he passed the garment off just as quickly, his touch lingered, his palm resting lightly against the small of my back. It was a steady, deliberate presence, guiding me forward through the sprawling hallway. His protectiveness was unmistakable, balanced delicately between reassuring and overbearing.

The polished marble beneath my boots betrayed me as I took a misstep, my sole slipping slightly. Before I could even gasp, Heck's arm encircled me, pulling me upright with practiced ease. "Careful," he murmured, his voice warm but firm. "Those boots are more trouble than they're worth. Come on, let's get you comfortable."

He led me to a plush sofa placed against the wall, his movements sure and unyielding. I barely had time to protest before he knelt before me, his focus entirely on the task at hand. With efficiency and surprising gentleness, he worked the boots off my feet, leaving me in soft socks that seemed to soak up the faint coldness of the marble floors. He glanced up, his eyes meeting mine as a faint smirk betrayed his satisfaction. "Better," he said as if this minor victory was crucial in his uphill battle to keep me steady.

"I'm fine," I replied, trying to maintain my independence—a phrase I'd repeated countless times since leaving the hospital. Helen and I exchanged an amused glance, our eyes rolling in unison at Heck's incessant fussing.

"Really, Heck, you worry too much," Helen chided gently, her voice laced with warmth and affection.

Heck took a deep breath and merely looked at his mother, his expression silently saying, *I can't help it.*

I smiled, appreciating his care even as it bordered on excessive. "Thank you, Heck. But honestly, I've got this."

I reached out both hands, and Heck clasped them without hesitation, his grip steady as he helped me rise from the sofa. Together, we wandered into the living room, our steps echoing faintly against the vast marble floor. I couldn't help but glance around, my eyes tracing the elegant archways and polished details. A flood of memories pulled me back to the first time I stood in this spot. Back then, my nerves had carried a spark of excitement as Heck proudly introduced me to his parents.

But tonight felt different. My chest still tightened with a nervous rhythm, but it was less intimidating—somehow, I felt more at ease. I instinctively clutched the sleeves of my white sweater, its soft fabric offering a small measure of solace after the day's hurricane. It was the same sweater I'd worn in the hospital that morning, a reminder of the chaos I was still shaking off. Heck had promised to swing by my apartment tomorrow to grab my clothes, and Helen had reassured me there were plenty of nightgowns and pajamas ready for the weekend. Their quiet acts of care poked gently through my anxiety, grounding me just enough to keep going.

The murmur of the hallway shifted as Hector emerged from the library, his presence unmistakable even before he spoke. At fifty-eight, he carried himself with the poise of a man accustomed to command, his tailored business suit crisp despite the late hour. Silver strands, meticulously combed back, framed a face marked by sharp eyes that seemed to survey everything and miss nothing. Yet, beneath that aura of authority, there was warmth.

He approached us with measured, confident strides, greeting Helen first with a tender kiss on her forehead. Then his attention turned to me, his firm grip enveloping my hand, steady and reassuring. "Sara," he said warmly, his voice rich and calm—the kind of voice that could ease storms. And for a moment, amidst all my unease, I felt just a little steadier.

"How are you feeling?" Hector inquired, genuine concern lacing his tone as he assessed me. News of the morning's incident had clearly reached him.

Before I could respond, Helen stepped in, recounting the day's events —from the meeting to the unexpected hospital visit. "Sara needs to rest and stay here for the weekend," she concluded. "It's safest if someone keeps an eye on her."

"I'm really fine," I interjected with a smile, a touch of stubborn independence in my tone. "I don't need you guys babysitting me."

Heck's voice was gentle yet firm as he countered, "It's about keeping you and the baby safe, Sara. We can't take any risks."

Hector's eyebrows shot up in surprise, the revelation striking him. "A baby? You're pregnant?"

Helen placed a reassuring hand on his arm. "Yes, but we'll have all night to discuss it. For now, let's get Sara settled upstairs."

With a resigned smile, I relented, allowing Heck to guide me up the grand staircase to the second floor. We moved toward the right wing, home to the guest rooms. As we entered my designated room, I was struck by its elegance. The space was vast, adorned with plush furnishings, a king-sized bed draped in fine white linens with soft gray covers, and large windows offering a breathtaking view of the moonlit gardens.

I stood there momentarily in awe. "This is beautiful," I whispered, turning to Heck. "I never realized this place had an actual backyard garden in the middle of the city." The moon shone brilliantly, casting a spotlight on a lone tree at the garden's center.

Heck approached, wrapping his arms around my waist and resting his hands gently on my abdomen. I leaned back against his chest, feeling the solid warmth of him. "That tree used to have a tire swing," he chuckled softly. "I broke my arm several times playing with it."

"I can only imagine your mother having heart palpitations every time," I laughed.

"And how many nannies were fired every time I did," he added with a mischievous grin, the shared laughter wrapping us in a bubble of warmth.

I turned around and wrapped my arms around Heck's neck, pulling him closer. I placed a soft kiss on his right cheek, feeling the warmth of his skin against my lips. "Thank you," I murmured, glancing around the room at the breathtaking view. "This room is truly beautiful."

Heck smiled, his eyes softening affectionately as he gently tucked a loose strand of hair behind my ear. "I want you to be comfortable," he replied, his voice tender.

A soft chuckle escaped my lips as I basked in the warmth of his affection. "You know, I could get used to this kind of treatment," I teased, a playful glint in my eyes lightening the mood.

Heck laughed, a sound that wrapped around me like a comforting blanket. "I think my plan for you to stay longer is working."

I tugged his face toward mine, our lips meeting in a soft, lingering kiss. I could feel the rhythm of his breathing intermingling with mine. "Heck, this won't change a thing. We're friends, okay? I'm not moving in with you," I whispered against his lips, though a part of me wished for more.

"I can live with that, Pender," he murmured, kissing me again, deepening the connection. This time, it was more passionate, charged with unspoken words and emotions. Our moment was eventually interrupted by Helen clearing her throat discreetly.

"Sara, there are pajamas, nightgowns, and new underwear in those drawers," Helen announced with a gentle smile, her presence a reassuring comfort. She walked to one of the white doors leading to a walk-in closet and bathroom. Curiosity piqued, I followed her inside. Neatly arranged, the drawers offered an array of luxurious underwear and silk nightgowns, while bathrobes in various colors hung in the closet behind glass doors. Shelves were lined with slippers and towels.

"Toothbrushes and some skincare products are on the bathroom counter," she added.

A delighted giggle escaped my lips as I placed a hand over my mouth, unable to contain my joy. "I could live here for a month without needing to fetch my clothes from my apartment!" I exclaimed, my eyes wide with wonder at the luxurious provisions.

Helen's warm smile wrapped around me like a comforting embrace. "Stay as long as you like, dear. You're part of the family now."

A swell of emotion rose within me, and I felt a deep sense of belonging. "Thank you, Helen. For everything," I said sincerely.

She embraced me gently, her warmth a cocoon of safety. "Have a good sleep, dear. You need your rest. Dr. Michaels will be here to check on you again tomorrow," she whispered, kissing each of my cheeks tenderly. At that moment, the world felt so right, and I was wrapped in the nurturing comfort of Heck and his family.

Helen then turned to Heck, cradling his face between her hands, her eyes brimming with love. "Good night, my darling. Let's leave Sara alone to rest. She's had a long day," she murmured, pressing a kiss to his cheek with a mother's affection.

"Yes, Mom," Heck replied, his voice warm with affection.

"Good night, Helen," I added, watching her leave and close the door behind us.

————

Before Heck left my room, he kissed me passionately. It was a kiss that held on—possessing. It was bruising but gentle at the same time. I wouldn't want to let go. I cling to him like he was my lifeline. Then he let me go. " If I don't stop now, Mom will haul me out of this room," he chuckled.

"You better go before I won't let you go," I said.

He kissed me once again and headed toward the door.

I quickly showered when Heck left to erase the day's tension. I selected fresh underwear from the drawer and a white, mid-thigh, ivory silk nightdress with a matching kimono. I looked at myself in the mirror. My stomach was still almost flat, but somehow, a slight bulge was already forming. My breasts are firmer. My body was doing wonders due to my pregnancy. My sex drive was more sensitive now. I was craving for Heck.

I closed the walk-in closet and settled on the bed, but sleep was elusive. What was Heck doing? I turned off the bedside lamp and went to sleep.

I was dreaming. Almost real. Heck's hand was all over my body, touching me until I cried for him to stop. Or not. That woke me up. I was perspiring. I looked at my watch. It was past midnight. Is this pregnancy hormone or what? I tried to go back to sleep. Closed my eyes. But the image of Heck from my dream kept haunting me.

I left the bed, gathered my kimono, and wrapped it around my body. I tiptoed the hallway. It was deserted as I walked into Heck's room. When I turned the knob, it wasn't locked. There he was, sleeping soundly naked from the waist up. He was still sleeping in his boxers. The single light from the bedside lamp illuminated his face.

I slowly removed my kimono and nightgown, leaving just my panties. I straddled Heck's waist and rubbed my breast across his chest. Suddenly, I felt both her hands on my buttocks.

"Oh God, Sara," he murmured as he claimed my lips. He was gentle yet hard. He's too careful and calculated.

"Heck, I won't break. Don't treat me like a china doll," I cried.

"You're beautiful," he moaned as he took my right nipple between his teeth. He sucked it so hard, and he pulled the other nipple with his fingers. I arched my back, wanting more. I cradled his head to my breast, not wanting to let him go.

"Please take me now, Heck," I begged.

He magically got rid of his boxers and didn't wait for me to remove my panties; he just slid them to one side and guided me to take him.

"Ahh, Sara! You're so warm. Wet," he moaned.

I rode him the way he wanted to. Slow. Hard. Fast. And when he touched my pleasure nub with his thumb, this drove me crazy. I don't know how long we lasted, but when we both came, it was glorious.

———————

The early morning light streamed softly through the partially drawn curtains, gently waking me. Panic flickered momentarily as I realized it was morning. Heck's arms were wrapped firmly around my waist, his grip gentle yet possessive. I turned to look at him, watching the peaceful rhythm of his breath as he slept soundly. With a delicate touch, I traced his lips with my forefinger, recalling where those lips had explored on my body. As if sensing my touch, a smile crept across his face in his sleep. I longed to linger in his embrace, but the thought of the house staff bustling about urged me to move. Carefully, I disentangled myself from his hold and slid out of bed, moving with the stealth of a whisper. I quickly slipped into my nightdress and panties, my heart beating a little faster with each quiet step I took out of Heck's room.

As I navigated the hallway, I felt a thrill in the secrecy of my movements, a playful mischief that made me smile. The idea of fooling everyone, even if just for a fleeting moment, added an edge of excitement to my morning routine.

Back in the guest room, I lay momentarily on the untouched bed, my mind wandering to how the Archibalds presented themselves for breakfast. It seemed trivial, yet the grandeur of their home made me question every detail. Opening the guest closet, I marveled at the selection of clothes perfectly suited to my size. The luxury of wealth, it appeared, anticipated every conceivable need—even those of surprise guests. After some contemplation, I chose black yoga pants and an oversized white t-shirt adorned with a whimsical black pipe print. After a refreshing shower, I blow-dried my hair and tied it back into a neat ponytail, slipping into black slippers. Standing before the full-length mirror, I noted the subtle curve of my stomach. "Well, here we go," I whispered to myself, steeling my nerves for breakfast.

The breakfast room was a welcoming sanctuary against the cold morning outside, the snow dancing gracefully beyond the glass doors and walls. The table was a feast for the senses: freshly baked croissants, vibrant fruits, perfectly cooked eggs, an assortment of cold cuts, crispy bacon, and a steaming pot of coffee. Helen, seated to the right of Hector, greeted me with a warm smile, her presence a comforting balm in the elegant setting.

At the head of the table, Hector looked up from his newspaper, setting it aside as he rose to greet me.

"Sara, good morning," he said, his voice carrying a hint of authority softened by genuine kindness. The housekeeper quietly approached, pulling out a chair for me—the seat next to Hector clearly reserved for Heck, which was still empty.

I was relieved to see Hector and Helen dressed casually, breaking the formality I had feared. Helen wore pink yoga pants and a white long-sleeved t-shirt, while Hector wore black joggers and a gray sweatshirt. Their relaxed attire matched the warmth of the room, a stark contrast to the snowy landscape outside.

"How did you sleep?" Helen asked, her eyes filled with concern.

"Very well, thank you," I replied, hoping my voice didn't betray the small lie. The truth of having slept in Heck's room was a secret I intended to keep.

Just then, Heck appeared, wearing black joggers and a t-shirt, his hair still damp from his morning shower. He kissed his mother, nodded a greeting to his father, and then made his way to me, placing a gentle kiss on my forehead before settling into his seat.

"Morning, everyone," he said, his presence adding a comfortable familiarity to the room.

As Heck settled in, I reached for the freshly squeezed orange juice beside me, savoring the sweet tang as I helped myself to eggs and bacon. The realization of my hunger hit me as the enticing aroma of coffee filled the air, swirling up from the cup being poured for Heck. Yet, I resisted, remembering my recent cutback on caffeine and alcohol.

Hector, folding his newspaper, shifted his focus to Heck. "Heck, join me on the Dubai trip next week. It's a two-day meeting, and we need their buy-in while the stocks are low," he instructed, his tone a mix of urgency and business acumen.

"Sure, no problem," Heck replied, nodding in agreement before turning his attention across the table. "Mom, aren't you coming on the shopping trip with us?"

Helen's eyes lit up with a smile. "I wouldn't miss it for the world." Then, she turned to me, her invitation warm and welcoming. "Sara, would you like to join me?"

"I'd love to," I began, my fork pausing mid-air as I considered my workload. "But we're in the middle of developing a major campaign, not only with Goldstar but another important account as well."

Heck leaned forward, his determination evident. "We can arrange something with Milliford. I'm sure they'd accommodate my request."

I shook my head, cutting him off swiftly. "Don't do that, Heck."

He looked puzzled. "Why not?"

"Because it wouldn't be professional. I don't want people thinking I'm receiving special treatment because of you," I explained, my tone firm yet appreciative of his willingness to help.

Heck shrugged, a playful defiance in his eyes. "It is what it is. And I don't mind pulling some strings."

"I don't want you to," I interjected firmly. Turning to Helen, I added, "I'd love to go shopping, but I really don't want to stir things up. You know what I mean. People are already talking, and I'm trying to keep a low profile," I said, my tone almost pleading as I looked back at Heck.

"What could they possibly be talking about?" he asked, his tone teasing, and I could feel my annoyance starting to bubble up.

"Heck, you're still married," I replied, my voice rising slightly. "I don't want to be seen as the other woman flaunting it in their faces!"

Realizing I'd gone too far, especially with his parents listening, I glanced at Helen, who was watching me with a knowing smile.

"Who's still married?" Heck queried, the playful curve of his lips suggesting he was enjoying this far too much.

"Very funny, Heck," I shot back, rolling my eyes as I bit into a strip of bacon.

"No, really. I'm not joking," he said, the laughter in his eyes undeniable. "You're looking at the most eligible bachelor," he paused for effect, "again… in New York City."

I turned to him, ready to swat his arm playfully, but caught sight of his parents, both suppressing grins. "Heck, are you serious?"

"I was going to tell you after the meeting, but then you fainted, and with the news about the baby, I figured it wasn't as important," he explained, his smile broadening.

"Oh…" was all I could manage, my mind racing to catch up with the revelation.

13

Monday mornings had never been my favorite, but this one felt utterly surreal—like stepping into a scene from someone else's life. The first week of spring was casting its spell over New York City, and the city was alive, shedding its winter coat. Patches of color began to bloom where bleakness once clung—bouquets of daffodils brightened window boxes, and hints of green peeked from the trees lining the streets. Adjusting my skirt, I stepped out of my building as Tony, the clean-shaven muscle assigned to me, opened the sleek black car door. Dressed in a black coat, he gave me a polite nod, like we were co-stars in some mob movie, and I, of course, was the clueless heroine thrust into a world of wealth and danger.

"Thank you," I mumbled as I slid into the car, clutching my bag tightly. This was my life now. Chauffeured. Guarded. Babysat. God, I missed the subway—and bumping into someone in a bad mood before 8 A.M.

"Have a good day, Miss," Tony said, holding his position by the passenger side door as I tried to dodge the world's gaze and sprint into Milliford.

I wasn't used to this. At all. I'd always been independent—proud of it, even. But things had shifted dramatically since... well, since I started carrying an Archibald. Heck, Helen and Hector had made it painfully clear that I wasn't just carrying a baby; I was carrying the most precious cargo. And because Heck's messy divorce was the kind that tabloids feast on, I'd been placed in this overly cautious bubble of protection. It wasn't just about me. It was about the baby—the

Archibald heir. Apparently, I needed to be treated like a Fabergé egg from now on.

Tony shadowed me as far as he could without following me through the office's glass doors, and as soon as I made it inside, I bolted for the elevator. The last thing I needed was Andi—or worse, Alexis—catching me climbing out of the Archibald Batmobile.

The office was its usual dull palette of assorted greys and whites, a stunning display of how much we pretended this place was "creative." Yet something in me felt lighter today. Maybe it was the hormones. Or the three croissants I'd inhaled for breakfast. But my good mood froze mid-step when Andi barged into my line of sight like the pixie tornado she was.

"Your lover boy is here," she announced, her trademark pink coffee mug poised dramatically in one hand, an iPad in the other.

"What are you talking about?" I blinked, half-distracted by her sudden transformation into a walking banana tree. Her pixie haircut—a shade of green not found in nature—perfectly matched her green onesie ensemble.

"He's in the conference room," Andi hissed as if confessing state secrets. "Big bosses. Lawyers. The establishment. And Heck Archibald himself, front and center."

I frowned, glancing at my watch. "It's barely nine in the morning. What could possibly be—"

"Exactly!" Andi interrupted. "What could be so important that he's here? And, for the record, don't pretend you have no clue. Like, seriously, Sara. You sleep in that man's silk sheets—don't look at me like that! Tell me you didn't at least giggle-pillow-talk whatever this is out of him."

"No!" I exclaimed, louder than intended. "I have no idea, Andi! He didn't tell me anything."

"Well." She smirked over her coffee, clearly unconvinced. "Guess you're about to find out."

Despite my protests, I couldn't help but glance into the conference room's frosted glass as I walked past. Shadows of sharply dressed figures moved inside—a mix of power suits, ties, and serious postures. My breath hitched when I almost caught sight of Heck's familiar silhouette. Almost. But if he saw me walking by, he didn't acknowledge it.

"What the hell is going on?" I muttered under my breath, more to myself than to Andi, who had already wandered off.

Sliding into my cubicle, I barely had a moment to gather my thoughts before Kelly, my famously no-nonsense boss appeared. One sharp flick of her manicured finger—bright red claws of intimidation—and I was summoned into her office.

I stepped inside, shutting the door softly behind me. Kelly didn't waste time.

"What's going on with Heck and the Gold Standard lawyers?" she demanded, her fingers tapping the desk rhythmically, like an impatient predator.

I blinked at her, caught off guard. "I honestly have no idea. Why is everyone assuming I do?"

"Well, gee, Sara," she said, throwing her hands wide in mock exasperation. "Could it be because you're basically sleeping next to one of the decision-makers?"

"Is that what everyone's calling it now?" I snapped, more defensive than I intended. "Where I rest my head at night is none of anyone's business."

Kelly waved a dismissive hand, clearly uninterested in the nuances of my personal life. "Fine. But this is serious. Are we losing Gold Standard?"

"I don't know, Kelly," I said firmly. "If Heck didn't tell me why he's here, do you really think he'd just casually drop that kind of game-changing news in bed?"

"I don't know how you people in relationships work!" she shot back, exasperated. "All I know is that this meeting is above my pay grade—and above my boss's pay grade—and everyone's on edge because no one knows what the hell is going on."

I folded my arms, tilting my head slightly. "Well, that makes two of us, because I'm just as clueless as you."

Kelly narrowed her eyes, studying me, as if deciding whether to press further. Then, with a dramatic sigh and an eye-roll reminiscent of a high school Mean Girl, she threw her hands up in mock surrender.

"Fine. But if you happen to find out—and I know you will—you'll tell me. Right?" Her tone was less a question and more an ultimatum from someone who expected information to be handed over.

"Of course," I replied dryly, already done with the interrogation.

"Good," she said, leaning back in her chair. "Now go figure out why the hell that man is here at the crack of dawn."

"Noted," I muttered, slipping out of her office.

Back at my desk, I settled into my chair, staring blankly at my monitor. Despite my efforts, curiosity gnawed at me, joining the buzzing anxiety that seemed to vibrate through the building. Whatever Heck was doing here, it wasn't trivial. And for the first time in a long time, I wasn't sure where I stood in all of it.

What was he keeping from me? And why did I feel like today was about to change everything?

———

The conference room remained impenetrable, its frosted glass walls guarding whatever monumental secrets were brewing. Hours ticked by. Food and refreshment carts rolled in at regular intervals, a parade of nervous assistants ferrying trays stacked with finger sandwiches, coffee carafes, and bottled water. Occasionally, the door would creak open as someone slipped out for a bathroom break, but the rest of us were left to speculate in utter ignorance. The opaque glass was a constant reminder that something *big* was happening behind it—and I wasn't part of it.

I stared at my computer screen, willing myself to focus. I typed, deleted, and retyped the same email at least three times before giving up and leaning back in my chair with a groan. Productivity was a joke today. How could anyone focus on that kind of tension radiating through the office? Nobody besides me seemed as curious about Heck and the Gold Standard lawyers as Kelly or Andi.

Since the morning Heck had dropped the mother of all bombshells about his divorce over breakfast, our dynamic had been... complicated. We were friends. We were more than friends. Technically, we were sleeping together, but there were no labels. We'd agreed to take it slow. And slow, for me, meant returning to my apartment after that fateful weekend. At least Veronica didn't seem to mind the circus this new arrangement brought into our building. Every morning, she peeked out her window as Tony opened the car door and escorted me to the sleek black SUV, grinning like a kid spotting a celebrity.

But I'd stood firm on some boundaries. Heck was welcome to visit— after work, during weekends, and definitely for the Central Park walks his mother insisted on accompanying us for. He was even allowed at my doctor's appointments, where Helen fussed and asked all the questions I never even thought of. Yet, his toothbrush still didn't have a rightful home in my bathroom, and his clothes didn't occupy a single drawer in my apartment. Independence meant that much to me. It was my way of holding onto who I was before all this Archibald business came swooping into my life.

Of course, that didn't stop the office gossip mill from spinning. Rumors bubbled, and whispers grew louder. But no one had clocked what should've been the juiciest part of the story yet—that I was carrying the next Archibald. My stomach barely showed at twelve weeks along, giving me the anonymity I still cherished. For now, anyway.

My phone buzzed on my desk, interrupting my train of thought. A sly smile crept onto my face as Heck's name flashed across the screen. I cradled the phone between my ear and shoulder and answered quietly, mindful of the others working around me.

"Hey there," I whispered, unable to hide the cheeriness in my voice.

"Hey," his voice replied, low and gravelly, tinged with exhaustion. "How are you feeling?"

"Good. No big events today, just some looming deadlines. You know, the usual," I said, rolling my shoulders out of habit to relieve the tension from staring at my screen. Pausing, I added, "But I can't say the same for you." The words slipped out before I could catch myself —I didn't want to sound nosy.

He sighed deeply, lingering silently for a beat too long. "I don't think this will wrap up in an hour or two," he finally said, his tone giving nothing away.

I bit the inside of my cheek, debating whether to push or retreat. Curiosity gnawed at me—damn, I hated this whole mysterious conference room situation. But I didn't want to pry openly. Instead, I took another route.

"Hmmm... Do you want to sleep with me tonight?" I asked, the playful tone in my voice deliberate.

For a moment, silence. Then, a chuckle—a husky one that told me he knew exactly what I was up to. "Now that I couldn't say no to," he said, amusement clear in his voice. "What did I do to earn this invitation?"

I leaned back, twirling a pen idly between my fingers. "Oh, nothing. Maybe I just miss you," I teased. "Or maybe I intend to bribe you for information."

He laughed outright this time. "Ah, now the truth comes out. Manipulative Sara makes an appearance."

"I might wear something sexy," I teased in return, keeping my tone light. "Because maybe, just maybe... I'll play interrogator tonight."

"Damn," he muttered, his voice dropping half an octave. I could almost hear the way his smile curved into that lopsided grin. "You really know how to get a man to talk."

"Or..." I continued, feigning innocence, "I could just skip the charade and answer the door naked. Save time."

"Sara!" His voice pitched higher for a moment before he caught himself, likely glancing around to make sure no one overheard him. "You're dangerous, you know that?"

I smirked, knowing I'd won this round. "Go back to your high-stakes meeting, Heck. I'll see you tonight."

"See you," he murmured, the smile still lingering in his voice as he hung up.

I set the phone down carefully, the grin lingering on my face far longer than it should've. While Heck hadn't revealed a single detail about the meeting, I felt a small measure of victory knowing I'd gotten him to unwind, even briefly. But as much as I cherished these little games between us, I couldn't help but feel the tension grow stronger by the minute.

What could be so important, so monumental, that Heck couldn't talk to me about it? Whatever it was, it felt like the answer would come sooner rather than later—and it might be too big for me to ignore when it did.

For now, I had a deadline waiting. But the weight of curiosity loomed over me like a storm cloud about to break. Tonight, I was going to get answers. I wasn't sure how or when, but I knew Heck couldn't keep me in the dark forever. Not this time.

———

The spoon hovered in my hand as I savored the last silky drop of chocolate ice cream, letting it melt luxuriously on my tongue. The sugar rush comforted me, as familiar as a warm hug on a rainy day. I lounged on the couch, knees pulled up, wrapped in an oversized black T-shirt dominated by an absurdly large neon-pink hashtag symbol. The hem barely grazed the tops of my thighs, where my matching pink cotton panties peeked out—a combo I'd worn a hundred times. Somehow, it felt softer tonight, maybe because I'd paired it with a lazy evening and my favorite dessert.

The low hum of the television filled the air, though I wasn't paying attention to the drama flickering across the screen. My mind was a soft swirl of contentment and curiosity—particularly about the mysterious project Heck had been working on with such intensity over the past few weeks.

The click of the apartment door stirred me from my thoughts. Heck stepped in, carrying with him the faint scent of cedarwood from his cologne mingled with the crisp air from outside. His arrival always ignited something inside me—the anticipation I could never quite describe.

"I was hoping to see you before you fell into a sugar coma," he teased, shrugging off his gray jacket. His fingers worked at the buttons of his perfectly white shirt, revealing a hint of that well-toned chest I never got tired of seeing. He didn't stop until the edges of his shirt fanned open just enough to drive me insane. With a weary sigh, he collapsed onto the couch beside me.

I tilted my spoon, the empty curve catching the dim light from the lamp. I knew better than to scrape the bowl—it'd make that awful sound—but my disappointment at finishing the ice cream was almost unmistakable. Before I could mope for too long, Heck leaned over, brushing his lips near my jaw to catch a stray streak of chocolate. His tongue dashed across my skin playfully, sending an electric thrill down my spine.

"Hey!" I laughed, swatting at him half-heartedly.

"You know," he began, smirking as he settled back against the couch, "I thought you promised to meet me at the door naked. Wasn't that a thing we discussed?" The arch of his brow and that infuriating smirk made it impossible to stay mad at him.

I leaned back and crossed my arms, a petty pout settling across my lips. "Maybe I forgot. Besides, what's the big secret brewing in the Milliford conference room today?" I countered, sliding closer to him until my head rested comfortably across his lap.

He started combing his fingers gently through my hair—a soothing, intimate act that felt as natural as breathing between us. My lips clung to the edge of the spoon, rolling it back and forth between my teeth as I watched him.

His eyes flickered down to meet mine, amusement dancing there before he murmured, "Can you keep a secret?"

"You know I can." I straightened up slightly, offering him my pinky for good measure. "Pinky swear?"

At that, he chuckled—deep, rich, and the most beautiful sound I'd heard all day. His larger pinky hooked around mine, sealing whatever fate lay between us.

Sliding his hand back into my hair, he leaned in conspiratorially. "Gold Standard is planning to corner Milliford," he said, glancing at his watch. "Ah, correction—we officially acquired it two hours ago."

"What?" The word burst out of me like a spark, and I bolted upright, staring into his smug, proud face. "Are you serious? Gold Standard? Your family's bank? Wait—does this mean you're technically my boss?"

"Unless you'd prefer a direct report," he quipped, laughing at my shocked expression. That boyish grin—it was dangerous in moments like this. Heck was giving me that *I-can-make-things-happen* look, which was even more dangerous.

"Heck! No! Do not pull strings for me!" I warned, jabbing a finger in his direction.

"Relax," he said, raising his hands defensively, though the mischievous glint in his eyes remained. "You're safe under Kelly—for now."

I leaned back, narrowing my eyes at him, before quickly returning to my curiosity. "What does this mean, though? For the company? For you?"

"It means expansion." His tone shifted, taking on a weightier, more serious edge—but not without a spark of excitement. His gaze drifted somewhere beyond the room as if he were staring into a future only he could see. "Southeast Asia, Europe—advertising is our next big project. Think of it as a prototype for broader bank investment initiatives. Just like real estate."

I blinked, momentarily stunned. "Listen to you! Months ago, you were all gallery openings, gray T-shirts, and jeans, living for the love of art. And now you're sitting here talking about global expansions. Investments!" I paused, gasping dramatically. "Who even are you, Heck Archibald?" I threw myself into a mock cry, rubbing fake tears into my oversized T-shirt.

He rolled his eyes half-heartedly, a soft laugh rumbling in his chest. "I'm still me... mostly," he admitted. His expression softened as he placed both hands on my stomach. The gesture melted away my playful act. "Little Hemingway just made me see things differently. Gave me a new perspective."

My heart caught at the way he said it, with such quiet reverence for a future he hadn't known to imagine until now. I studied him briefly, the boy I'd met and fallen for so quickly, and now the man he was becoming. His ambition didn't scare me the way I thought it might. It grounded me, making me feel like I was stepping into a life that felt impossibly right.

I cupped his face with both hands, trailing my thumbs along the strong edges of his jawline. He had become so much more than I had dared to dream for myself, yet here he was, looking at me like I was his whole universe.

With a surge of emotion that defied words, I kissed him—fully, deeply, unwaveringly. My lips pressed into his with all the weight of my heart, carrying every unspoken thought, every buried feeling that language could never hold. It wasn't just a kiss; it was gratitude, raw and unfiltered. It was love—boundless, consuming, and undeniably real. My hands trembled against his chest as the warmth of his skin radiated through me, anchoring me in the present. Time felt suspended, the world around us fading into nothingness as I poured every ounce of myself into that kiss. It was a plea, a promise—I wanted to stay here, bound to him, tethered to a perfect moment that somehow held everything we were and everything we could be. The air between us felt electric, our connection deep and unbreakable, and as I pulled away, the whisper of his breath on my lips lingered like an unspoken vow.

When I pulled back, meeting his gaze, Heck rested his forehead against mine. His breath fanned warmly over my lips before he murmured, "I'm not going anywhere, Sara. Not now. Not ever."

Neither was I.

14

The cat was already out of the bag. As far as Milliford was concerned, I was pregnant with the child of Gold Standard Bank's top boss. While we never officially confirmed it, the whispers had turned into an open secret. Kelly still treated me much the same, but her demeanor had softened slightly; I could almost catch glimpses of a maternal side to her. Despite the circumstances, my workload remained unchanged. Heck and Raul had explicitly requested that I take the lead on the bank's social media messaging. Following protocol, I ensured that everything went through Jen first, even though she seemed determined to make my job more challenging. Fortunately, Kelly had my back, insisting that all communications be copied to her and the entire team, including Heck, which helped keep things in check.

The conference room at Gold Standard Bank was becoming my second home—a corporate cocoon of glass walls, a polished walnut table that gleamed under the soft lighting, and ergonomic chairs that promised more comfort than they delivered. The near-constant hum of the central air conditioning blended with the distant murmurs of employees bustling in nearby cubicles. A faint smell of fresh coffee lingered, courtesy of the break area just down the hall. It was my usual day to be at their office, presenting the weekly report and outlining plans for the week ahead. I typically spent the entire day in the conference room, poring over data and reviewing feedback from the bank branches. With my pregnancy becoming more noticeable, I'd retired my tight jeans in favor of comfortable dresses—a choice that felt both practical and freeing.

My laptop was open, its screen glowing with a tangle of spreadsheets, engagement metrics, and chart presentations for this week's social media performance review. My fingers hovered over the keyboard as I adjusted key points for upcoming posts. The table around me was cluttered with files, annotated notes on sticky pads, and two tall bottles of water I'd promised Helen I'd drink throughout the day.

I absentmindedly smoothed the fabric of my emerald A-line dress over my growing belly. It was getting harder to hide now—not that it mattered much. The office gossip had already run wild, crafting fantastical stories about my mysterious pregnancy. From whispers about a scandalous Parisian affair with a married man to curious speculations about what the Gold Standard Bank's elusive heir was doing with me, the rumors had taken on a life of their own. Heck found the chatter amusing; I found it exhausting.

A shy knock on the door cut through my thoughts. When I looked up, a young woman with wide, curious eyes peeked through the frosted glass.

"Hi, Sara," she said, her voice soft but hopeful. "Do you need anything?"

I smiled at her, gesturing for her to come in. "Oh, I'm fine. But if you're up for it, I could use a second pair of eyes on this data."

"Sure!" she said eagerly, stepping inside. She closed the door behind her with just a little too much care, and I recognized the telltale awkwardness of someone new to the corporate world. Cindy was petite, with a short bob of jet-black hair tucked neatly behind her ears. She wore a bright blazer that was just slightly oversized, a sign that she hadn't yet found her footing between trendy and professional. Her enthusiasm, however, was unmistakable.

She settled into the chair beside me, her fingers nervously fiddling with the USB drive hanging from her lanyard. I slid my iPad toward her, showing her the engagement graphs I'd been working on.

"These are last week's metrics," I began, pointing at the screen. "The blue bars represent comments, and the green is for reactions. I'm trying to identify the messaging types that resonate with our audience—what gets them talking versus what gets them clicking that heart button."

Cindy nodded intently, her laptop already flipped open in front of her. "Would it be okay if I airdrop this to my computer? I might be able to pull some benchmarks to cross-check."

"Go ahead." I smiled as she began working diligently. "You've got a knack for this, Cindy. Have you always been into social media analytics?"

She looked up, slightly startled but pleased. "I... yeah. Kind of? I mean, I love how you can tell so much about people and trends just from data. It feels like piecing together a puzzle."

Cindy and I pored over the metrics for the next two hours, bouncing ideas back and forth. Her confidence blossomed as she found insights I hadn't considered, and I had to admire how effortlessly Gen Z seemed to decode social media language.

A soft knock at the door interrupted our flow. This time, it was Heck.

The sharp cut of his tailored charcoal suit demanded attention, elevating his usual charm with effortless elegance. The open collar— just undone enough to toe the line between polished professionalism and rogue confidence—only added to the effect. He lounged against the doorframe as if it were his rightful place, hands buried casually in his pockets, that boyish grin spreading across his face like both a shield and a weapon.

"Howdy! Mind if I interrupt a bit?" His voice carried the familiar teasing drawl that never failed to disarm me, no matter how much I pretended otherwise—a maddening mix of smug and sweet.

I couldn't help the grin that tugged at my lips. "Only because you said 'Howdy,'" I shot back, my words laced with mock surrender.

Cindy, perched on the edge of her seat, sprang into motion, gracefully collecting her things with as much composure as she could muster. "Uh, I'll go finish those cross-checks at my desk," she murmured, her cheeks warming with the faintest blush.

"Thanks, Cindy," I said, keeping my tone genuine despite the faint amusement bubbling beneath. Her diligence was always appreciated, even as the moment took a decidedly different turn.

She offered a slight nod before slipping past him, her presence quickly replaced by the weight of his attention. His grin deepened, and I fought the urge to roll my eyes, knowing all too well just how much of an effect he intended to have.

Once she was gone, Heck stepped inside, closing the door with a soft click. He crossed the room with an easy confidence, leaning down to kiss me. His lips brushed mine briefly before he sat beside me and reached for my hand, his touch warm and comforting.

"You look beautiful today," he murmured, his voice low and meant just for me.

"So do you," I replied, running my finger along his jawline to wipe away a faint trace of my lip gloss.

His hand found its way to my stomach, his fingers gently resting against the slight curve of my belly. "Did you give Mommy some hard kicks today?" His grin widened, his tone light and playful.

I laughed softly. "It's too soon for that, Daddy." I couldn't help but mimic a sing-song tone.

He chuckled, then adopted a mock-stern expression. "Mom asked me to check on you—again. Did you take your vitamins? Have you eaten? Fruits and milk?"

"You and Helen are ridiculous," I teased. "Of course I did! How could I forget when she texts me reminders every few hours?"

He leaned back in his chair, his expression softening as a tinge of seriousness crept in. "I hate the rumors, Sara. They're not funny anymore. Mom and I talked... and we have a plan."

"A plan?" I asked, tilting my head. "What plan?"

"Don't freak out, okay?" he started cautiously, his crooked smile suggesting he was about to do something bold.

I narrowed my eyes, leaning back as he fished something from his inner coat pocket. Out came a small black velvet box. My heart stopped.

"Heck," I started, my voice barely above a whisper.

"I know we've talked about this." His voice softened, his usual confidence tempered by something more vulnerable. "I'd ask you to marry me, but I know it's too soon—it's not what you want right now."

My chest tightened as he opened the box, revealing a breathtaking emerald set in white gold, surrounded by a halo of diamonds.

"This isn't an engagement ring," he said quickly, his words tumbling out as if they couldn't wait to reach me. His hands fidgeted, almost nervous, but his eyes stayed steady on mine. "It was my mom's. My dad gave it to her the day she found out she was pregnant with me."

He paused, the weight of the moment settling between us before he continued, his voice softer now. "She wanted you to have it. She said it was time for it to be passed on. And… one day, when the time's right, you'll pass it to Little Hemingway's girl. Keep it in the family, you know?" His voice cracked slightly on the last words, and the emotion in his gaze was undeniable.

"Oh my God," I whispered, my voice barely audible as tears welled in my eyes. The ring rested in his palm, catching the light just enough to cast a soft shimmer. It was beautiful—understated yet timeless, as if it carried decades of stories within its elegant curves.

"Will you wear it?" he asked, his voice steady, though his eyes held the weight of something fragile—hope, maybe fear, or both.

"Yes," I breathed, the word quivering, laced with everything I couldn't say. "Yes, I'll wear it."

He reached for my hand with such care, as if the moment held its own gravity, pulling us into a world where nothing else mattered. Slowly, he guided the ring onto my finger, his fingers brushing my skin, igniting a warmth that bloomed through me. We stayed like that for a second—forever compressed into a heartbeat—before he closed the space between us.

The kiss wasn't urgent, but it consumed me all the same. His lips found mine, gentle at first, his touch a question, a whisper of emotions too vast to translate. Then, as if understanding there was nothing left to hold back, he deepened it, and the world dissolved. It was the kind of kiss that unraveled everything. Like words unspoken found their way through the press of lips, the tilt of his head, the way his hand cupped the curve of my jaw. Slow and aching, it carried promises we hadn't spoken yet, vulnerabilities we hadn't fully unwrapped.

His other hand wove into my hair, tilting my face closer, and in that moment, I felt something shift. This wasn't just a kiss—it was an unspoken vow, one that existed beyond tradition, beyond rings or words. Somehow, it was raw and tender all at once, breaking me open and stitching me back together in the same breath.

When the kiss finally broke, our foreheads rested against each other, his fingers still lightly curled around my face as if afraid to lose the moment. The edges of his smile curved against my skin, a tether back to reality. But for a beat, all I could feel was him—the taste of him lingering on my lips, the steady rhythm of his breathing aligning with mine.

It wasn't an engagement proposal. But with that kiss, it became something else entirely—a promise, a beginning, and the end of every doubt that had tried to creep between us.

For a moment, it felt like the closest thing to an engagement proposal.

15

Saturday.

The smell of fresh paint lingered in the air, carrying a hint of lavender from the diffuser Heck insisted we use to combat the fumes, though I'd told him twice already that I kind of liked the smell. We stood in the middle of my apartment, surrounded by open boxes, tiny furniture pieces, and rolls of wallpaper with pastel animal prints I couldn't decide between. The space was chaos. Beautiful chaos. And yet, I couldn't stop grinning.

"Are you sure the dresser doesn't look crooked from this angle?" Heck stood back, tapping his chin with his forefinger, the instruction manual dangling from his other hand. The man had been obsessing over corner angles for the last fifteen minutes, and I wondered if the baby would inherit his perfectionist streak.

"It looks fine. Perfect, even," I said, stepping close to pinch his arm playfully. "Though at this rate, the baby will be in college before we finish."

He smirked, playfully brushing a streak of paint off my cheek. His eyes softened for a moment as he looked at me—like he was already imagining me here, cradling our child. I was already in my 27th week, and the baby bump was prominent. My heart swelled at his expression. All the discomforts, the hormonal mood swings, the growing pains—everything I'd endured so far—felt worth it in that moment.

The nursery in my apartment was a small haven crafted with care. Pale mint-green walls bathed the room in a soft, soothing glow, while crisp white trim and furniture added a touch of simple elegance. Every detail had a purpose, chosen to create a space that felt both calming and full of quiet joy.

By the window stood my favorite feature—a cloud-shaped bookshelf, its whimsical design making it feel like a little piece of the sky had drifted into the room. It was already filling up with storybooks, some lovingly selected by Heck during our trips to the shops. I couldn't wait to read each one, to tell Little Hemingway the characters and their stories. That reading nook made the nursery feel more alive. It might have been small, but every corner of that room felt like it belonged to something bigger, something brimming with love.

"I'm serious," he added, dragging his hand through the mess of his hair. "If this dresser isn't level, the drawers are going to slide open on their own. Baby-proofing nightmare."

"And yet," I teased, supervising as he crouched to adjust the legs once more, "this from the man who managed to assemble the crib upside down last week."

"An honest mistake! They shouldn't make those instructions so vague," he replied, his voice warm with mock indignation.

I knelt beside him, pressing a light kiss to his cheek. "I think you're doing an amazing job, Heck. You are going to be the best dad. Even if you do lose wrestling matches to furniture."

He reached for me, gently pulling me into his arms as we lay sprawled on the soft, carpeted floor. I tumbled into his side, laughter spilling out as my shoulder pressed into the curve of his chest. The dresser was forgotten, replaced by the warmth of us together.

I turned my face to his, running a finger softly along the curve of his lips. "I hope our son gets your eyes," I said, my voice barely above a whisper. His gaze locked on mine, steady and searching, as though he wanted to memorize the contours of this memory.

He leaned in, answering with a kiss—slow at first, but full of meaning, his hand cradling my face. His thumb brushed along my cheek, grounding me in the moment as the world outside the nursery seemed to dissolve. His other hand slid around my back, holding me close as though he couldn't bear even a breath of space to separate us.

When we finally pulled back, his forehead rested against mine, our breaths mingling in the quiet air. "You're so beautiful," he said, the words brimming with silent reverence, as though he were speaking a truth he could see, but I couldn't.

A lump caught in my throat, and I shook my head lightly, the vulnerability of the moment nudging at my heart. "I look hideous. And huge."

He tipped my chin up with gentle fingers, his gaze unwavering. "No, you're one hot mama. And I couldn't keep my hands off you if I tried," he said, his voice low and full of warmth. He removed my top, revealing my so-ripe breasts. "And these? Made you even sexier," he moaned as he took the nipple to his mouth and gently sucked it.

I laughed softly, the tension breaking as I leaned into him, feeling the love and reassurance in his touch. At that moment, surrounded by the chaos of the nursery and the quiet anticipation of what was to come, everything felt right.

The nursery's woes and the lingering scent of fresh paint faded into nothingness as Heck, and I found each other beneath the soft glow of the stars scattered across the ceiling. Their faint shimmer cast a tender light over us, but it was his warmth, his presence, that truly filled the room.

Lost in his arms, time seemed to stop, the outside world vanishing like a forgotten thought. It was just us, wrapped in each other, anchored by a love that made even a simple nursery feel infinite and sacred. The stars above watched quietly, bearing witness to a moment that belonged completely to us. The world beyond those walls didn't matter. Only us.

The next day, when we'd finished, I stepped back to take it all in. The crib sat perfectly by the far wall, flanked by soft gray curtains that pooled lightly on the floor. A vintage rocking chair—one Heck had refinished—balanced the space near the pastel bookshelf. There were touches of warmth everywhere: a woven rug with star patterns, a framed family photo hung carefully by the changing table. Every part of this room reflected a piece of us, of the life we were about to share.

"Do you like it?" I asked, glancing at him.

"It's perfect," Heck nodded, slipping an arm around my waist. "Almost as perfect as you."

My cheeks flushed, and for a second, I wondered how someone could always seem to find the right thing to say.

However, the nursery at the Archibald estate was an entirely different story.

"Oh, we are *not* skipping the chandelier!" Helen declared, her tone making it very clear this was non-negotiable. She swept her hand dramatically toward the ceiling of what had once been some kind of parlor room, now stripped bare save for a ladder and paint cans. "This room demands elegance. My grandchild deserves nothing less!"

"I'm not sure the baby will even notice the chandelier," I tried to reason, though I knew it was futile. You didn't *reason* with Helen.

"I do," Helen replied with an air of finality.

Heck snickered quietly beside me, clearly enjoying the exchange. "I mean," he murmured under his breath, "what's a nursery without a chandelier, anyway?"

"Don't encourage her," I whispered, giving him an exasperated look. Helen, however, hadn't missed his comment and was now beaming at him as if they'd just co-conspired to create the most decadent baby room in history.

Despite her dramatic nature, Helen's ideas weren't all bad. The nursery here was grand, yet it still felt surprisingly playful. The walls were painted a soft cream, with golden accents along the crown molding, which Helen had gleefully insisted on keeping. A luxuriously cushioned window seat overlooked the garden, and I could already imagine curling up there with the baby. On the walls, a mural of woodland animals had been hand-painted by one of Helen's contacts —a local artist she'd flown in specifically for the project.

"It's coming together," I admitted to Heck as we watched Helen briskly interrogate a contractor about floor trim measurements.

"It is," he nodded, looping an arm around my shoulders. His voice softened as he added, "I can tell you're starting to get used to living here."

Living here. Permanently. The thought was still so surreal, but watching everything come together in this room made it feel real. It felt... right.

"I guess I am," I said with a smile.

By the time we returned to my apartment that evening, we were both too tired to do anything but collapse on the couch. My hand instinctively rested against my growing belly as I looked at Heck beside me.

"Our baby's going to be so spoiled," I laughed.

"Definitely," Heck agreed, grinning. "But I don't think there's anything wrong with that."

And in that moment, surrounded by the quiet hum of my apartment and the knowledge of everything we were building together, I didn't think so either.

16

The rich aroma of roasted lamb, laced with fragrant herbs, wafted through the grand dining room, weaving itself into the soft flicker of candlelight that danced against crystal goblets and gleaming silver. It was beautiful, undeniably so. The table looked like something out of a storybook—every detail perfectly polished, every moment measured. And yet, the tight knot in my stomach refused to ease.

Sunday dinners at the Archibalds had a rhythm I hadn't yet learned to follow. They were elegant, deliberate events where formality wasn't just expected but required. I sat there, outwardly composed, part of the intricate performance that seemed effortless for everyone else. But inside, I longed for something far simpler. I pictured a messy, joyful chaos instead—not lamb and linens, but hot dogs and pizza scattered across a coffee table. A Sunday filled with laughter, mismatched sweatpants, and little hands grabbing slices, choosing fun over proper utensils.

Hector carried most of the conversation, his voice steady and confident, filling the spaces between carefully practiced pleasantries. We nodded and smiled, our responses precise and courteous. It wasn't unpleasant—not at all. The food was exquisite, and the atmosphere was refined. But it felt like slipping into a role that didn't quite fit, like stumbling around in someone else's shoes. Everything here whispered of tradition and perfection, yet I couldn't shake the feeling of being an outsider.

I glanced at Heck. He was at ease, his place at the table undeniable.

This world was his. Whether I liked it or not, it was mine now, too. My life had changed, and I would have to find my way within these walls of quiet opulence and unspoken rules. I took a small breath, gripping my resolve as tightly as I gripped the polished silver fork in my hand. No matter how much I missed the comfort of something messier, something more familiar, this was the life I'd chosen. And for him, I would learn to belong.

Then Hector cleared his throat—a deliberate sound, weighted with intention—and just like that, the air around the table shifted, as though we were all holding our breath, waiting for him to speak.

"Tony will be your full-time driver from now on. He won't just drop you off; he'll stay with you until you've reached your floor. Your safety is his priority, Sara," Hector said, his voice firm as it cut through the clinking of utensils.

I froze mid-bite, the savory flavors on my tongue suddenly tasteless. "Hector, I appreciate that, but I really don't think it's necessary," I began, setting my fork down gently. "I don't even take the Metro. I'm driven from my apartment to work. I'll be fine."

Beside me, Heck shifted in his seat. His jaw tightened, and when he spoke, his voice carried a mix of concern and frustration. "Sara, I know you hate losing your independence, but you're pregnant. It isn't safe."

His words stung more than I wanted to admit. I looked at him sharply, searching his face for something—or maybe just trying to figure out why he seemed so adamant. When he glanced at his father, a silent exchange passed between them. That was when I realized—they were keeping something from me.

"What's going on?" I asked, my voice sharp at the edges, though a slight tremor betrayed the calm I was trying to hold onto. My gaze darted to Helen, searching her face for answers.

She offered me a small, tight smile—more resigned than reassuring. "Nothing to worry about, dear," she said, her tone gentle but fraying at the edges. Despite her words, the worry etched in her features told a different story entirely.

"Is there something I should know?" I asked Heck, trying to keep my voice steady but failing miserably.

He opened his mouth to respond, but Hector beat him to it.

"Peter Sullivan. Sophie's father," Hector began, his commanding tone nearly void of emotion. "He's in deep trouble—financial trouble. He owes money to some very dangerous people, and he was banking on Sophie's marriage to Heck or at least a large divorce settlement to cover his debts."

The knot in my stomach tightened. I couldn't speak, couldn't move. I gripped the edge of the table as Hector continued, each word heavier than the last.

"Sophie signed a prenuptial agreement. The child she's carrying isn't Heck's, and she has no legal claim to his inheritance. She can stay at Heck's apartment, but she can't sell it—though she's already tried, weeks ago." He paused, setting down his silverware with such precision it sent a shiver down my spine. His gaze met mine, unflinching. "Sophie and her father blame you for all of this."

A chill coursed through me as my mind raced, trying to piece it all together. None of this made sense. "What does that have to do with me?" My voice was smaller than I intended, strained. "I'm not married to Heck. I'm not even engaged."

"Sophie and Peter don't care about logic," Heck interjected, leaning closer. His voice was soft but firm, trying to bridge the gap between concern and desperation. "They blame you because they think... you've taken everything from her. He's angry, Sara. And people like him—they don't always think rationally."

I leaned back slightly in my chair, feeling the blood drain from my face. "Angry enough to hurt me?" My voice cracked, and I didn't care. The words just spilled out.

"They may try to intimidate you... or get to you," Hector said, his tone as steady as the ticking clock in the corner of the room. "And while they haven't crossed any legal lines yet, we're not taking any chances. I'll make sure you're safe—this isn't just about you. Helen will have her own bodyguard, and so will Heck. And we're assigning Tony to you."

The formal dining room suddenly felt suffocating, its grandeur mocking the rising panic in my chest. "But the police..." I started, reaching for some fragment of reassurance that wasn't coming. "Can't the police do something about this?"

"As far as the authorities are concerned, Peter Sullivan hasn't done anything criminal," Hector said. His calm delivery was almost maddening.

I reached for Heck's hand under the table, my grip tightening until my knuckles turned white. He didn't pull away. Instead, his other hand cradled mine, his thumb instinctively brushing small circles along my trembling fingers.

"I'll drive you to work myself," Heck offered, his voice dropping to a whisper meant only for me. "Every day if I have to. I'm not letting anything happen to you."

My eyes blurred with threatening tears. "No." I shook my head vehemently. "No, that's unnecessary. I don't need you shadowing me. I'm fine—"

"This situation is far from fine!" His sudden outburst startled me. The firm intensity in his voice sent me reeling as I stared into his darkening eyes. "I can't take that chance, Sara. Not with you. Not with the baby."

His words struck a raw nerve, but it wasn't anger that surged to the surface. It was the naked vulnerability in his voice—the fear he wasn't trying hard enough to hide.

I swallowed the lump in my throat and placed his hand over my growing belly, holding it there as if that connection could somehow calm us both. "Then promise me, Heck," I said, my voice breaking, "promise me I won't lose myself over this. My independence, my strength—I won't lose it all because someone else can't handle their

133

own choices in life."

He softened, his hand pressing slightly into my stomach, feeling the faint movement beneath the surface. "You won't," he said, his voice tremulous and low. "I swear you won't. You'll never lose who you are."

His words wrapped around me like a shield, but the doubt lingered. Dinner carried on as though the heaviest conversation of my life hadn't just happened. Plates were taken away, and dessert was served, yet the tension hung thick even as Helen made perfunctory comments about the chef's walnut tart.

When we returned to my apartment, exhaustion hit me like a wave, but I couldn't quiet the thoughts swirling in my mind. Heck pulled me onto the couch beside him, a blanket already draped over my lap before I noticed he'd reached for it.

"You don't have to be strong all the time, you know," he said softly, pulling me closer. "If you're scared, it's okay. I'll be here. I'm not going to leave your side."

Tears finally slipped free, and no dam was left to hold them. "I'm scared," I admitted, my voice trembling as I buried my face against him. "But I won't hide away, and I won't just give up because they want me to."

He held me tighter, like he was anchoring us both. "Then we fight back," he whispered, his voice warm against my hair. And in its quiet resolve, I found just a tiny flicker of courage to keep going.

17

My daily routine had narrowed to two locations—home and work—a carousel of predictable stops dictated by necessity. Every morning, Heck would either fetch me himself or send one of his suited men to drive me. He'd drop me off before heading to work, leaving Tony, my shadow for the day, to escort me upstairs to my office. At first, Tony's presence felt overbearing, but I'd started to find a strange comfort in it; he was the silent wall between me and the unnerving whispers of danger creeping into my life.

The hum of fluorescent lights greeted me as usual when I stepped onto my office floor. My cubicle was tucked neatly in the corner, away from the bustling chatter of my coworkers. I set my bag down and plopped into my chair, leaning back just enough to give my increasingly heavy belly some reprieve. Thirty-four weeks along, and I felt every ounce of it.

The distant sound of heels clicking knew no stealth—Kelly's brisk steps were as familiar as my own heartbeat. She paused at my workstation on her way to her office, her navy blazer as sharp as her tone.

"Sara, how are you holding up? We're headed to Gold Standard HQ in an hour," she said, smoothing the papers in her hand.

I glanced at my calendar and exhaled deeply. "I'll manage. Just feeling a bit weighed down these days," I admitted, my hand instinctively resting on the curve of my belly. There was only a little more than a month before I'd finally meet this little life growing inside me. Heck and Helen had been gently nudging—practically begging—me to start my maternity leave early. They worried, fussed, and wanted me to rest. But I'd insisted—just two more weeks of work, I'd told them. Without it, I'd go stir-crazy waiting for my due date to arrive. "Don't worry," I added with a small, determined smile, pulling my focus back. "I'll have the report done in thirty minutes."

Kelly offered a rare smile, brief but genuine, before she strode off. I exhaled deeply and turned to my laptop, focusing on consolidating data for the presentation. The familiar rhythm of work always had a way of steadying me, though my mind wandered with anxiety about entering Gold Standard Bank's formidable boardroom—a space that always felt too big, too cold.

Tony waited patiently for the time to leave, as usual. The sleek black car saved us the hassle of booking an Uber, and with only Kelly and Alexi accompanying me, the ride was comfortably quiet. But my chest grew tighter as we neared our destination, its polished façade reflecting the city like a fortress.

Once inside, I tried to shake my unease, focusing instead on the purposeful click of heels along the marble floor. I still hadn't gotten used to the enormous conference room, its glass walls allowing light to seep in while reinforcing its sterile professionalism. Today's absence of Heck and Raul was notable; instead, Jen and her marketing team ran the agenda efficiently.

Jen was all business as she discussed the campaign progress, flipping through screens projected on the wall that detailed metrics and implementation strategies. Kelly chimed in occasionally, her voice strong and decisive, while Alexi remained focused on his notes. I tried my best to stay engaged, though my mind kept circling back to the distant hum of whisper campaigns surrounding Milliford's acquisition by Gold Standard Bank—the secret was out, even if we weren't speaking about it publicly yet.

And then the door slammed open.

It happened so fast that my heart skipped a beat. Sophie stormed in, her presence exuding chaos despite her pristine appearance. Her tight black pants contrasted sharply with the oversized white shirt cascading over them. Her blonde hair gleamed, catching the late morning sun filtering in from the windows. She was painfully beautiful, radiant even, and a pang of envy hit me as I glanced down at my loose yellow maternity dress hanging awkwardly on my frame.

"Where's Heck?" Sophie's voice was sharp, cutting through the room like a knife.

Jen didn't even flinch. "Excuse me?" Her disdain was thinly veiled, her polished professionalism intact but teetering.

"Are you deaf or something?" Sophie's tone was a mixture of venom and desperation.

Jen rose to her feet, her eyes narrowing. "As far as I recall, you've no business here. If you need to speak with him, I suggest you contact his assistant and see if you can make his schedule." Her words were icily clipped, her posture shifting into quiet defiance.

That was when Sophie's eyes locked on me. Predatory. Unflinching. The kind of gaze that pinned you in place, trembling before the strike.

"What the hell are you doing here?" she snarled, taking a step forward.

The table was long, an ocean of polished wood separating us, but I swore I could feel the heat of her anger burning through it. I opened my mouth, hesitant, trying to bring calmness into my voice.

"She is working on the Gold Standard campaign," Kelly said simply, keeping her tone measured. My hands shook under the table. Fear coiled tightly in my stomach as adrenaline prickled along my skin.

"You bitch. You ruined my life!" Sophie shrieked, her voice cracking. She moved toward the side of the table like she intended to come at me, her hands trembling, her face twisted in anger.

Alexi was out of his seat before I could process what was happening, stepping in just as Sophie looked ready to lunge. The room erupted into chaos, voices overlapping, my breath quickening as my pulse pounded in my ears.

And then he was there. Out of nowhere, Heck rushed into the room, his figure tall and imposing, his presence anchoring the spiraling frenzy.

"What's going on?" he demanded, his voice low but taut, fraying at the edges. His sharp eyes scanned the room before immediately landing on me. His steps quickened, and he knelt beside me, his hand cradling my cheek tenderly. His thumb brushed against my skin as he tilted my face toward his. "Are you okay?" he asked, his voice softer now, edged with worry.

"I'm…" I tried to answer, but his attention snapped like a whip to Sophie before I could finish. His features hardened, his jaw locking as he stood, positioning himself between her and me in a single, deliberate motion.

He barely waited for my response before turning to Sophie. "What the hell are you doing here, Sophie?" The venom in his voice was cold and controlled, but I could sense the fire building just beneath the surface.

Sophie's anger, fierce and volatile when she first stormed in, seemed to crumble under his glare. She stepped back as if the weight of his fury was physically pushing her. "You wouldn't answer me," she said, her voice trembling, cracks of desperation breaking through. "You ignore my calls, my messages. What choice did I have? I had to see you…" Her words faltered, tears spilling freely now. "Heck, please. I'm begging you."

"There's nothing left to say," he bit out, each word sharp and unrelenting. "Whatever this is—us—it's over. You don't get to come in here, cause a scene, and harass her."

"I don't want to fight," Sophie choked out, clutching the edge of a nearby chair as though she might collapse. "I just… I just need five minutes. I just need you to listen. Please!"

"Goddammit, Sophie!" The anger escaped him then, fierce but

restrained, his body rigid with the effort of holding back more. "You're making a fool of yourself. We're done. I told you before—don't come near her. Leave."

Her shoulders sagged under the weight of his words, but her eyes darted toward me, blazing anew with accusation and hurt. "This? You threw everything away for this?" Her gesture at me was sharp, almost feral, like she couldn't decide whether to cry or scream. "You're choosing her over me, after everything we've been through?"

"I'm not choosing," Heck growled, his voice darkening. "This was never about a choice. You and I—we ended long before she came into the picture. Don't twist this."

"She doesn't deserve you," Sophie spat, her composure finally splintering into jagged pieces. "She doesn't even know you like I do."

"That's enough!" His voice cut through her protest like thunder, reverberating between us. He tugged me closer to him, wrapping an arm around my shoulders protectively. Even as the tension crackled in the space, his hold on me was an anchor, steadying me against the chaos. "You've crossed a line, Sophie. Whatever you think you're doing, stop. Right now."

Trembling, I instinctively reached for his arm, my fingers curling over his forearm. "Heck," I whispered, my voice soft, pleading. "Maybe she just—she just needs—"

He turned his face toward me, his expression softening just enough for me to see the guilt and fury warring in his eyes. "No," he said firmly, though his touch against my shoulder was careful, grounding. "You don't deserve this. She's made her bed, and she doesn't get to disrupt our life like this."

"Heck, please…" Sophie's voice broke behind him, small and fractured now, as though even she was realizing there was no fight left to win.

But Heck only wrapped his arm around me, pulling me into him firmly. "Not today, Sophie. Leave," he said coldly.

Jeffrey, his assistant, appeared then, flanked by two broad silhouettes. "Mr. Archibald, I'm so sorry," Jeffrey stammered, gesturing toward the guards.

Without hesitation, Heck waved toward Sophie with a finality that chilled the room. "Get her out of here," he instructed, his tone devoid of anything but authority.

Two security guards stepped forward, gently but assertively guiding Sophie toward the door as she struggled, her cries echoing in the room. "Please, Heck! Please!" Her resistance faltered, and soon, she was gone.

He didn't turn to face her. Instead, he cupped the back of my head, pressing it gently against his chest as though shielding me from everything happening behind us. It didn't matter that we weren't alone, surrounded by people we worked with. The silence that followed was deafening, but Heck didn't move. His arms tightened around me as though he thought I might vanish, as though he could shield me from even the memory of what had just happened.

"I've got you," he murmured. "I won't let anything happen to you. I promise."

I nodded against him, not trusting my voice. The tears I hadn't even realized I was holding back trailed silently down my cheeks. "Promise me you'll talk to her."

He nodded. "I'll never let anyone hurt you," he murmured again, pressing his lips softly to the top of my head. And the way he said it, low and fierce, left no room for doubt.

I closed my eyes against the fabric of his shirt, the solid beat of his heart steadying me as I tried to catch my breath.

PART TWO

"No matter how far I ran, how hard I fought, the leash was always there.
Loose enough to keep me running in circles, but never enough to set me free."

- STEVEN

18

The hospital corridor seemed endless, stretching like a hollow labyrinth beneath the harsh glare of fluorescent lights. I was slumped in an oversized plastic chair, my head resting against the cold wall, my hands instinctively cradling my swollen belly. I was so tired. God, I was exhausted. My baby, still safe within me, was due in two to three weeks, but the thought of holding him now felt surreal amid the nightmare unfolding around me.

The sharp, metallic tang of antiseptic clung to the air, mingling with the faint, unmistakable smells of iodine and latex gloves. It stung my throat with every shallow breath. Around me, chaos raged. Doctors and nurses in scrubs the colors of twilight—blue, green, and pale lavender—hurried past, their shoes squeaking on the polished floors. Clutching charts and murmuring orders, they moved with purpose, rushing to operating rooms or heading off to patient rounds. Their movements were efficient, almost detached. But for me, time refused to move. It crawled, stretching painfully between the hollow beats of my breaking heart.

Somewhere beyond those doors was Heck. My Heck. My heart splintered at the thought of him lying there, his body broken beyond recognition. His face, somehow spared, bore only a few bruises, but inside, his organs were mangled. His liver and kidneys had failed. The Heck I knew—the quick-witted man who navigated life with quietly magnetic ease—was slipping away, piece by piece.

I couldn't take it anymore.

I glanced down the corridor, where Heck's dad stood, his broad frame stiff, issuing clipped commands to the doctors. His voice was anything but calm. Desperation lingered just beneath the surface, buried beneath his brusque tone. It didn't matter that he was Hector Archibald III, a man whose wealth could bend the world; even he couldn't buy the one thing we needed most—time. Still, I could see him trying. He was rallying every dollar, calling in every favor, pushing Heck's name to the top of donor lists in an impossible race against fate.

Behind Hector stood Helen, her red-rimmed eyes unfocused, her fingers clutching the thin gold chain around her neck as if it were the only thing anchoring her to this moment. When her gaze finally lifted and met mine, she smiled. It was meant to reassure me. But the smile was thin, fragile, already unraveling at the edges.

Today was supposed to be ordinary. Just another day of wandering through aisles of impossibly tiny baby clothes. Helen had insisted we go shopping again, even though the nursery could already clothe an army of babies. "You need a distraction," she had said, her tone brooking no argument. "Get your mind off the countdown to labor." I had agreed, thinking, Why not? At the time, her logic made sense.

I had been holding up a pastel onesie adorned with chubby little elephants, its softness melting a small corner of my weary heart. "What do you think?" I asked, glancing at Helen. But her phone buzzed before she could answer. She gave me an apologetic smile as she glanced at the screen.

"Oh, it's Hector," she said, her expression briefly brightening. Tucking the phone to her ear, she added, "I'll be right back. But I think we're definitely getting that onesie. It's too cute to leave behind."

I nodded absently, turning my attention to another rack of impossibly adorable options. At first, her voice was light, almost cheerful, as she walked a short distance away. I could still hear snippets of her conversation breaking through the quiet hum of the store.

And then there was silence.

I turned to look at her. Helen had stopped mid-step, her body frozen as though someone had pressed pause. The vibrant energy she carried moments ago had drained away. Her face went pale, almost translucent, and her free hand flew to her mouth, trembling fingers pressing hard against her lips.

A knot of unease coiled tighter in my stomach. All I could hear now was the faint sound of her breathing—shallow, uneven—with the low murmur of whoever was on the other end of the line punctuating it. My heart began to pound painfully against my ribs. This wasn't normal. Something was wrong.

"Helen?" I asked, my voice gentle but weighted with uncertainty. None of this made sense. "What's going on?"

She didn't answer.

Her gaze remained fixed somewhere in the distance, her eyes glassy and unfocused as if she were staring at something I couldn't see. Her hand fumbled with her phone, trembling as she ended the call. Slowly, she turned to face me. Her expression was raw, unrestrained, and intensely serious.

Without a word, she grabbed the little onesie I was holding, along with the other items draped across my arm, and handed them over to the sales clerk assigned to us. Her movements were jerky, almost robotic, and her focus narrowed to one undeniable goal: escaping the shop as fast as possible.

"We'll take these. Charge them to my account and have them delivered to my address on file," she snapped, her voice tight, unfamiliar. She shoved the rest of the baby clothes into the startled clerk's hands without so much as a glance.

Before I could ask anything else, she turned on her heel and grabbed my wrist with unexpected force. "Come on," she muttered through gritted teeth, dragging me toward the exit.

"Helen! What the hell is going on?" My words fell flat, swallowed by the pressure thickening around us.

She didn't answer. Her grip on my wrist stayed firm, and the cold, fearful set of her features scared me more than anything she might have said. Whatever had happened, whatever she'd just heard, had shaken her to the core.

"Helen?" I tried again, my voice sharper this time. The chauffeur opened the car door, and she practically shoved me inside before sliding in after me.

The moment the door shut, I grabbed her arm. "Helen, you're scaring me! What is going on?"

Her hands found mine, her grip firm but icy, trembling slightly. For a moment, her lips moved without sound, as though the words were stuck somewhere deep, heavy with the burden of speaking them aloud. Finally, her voice came, hushed and broken. "It's Heck. He's been in an accident."

My stomach plummeted. Blood pounded in my ears, drowning out the sound of the car engine as it roared to life. "What? How bad is it? Where is he? What happened?!"

"We don't know much yet." Her voice quivered as she squeezed my hands. Turning sharply to the driver, she added with urgency, "We're going to Mercy West. Now."

The rest of the drive passed in agonizing silence, broken only by the uneven sound of my breathing. I stared out the window, the city blurring into streaks of light and shadow, denial and panic waging a relentless war within me. This couldn't be real. It couldn't be.

When we arrived at the hospital, Heck's assistant, Jeffrey, was pacing near the entrance. He froze when he saw us, his face etched with worry, and rushed over. Helen immediately launched into questions, her words quick and cracking under the strain, but I beat her to it.

"Jeffrey." My voice trembled, threatening to break. "What happened? How is he? Is he okay?"

He raked a hand through his disheveled hair, the tension carving lines deep into his face. "He's still in surgery. They're working on him." He swallowed hard, struggling to keep his composure. "It's… not good."

The world spun. My knees wobbled, and Helen steadied me with a hand on my shoulder, but her eyes mirrored the panic tearing through me. "Not good?" I repeated, the words alien as they left my lips, sharp edges that didn't belong in my reality. "How did this happen?"

Jeffrey shook his head, his tone hushed and apologetic. "I don't know. A collision, I think. He was driving back from… something. The details are still unclear."

"Is Hector here?" Helen's voice cracked as she spoke his name.

"Yes, he's upstairs. The doctors are updating him as they can," Jeffrey replied, his words careful, deliberate. "But the situation is… delicate."

We didn't wait for permission. Helen and I almost ran for the elevators, driven by purpose, Jeffrey trailing close behind like a silent shadow. The moment we stepped onto the surgical floor, the air shifted. It hit me like a tangible force—cold, sterile, carrying that faint metallic tang that clung to the back of my throat.

Hector stood at the far end of the hallway, his back turned to us, his gaze locked on the double doors in front of him. His frame was stiff, unmoving, except for the steady rise and fall of his shoulders. I'd never seen him like this. Hector Archibald, the man whose name could command industries, now looked… fragile. He seemed like a fabric stretched to its breaking point.

Helen didn't hesitate. She crossed the distance in a few quick steps, falling into his arms as if trying to shoulder some of his weight or offer him a measure of hers.

"Please," I managed to choke out. The desperation made my voice barely audible, cracking under its weight. "Please tell me he's okay."

Hector's head turned slightly, his arms tightening protectively around

Helen. For a moment, I thought he might offer some reassurance, the kind of calm certainty he'd always seemed capable of summoning. But instead, his face faltered. His expression wavered, and what I saw there shattered any illusions I had left. "Sit down, Sara," he said softly, motioning to a nearby row of cold, unyielding waiting room chairs.

My legs felt weak, uncertain beneath me, but I obeyed. When Hector's gaze shifted to Jeffrey, his voice took on the faint edge of authority, though it carried a tired weight. "Jeffrey, get her some water."

"Yes, sir." Jeffrey nodded and hurried down the hallway, his footsteps fading quickly.

I lowered myself into a chair, the flimsy cushion beneath me doing nothing to ease the growing ache in my chest. My hands fidgeted restlessly, my fingertips drumming against my knees as I tried in vain to steady myself. All I could do now was wait, drowning in a silence too heavy to bear.

Seconds later—though it felt like an eternity—Jeffrey returned. He handed me a bottle of water, already opened, his movements deliberate yet silent. I accepted it wordlessly, staring at the plastic in my hand as though it held all the answers I sought.

Hector cleared his throat, the sound brittle, almost hollow. Straightening his posture, he seemed to summon what little composure he had left, though weariness clung to him like a shadow. "We don't know yet," he said, his voice taut, every word unraveling under the weight of uncertainty. "He's still in surgery."

The room seemed to shrink around me, the air thinning as his words stole something vital from it. They hovered, unreal, refusing to sink in. I couldn't grasp their meaning, couldn't feel the sting of their reality. It was as if they existed in a place too far away for me to reach. "Oh, God," I murmured, barely recognizing the sound of my own voice. The words slipped out as more of a prayer than a thought, drifting upward into the void.

Helen collapsed into Hector's chest, her sobs muffled against him, her grief finding an anchor. But me? I remained frozen, untethered, unsteady as silence pressed down on me with crushing weight. Alone in a room full of people, I spiraled, each breath a struggle against the tightening grip of fear. My lungs constricted, the world narrowing to a single, suffocating point.

I wrapped my arms around myself, not for warmth but to keep what little remained of my strength from slipping through my fingers. It felt as though I could crack apart at any moment. And still, the words lingered in the air, heavy and unbearable, suffused with an ache that defied endurance.

The world blurred into an endless stretch of waiting. I stayed in that chair, gripping the water bottle like it was a lifeline. My gaze remained fixed on the beige floor tiles, their dull patterns an unwelcome canvas for my splintering thoughts. Time moved strangely, sometimes dragging, sometimes leaping forward in uneven jerks, marked only by the faint squeak of sneakers or the monotone hum of distant machines.

Doctors appeared periodically with updates, their words rehearsed, clinical, and detached, as though they had been drained of emotion. "He's still in surgery," they would say. Four words, neutral in delivery but with the force of a blade, each one carving deeper into my already battered heart.

Helen paced the floor relentlessly. The sharp staccato of her heels broke through the oppressive silence, a rhythmic sound that I latched onto in a desperate attempt to feel grounded. But my thoughts betrayed me, tugging me deeper into memories, deeper into what could be lost.

This wasn't supposed to happen.

Heck was supposed to be beside me when I brought our baby into the world. He was supposed to hold my hand, tell me I was strong, that we could do this together. He was supposed to cut the cord, to be the calm when things felt too heavy. We had imagined it all so vividly, painted a future in brilliant colors—but now that vision was unraveling, thread by fragile thread.

There was nothing to do but wait. Wait, pray, and cling to Helen in this shared, unbearable suspension of time.

Minutes bled into hours that felt like decades. Finally, a surgeon emerged, his scrubs untidily smeared with the toil of the day. Without preamble, he walked directly to Hector. I caught fragments of his words. "His liver and kidneys were severely damaged…"

That was all I needed to hear. I couldn't sit any longer. Fear and hopelessness propelled me forward, and before I knew it, I was on my feet, stumbling toward them. The words spilled out of me, raw and frantic.

"Take mine!" I cried, clutching the fabric of the surgeon's sleeve as tears streamed unchecked down my cheeks. "Take my kidney, my liver, whatever you need! I'll do it! I'm healthy! Please, just save him!"

For a moment, the room seemed to hold its breath. An unnatural stillness settled, sucking the air from the space. Helen's wide, tear-filled eyes locked onto me, her expression twisted in a mix of anguish and disbelief. Hector, caught mid-sentence, turned to stone, his phone slipping silently to his side. The doctor shifted uncomfortably. His professional veneer cracked at the sight of a heavily pregnant woman, desperate and pleading, offering pieces of herself to save someone she loved.

It was Helen who broke the silence. She crossed the distance between us with trembling steps, pressing her cool fingertips to my lips to hush the torrent of my cries. "No, Sara," she said softly, her voice fracturing under the weight of her own emotions. "Please, don't. Heck wouldn't want this. None of us wants this. The only thing you should be worrying about is that beautiful boy inside you."

Her arms enveloped me, warm and grounding, holding me together when I most felt like dissolving into fragments. She kissed my forehead, her lips trembling, dampened by the salt of her tears.

Behind her, Hector stood silent, his shoulders heavy with the weight of helplessness he couldn't outrun. Slowly, he reached out, resting his hand on Helen's as she held me. It was a gesture that almost seemed tentative, as if too much pressure might splinter the fragile barrier holding grief at bay.

For that moment, we were frozen in place, a tangle of raw desperation and fragile resolve, anchored to one another, yet each bearing our own unbearable pain.

Seconds later, the fragile silence shattered like glass. A young doctor in blue scrubs stepped hesitantly forward, his face careful, almost apologetic. He cleared his throat, the sound slicing through the oppressive quiet.

"I don't mean to intrude," he began cautiously, his words slow and deliberate, "but... is there any chance of a sibling? An immediate biological relative? It could expedite the search for a match."

The question dropped into the room like a grenade.

Hector's shoulders tensed first, the movement subtle but unmistakable. His jaw clenched, and his entire frame stiffened as if bracing for some invisible impact. His silence was sharp, cutting through the space like the flash of a blade.

Before he could respond, Helen's voice broke through, trembling yet resolute. "Hector..." she murmured, her tone laced with a plea impossible to miss. She turned toward him, her hand gripping his arm tightly, almost desperately. "Please, find him," she whispered.

I flinched, instinctively leaning away from where Helen had been supporting me just moments before. My pulse raced, each beat thrumming faster and harder as I looked between them. Helen's expression was drenched in fear and urgency, while Hector's face—so typically composed—was a tempest, wild and unreadable.

"Who's him?" The question stumbled out of me more like a breath than a demand. I knew I had no right to ask or insist, but it was Heck's life, his survival, hanging in the balance. My gaze darted back and forth between them. "Who is it?"

Hector raked a hand through his salt-and-pepper hair, the crack in his composure widening. His posture sagged, the weight of the moment dragging him deeper into himself. When he spoke, his voice was low, almost hollow. "We... we couldn't ask him, Helen," he muttered shakily, his eyes dropping to the floor.

Helen's grip on his arm tightened suddenly, her knuckles whitening as though sheer force alone could compel him into action. "Hector, please," she choked out, her voice raw, breaking with the effort. "I'll beg him if I have to. I don't care—I'll do anything. There's nothing I wouldn't do. I can't... we can't lose him." The last words fractured on her tongue, splintering under the weight of her agony.

"What are you talking about?" My voice rose now, trembling with disbelief. "Tell me! Tell me what this is about!"

Helen turned to me, her tear-swollen eyes meeting mine. Slowly, she took both of my hands in hers. They were trembling, damp, and cold, but her grip was firm enough to keep me steady, fragile enough to reveal her own barely-held-together state.

"Sarah..." she whispered, her breath hitching. "He wasn't... as we always told people..." She faltered, guilt tightening her expression, every muscle on her face twisting with the agony of what she was about to confess. Finally, with a sharp inhale, the words fled her lips. "Heck wasn't an only child."

The revelation was a tidal wave, pulling me into its icy depths. I froze, staring at her, unwilling to comprehend what she had just said.

Helen's voice cracked again, and she pushed forward as if rushing through the words would numb their weight. "He has a brother," she said, her voice trembling. "A half-brother. Hector's son... from another woman." Her voice broke entirely, and her grip on my hands slackened as though preparing for me to pull away in shock.

My breath caught, and the world tunneled for a moment. "A brother?" I echoed faintly, the words barely forming as they slipped through the lump in my throat. Turning to Hector, fresh tears spilled over as I cried, "Then find him!" The surge of desperation propelled me forward—I gripped his arm, my fingers digging into his sleeve as though I could physically push him into action.

151

"Please!" The plea burst from me, raw and ragged. "I'm begging you! Find him and save Heck!"

Hector didn't respond immediately. His eyes shut tightly, his lips pressing into a thin line as he swallowed the tension shimmering around him. Finally, with visible effort, he opened his eyes, stepping closer to Helen. He cradled her face and placed a soft kiss on her forehead. It wasn't a reassurance, not entirely, but it was a promise, unspoken yet heavy between them. Then, without words, he turned and pulled out his phone, striding purposefully down the corridor.

"Find him, Hector," Helen whispered brokenly, tears falling unchecked. Her voice was quiet, but resolute. "Do this for our son."

The echo of her words lingered as I collapsed back into my chair, cradling my swollen belly. Somewhere deep within, I felt my son stir just slightly, his faint kick grounding me for a fleeting moment. Tears blurred my vision as I closed my eyes, clutching that small movement to my heart.

"Please, save him," I whispered into the stillness, my prayer trembling on the verge of desperation. A final, breaking plea. "Please, God, save him."

19

Mercy West's intensive care unit felt like a world apart—suspended in a strange, sterile limbo, untouched by the rhythm of life beyond its cold, unfeeling walls. Thirty-six hours had crawled by since they wheeled Heck out of the operating room. Despite all my bracing, the sight of him had shattered me. He looked fragile, almost unrecognizable, tangled in a maze of tubes and wires. Machines beeped and hummed steadily, performing the tasks his body could no longer manage. And worst of all—he hadn't opened his eyes. Not once.

I didn't want to leave him. The mere thought of stepping away felt like a betrayal, like I was severing some invisible thread between us. But Hector and Helen had insisted. They brought me back to their home—not to my apartment, where the silence would have been deafening, but to their place, where I wasn't alone. Still, the hours away from Heck stretched unbearably thin, my every thought consumed by images of him lying there, unmoving. They promised me they'd take me back the moment there was any change, but my heart ached to be near him.

Now, I was allowed to stay during the day. And so, here I stood, outside the intensive care unit.

My hands pressed flat against the icy glass window that separated Heck from me. The chill bit into my skin as I stared at his bed. His chest rose and fell in shallow, mechanical motions—the only sign that he was still tethered to this world. I didn't move. I couldn't. Every part of me felt raw, as though the sharp edges of my emotions had scraped me hollow.

It was the third day. Three days spent desperately watching, waiting for something—anything. Three days of clinging to the rhythmic pulse of the machines, willing him to find his way back to me. The stillness in his room was maddening, as though time had stopped there while the rest of the world spun on without us.

I shifted my weight, my legs stiff from standing too long. But I couldn't pull away—not even for a moment. My hope hung by a delicate thread, stretched taut between my prayers and the faint, unchanging rise and fall of his chest. With every passing second, the ache in my heart grew heavier.

Three days. Three days of begging the universe to give him back to me. Three days of murmured prayers, whispered promises that I'd do anything—anything—if it meant seeing his eyes open again. I needed him to wake up. I needed to hear his voice, feel his hand in mine, and know this wasn't the end.

But all I could do was stand here, powerless, staring into that silent room and holding onto the fragile hope that tomorrow, something might change.

The air felt heavy, thick with the hum of ventilators and the rhythmic beep of heart monitors. Beneath it, the sharp smell of antiseptic lingered, clawing at my exhausted senses. I leaned my forehead against the glass, closing my eyes for just a moment. My reflection stared back at me—pale and drawn, with deep shadows beneath tear-swollen eyes. I hardly recognized myself.

Doctors moved purposefully through the hall, their soft conversations blending into a murmur of medical jargon I couldn't understand. Occasionally, I caught the metallic clink of trays or the hiss of nearby machinery, but mostly, the sounds passed over me like distant storms. Nurses hurried to and from Heck's room, adjusting tubes, jotting notes, and checking the machines surrounding him. The sight of them bustling around made my chest tighten. It was a dance I couldn't engage in or interrupt—though every fiber of my being screamed to burst in there and will him awake.

Beyond the glass, Heck lay as he had for days—a tangle of wires and pale skin. The strength his body once carried, something I'd always admired, now seemed like a distant memory. He looked impossibly fragile, the bruises mottling parts of his body leaving his unscathed face a cruel reminder of just how broken he was beneath the surface.

For a moment, I imagined him waking up, tilting his lips into that crooked smirk I loved so much. I imagined those cerulean eyes bright again, teasing me when I scolded him for scaring us so badly. But it was just that—an imagining. The reality was heartbreakingly far from it.

The baby kicked hard, jolting me from the fog of my thoughts. I sucked in a sharp breath, instinctively pressing both hands to my belly. "Easy there, sweetheart," I whispered, cradling the swell of him as if my touch could soothe his restless energy. For a moment, the desperation weighing me down eased, just a little. His nudges felt like proof of life —of strength in a world that suddenly felt so fragile.

A dry, shaky laugh escaped me, though it burned my throat after days stained with tears. "Pray for Daddy to get better," I murmured, my voice barely holding steady as the words left my lips. The heaviness began to creep back in, pressing against my chest, unwelcome and relentless.

"That's the most powerful wish," a voice said from behind me, low but carrying a quiet strength. I hadn't heard anyone enter. Startled, I turned, my pulse quickening, instinctively protective of myself and the life I was carrying.

The man standing there exuded a serene stillness that felt almost out of place in the suffocating tension of the ICU. His voice grounded him—a surprising softness woven through every word. "He's yours?" he asked, his tone respectful but tinged with something deeper, something I couldn't quite name.

I blinked at him, my mind catching up to his presence. He certainly didn't belong in scrubs. Instead, he wore a simple black T-shirt tucked neatly into faded jeans. Despite his casual clothes, his posture was calm, almost commanding. Long black curls cascaded just past his shoulders, and dark stubble, hinting at days of growth, shadowed his angular jaw. Tattoos snaked along his left arm, disappearing into the short sleeve of his T-shirt like deliberate strokes of ink on weathered parchment. But it was his eyes that struck me the most.

They were heavy. Sad. And hauntingly familiar.

"Yes," I said, my voice soft, almost hesitant. My hand drifted to the emerald ring twisting on my finger, its coolness grounding me in a way nothing else could. It was a quiet, unyielding thread connecting me to Heck. Hector had given it to Sylvia when she was pregnant with him, and now it had been passed on to me. If Heck had his way, there would already be an engagement ring on my finger, but I had said we should wait—it felt too soon. He had just wrapped up his divorce from Sophie. This ring, for now, was the closest I had to a pledge to our promises, to the family we were building. So I said, "He's my fiancé." The words rolled off my tongue, laced with both pride and an ache I couldn't entirely bury.

The stranger didn't look away, his gaze lingering a beat longer than I expected. There was pain in those eyes—not obtrusive, but present, as though he carried something with him that he hadn't yet unpacked. Still, he didn't say anything more, as if waiting for me to decide whether there was anything else to say. Something about him—his calm, quiet weight—unnerved me, but at the same time, it steadied me in a way I couldn't understand.

His gaze never left the glass window before us. "And you—are you waiting for someone?" I asked cautiously, almost out of instinct. Something about his presence felt... different. Grounded but fractured —as if his strength had been shaped by pain.

His lips parted as though he might answer, but he didn't. He just nodded faintly, his gaze distant. And then, before I could press further, rapid footsteps broke through the steady rhythm of the hallway. I turned to find Helen approaching, her steps hurried, with Hector just a breath behind her.

"There you are, my dear." Helen reached for me immediately,

gathering my face in her hands before gently kissing each cheek. Her touch brought comfort, yet it deepened the ache in my chest. Her grief reflected mine so perfectly it hurt. But her attention wasn't on me for long. She turned, her wide, tear-glimmering eyes settling on the man beside me.

"Steven," she breathed, her voice trembling with a charged mix of relief and sorrow.

The words struck me like lightning. I inhaled sharply, glancing between Helen and the man like a camera haphazardly snapping photos. It clicked—the familiar shape of his jawline, the way his eyes softened despite their burden. He didn't look away from her or flinch under the weight of her gaze. Slowly, I watched his expression shift, the complex threads of distance glinting for just a fleeting moment before his shoulders softened.

"Helen," he murmured, his voice laden with something I couldn't quite place—guilt? Pain? Love?

Helen's breath hitched, her hands reaching instinctively for his arm before halting, hovering, uncertain if she had the right to cross that boundary anymore. Her lips parted, forming soundless, half-shaped words as though she were searching for some fragment of language that might carry the weight of this moment. Finally, her voice, fragile and trembling, broke the silence. "You came..." she whispered, the words raw with disbelief as tears carved silent paths down her cheeks. "You really came."

The man held her gaze for a long, suspended moment, his expression unreadable yet heavy with something he wasn't quite ready to name. Then he closed the space between them in one deliberate step and pulled Helen gently into his arms. "As fast as I could," he murmured, his words quiet but full of intent. His gaze flicked momentarily toward Hector, who stood behind Helen, a glimmer of something unspoken passing across his expression—resentment, acknowledgment, or perhaps both—but it lingered only an instant before vanishing into composure.

Helen exhaled shakily and closed her eyes, allowing herself to lean into his hold and rest there, even for a moment.

I hadn't realized until then how silent I'd become, how tightly I'd gripped the edges of my own pain as the scene unfolded in front of me. My throat felt dry, and my lips hesitated over words that tumbled out faster than I could stop them, spilling into the thick air. "You're here... for Heck..." The way I said it wasn't a question—it was hope, fragile and desperate, barely able to breathe.

His focus shifted to me, his measured gaze locking onto mine with a steadiness that almost felt like gravity, pulling everything in. Slowly, he released his hold on Helen, and the air between them seemed to loosen with it.

"I'm Steven," he said, extending a hand. It was stiff, formal—awkward, even—but I took it anyway. His palm was warm and solid, grounding me, if only for a moment.

"I'm Sara," I replied, my name barely more than a whisper.

He studied me, his expression calm yet a fortress I couldn't breach. Then he spoke, and his words carried a weight too heavy for the space they occupied. "Anything and everything for my brother," he said, his voice low, deliberate—like the click of a long-sealed lock finally turning.

Relief sliced through me, sharp and unexpected, catching me off guard. My hands flattened against the window frame, palms trembling as though the fragile pane beneath them might shatter under the weight of it all. My knees wavered, threatening to buckle under the rush of emotions I could no longer contain—grief for the days we'd teetered on the brink of collapse and a flickering, fierce hope that, perhaps, we hadn't run out of chances just yet.

20

The hospital conference room was a stark contrast to the cold, clinical sterility of the ICU. Its dark mahogany-paneled walls, adorned with oversized gilded frames holding abstract paintings, felt strangely out of place—like they belonged to a different world. A long, polished table stretched the length of the room, its glossy surface catching the dim light from brass sconces mounted above. The forest-green chairs, high-backed and formal, encircled the table like silent observers. They weren't comforting—no, they were stiff and uninviting, the kind you'd expect in corporate boardrooms, not in a space meant for moments like this.

The quiet hum of the overhead vent did nothing to ease the suffocating tension. Each breath felt louder, heavier, amplifying the unease already tightening the air. Steven's arrival had called for a family meeting, and the medical director had graciously offered us this space for privacy. Yet, as I glanced around the room, a queasy thought crept up on me— this was a discussion reserved for family members only. I wasn't sure what I was doing here or if I even belonged in this meeting at all.

The door shut behind us with a solid thud, and I felt the walls close in. Helen sat beside me, clutching a tissue in one hand while the other trembled against her lap. Hector had taken his seat at the head of the table, his usual place of authority, though every line on his face betrayed how hard he was fighting to hold himself together. His fingers tapped against the wood—not in impatience, but to mask their slight tremor. Steven stood at the far end, his stance rigid, his jaw tight as though holding back a storm. His presence sucked the air out of the room, his anger simmering just below the surface.

Steven's voice cut through the heavy silence, sharp and unrelenting. "How'd this happen?" He didn't sit. His arms were crossed, his broad shoulders square as though bracing himself for what was to come.

Hector's eyes darted toward Steven but quickly shifted to the polished table. For a moment, he said nothing. The weight of the question lingered in the space like a live wire, sparking tension no one dared to touch.

"It was Peter," Hector finally said, his voice low and deliberate, though his words felt like they'd been wrung out of him.

Steven's brows furrowed in confusion. "Peter? Who the fuck is Peter?"

Hector exhaled heavily, dragging a hand down his face. His mask of composure cracked for a fleeting moment, and he clenched his fists on the table. "Heck's ex-father-in-law. Sophie's father."

At that name, Helen gasped audibly, her hand flying to her mouth. Tears pooled in her eyes as she whispered, "Oh my God..."

"You mean to tell me," Steven growled, taking a step closer to the table, "that the man who should've been rotting in obscurity—thanks to your connections and control—is the one who almost killed my brother?" His voice climbed steadily with every word, like a blaze catching hold. Then, as if unable to restrain himself, he slammed his fist down on the table, the sound reverberating like a gunshot. Helen flinched, clutching her tissue tighter.

"I thought we took every precaution," I said, my voice breaking mid-sentence as tears swelled in my throat. My hand went instinctively to my belly, cradling the life inside me. "I thought Heck was protected—how could Peter get to him?"

Hector's voice was low and strained, every word dragging like it hurt to say. "Someone lured him out... maybe Sophie," he asserted, the name heavy enough to suck the air from the room.

160

The cold hit me first, sharp and unforgiving, before the panic flooded in, rushing through my veins like ice. "Oh my God," I whispered, my voice cracking as dread consumed me. The realization swallowed me whole. "I told Heck to see Sophie after her outburst at the office," I stammered, the words rushing out in a breathless spiral. "I asked him to talk to her—to fix things! I pushed him there!" My hands trembled, the weight of guilt pressing down like a vice, threatening to pull me under.

"Sara, stop." Hector's gaze locked onto mine, steady, firm. "No. Heck wouldn't go to her because you told him to. It wasn't that." His tone softened but didn't erase the anguish threading through his words.

Before I could reply, Steven's laugh cut through the tension—not warm but bitten and bitter, a jagged edge slicing into the moment. "This wasn't an accident, was it?" he accused, his voice cold and raw. His eyes burned as they bore into Hector's—accusatory, unflinching.

The room fell silent, held in a fragile stillness, the weight of Steven's words crashing over us like thunder waiting for lightning.

Hector's lips tightened. His knuckles went white as his fists clenched even harder. "No," he admitted, his voice raw. "It wasn't. They shot him. They tortured him. They..." He faltered, closing his eyes as if to ward off visions too unbearable to speak of. "They electrocuted him, drowned him. I saw the burns. The water in his—" His voice broke off abruptly, and he turned his head away, biting his lip. Hector Archibald, usually so composed, looked utterly broken. "They drugged him and made him escape."

Helen moaned quietly, tears slipping freely now, and buried her face in her hands. My heart twisted painfully at the image of Heck enduring that kind of cruelty. It was enough to make my knees buckle under me.

"Fuck!" Steven exploded, his voice carrying the full force of his fury. He shoved one of the chairs violently, sending it crashing onto its side. Before I could react, he stalked to where Hector sat, towering over him with fists shaking like coiled thunderclouds. "You... YOU were supposed to protect him!" he bellowed. "You always have your goddamn goons ready to shield you without hesitation, but your own son? You can't be bothered!" He leaned in closer, his face a mask of raw fury. "You protect everyone else. Everyone. Your money! But not your family—not us, not HIM!"

Hector's chair scraped as he stood abruptly, facing Steven head-on. "You don't know a damn thing about what I've done for this family! You've been gone too long. Twenty years, Steven!" Hector shouted, his voice cracking into unfamiliar territory. His chest heaved as though every breath cost him. "You think I've sat idly while you ran away? While Heck is fighting for his life?!"

Helen sprang to her feet, inserting herself between them with desperate cries. "Steven! Hector! STOP! Please!"

Steven shoved away from her, slamming his fist into the nearby wall with a sickening crack. His face twisted in pain, but he barely flinched. Blood trickled down his knuckles as he turned back toward Hector, his face awash with unrestrained rage. "You care about your bank account. How many more fucking zeros you can add to those already bloated figures! The damn empire you maintain. We've never mattered to you!" His voice broke slightly, and he turned abruptly, running both hands through his hair in anguish and frustration.

The room felt charged with emotions too volatile to contain. The storm brewing in Steven, Hector's unraveling composure, Helen's quiet sobs —it was too much.

And I had to end it.

"Heck wanted to name our baby Hector Archibald V," I said, my voice trembling. It cut through the tension like a fragile plea. All eyes turned to me as tears spilled freely down my face. "He loved this family more than anything. He wanted that name to connect to his duty as your son —even if it meant giving up everything he loved. Everything." I choked on a sob. "That's how he sees this family. How important it is. In the end, he wanted to fulfill the role he was entrusted with the moment he was born... despite wanting to do something else. Be someone else."

I turned to Hector and Helen, my voice wavering but steady enough to carry the weight of what I needed to say. "The happiest I've ever seen him… it was in Paris. He was painting and writing poetry—he was alive in a way I can't describe. He was living for himself, not for anyone else. That was the Heck you've never seen. And he gave it all up—for this family." My throat tightened, but I forced the words out. "Do you know what that kind of sacrifice feels like? Because I don't think I could do it."

"I'm sorry, Sara…" Steven's voice was barely above a whisper, frayed and heavy, as though it carried the weight of something too big to hold. Slowly, he sank back into his chair, each movement sluggish, pressed down by the burden of his apology.

"When he wakes up… when he's well…" My voice trembled, flickering like a fragile flame trying to stay lit. I clung to those words, to the hope buried deep within them. "I'll ask him to go back to Paris with me. Just us… the three of us." My hand instinctively rested on the gentle curve of my belly, where my Little Hemingway was safely nestled. The thought of Heck, of healing, carried me forward. "…and Guernsey," I added softly, my memories of him on that island thick with warmth. "He traced his great-grandfather's love story there. He blended in with the locals like he'd lived a lifetime among them. I wish you could've seen it. He laughed with them… laughed in a way that made him feel like he belonged." My breath hitched as a tear slipped free, quickly wiped away with the back of my trembling hand.

My gaze settled on Hector, steady despite the storm surging inside me. "No responsibilities. No demands. Just poetry, art, and the life he loves. I'll make sure he gets back to that." My voice strengthened, rooted in the promise I refused to break. "I know that's not what you want for him, but I don't care. Heck loved those things. He gave them up—for you. Because he loves you. It was his sacrifice. Selfless. Yours… over his."

Before Hector could respond, Helen moved toward me. She reached me in seconds, her arms enfolding me in a fierce, maternal hug that made my knees tremble under its force. Her sobs finally broke free, each one full of promise and grief. "I'll make sure he gets that," she whispered, her voice filled with a raw determination that cut through every ounce of pain in the room. And in her words, I felt something rekindle between all of us, a fragile but unspoken vow to give Heck the life he deserved.

I sank against her, my tears spilling freely. My body shook in her hold, but I forced myself to lift my head, turning to Hector with tear-streaked cheeks. "Get Peter," I said, my voice soft but steady, like steel wrapped in desperation. "I don't care if he rots in a cell or is wiped off the face of this earth. Do whatever it takes. He must pay. And Sophie, too."

My attention shifted to Steven, whose fury still burned under the surface. "I know you're angry," I said, willing my voice to stay strong. "But anger won't help us—not now. Heck needs you. We need you. He has to be put back together, Steven, and I need your strength for that. I know it's not easy, and asking this of you is like asking someone to move mountains. But we have no one else to turn to." My breath hitched. "If I could give my life for his... I would."

Hector's reply came, his voice thick with strain but as steady as the room's unflinching air. "You have my word," he said, his gaze hard as it swept from Steven to Helen to me. "Peter won't escape. He'll pay for what he's done. That I promise you. Both of you."

His eyes rested on Steven. "This isn't on you. It's not your weight to carry. I won't bore you with the details—because that isn't your job. But know this... I may not be the father you and Heck wanted, but when it comes to this family, no one—no one—will harm what's mine and walk away unscathed."

Steven's jaw tightened, his fury still storming below the surface. His voice was low when he spoke, but each word cut like a blade. "You better mean that. Because if you hesitate... I will handle it. And when I do, I'll make sure Peter doesn't take another breath."

The room fell into a throbbing silence, all too worn by emotion and pain to say more. Yet in that silence was a resolve—a shared determination to fight because we had no other choice. We couldn't fall apart now. Everything depended on the love, the rage, and the desperate hope we carried for the man who lay broken and unresponsive. For Heck.

I Love You, Sunday Sunset.

21

The day sped past me, every hour rushing by like water slipping through my fingers. Everything blurred—a relentless storm of doctors bustling past, whispers fading before I could catch their meaning, and the sharp cadence of hurried footsteps ricocheting off cold, sterile white walls.

Steven and I barely exchanged more than a few words after that day in the hospital conference room. But then again, words felt secondary to the weight of what lay ahead. This man—this near stranger who bore fragments of Heck in every thread of his being—was preparing to risk his life for someone he hadn't spoken to in almost twenty years. His sacrifice spoke volumes, echoing far louder than words ever could.

This morning, when Steven stepped into the meeting room to talk to the team of doctors prepping for Heck's surgery, I lingered outside. I leaned against the cold glass window lining the corridor, my arms wrapped instinctively around my belly. Through the slats of the vertical blinds, I caught sight of him inside. He stood upright, his posture rigid, as if bracing himself against an invisible weight. The movement of others around him barely seemed to register. His broad shoulders held firm, even as the tension threatened to bow them. Occasionally, he would nod—a small, measured motion that betrayed the strain etched into every line of his frame.

Archibald's blood was impossible to miss: the angled jawline, the proud lift of his nose, the depth in those cerulean eyes that so clearly marked who he was. It was eerie, almost unnerving, to see so much of

Heck reflected in him—the same sharpness of their features, the way they moved with quiet confidence.

Yet Steven carried something else, too. The hard edges of someone who'd built his life alone. His darker skin, the unruly curls falling casually over his face and shoulders, and the restless energy in the way he stood—he was entirely his own man, both part of this family and decidedly apart from it. Scrawled tattoos covered his forearm, detailed and intricate, but the most striking was the delicate line of what seemed like a tree climbing toward his elbow. I couldn't help but wonder what that tree meant to him, what memories it held. He looked every bit the wandering soul—the kind who might play guitar in smoky bars and never stay long enough for life to pin him down.

The thought made me smile, fleeting as it was. He reminded me so much of Heck when we first met, with his messy curls and hipster charm, like someone who'd always been halfway out the door to his next great adventure. Shaking my head, I pressed my back to the wall and slid into one of the chairs lining the hall.

When the doctors rushed out of the room, I stayed where I was, alone. Helen, Hector, and Steven remained inside. I'd decided to give them that space, that moment to reconnect with the son who, for too long, had been a distant shadow in their lives. It had to be their time. Mine would come later—after Steven saved my Heck. If I thought too much about what that meant—the giving of flesh and bone, the sacrifice—I'd crumble under the weight of it.

Selfishly, I couldn't even bring myself to feel guilty. I was desperate. My world had narrowed to this one goal, this single aching prayer whispered at every opportunity: *Let him wake up. Let him come back to me. I don't care what it takes.* Even if it meant part of Steven had to bleed to save him, even if it felt unfair or cruel. All that mattered was that Heck woke up, strong enough to see our son and hold us both through the life we'd dreamed of together.

The sound of Steven approaching broke the swirling chaos of my thoughts. I shifted in my seat, watching him lower himself into the chair next to mine as though the weight in his steps had grown heavier. For a few moments, we sat in silence, both staring straight ahead at the endless length of the corridor before us. It wasn't uneasy —it was just still.

"It's been almost twenty years," he said, his voice quiet yet steady. "We never reconnected. I chose that. I didn't want to intrude on their lives... didn't want to ruin their family."

His words hung in the air, heavy with unspoken pain. My gaze drifted from him to the narrow bands of light slipping through the blinds, and I leaned slightly, trying to catch a glimpse of Hector and Helen. They were still seated, their heads closed as they spoke in hushed tones. Despite the tension that had simmered between us all, there was something about the way they sat that felt... unified.

Steven noticed my lingering glance.

"I'm giving them space," he said simply.

"You're part of the family, too," I replied quietly, still not meeting his eyes. My voice was soft but unyielding, the truth of my words sitting between us like an unspoken demand.

He didn't answer right away. I could feel his pause, how he seemed to turn my words over, testing their weight. Finally, his voice reached me again, gentler this time. "When are you due?" he asked, the shift in his tone catching me off guard. There was a hesitation there, almost as if he were afraid of stepping into something too fragile.

"Anytime now to two weeks," I replied, letting my hands drift instinctively to my belly. The baby shifted then—just a slight nudge, enough to remind me why I needed this to work. Finally, I looked at Steven more closely. Those familiar, piercing Archibald eyes met mine, shining with something I couldn't name.

A faint smile curved his lips, low and bittersweet but sincere. "You're going to need some rest before he gets here," he said, his voice softer than I expected. There was warmth in his words, a quiet kind of encouragement that felt like a small balm against the weight of it all. Then his smile deepened slightly, touched by a memory. "Time moves faster than you think. Twenty years, but it feels like yesterday that

Heck and I were raising hell together, giving everyone headaches." His eyes drifted for a moment, distant, and his voice softened even more. "Kids grow up fast. One minute, you're trying to figure out how to hold them… the next, they're out in the world, blazing a path of their own."

His gaze returned to me, steady and knowing. "You'll blink, and he'll be here. And when he is, everything will change. But it's the kind of change you hold onto, the kind that makes you realize it was all worth it."

I smiled then, if only briefly. "I just want a world where his father is there to meet him."

"You'll have that," Steven said, his voice steadier now. He nodded toward my belly before lowering his gaze. "I'm sure he'll be handsome like Heck. And maybe, if you're lucky... not such a handful."

"Or stubborn like his uncle Steven," I teased, trying to pull the moment into something lighter.

He chuckled softly, the sound echoing just enough to feel warm in this cold, clinical place. "Maybe so," he said with a faint shake of his head. "But I like it... being called an uncle. It's new to me, but yeah—I'm liking it."

"I'm glad Heck has a brother, after all. Imagine my boy not getting enough toy cars on his birthday," I teased, a laugh slipping out, relieved as the weight in the room began to lift.

But the reprieve hung lightly, fragile, and after a pause, he adjusted in his chair. His gaze dropped momentarily before returning, steady but edged with gravity. "They'll prep me soon," he said, his voice softer now. "Tests first, and then I'll go wherever they need me. The kidney and the liver are all to buy more time. Once it works, the doctors... they'll take it from there, stabilize him however they can."

The words settled heavily between us, too stark to fill with more banter. I swallowed against the lump rising in my throat, the earlier warmth still lingering but now weighed down by everything unsaid. I reached out carefully, my fingers brushing against his hand where it rested on the armchair. "Steven," I began, my voice trembling, fragile under the enormity of what I felt. "I don't even have the words. This... what you're doing—I'll never be able to thank you enough. For this. For being here, for trying to save him." My voice wavered, cracking under the strain of emotions too vast to fully contain.

"You don't have to say anything," he said simply, turning his hand to give mine a slight squeeze. His tone softened, like he could feel the cracks splintering in my chest. "One step at a time, Sara. No one's prepared to do any of this, but we do it anyway."

Tears stung the edge of my lashes, but I blinked them away quickly. I nodded, my voice failing me for the moment.

"And you," he added, sitting up straighter now, "you need to take care of yourself. Go home tonight. Eat, sleep. There's not much you can do here."

"I'll try," I murmured, though I wasn't sure I believed myself.

He sighed softly, then lifted one brow toward me in an almost playful exasperation. "No promises, huh? Fine. But you'll need your strength in two weeks. That baby will need its mama at her best."

For the first time in what felt like forever, a small, hesitant smile broke through—a whisper of hope stirring awake. "Alright," I said softly, the word carrying a quiet strength, as if speaking it made the possibility of brighter days feel just a little more real.

Maybe tonight, I'll actually sleep.

22

The Archibalds didn't waste time—getting down to business was second nature. Steven's arrival was no exception. After meeting him outside the ICU and the shock of our earlier encounter in the conference room, I'd barely caught my breath before we were ushered into another room. This one wasn't nearly as intimidating. It was simple, a quiet space designed for doctor-patient-family meetings. A small rectangular table sat in the middle, flanked by utilitarian metal chairs. The walls were painted a stark, sterile white, and vertical blinds covered the glass windows, providing privacy from the bustling corridor just beyond.

Dr. Arnolds sat at the head of the table. He was the kind of man who exuded calm authority—the lead surgeon overseeing Heck's case. Beside him was Dr. Kevin, the cardiologist—older, sharp-eyed, and intimidating in his confident posture. Three younger resident doctors stood discreetly near the edges of the room, scribbling notes onto their clipboards as if every word might be life-altering. Across from Hector sat a fourth doctor. I didn't catch his name, but his presence carried a quiet weight, as though he'd been in this type of room far too many times before and understood the stakes better than anyone else.

Helen fidgeted beside Hector, her hands clenched tightly in her lap. Steven, by contrast, sat between me and Helen, his shoulders relaxed, his expression calm. I couldn't tell if it was natural composure or if he was bottling his anxiety so tightly that it simply couldn't break the surface. No one said a word at first. My heart pounded against my ribs, filling the silence with its own rhythm.

Dr. Arnolds broke the stillness. "Thank you all for coming on such short notice." His voice was deep and steady, the kind of voice you wanted to trust with something as fragile as a life. He glanced at Steven. "Thank you for agreeing to do this. The nurse will discuss some forms for you to sign, and I'm sorry to meet you under such unusual circumstances."

Steven nodded.

"We've thoroughly screened and confirmed the compatibility between Mr. Steven Archibald and the patient. The results make him an excellent candidate as a living donor," Dr. Arnolds continued.

Hector nodded once, somber, though his fingers kept tightening and loosening on the table's edge, betraying his nerves.

Steven spoke up, his calm voice cutting through the tension like a balm. "What does the procedure look like—for both of us?"

Dr. Arnolds leaned slightly forward, threading his fingers together on the table. "We'll be performing a dual transplant," he began, his tone steady but weighted with the gravity of the situation. "Heck will receive both a kidney and a portion of a liver from you, Steven." His eyes scanned the room before settling on Hector, as if ensuring everyone understood the critical nature of the situation. "The liver is unique—it can regenerate after a segment is removed, both in the donor and the recipient. For you, Steven, this means we'll remove approximately 60 to 70 percent of your liver, and within several months, it'll regenerate to its full size. The same will eventually happen for Heck, assuming his body embraces the graft."

He paused, letting that hope linger briefly before addressing the hard truths. "But Heck's case is far from straightforward. His injuries are catastrophic. Drowning and electrocution alone would strain anybody, but when you add in the trauma from torture and days in a coma… his organs have been pushed past their breaking point. His kidneys are no longer functioning, and his liver has sustained irreversible damage. He's in critical condition, and right now, those failing organs are poisoning his system. His body can't heal while it's fighting its internal collapse."

The air in the room seemed heavier, and I realized I had been holding my breath.

"The transplants," Dr. Arnolds continued, his voice a measured anchor in the storm of emotions, "are not about curing him immediately. They're about giving him a fighting chance. Heck's damaged kidney and liver can no longer do their jobs—filtering toxins, processing nutrients, and regulating his body. Without replacements, the rest of his systems will begin to fail." He glanced at Steven, his expression softening. "That's where you come in. By providing him with a functioning kidney and part of your liver, we're stabilizing his body's foundation. The new kidney will take over waste filtration, relieving the pressure on his other organs. The transplanted liver, once integrated, will begin detoxifying his blood and producing the essential compounds his body needs to recover."

Dr. Kevin, the cardiologist, chimed in at this point, his voice clinical but not cold. "It's important to remember, though, that we're dealing with a body that's been through deep trauma. Even with the transplants, Heck's recovery hinges on how well his systems adapt post-surgery. The surgery itself will be grueling. His immune system is compromised, his body has endured prolonged stress, and these factors increase the risk of complications—rejection, infection, or internal bleeding."

Dr. Arnolds nodded in agreement. "Exactly. That's why these next steps are so critical. The transplants will address the immediate crisis, but recovery will be a long, uncertain road. He'll remain intubated and sedated after the surgery, giving his body the chance to focus its energy on healing. Even then, there are no guarantees. He could remain unconscious for days, weeks, or longer. But without this surgery, there is no path forward."

I felt my chest tighten as each word sank in. They weren't offering miracles—they were offering hope, fragile as it was. Steven spoke up again, his calm voice cutting through my racing thoughts. "If we go through with this, and his body accepts the transplants, will he have a shot? Will the transplants give him enough to recover, even with everything else he's fighting against?"

Dr. Arnolds straightened slightly, his expression resolute. "It gives him the only shot he has. The transplants will replace what his failing organs can no longer do. But beyond that, this surgery creates the opportunity to address the damage caused by his injuries—the severe metabolic imbalance, the organ shutdown, and the lingering effects of his coma. It buys us the time we need to help his body stabilize and repair itself. The road ahead will be uncertain and, honestly, brutal. But without this, we're out of options."

Silence wrapped around the room like a tightening noose. Hector stared at the table, motionless, while Helen wiped at her eyes with a trembling hand. Steven, composed as always, gave a slight nod. "Then we do it. Whatever it takes, we'll do it."

Dr. Arnolds gave a thin, approving smile, the weight of responsibility visible in the set of his shoulders. "We'll give Heck the best possible chance. From here, it's a waiting game. The surgery, grafts, and recovery are all part of a larger battle. His body will need time and strength. And we will need to be patient. The waiting will be hard, but every step forward, no matter how small, will matter."

"Yes, but," Hector interrupted, folding his arms tightly across his chest. "What about Steven's safety? If something—to be blunt—if something goes wrong, what happens to him?" He gestured toward Steven as if the question weren't unsettling enough without the pointed emphasis.

It was Dr. Kevin, the cardiologist, who answered. His tone was measured and practical. "For a healthy individual like Steven, the risks are minimal but not nonexistent. The surgical team will remove about four centimeters of his kidney and a segment of his liver, both of which are procedures we've refined over decades. Recovery for the donor is generally straightforward. Some post-operative pain and fatigue are to be expected, but long-term issues are rare. Steven will stay in the hospital under close observation for a few days to ensure there are no complications, after which he can go home to recover fully."

Steven didn't flinch. "And for Heck? What happens immediately after the transplant?"

Dr. Arnolds shifted in his seat, tilting his head slightly as he considered his response. "For Heck, the post-surgery phase is critical. While the new kidney and liver will function independently right away, his body's immune system will see these organs as foreign. We'll administer immunosuppressive medications to prevent rejection, but this comes at the cost of making him more vulnerable to infections. The first 48 to 72 hours will tell how his body reacts to the surgery, the organs, and the medications."

I couldn't stop myself. "And how long before we know... before we know if it worked?"

The fourth doctor's sharp gray eyes softened just a touch. "It varies. The kidney graft should start showing signs of function almost immediately, flushing out toxins and regulating fluids. The liver is trickier. Though it will begin working to some extent, full integration into Heck's system can take weeks. During that time, we'll be monitoring for complications, including bleeding, infection, and, of course, organ rejection. And, yes, there's also the waiting game." He exchanged a glance with Dr. Arnolds as if passing the baton of explanation.

Dr. Arnolds nodded. "Waking up." He said it bluntly but without coldness. "With major surgeries like this, some patients remain unconscious for longer than expected, even if the procedure itself is successful. It's the body's way of protecting itself while it adjusts. Once Heck wakes, we'll still need to closely watch for signs of rejection or other post-surgical challenges, especially given the complexity of a dual transplant like this one."

The words sank in, weighty and unrelenting. Still silent, Hector finally whispered, "And what if... what if he doesn't wake up?" His voice cracked slightly, and Helen's hand darted to his arm.

"Every effort will be made to ensure he does," Dr. Arnolds replied gently. "But there's no precise timetable for recovery. It may take time —sometimes days and, on rare occasions, weeks. That doesn't mean the organs aren't working. It just means his body is adapting at its own pace. The waiting can be excruciating, but it's not unusual in cases as complex as this."

Steven leaned forward slightly, his calm voice steadying the room once again. "And what can I do to ensure his recovery after the transplant?"

The smallest flicker of gratitude crossed Dr. Arnolds' face. "Heck will need support—mentally, emotionally, physically. The healing process isn't just medical. It's holistic. Family involvement often improves outcomes, so being there for him, much like you're doing now, is key." He looked at us, his gaze softening. "In Heck's case, family support is very strong, from what we've seen so far."

The room grew quiet again, the weight of the information pressing down on all of us. I felt Steven's hand brush mine under the table—a small, steadying motion. I didn't look at him, but I held on. He didn't say a word, but his presence said everything. We'd get through this—somehow, some way. We had to. Because, for Heck, this was it. His only chance.

Hector finally exhaled and leaned back. "Okay," he murmured, looking at Steven. "Okay." It was as much for himself as for anyone else.

The meeting ended soon after, the doctors shuffling out one by one. When we were left alone, Hector dropped his head into his hands, and Helen softly rubbed his back. Steven stood, stretching his neck, and glanced at me with a small, almost invisible smile.

"We got this," he said quietly, his confidence unwavering.

I wasn't sure if he was trying to convince me or himself, but for now, it was enough.

23

The day before the surgery unfolded in a fog of heavy decisions and smiles stretched too tight to feel real. We sat in the doctors' cafeteria, its harsh fluorescent glow casting long shadows over trays of untouched food. The metallic hum of a vending machine filled the silence we didn't know how to break, a nonstop reminder of how time dragged on.

We were deciding whether to go home—or at least Helen and I were. Exhaustion hung heavy between us, pressing into every sigh and glance until it felt like even the air was too tired to move.

Then Helen turned to Steven, breaking the silence with words that weren't framed as a suggestion. "You should come with us," she said. Her voice carried no polite invitation; it was more of a plea. "You can't keep flitting between hostels, Steven. You have a home." Her tone was firm and maternal, yet it wavered just enough to reveal the guilt she couldn't hide. Her eyes softened as she looked at him, silently pleading for him not to argue.

And how could he argue? Steven looked every bit as frayed as his old backpack slumped at his feet, its worn straps and thinning fabric a physical mirror of the man carrying it. He shifted in his chair, the movement stiff, his head dipped as though the weight of everything he wasn't saying had bent him inward. His shoulders curved under the silent strain, the lines of his face a map of sleepless nights.

The hospital had drained us all. The endless waiting slowly chipped away at our spirits. Living in its sterile corridors, trapped between hope and despair, made even breathing feel like an effort. But Steven... Steven looked like he was barely holding himself together, his grip slowly loosening on whatever kept him upright. That backpack, sagging against the floor, was all he had left. His whole life boiled down to what could fit inside it, and the sight of it made something twist in my chest.

Helen said nothing more. She didn't have to. By now, we were all clinging to the hope of feeling normal again, even if just for a fleeting moment—to catch our breath amidst the chaos. Deep down, we knew this burden wasn't going anywhere, not yet. The unspoken truth, heavy and tangible, hovered around us, lingering like a ghost we couldn't escape.

"You need real rest, Steven," I said, forcing the words out more firmly than I thought possible. My voice trembled, betraying the layer of worry beneath my resolve. His gaze didn't meet mine, and I pressed on. "You're going into surgery tomorrow night. You know you can't keep ignoring what you need. No excuses."

His fingers brushed the edge of the table like he was tracing lines only he could see. Before he could respond, Helen swooped in, her words softer, more coaxing than mine. "Your old room is waiting for you," she said with a hopeful kind of warmth. "Heck wouldn't even let me touch it. Not even when I suggested turning it into the baby's nursery." She gave a small, almost nervous laugh, but it wavered in the air like a fragile thread.

I watched Steven's expression carefully. His tired smile flickered, one of those faint, fleeting expressions that didn't quite reach his eyes. He glanced between us, calculating whether arguing with us was worth his energy. Finally, he sighed and gave in. "I'll take you up on it," he said, his voice gentle but worn, frayed at the edges like himself. "Anyway, I need a washer. I only packed for three days."

Helen seized on his acceptance as if it were a life raft. Her eyes brightened, and her words tumbled out with quick enthusiasm. "There's a closet full of clothes in your size," she said quickly. "I asked Jeffrey to pick out a few things for you. He was... well, he wanted to feel useful." Her voice cracked just slightly around the mention of Heck's assistant. That guy—always hustling, always buzzing with energy—had been quiet lately, lost in his own helplessness. I didn't think any of us knew what to do about it.

Steven waved his hand dismissively, shaking his head in that quiet, tired way he had. "You didn't have to go through any trouble," he murmured, almost as if he wanted to change the subject entirely. His reluctance was obvious, almost like the weight of being cared for was harder for him to carry than any backpack filled with his whole life.

But Helen wasn't having it. She stood her ground, her tone firmer now but still carrying the tenderness of someone who truly cared. "It's the least we could do for you," she said firmly. And though she didn't say it outright, the words felt like an apology, like she was trying to balance the scales for a debt none of us could articulate. Gratitude, regret—whatever it was, I could feel it in the air.

The silence that lingered afterward was thick, pressing down on all three of us, stuffed with the weight of things we wouldn't—or couldn't —say out loud. The only sound came from the faint hum of the overhead lights, a distant buzz that made the stillness even heavier.

Steven looked up after what felt like ages, but his gaze wasn't sharp or defiant. If anything, it was faintly resigned, softened by the kind of weight you carried for too long. "Don't mention it again," he whispered, the words so quiet they barely made it across the room.

His voice held a sense of finality that none of us dared to question. I looked at Helen, expecting her to protest or say something more, but she just sat there, her hands clasped tightly together on the table. I don't think either of us knew how to push further without crossing some invisible line Steven had drawn.

The tension in the room didn't break right away. It hovered, hanging over us like storm clouds that didn't quite know if they wanted to rain. Steven leaned back in his chair slightly, his exhaustion almost unmistakable now. The set of his shoulders and the way his head dipped forward spoke louder than words.

"You'll get used to us fussing again," I said finally, my attempt at lightening the mood falling short but at least breaking the silence. I tried to smile, and maybe it even looked genuine. "You know... women."

Steven chuckled softly, barely more than a breath of sound, but still, it was there. "Yeah," he said, almost to himself, "I guess you do."

Helen reached across the table then, her hand resting lightly on Steven's forearm. "We'll leave in an hour," she said, her voice soft but steady. "I'll call home, ensure everything's ready, and prepare dinner. We all need something real to eat—none of this cafeteria food we've been forcing down. You need a proper meal, Steven."

Steven nodded at that, but it was a slow, deliberate motion, like every agreement he gave now cost him something. "Thank you," he said simply, raking a hand through his hair. It was such a stark, quiet thing to say, but it carried more weight than a dozen flowery words could have.

None of us had anything else to add after that—not really. We just lingered there in the quiet for a while, each caught in our own thoughts.

Morning came too quickly. My alarm stirred me at six, the soft chime feeling like a distant echo of another life—one where mornings weren't met with dread and waiting. I rubbed my eyes and sat up, the autumn chill seeping into my bones. Fall had arrived in full swing, bringing cold mornings that smelled of earth and dying leaves.

Slipping on an oversized purple hoodie over one of Heck's old gray T-shirts and my stretched black maternity yoga pants, I shuffled to the window. My room overlooked the back garden—a space that felt like an oasis in the middle of the urban jungle called New York City. The garden was framed by rows of saplings slowly shedding their amber and russet leaves. Early light spilled over the dewy grass, casting long shadows that felt like they belonged in a storybook rather than reality.

And there, in the distance, on the weathered wooden bench beneath the old sycamore tree, sat Steven. His back was to me, his broad shoulders slightly hunched as if he were carrying more than his own weight. His olive-green jacket contrasted against the bench's faded brown. The muted colors—his coat, the bench, the tree—whispered of quiet sorrows. The scene felt fragile, like a still life too heavy with meaning to disturb. Sad. Lonely.

I stood there for a moment, feeling like an intruder. He didn't move. Something about the way he sat—so utterly motionless—set a stone in my chest. There was no rest in his stillness, only the kind of pause that comes when you're trying to keep yourself from unraveling. His breath might have been even, but the air around him carried a tremor, the kind only felt, not seen.

I was halfway to grabbing my towel to shower when I stopped. My feet found their way back to the window. I swallowed hard as my gaze returned to him, pulled like a tide to shore. I hated seeing him like this —lost in some inner place I couldn't seem to follow, couldn't quite reach. But maybe part of me… didn't hate it. Maybe part of me recognized it too well. A reflection. A mirror of my own.

I left my room and padded quietly to the kitchen. The house stirred faintly behind me—dishes clinking in the sink, the hum of life I wasn't entirely ready to face yet. The smell of freshly brewed coffee reached me as I stepped into the kitchen, the housekeepers moving wordlessly in the corner. I poured two mugs from the pot, the steam curling tenderly into the chill of the morning air. I hesitated, my fingers curled around the handles of the warm ceramic. The weight of both mugs carried questions I wasn't ready to answer yet.

If I walked outside and took this to him, it would mean opening something—something neither of us had touched in weeks. Did I want that? Could I handle it?

But then I thought of his shoulders, hunched, staring at the old sycamore, and all the questions faded into what I already knew.

Quietly, I stepped past the threshold and crossed the lawn, the damp grass cool beneath my bare feet. It was a habit I couldn't shake—walking barefoot. The cool air bit at my cheeks and pricked my lungs as I crossed the garden. By the time I reached him, mug handles warm against my fingers, he still hadn't moved. I thought about turning back for a brief, weightless moment—but the words came before I could stop them.

"You look like you could use this," I said gently, holding out the coffee.

Steven turned his head slowly, as if the weight he carried seeped into every movement. His tired eyes met mine, dark shadows underlining them, but even through the exhaustion, a faint smile appeared. "I wouldn't say no to that," he murmured, gesturing to the empty spot beside him on the bench.

I eased down next to him, careful not to spill the coffee. His gaze dropped to my bare feet, questioning. I couldn't help but laugh and shake my head. Without a word, he shrugged off his jacket, placed it on the ground, and gently tucked it around my feet.

"Thanks," I whispered. Our shoulders hovered just inches apart, and for a while, we stayed like that—quiet, watching the day stretch out before us in muted shades of gray and gold.

After a moment, I broke the silence. "You're thinking about Heck," I said. It wasn't a guess; it was a truth I didn't need him to confirm.

Steven didn't reply right away. Instead, he nodded toward the tree, his expression softening with a distant familiarity. "There used to be a tire swing on that branch," he murmured, his voice quiet, almost reverent. His eyes lingered there, as if he could still see it swaying gently in the breeze, suspended in time. It reminded me of how Heck had looked at that exact spot the weekend I first came to stay—the weekend he learned I was pregnant. There was something unspoken in both their glances, as though they were sifting through the same well-worn memories, searching for something they'd both once held and maybe lost along the way.

I tilted my head, trying to picture it. "From what you've told me, I'm guessing it became another Archibald trouble spot?"

His laugh was low and warm, like an ember struggling against the cold. "Definitely. We used to race to it, sometimes wrestling until one of us got the swing. Usually ended in scrapes, tears, or black eyes—and a nanny ready to quit."

"I can almost see you two terrorizing the maids."

"You bet! But Heck was way too smart for his own good," Steven said, a grin tugging at his lips as he drifted into a memory. "Back then, I was clueless when it came to the internet. We were trying to get onto some site we definitely weren't supposed to. I was at the computer, and Heck—he was behind me, doing his best impression of a backseat driver."

I raised an eyebrow, already suspicious. "I'm not even going to ask what site you two were trying to access," I said, blowing on my coffee to hide my smirk.

Steven laughed, shaking his head. "We were teenage boys. You can probably guess. Anyway, I was typing in my email to sign up for something—StevenYArchibald92@gmail.com, mind you—and Heck just smacked the back of my head. Hard. Then, in that dramatic way of his, he goes, *'Stevie, are you mental?!'* And I'm sitting there like, what? What'd I do? Then he points at the screen and says, *'You put your actual name on there. Do you want those creeps to just show up at our house or what? Worse, they'll steal your identity!'"*

By now, I was laughing so hard I nearly spilled my coffee. "You've got to be kidding me. What the fuck, Steven? Let me guess—you're 33 years old now."

"How'd you know?"

"It isn't rocket science, is it? Seriously, who the fuck puts their birth year in their email handle?" I felt like joining Heck in mocking him.

Steven leaned back, grinning so wide it was contagious. "That's exactly what Heck said! Except, of course, with way more attitude. C'mon, cut me some slack, alright? I wasn't internet savvy back then."

We both burst out laughing, the sound filling the space like a much-needed breath of fresh air. Somehow, for those few moments, the looming weight of the surgery and the uncertainty of it all faded into the background.

His soft chuckle trailed off, and the stillness returned. I looked at him again—really looked. He wore the weight of his family's name with such quiet grace, though the cracks in his armor were starting to show. He was handsome, dangerously so, but in a way that was deeply human. Nothing about him felt untouchable, and for a brief, foolish moment, I allowed myself to notice. Guiltily, I admitted to myself just how attractive he was. I shouldn't, right? Not when I was engaged to Heck. Not when Steven would soon be my brother-in-law. Not when Heck was still out in the other room fighting for his life...

But before I could stop myself, he caught me staring. His brow lifted, confusion flashing briefly across his features before he offered a teasing wink. I rolled my eyes and sipped my coffee, trying to play it off, but the heat rising up my neck betrayed me.

I rested my hand on my stomach. The weight of the baby growing inside me was more present every day. At that exact moment, a sudden kick made me flinch slightly. My hand pressed instinctively against the spot, and my eyes wandered downward.

Steven noticed, of course—he saw everything. "Whoa!" he exclaimed, his eyes widening with mock astonishment, his voice teasing. "Is my nephew training to be a football player already? Just like his dad and his Uncle Steven?"

I chuckled as I shifted in my seat. "Lately, he's been practicing those moves nonstop," I said, taking a deep breath. Then, grinning, I looked at my belly and said, "What do you think, Little Hemingway? Should we ask Uncle Steven about his love life?"

He laughed, shaking his head. "Hmm, colorful and black," he quipped, his smile a little mischievous. Then his expression softened as his gaze settled on me. "You're a writer, aren't you? Helen mentioned it."

"Trying to be," I said with a slight shrug. "My manuscript's still with my agent. Probably busy collecting rejection letters." I chuckled lightly.

"That's just part of the process," he said with a knowing smile. "The waiting game."

"Yeah, I've come to terms with it, though. It won't stop me from writing. It's just... in my bones. I've fallen in love with my characters, and I feel like I owe it to them to tell their stories."

He grinned and leaned back against the bench. "See? Writers and musicians—we're cut from the same cloth," he said, settling comfortably. His smile softened into something distant, almost daydream-like. "We're hopeless romantics, you know why? Because we feel everything. Every little thing. Writers weave all their feelings into words, and musicians..." He tapped his chest gently. "We carry it right here. We live in those feelings. We fall in love, completely, recklessly... every single day."

I tilted my head, curious. "Speaking from experience? Did you leave someone back in L.A.?"

"Nah. Not anymore," he said, his voice tinged with something more complex to place. A silence lingered before he spoke again, more slowly this time. "I was in love with someone," he admitted, his tone dipping steeply into something quieter, more vulnerable.

"Was?" I prompted gently.

"Yeah," he said, his jaw tightening just enough for me to notice. "We had a great life together... until we didn't."

I frowned. "What happened?"

He hesitated, and for a second, I thought he wouldn't answer. But then he exhaled, a sigh that felt years in the making. "She left me. For someone else."

The words came out coolly, matter-of-fact, but the way his shoulders tensed told another story.

I bit my lip. "Why?" I asked before catching myself. "Sorry, I shouldn't have—"

"Nah, it's okay," he interrupted, brushing it off like he was used to carrying this weight. "She wanted something more stable. She wanted a good life—the kind where she didn't have to worry whether the rent would get paid or where her next vacation would come from." He glanced at me sidelong, his mouth tugging into a faint, bitter smile. "She was tired of struggling. Tired of being with someone who was fighting to make ends meet every single day. And I couldn't blame her, Sara."

"That's not fair," I blurted out, heat rising in my voice. I didn't know her, but the thought of someone leaving Steven—sweet, talented, and obviously trying his best—infuriated me.

"Who said life's fair, Sara?" he said, his smile softening, though it didn't quite reach his eyes. There was no anger in his voice, just a raw acceptance that hurt more than any outburst of rage could have.

I didn't know what to say. What could I say? I wanted to argue—about fairness, about how anyone could leave someone like him—but the sorrow in his voice silenced me. Instead, I reached out and took his hand, letting it rest in mine. He froze for a moment, then gave a soft, careful squeeze.

We sat like that for a while, looking at the tree. The silence between us was both heavy and oddly comforting, as if it permitted us to hold the broken pieces of ourselves without needing to say anything at all. For a while, that was enough.

I Love You, Sunday Sunset.

24

The afternoon light sliced through the sterile hospital blinds with a charm that seemed at odds with the weight in the air. The golden, warm sun fell across Heck's face, its rays softening the stark angles left behind by the accident. I sank into the chair beside his bed, my fingers trembling as they wrapped around his hand. The weight of those same fingers used to anchor me, but now they felt so fragile, almost lifeless beneath mine.

Today was the day. The surgery. The one whispered about in hushed voices down every hallway. Two brothers, separated by years and miles of silence, now tied together by something no one could have imagined. The tabloids had sniffed out the story, no matter how much Hector tried to keep it quiet. Someone, somewhere, had leaked it; it was too sensational for them to resist. The prodigal son returning—not with words, but with a piece of himself to save his brother. It had the makings of a biblical tale, something too grand to keep hidden, yet so fragile that speaking it aloud felt dangerous, as if even the air might split under its weight.

We hadn't seen a single tabloid story, but somehow, they'd found a picture of Steven—one we didn't know existed. At this point, we didn't care.

For the medical team, this was the turning point. The procedure could be the miracle that tipped the odds in Heck's favor or the moment everything collapsed.

I sat frozen, my eyes locked on the monitor. The rhythmic beeping was all that told us he was still here. Barely.

His hand felt so familiar in mine. Smooth, warm—almost how I remembered it before all this. A part of me wanted to cling to those feelings, to imagine him waking up tomorrow, whispering my name in that deep, steady voice, smiling the way only he could. I pressed his hand softly to my stomach, where his son stirred beneath my skin. "Your son is waiting for you, you know. He kicked twice this morning —he's getting restless. Just like you do when you're forced to sit still for too long," I murmured, a sad smile tugging at my lips. "Heck, you have to get better. I want you to wake up. I want you to be the first person he sees when he opens his eyes. Promise me you'll fight for that."

I stayed like that for a long while, my hand resting lightly on his as though the warmth of my touch might anchor him to us. I spoke to him about the little things, the fleeting moments that still seemed to matter today—the way Helen and Hector flitted around the hospital like restless birds, their nerves practically buzzing through the air. The way Christine, his nurse, always managed to find the right joke at the right time, coaxing laughter from me even when it felt like my world was buckling under the weight.

Leaning closer, I gently brushed a loose strand of hair from his pale, unmoving face. My fingers lingered there for a moment, as if I could pull him back to us through touch alone. "I met Steven," I began, my voice barely more than a whisper, brittle with the weight of so many unsaid things. "Steven's home again, Heck... not fully, not yet, but he's finding his way. He stayed in his old room last night." I paused, a faint, wistful smile tugging at my lips. "I saw him in the garden earlier. He was just sitting there, staring at that old tree. You know, the one where your swing used to hang?" A soft laugh escaped me, a fleeting crack in the tension wrapped tight around my chest. "He mentioned how you two used to fight over who got to use it. He even remembered how you'd cheat to get one more turn." My smile faded, replaced by the ache of too much time lost. I kissed his hand, my heart leaning into the memories that felt both sweet and unbearably heavy. "You and Steven... you both deserve this chance. To be brothers again. To be in each other's lives. For real this time." The words caught a little in my throat as I searched his quiet face for the slightest hint of movement, my own hope teetering between belief and despair.

"I know he's special to you, Heck... and I know you're hurting. You're burying those memories because it's easier than facing the pain—because you love him. And I've never doubted, not for a second, that he loves you, too," I said, my voice softening, now laced with a tenderness that threatened to undo me. "He's selfless—the kind of person who would give everything he has, without hesitation, for the people he loves. And most of all, he's here. For you. No questions, no second-guessing—just a heart wide open, ready to give whatever it takes to save you. That's what a brother does. That's who he is." The word caught in my throat, heavy and raw, but I swallowed hard and forced myself to keep going. My hands clenched in my lap now, gripping that fragile thread of hope that seemed ready to snap at any moment. "You and Steven... you have so much time to catch up on, years and years of life you've missed together. But to get that—" I paused, my breath hitching as though the words might not come, "you've got to fight, Heck. Please, wake up."

The room held its silence tightly, answering with nothing but the rhythmic hum of the machines, the rise and fall of his chest. I leaned in closer as though some part of him could feel the pain in my words. "I hope you hear me. I hope you know how much I need you... how much we need you. We're all rooting for you to come back to us."

Silence followed, settling into the room's stillness like a weight I couldn't shake as I stayed there, trembling fingertips brushing against his hand, waiting for something—anything—that felt like it would never come.

"Good morning, Sara." A soft voice broke through the quiet. I glanced up to see Christine tidying a small cart of supplies as she stepped into the room. Her petite frame and warm smile always brought a strange kind of comfort amid the chaos. Filipino nurses had a magic sort of way about them, and Christine was no exception. "I hate to interrupt, but I'll need to get him prepped soon."

"It's alright, Christine," I said, rising slowly and smoothing my dress over my belly. "Can you tell me—did they wheel Steven into the operating room yet?"

Before she could answer, a familiar figure stepped in. Helen. Behind her strolled Hector, silent and stone-faced, his hands in his pockets, shoulders tense with worry. Helen crossed the room with a quiet urgency, her maternal calm doing its best to mask the storm brewing behind her eyes.

"Hello, dear," she said softly, placing her hand on my arm.

I kissed her cheek gently, then met Hector's gaze briefly, my nod accompanied by a sad, fragile smile that carried more than words could say. "I'll leave you to him," I said, sensing they needed this moment as much as I had. "I'm heading to check on Steven before the surgery starts."

"Thank you, Sara," Helen said as she took the chair I had vacated. Her expression softened slightly, but there was no hiding the weariness etched into her features.

Tipping my head toward the bed, I sighed before slipping out. The door shut with an almost imperceptible click, and I leaned against it for a moment, taking a deep breath. The hallway stretched before me, muted voices blending with the faint hum of machines and the occasional squeak of carts being pushed through.

I headed toward the surgical wing, my shoes tapping softly against the floor. The air felt heavier there, more clinical.

25

The hallway outside Steven's room was eerily silent, the stillness broken only by the faint hum of nearby machines and the occasional murmur from the nurses' station down the corridor. I stopped just outside his door, my hand pressing against the cold metal frame as if it could steady the storm inside me. Gratitude swirled uneasily with guilt in my chest as I drew a shaky breath. Steven had chosen this. He could have said no, but instead, he was here, waiting for the surgeons to take what they needed from him to save Heck.

I didn't have to look inside to know Steven was there, calm and steady as always. Even now, as he prepared to give away a piece of himself for the brother he'd spent his childhood wrestling with and teasing at every turn. He was doing this—for my Heck, the man I couldn't imagine living without.

The enormity of it all hit me again, sharp and new. How many people could love so selflessly? How many people would?

We were raised to believe family meant more than just blood—it was built through love, forgiveness, and holding on to hope when everything told you to give up. And now, as Steven sat inside that room, ready to prove all that with the most selfless act of his life, he became the very definition of it. Blood and love, bound together in a way that left no room for doubt.

When I stepped inside, the room was bathed in golden light—it was almost sundown. Steven sat propped against crisp white pillows, his hospital gown wrinkling slightly as he leaned back. A nurse hovered by his side, taking his blood pressure with practiced efficiency. He glanced up as I entered, his expression shifting into an easy, almost mischievous smile that softened the sharp edges of the moment. Flustered by his charm, the nurse ducked her head, her cheeks pink as she focused on the cuff wrapped around his arm.

"Sara," he greeted, his voice steady and casual, as if we were meeting for coffee instead of standing on the cusp of something life-defining. "You doing okay?"

The question caught me off guard, and I blinked back the burning in my eyes. I managed a small, wavering smile. "I should be asking you that," I said, my voice softer than intended. "You're the one about to go under the knife."

Steven chuckled, the sound rich and warm despite the sterile atmosphere of the room. "I'm in good hands," he quipped, his gaze flicking conspiratorially toward the nurse, who was now gathering her equipment with quick, jerky movements. "Right?" he added, a wink flashing in her direction.

The poor nurse looked like she might evaporate from sheer embarrassment. She mumbled a hurried goodbye and practically fled the room. For a brief moment, the tension lifted, and I found myself laughing—really laughing—for the first time in what felt like forever.

"Do you realize you just gave her a mini heart attack?" I said, still chuckling.

"Me?" he shot back with an innocent, boyish grin. But I wasn't fooled. He knew exactly the effect he had on women.

I sank into the chair beside him, my hand reaching for his without thinking. His hand was warm and steady, anchoring me in a way I desperately needed. "Thank you," I whispered. Those two simple words felt heavier than they should, my voice cracking as emotion threatened to spill over.

Steven's grip tightened briefly under mine. "Just take care of him, okay?" he said simply. His tone was serious now, his easygoing charm replaced by something heavier. "And make sure he knows he owes me big time when he wakes up."

"Never let him forget that," I said, managing a quiet laugh through the tears threatening to slip down my cheeks. "You and Heck have a lot to make up for."

"Sure we do," he said, smiling faintly, his dimple appearing on his right cheek. I'd never noticed it before, but now it felt strange to see Heck's smile reflected in his brother. It was softer, less practiced, but no less authentic, and for a fleeting moment, I saw a side of Steven I hadn't quite known existed.

"How long will it take you to recover after... you know, all of this?" I asked. I knew it was a stupid question—the doctors had already explained it—but it was the only one I could voice amid the storm of thoughts swirling in my mind.

"A couple of weeks," he answered with a shrug, leaning back further against the pillows. "Lucky for me, I'm healthy. Turns out yoga really did pay off."

"You do yoga?" I asked, raising an eyebrow in genuine surprise.

He grinned. "What, you think I just lift weights and bench press dudes at the gym?"

"That seems more on-brand," I replied, smirking despite myself.

He laughed, the sound light, almost careless. "Nah. Yoga keeps you balanced—mind, body, and all that. Plus, the liver? It'll grow back, and we only need one kidney to live a healthy life. I'll be back in shape before you know it."

"You make it sound so simple," I said, shaking my head slightly. His modesty only made his actions weigh heavier in my chest.

"It is simple," he said firmly. He released my hand and rested his palms on his knees, leaning forward slightly. "You're marrying him,

Sara. Which means you're family now. And family? It's everything. We don't get second chances often, but Heck and I? We have one now. And I'm not wasting it."

A lump formed in my throat, making it impossible to respond. Instead, I smiled, willing myself to hold back the tears threatening to break free again.

Steven leaned back once more, a cheeky smirk tugging at his lips. "Besides," he added, "Heck would never survive without me reminding him how much cooler I am than he'll ever be."

I couldn't help but laugh, a sound that felt foreign and fragile but filled the room nonetheless. Before I could respond, the door opened, and an orderly stepped in. It was time. The words hung unspoken in the air as we both looked toward the bed.

Steven exhaled slowly, the confidence and humor still faintly lingering on his face as he shifted to make himself comfortable. He glanced back at me. "Be ready, Sara. After this, I'm coming for you. We're going to get to know each other better—you know, sister-in-law bonding and all that."

"I'd like that," I replied, standing as two nurses moved to wheel the bed toward the door.

The room filled with a burst of bittersweet laughter from both of us as they began to move him out. I followed at a slight distance, watching as they wheeled him into the hallway. Just before they turned the corner, he looked back briefly, throwing me a wink that left me smiling and tearing up all at once.

And then he was gone, disappearing behind the double doors leading to the operating theater. I stood there for a moment, staring at the empty space where he had been, before finally turning away.

A faint thread of hope clung to me as I made my way back to Heck's room, only to find it empty. He had gone, too, joining Steven in the operating room. It wasn't over—not yet—but even amid the fear and the crushing weight of it all, I could feel it. The promise of something better. Something waiting just beyond this moment.

Warm arms wrapped around me, drawing me back to the present. Helen's familiar voice was soft in my ear.

"Everything's going to be fine now," she whispered.

And I nodded, my voice steady, though quiet. "I know."

We stood there in silence, her presence steadying me, anchoring me to a fragile but unyielding hope. We were going to make it through this—we had to. Heck was fighting. Steven was giving everything he had. And now, it was my turn to fight. Not just for Heck, but for the life growing inside me. For this boy who hadn't even seen the world yet, but whose future I was determined to protect. I wouldn't give up. Not for a second.

26

Helen begged me to go home, to step away from the sterile walls and relentless beeping machines. Her voice was heavy with worry, but I couldn't leave—not while Heck was in surgery, suspended between life and whatever came next, tethered by wires, scalpels, and fragile hope.

Of course, Helen, always one step ahead, had already done what I wouldn't. With Dr. Michaels' help, she arranged for me to stay. An adjoining suite had been secured for me and Heck next to Steven's, and before I could protest, I was officially admitted to the hospital. My delivery was close, and they weren't taking any chances.

That night, as we waited for the surgery to end, I tried to rest. The small hospital bed beneath me felt stiff and unfamiliar, its sterility only amplifying my discomfort. Sleep wouldn't come. My mind was too full, churning with fear, hope, and a thousand unspoken worries, all swirling too fast to allow even a moment of peace.

"You're barely upright, Sara," Helen had whispered with quiet insistence, her hands gently guiding me toward the bed. "Please. If the surgery is over, they'll find us right away." Her words, soft but steady, anchored me enough to concede. I lay down reluctantly, even as my heart remained rebelliously alert.

Now, the world felt sluggish and hazy. I curled up on the hospital bed, staring at the dim glow of the room, trying to push past my never-ending worries. Helen sat by my side, silent but steady, her delicate hands threading through my tangled hair. There was something achingly comforting in the motion—the soft, rhythmic brushing was oddly soothing, like she was smoothing down not just my hair, but the ragged edges of my soul.

Her presence anchored me in a way words couldn't. For now, that small comfort had to be enough.

"Do you know," she murmured, her voice so soft it melted into the room, "I always wanted a daughter, Sara?"

I tilted my head slightly, looking up at her. My tired eyes caught the wistful curve of her lips, that faraway look in her gaze. "Really?" I asked, only half surprised. "I didn't know that—but I can imagine. She would've been glamorous, just like you."

Helen laughed under her breath, the sound like a lilting melody. "You always know what to say, my darling." Her fingers paused in my hair, resting lightly against my temple. "If I'd had a daughter, I imagine she'd be as clever as you. And as stubborn."

"It's easy to talk with you," I admitted. Then, hesitating, I added, "Why didn't you have one? I mean—money was never an issue for you and Hector, right? I'd have thought... you'd have tried."

Her smile faltered, just slightly, as her hand stilled. "It was difficult for me to conceive," she admitted. Her voice was steady, but I could hear the crack beneath it, the delicate fracture where years of pain lingered. "I thought I'd never have a child. Hector and I waited too long. We were so busy building our lives. And when we finally tried... it just didn't happen for years."

I watched her face closely as she spoke, her profile regal and composed, but her eyes betraying the memories that haunted her. "Hector loves me," she said, her voice softening to something fragile, almost breakable. "I've never doubted that. But he wanted an heir, Sara. Needed one, really. The Archibalds... they're like royalty, you know? An unbroken lineage to protect, a legacy carved out over centuries." A dry, bitter laugh escaped her lips. "And when it seemed I couldn't give him one..." She paused, her words hanging like a delicate thread about to snap. Slowly, she pulled her hand away from my hair, folding it carefully, almost methodically, into her lap. "He had an affair."

The words landed like a stone in my chest. I sat up quickly, reaching for her. "Helen," I whispered, my voice aching for her pain. "I'm so sorry."

She gave me a small smile, one that didn't quite reach her eyes. "It was a lifetime ago," she said, brushing the jagged edges of her confession aside. "But then, two years after that... Hector came to me. He told me about a boy."

I blinked, my heart sinking further under the weight of her words.

"He asked me if I could accept him," she said, her voice trembling now but still firm. "This child. Flesh of his flesh. He wanted the boy to be ours. But how could I, Sara?" Her hands squeezed mine tightly, her grip a lifeline. "I loved him—I do. But having a child from someone else? It was pain beyond anything I can explain."

I swallowed the lump climbing up my throat, doing everything I could to hold back the questions that wanted to spill out. "What did you do?" I asked softly.

Helen exhaled slowly, shakily, like she was unwrapping the years one at a time. "We tried again, Sara. A year later... against every odd imaginable, I became pregnant." Her smile bloomed now, genuine and bright despite the old sadness clinging to her edges. "It wasn't an easy pregnancy. I fought for it every single day. But in the end, Heck arrived. He was the most beautiful baby in the world. The second I held him, I knew—it was worth every sacrifice, every tear."

"Hector must have been thrilled," I said, leaning forward, imagining her yielding strength and love through that storm.

"Oh, he was beyond thrilled," she confirmed, her laughter threading through the soft light of the room. "Finally, I gave him the heir he wanted." Then, shaking her head with a grin touched by pride, she added, "Heck was a little terror though—stubborn, impatient, always pushing the limit."

We both laughed, the memory of Heck's fiery, uncontainable spirit warming the air between us. Helen's voice carried that familiar, fragile pride whenever she spoke of him—a note tucked so deep it was almost hidden.

"But the past has a way of circling back," she murmured at last, her tone dimming to a shadow of itself. "When Heck was ten, Hector came home with devastating news. The boy... his other boy... he needed a home. His mother had passed, and there was no one left."

My breath caught. "Steven?" I asked, though every instinct warned me to tread carefully.

"Yes." Her voice cracked—soft yet heavy—and her hand tightened on mine. "He was twelve when he came to us. I wasn't ready for that. But Hector? Oh, he was determined. He wanted to bring his son home."

"And what about Heck?" I ventured.

A faint, sad smile flickered across her face. "He was ready. More than ready. He welcomed Steven into his world with open arms." She paused, glancing away for a long moment. "And me? I tried. But the truth? I struggled."

My voice dropped to a whisper. "Did you?"

Helen nodded, her lips trembling, her gaze dissolving into unspoken memories. "Hector brought Steven home, and from that moment, nothing was the same."

I hesitated, weighing my next question, but decided it was best to stay silent. Helen, however, pressed on, her words spilling out like she'd kept them bottled for too long. "Steven... he was his mother's reflection. She was beautiful," she said, her voice soft and raw. "And every time I looked at him, all I could see was her. And Hector's betrayal."

Her expression clouded with pain, but after a moment, warmth flickered back into her eyes. "But Heck? Oh, he adored Steven. Idolized him. He copied everything he did. Steven doted on him too—spoiled him, even. Their little adventures constantly had them knee-deep in trouble."

I couldn't help but chuckle. "I can only imagine! Must've kept you on your toes."

"You've no idea," Helen sighed, a weary smile tugging at her lips. "We went through nannies like water. Heck lived for summer camps and Christmas vacations because of Steven. His world revolved around him."

The air shifted as Helen hesitated, debating whether to say more. I waited, letting the silence stretch into something fragile but not oppressive.

Finally, she broke it. "On Steven's thirteenth birthday, Hector and I had an argument. It was late—we thought the boys were asleep. We were in Hector's study, trying to keep our voices down, but..." Her words trailed off, but the ache lingered.

"What happened?" I asked gently.

"The next morning, Steven was gone." Her voice barely rose above a whisper.

I blinked. "He ran away? Do you know where he went?"

"We searched for days. The police got involved. And then... one day, Hector stopped. He never said anything, but I knew—deep down, I knew he found him. And he... he let him go." Her voice cracked again, and I braced myself for more, feeling her pain like it was my own.

"But he was just a child," I said, my voice trembling.

Helen nodded, her shoulders curling inward. "He was. And I've carried that guilt for so long. He was just a boy. And the world?" She took a shaky breath. "The world is cruel. Heck was shattered. He blamed us—blamed me entirely. He said if I had treated Steven like my own, he would've stayed."

"Did you ever think about trying to bring him back? For Heck's sake, if nothing else?" I asked, the words tumbling out awkwardly. I winced inwardly, knowing it was too late to take them back.

"I begged Hector to bring him back home," she said, her voice heavy with regret. "But he wouldn't hear of it. He told me to let him go—to erase him from our lives completely."

Her words were razor-sharp, each one cutting into the air between us. "I'm sorry," was all I could manage.

"From then on, Heck drifted away. I lost my bright, joyful boy. He became rebellious, angry, and restless. And then one day, when he was fifteen, he begged for a loan to buy this old car he wanted to fix."

I smiled faintly, recognizing the moment. "I think I know about that."

Helen's lips curved into a bittersweet smile. "After that, art became his escape. Even then, I knew… I'd never fully been forgiven. Not for that."

"You don't know that," I said softly.

She shook her head. "Maybe not. But when you showed up in our lives… you gave us a chance. A chance to do right by you, to make up for the things we didn't do for Steven."

I opened my mouth to respond, but no words came. The silence between us grew heavy, laden with years of pain and regret. Yet, in that moment, something else lingered too—a quiet understanding, an unspoken forgiveness neither of us could yet name.

We sat together, lost in the echoes of the past but bound by the stubborn hope that healing might still be possible. There was more to her story. I could feel it. But for now, we stayed in the quiet, two women tethered by the weight of memory and the faint, distant light of what might yet come.

I Love You, Sunday Sunset.

27

I woke to muffled footsteps outside the door—insistent, like a whisper piercing the fragile threads of my dreams. My eyes flew open, darting around the room. Light spilled through the curtains in harsh, jagged streaks, cutting through the dimness like broken glass.

It was past noon. My body felt leaden, as if sleep had wrapped itself around me and refused to loosen its grip. For a fleeting moment, I couldn't remember where I was. The weight of reality hovered just out of reach until, all at once, it came rushing back. The memories hit like a storm, sharp and unforgiving, forcing me to face everything I had drifted away from in those few stolen hours.

The hospital suite wore a thin disguise of warmth, but it didn't fool anyone. The pale walls, broken only by a strip of flimsy wood trim, hemmed in the room with a suffocating sterility. On a small table near the window sat a vase of carnations, their edges curling inward, their petals sagging as though weighed down by the lifeless stillness of the room. A faint trace of lavender and rose lingered in the air, clashing with the sharp bite of antiseptic in a tenuous effort to counteract the clinical chill. Against the wall, a lounge chair stood stiff and uninviting, its posture angled awkwardly, echoing the restless hours of waiting that had passed in its shadow. The room felt like a reluctant pause, caught between pretense and reality.

"Heck?" I rasped, the word clawing its way out. My voice startled me. It sounded raw and scraped, hollow with worry. "Heck?" I repeated, my heart clenching.

Helen stood by the small table. When she heard me, she turned immediately, her face softening into a tired but relieved smile as she crossed the room. She was still in the same clothes from the night before—now wrinkled and slightly disheveled. A delicate, understated necklace caught the light as she moved closer.

"There you are," she said gently. "You were sleeping soundly for once. I'm so glad you got some rest." Her hand touched my forehead, cool fingers brushing against my skin. The gesture felt maternal in a way I hadn't expected, and I leaned into her touch without meaning to.

She perched on the edge of the bed. "I asked them to bring you some breakfast," she added, her voice soft but insistent, as though the food might mend what was broken inside me.

"Heck?" I asked again, my chest tightening around his name. That single syllable held everything—all my fear, hope, and desperation. I could feel its weight pressing on her, too.

Helen hesitated. Her dark eyes flickered for a second, a crack in the strength she was trying to project. "Two surgeries were completed last night," she said carefully. "Both went well, and he's in the recovery room. But..." She paused, the silence dragging painfully. "He hasn't woken up yet. The doctors say it's to be expected."

"To be expected." The words felt like a cruel joke.

She tried to smile, but I saw the worry in the tight lines around her mouth and the way her hands fidgeted in her lap.

"And Steven?" I asked, my voice breaking slightly. No one talked about him. Every conversation, every update, every life-or-death glance from a doctor seemed to orbit solely around Heck. But Steven—God, Steven had given more than anyone else in this mess.

Helen's expression softened at the mention of his name. "He's strong," she said, placing her hand over mine. "He's recovering well in his room next door. The doctors are optimistic. They say he should wake up anytime now."

A lump formed in my throat, thick and unmoving. My heart swelled, weighed down by the endless worries. "Heck isn't out of the woods," I whispered, my voice cracking. "They'll need him strong enough for the next surgery, right? He still has more to go?"

Helen's features softened, though exhaustion lingered in her eyes despite her best efforts to hide it. I thought she might not answer for a moment. Then she nodded, her voice steady yet heavy. "He needs time to heal. But he's strong, Sara. You know that. Stubbornness runs in his blood—just like his mother's."

Her quiet conviction should have been a comfort, a steadying force, but instead, it pressed heavier against my chest, smothering the fragile hope I was desperately trying to cling to. I dropped my gaze and rested my hand on my abdomen, where faint, restless flutters rose beneath my palm. My tiny boy. His tiny, defiant movements. Restless, just like us. Determined to remind me he was still here and ready to meet the world.

"Maybe you should head home for a little while," I said gently, keeping my voice steady, though the edge of worry crept into my words. "Change into something comfortable. Get some proper rest. The surgeries are done for now, and sitting here like this—it's not helping anyone."

Helen's face softened, faint relief spreading across her features. For the first time, she seemed to take stock of herself, the rumpled lines of yesterday's clothing still clinging to her. She gave me a slight, approving nod. "That's a good idea," she said softly. Her hand found mine, warm and steady, and gave it a reassuring squeeze.

"And I'll call you the moment anything changes. I'll send someone for you as soon as Heck wakes up," I added, trying to sound surer than I felt.

She nodded again, though the uncertainty in her expression mirrored my own, pooling at the edges of her resolve. "Are you sure? Can you manage on your own? I could ask Jeffrey to stay with you," she offered tentatively.

I smiled faintly. The weight in my chest lightened just enough for humor to break through. "I'm surrounded by doctors and nurses. This is probably the safest place in the world for me," I said with a soft laugh, though it faded quickly as another thought surfaced. "I need to check on Steven," I murmured after a beat, the words heavy with unspoken intention.

"Of course." Her smile flickered, bittersweet in its brief bloom. It held approval, but there was something else there, too—silence dressed in sadness. She adjusted the blanket across my lap, her attention so delicately focused on me that I felt fragile in a way I hadn't before. "Sara, stop worrying about everyone," she said softly, her voice laced with an honesty that almost undid me. "You've been so strong. For all of us. For Heck. For Steven. I couldn't have done it without you. But you deserve room to breathe, too."

Something in her words cracked me open, but I masked it with a shallow breath. "You keep saying that," I whispered, unable yet to meet her gaze. "But I don't feel strong. Not at all. Most days, I feel like I'm barely holding it together."

Helen leaned in closer, lifting my chin so our eyes finally met. Her face was worn with worry but still illuminated by a fierce tenderness that made my resolve falter. "You don't have to feel strong for it to be true," she said firmly, each word anchoring me with quiet certainty.

I bit my lip hard, swallowing back the tears threatening to spill over. Crying felt like it would unravel every thread keeping me together. Not here. Not now. But her words nestled into the raw, breaking part of me I hadn't realized was still exposed.

"Go," she urged gently, her voice brimming with care that steadied something deep inside me. "See Steven. Then, take one small moment for yourself. I'll return in the morning."

I nodded.

28

The air in Steven's suite was cooler, carrying the faint medicinal smell that seemed to seep into every corner of this place. I eased the metal door open, cringing at the soft creak as if it might echo through the halls. I didn't want to wake him. But as I peeked inside, I saw that he was already awake and turned slightly toward the door. His sharp eyes, though tired, still held that familiar glint of humor.

"Hey," he greeted, his voice gravelly but light, a ghost of a smile tugging at his lips.

"Hey," I echoed softly as I stepped inside, letting the door close quietly behind me. "I was just dropping by. Heck is still in the recovery room," I explained, unsure why I felt compelled to justify my presence. "How are you?" The question felt ridiculous the second I asked it, given the state he was in.

He smirked faintly, pressing his head back against the pillow. "Fucking bored," he admitted with a chuckle that seemed to take more effort than he had to spare.

The corners of my mouth lifted in spite of the ache in my chest. "Would you mind if I hang out for a bit?" I asked hesitantly, stepping closer.

Steven raised an eyebrow in mock surprise, though his gaze softened with warmth. "Of course not. Hell, I've been hoping for company. I mean, who else am I supposed to charm if not my future sister-in-law?"

I laughed quietly, slipping into the chair beside his bed. "Oh, there's not much to charm. My life isn't exactly a page-turner," I replied, tucking a strand of hair behind my ear.

He dismissed my remark with a theatrical wave of his hand, weak though it was. "Not buying it. You're marrying my crazy little brother. That demands a kind of bravery I can't imagine."

I smirked and rested my hands on the edge of his bed. "What about you? I've heard whispers about your life. Sounds like you've got all the colors of an amusement park packed into it."

Steven chuckled, his laugh rasping through the quiet. "Psychedelic colors," he corrected with a crooked grin. "It hasn't always been pretty, but it's never been dull."

Instinctively, my hand moved to my stomach, feeling the faint flutters beneath my palm that reminded me of life, small and relentless. My voice softened, my words as much for the tiny being inside me as for the man before me. "Little Hemingway," I murmured, affectionate. "Your Uncle Steven here will tell us stories about your dad. Mischief, danger... probably things I'll never want you to repeat."

Steven's grin widened, though it seemed to cost him more energy than he had. His gaze flickered to my hand, his voice quieter now, threaded with a quiet reflection. "Your dad... yeah. Mischief is putting it lightly. He's always had a way of finding trouble and dragging everyone along for the ride." His smile lingered, but something bittersweet shadowed it.

I eased into the chair, leaning forward to rest my elbows on the edge of the bed, my hands clasped loosely. I studied him for a moment, his face taut with fatigue. Seeing him in a hospital gown with wires snaking across his skin felt surreal. When I spoke, my voice was cautious, as though the question might stir some delicate memory. "You two must've been unstoppable back in the day. What was he like? Before all of this?"

Steven tilted his head slightly, his expression hard to read. "Heck...
where do I even begin?" He laughed softly, though it didn't quite
touch his eyes. "He's the kind of guy who'd pick a fight with the world
just to prove he could win. Stubborn as hell. But he cares, you know?
Sometimes, too much. Always carrying more than his share, even
when it wasn't his mess to carry."

I nodded, my throat tightening as the image of Heck lying still and
silent in the other room crept back into my mind. Waiting to heal.
Waiting for yet another battle he didn't deserve.

"He's one of the good ones," Steven added after a pause, his voice
softer now, his gaze distant. "But not everyone sees that. They see the
chaos, the impulsiveness, but not the heart behind it."

I didn't trust myself to speak. I was afraid that if I opened my mouth,
all the emotion welling up inside me would spill out in a torrent of
sobs. Instead, I reached out, letting my hand rest lightly over Steven's.
His skin was warm, but the veins beneath pulsed with exhaustion,
countless hours of strain etched into every line.

"And you?" I asked after a moment, my voice steady despite the pull
of emotion in my chest. "What about you, Steven? You seem like the
same kind of trouble, only quieter."

For the first time, he really laughed, the sound small but genuine. "Oh,
I've had my fair share of scrapes," he admitted, his grin rueful. "But
mostly, I'm just the guy who shows up when someone needs him.
That's my thing, I guess. Being useful."

His words struck me deeply, and I found my voice thick with
gratitude. "You've been more than useful," I said softly. "You've given
more than anyone could've asked of you, Steven. Don't think for a
second that anyone could forget that."

He shrugged, but his gaze lingered on the ceiling for a moment. His
expression grew distant. "If there's one person who loved me
unconditionally, apart from my mom... it's Heck. And now, he needs
me." The way he said it, matter-of-fact and simple, carried the weight
of something unspoken. .

The room settled into a fragile quiet, broken only by the steady rhythm of the machines. The light from the dipping sun spilled through the window, painting the room with streaks of gold and lilac. The harsh lines of the machinery softened, and even the shadows beneath Steven's eyes seemed gentler under the warm glow. For a moment, it felt like time itself had paused, the world outside oblivious to the weight we carried here, in this small, hushed space.

I moved to sit on the edge of his bed, the blanket rough beneath my fingers as I steadied myself. Steven shifted to make room, his legs stretched before him, one foot bouncing lightly against the bed rail. We both stared out the window. It was easier that way. Watching the sun flirt with the horizon meant we didn't have to meet each other's eyes.

"So," I began softly, breaking the silence. "I want to hear your story."

Steven tilted his head toward me, a crooked smile creeping across his lips. "I don't think my story's all that entertaining," he said with a dry chuckle.

I shrugged, leaning back slightly and letting one hand rest on my belly. "I still want to hear it. How you and Heck met… and why you didn't reconnect." My voice trailed off on the last bit, hesitant and curious but not wanting to pry too deeply.

He exhaled softly, like he'd been expecting the question but still wasn't ready to answer. "My life was pretty normal for a boy in West Virginia," he said at last, his voice falling into a rhythm as he sifted through the clutter of memory. "It was just me and my mom, but she made it feel like it was the whole world. Hector... Dad," he paused, a shadow flickering across his face, "he was barely a name in our house."

I glanced at him sideways, my brow arching slightly as his words hung there. Steven caught the look and let out a low chuckle, shaking his head, almost wistful. "He didn't show up much. Not for Christmas, not Thanksgiving." He shrugged. "Usually, he'd roll in for my birthday… but even that was rare. I hardly remember what that felt like."

He paused again, his hand twitching slightly, like he was reaching for something that wasn't there. Maybe a cigarette. I didn't know. When he saw me watching him, a small smirk tugged at the corners of his mouth, and he forced his hands to still. I arched a brow in disbelief, earning a soft laugh that released some of the tension in the room.

"Our life was simple," he continued after a pause. "Happy enough. We lived in this old house—big but creaky, with warm sunlit rooms." A small, wistful smile flickered across his face. "Church potlucks on Sunday. Neighborhood kids gather on the porch with popsicle-sticky fingers and scuffed knees. And my father..." His voice trailed off, the smile faltering. "My father's name was just... an echo. Something people whispered about when they thought I wasn't paying attention. There was envy there. Or maybe pity. Probably both."

"She must've been beautiful," I said softly, meaning his mother.

Steven's gaze softened, falling to his lap. "She was," he said simply. His voice grew tight for a moment and then cracked, just slightly. "But Fate... she's got a dark sense of humor."

The room seemed to hold its breath. Steven's laugh came bitter and hollow. He rubbed the edge of the blanket between his thumb and forefinger, as though the tactile distraction could keep him from completely unraveling. "She was always like the sun—so bright it almost hurt to look at her directly. And then one day, the light was gone..." He trailed off, licking his lips, his voice lowering to a murmur. "...fading into rain-soaked Virginia ground."

My stomach twisted at the thought. Steven, just a boy, all elbows and knobby knees, standing at a graveside too grand for someone taken too soon. The muffled sound of church bells ringing, umbrellas popping open against a steady drizzle, voices blending into the patter of rain. And then... nothing. Only loss filling the space where love used to be. My hand brushed instinctively over my belly, my throat tightening at the thought of my Little Hemingway. The thought of him living in this world without me—or without Heck—sent the pain rippling down to my very core.

"I was twelve then," Steven's flat voice brought me back. His jaw tightened, his gaze distant but sharp as he added, "And just like that, they told me to live with a stranger."

I blinked. "Your father," I said, the words more a statement than a question.

"Yeah. My father," Steven repeated, his tone carrying just the faintest trace of venom. "Or the stranger everyone liked to call that." His eyes flickered toward me, and I caught something there. Anger, yes. But also sadness. Both too old for his face but too familiar to ignore. "They shipped me off to New York. Said I didn't have much of a choice. And," he muttered darkly, "children don't get to choose."

I opened my mouth to respond, but he shrugged, brushing off his own pain like a piece of lint on his shirt. "The Archibald mansion," he said, his voice lighter now, though the nostalgia lay heavy beneath it. "A tower of luxury, rising like some grand cathedral over streets too clean to touch. I hated it the moment I saw it."

I raised an eyebrow faintly. "Too clean?" I asked. I'd thought the same, the first time I'd seen it too.

Steven grinned at the memory. "Far too clean," he said with a touch of humor. "Nothing like home. Not like Mom's. I kept thinking... she'd hate it too. But then... there was this tornado of wild hair that smelled like peanut butter..."

The softened sadness in Steven's face cracked, replaced by something brighter. A grin that didn't struggle to reach his eyes this time. "And there he was. Heck. He didn't wait for me to even put my bag down. He ran full-force," Steven gestured faintly, "smacked right into me, and we both went flying." He laughed, shaking his head. "That was it. A 10-year-old whirlwind in a mansion way too clean for either of us."

His laughter was full and real, and for the first time that day, I laughed with him.

"From then on," Steven continued, his voice a mix of disbelief and affection, "we were the housekeepers' absolute worst nightmares. I mean it, Sara. I think we aged a few of them prematurely." He chuckled again, that deep, raspy sound edged with exhaustion but unmistakably genuine.

"No doubt," I said, leaning forward, caught up in his joy for a moment. "Heck must've been your greatest—and happiest memory."

Steven tilted his head, his gaze softening as it drifted to some distant place. "Yeah," he murmured. "Heck helped me... helped me forget the sadness, even if it was just for a little while. After that first day, we were inseparable. At night, when the nannies shut their doors and finally went to bed, we'd sneak off to relive whatever chaos we hadn't managed to pull off in daylight." He smirked, shaking his head. "The first nanny quit after a week."

"A week?" I raised my brows, stifling a laugh. "What did you do? Actually, scratch that. I probably already know the answer. You two must've been a real handful."

"Oh, we were worse than that," Steven said, his voice warming with humor as he leaned into the memory. "It started innocent enough. Stuff like me teaching Heck to fold a proper paper airplane in the drawing room. Hector and Helen were away on some business trip, so we had the place mostly to ourselves."

He paused, the grin tugging at his lips now unmistakable. "But, of course, Heck couldn't just make paper airplanes like a normal kid. Plain paper wasn't good enough for him. No, he needed a twist."

"A twist?" I asked, already smiling despite myself.

"Chocolate pudding," Steven replied, maintaining a perfectly straight face for half a second before breaking into a grin. "The kid decided paper aviation needed to evolve. He ran straight to the kitchen and came back with not one, but two pudding cups. Held them up like trophies and stood there, smug as hell, saying, '*Imagine it, Stevie. Turbo jets. Chocolate-powered aviation.*'"

A laugh bubbled from my chest, and I pressed a hand to my stomach, feeling the gentle kicks of my little one. "Oh, my God. That's absurd."

"Absurd doesn't even cover it," Steven said, his laughter mingling with mine, rich and genuine. "The next thing I know, chocolate streaks are flying through the air like fireworks. It hit everywhere. The walls, the carpets, and even the chandelier weren't spared. And the nanny? Her blouse took the worst of it. She screamed so loud I'm pretty sure half the block could hear her." He paused, his grin widening as the laughter stayed in his voice. "Meanwhile, Heck and I? We were on the floor, clutching our stomachs, laughing so hard we could barely breathe. I don't think I've laughed that hard since."

"And the dining room?" I asked, covering my mouth as the picture came together in my mind.

"Oh, the chandelier still had chocolate smudges a month later!" he said proudly, leaning back slightly. "That poor nanny? She lasted three days before she packed up her bags, swore she'd never work for the Archibalds again, and walked out the door."

"Three days..." I shook my head, laughing softly at the sheer insanity of it. "You two must've been unstoppable."

Steven's smile lingered, but it softened at the edges, taking on a quiet weight. "We were," he said simply. "Heck had the confidence, the chaos. I just gave us a plan, enough strategy to turn whatever crazy thing he dreamed up into something we could actually pull off."

I nodded, imagining the pair of them, a whirlwind of boyhood energy and wild ideas, testing the limits of what childhood in a mansion could be. "Helen must've known," I said softly.

"She did," Steven admitted, his tone gentle but certain. "I'm sure she knew about all of it. She just... never stopped us."

We sat in silence for a moment, the laughter fading into the quiet. Long shadows crept across the room as the last of the sunlight stretched thin against the bed and walls. Steven's face, once lit by the glow of the setting sun, dimmed slightly, and I caught the faint lines of tiredness returning, heavy and unforgiving.

"She just wanted Heck to be happy," I murmured, my words quiet, almost to myself.

"Yeah..." Steven echoed, his voice low but steady. His gaze remained fixed on the window, where the final sliver of daylight disappeared beyond the horizon. And then, so softly I almost didn't hear it, he whispered, "Me too."

I reached out and squeezed his right hand, the one free from wires and tubes. The cool twilight filled the room now, a faint glow lingering against the hospital walls. Steven stayed still, his broad shoulders seeming impossibly weighed down by years of burdens and memories too heavy to share. I didn't speak, didn't move. I just stayed there, my presence a quiet offer of understanding.

"When the whispers turned to jeers at school," Steven began again, breaking the silence, "Heck was always the first to defend me." His voice was quiet, sharp in its focus. His reflection in the window looked distant, like he was speaking not to me, but to the boy he used to be. "Once, this older kid cornered me after class. A real piece of work. Twice as big as either of us. Called me a charity case, said I wasn't even a real Archibald, just some stray Hector decided to feel sorry for."

He laughed faintly, but it wasn't a happy sound. "Before I could get a word out, Heck stepped in. God, he must've been... ten? Barely up to the guy's chest. But there he was, fists clenched, his feet planted like he was ready to try and take down the whole damn world. *What did you just say?*' he demanded, his voice cracking on the word. But he didn't back down."

I smiled at the image of young Heck, impossibly brave and headstrong. "That sounds exactly like him," I said softly. "He always stood up for people. Always fought for those who couldn't fight for themselves."

Steven turned, just enough for me to see the flicker of pride mingling with the sadness in his expression. "He threw the first punch," he said, a faint laugh breaking through. "Before I knew it, we were both swinging. It didn't matter that we weren't winning. Hell, we didn't even come close. The guy had us both on the ground in seconds. But

Heck? He wouldn't stop. Kept shouting at him. Calling him every insult he could think of until a teacher finally showed up and dragged us apart."

He paused, his gaze dropping to the floor. His fists clenched briefly before releasing. "Hector smoothed it over, like he always did. His connections made problems disappear. But he was furious all the same. At family dinner that night, he didn't say a word. He didn't have to. The silence was loud enough."

I swallowed thickly, picturing the scene, its weight hanging heavy between the clinking forks and perfunctory conversation. "You must've felt so alone," I said, my voice barely louder than a whisper. "But Heck…"

Steven smiled faintly, though his eyes shimmered with something unspoken. "Yeah," he said hoarsely. "Heck loved even a wrench like me."

"You're not that," I interjected, my voice firm but gentle. "You were lost. Hurt. That doesn't make you a wrench, Steven. You… you didn't know any better. And even if you had, you were just a kid."

He blinked a few times, then offered me a slight nod, the corner of his mouth twitching upward. "Thank you, Sara," he said softly. "I don't think I've heard that in a while."

I gave him a reassuring smile, and for a moment, the room settled into quiet. Then Steven turned back to the window and continued. This time, his voice was steadier, though the weight of his words only seemed to grow.

"There were too many adventures with Heck to count," he said, his tone lighter, almost whimsical. "How many bones we fractured during ski seasons or how many times we got thrown out of summer camp for one scheme or another…" His smile faded as he trailed off. "Then there was my thirteenth birthday. That one… that one sticks with me. It started like any other. Pancakes. Heck singing 'Happy Birthday' loud enough to wake half the street. Helen gave me one of those half-hugs, the kind that felt more about appearances than affection."

I nodded silently, recognizing that polished distance Steven so effortlessly described.

"That afternoon, Hector called me into his office," Steven continued, his voice hardening. "He handed me this pitch-black folder. Inside were cards, codes, numbers... enough zeros to make my head spin. My trust fund. My first taste of the Archibald name in monetary form."

"Did you feel... proud?" I asked cautiously, though I already sensed his answer.

Steven shook his head without hesitation. "No," he said flatly. "It felt like an apology I didn't ask for. A bribe to keep me placated. I didn't even open it properly. Just left it in my room and tried to forget about it. Money was never something I needed—or wanted. Helen's allowance was enough to keep me comfortable. But love? Purpose? Those things money can't buy."

His words lingered in the sterile air, wrapping around the space between us like a heavy fog. His reflection in the window looked sharp and fractured, a stark contrast to the quiet man beside me.

"My birthday ended like usual. Cake. Expensive candles that Heck insisted on lighting himself, even though he burned his thumb. Sometime after midnight, I woke up craving one last slice. I snuck down to the kitchen, my steps careful not to wake anyone. But..." He paused, his voice dropping to almost a whisper. "I never made it to the cake."

I leaned back instinctively, holding my breath. The room felt suddenly still, suffocatingly quiet. Steven broke the silence with words like sharp edges, cutting through the air.

"I heard voices. Helen and Hector. They were arguing in the study, and the door was cracked just enough for me to hear. *'He doesn't belong here, Hector!'* Helen shouted. I froze. It was all about me. Every word. She said I was... a reminder of his mistakes, of his infidelity. Hector tried to calm her down, but her voice just kept cutting through. Sharp. Unrelenting."

My chest tightened, imagining Steven as a boy, standing frozen in the dark, paralyzed by the weight of words never meant for his ears. I caught a quick glimpse of his strained expression as he swallowed hard, his throat bobbing visibly.

"That night, I didn't sleep," he admitted, still facing the window. "At dawn, I packed my bag. Just a few clothes, a jar of peanut butter I stole from the pantry, and the fifty-three bucks I'd been saving since I was a kid. Left the black folder on my desk. I didn't want their money. Didn't want anything from them. And before anyone woke up, I was gone."

His voice cracked faintly at the end, and for a moment, I thought he might stop there. But then he added, quieter this time, "The hardest part was walking past Heck's door. I stood there for a long time, my hand hovering over the knob, part of me screaming to wake him up, to tell him everything. But... I knew he'd try to stop me. And he was the only good thing I had left. I couldn't ruin that for him."

A hollow ache settled beneath my ribs, constricting my chest. "Steven..." I whispered, my voice trembling under the weight of his confession. I wanted to reach for him, to close the impossible distance between us and make him feel truly seen. But I stayed rooted in place, afraid that any movement might shatter the fragile air around us.

"Heck would've wanted me to stay," Steven said finally, almost to himself, his voice raw with regret. "But I couldn't. Not after I saw what my presence was doing to them—to that family. To Helen. To Hector. To Heck. I was like a termite, eating away at something they'd built so beautifully."

His breath caught faintly, so soft it was almost imperceptible. "I thought leaving would make it easier," he murmured, his voice breaking like waves retreating from the shore. "For everyone."

His words hung in the air, brittle and raw, as the night pressed deeper around us. And in that moment, I realized just how much of Steven had been left behind in that house. How much of him was still standing outside Heck's door all those years ago, trapped in the quiet agony of that goodbye.

The room had settled into an uncomfortable stillness, broken only by the faint hum of hospital machines. Steven leaned back against the bedframe, his fingers drumming a soft, uneven rhythm on the edge, while his other hand remained beneath mine. His gaze stayed fixed on the city skyline in the distance, as if it held the answers he sought but couldn't ask for. I sat beside him, frozen, the air between us thick and fragile. My free hand instinctively rested on the curve of my belly, a silent reminder that even in the shadow of grief, life could persist.

"I walked all the way to the subway," Steven began again, his voice distant, almost hollow. "And rode it to the Port Authority Bus Terminal. But when I got there, the prices on those digital boards..." He exhaled sharply, almost a bitter laugh. "It felt like they were mocking me. California—I kept thinking about it. Figured it was as far from Hector as I could go. But the fare would've drained every dollar I had, and I still needed to eat. I couldn't risk it."

He shook his head, a humorless smile tugging at his lips. "I left the terminal and started walking. No plan. No destination. Just... away. Away from New York City."

Tears burned at the edges of my eyes as I clasped my hands over my mouth, horrified at the thought of a young boy, barely more than a child, wandering alone along the highways. "Oh, Steven..." I whispered, my voice breaking, the words thick with sorrow. I felt something twist inside me as the image of Helen and Hector blurred into colder, crueler shapes, their polished exteriors cracking beneath the weight of his story.

I stayed silent, watching him. He didn't turn away from the window, his reflection fractured across the glass as the city lights began to flicker in the distance. His jaw tightened before he finally spoke.

"Cars roared past me in waves at first, headlights cutting through the dark. Most didn't stop. The ones that slowed down..." He paused, a faint smirk tugging at his lips, though it held no humor. "They got a good look at me—a scrawny teenager carrying a ratty backpack—and kept going. Mothers gripped their steering wheels tighter, pulling their kids closer as they passed. Truck drivers glanced at me and sped off. I guess I just looked like trouble."

He hesitated, his voice softening. The smirk faded, replaced by something heavier. "Occasionally, someone would stop. Usually older men. Decent folks, I think, with tired eyes. They'd take me as far as they could, drop me off with an apologetic smile, then drive away before they thought better of it." He exhaled sharply, his fingers twitching against his arm. "I was lucky, that time. No one hurt me. If they had…" He trailed off, his voice sinking into silence.

I couldn't stop myself. "But you were just a boy," I said, my voice trembling faintly around the edges. "How could they… just leave you?"

Steven turned his head slightly, enough for me to catch his faint, knowing smile. "Life on the road, Sara? It doesn't care about age. It just swallows you whole."

I swallowed hard, fighting the lump forming in my throat as he continued. "For days, I walked. The gravel ate through my sneakers, every step feeling like it might be the one to break me. I got so hungry, it hurt. My stomach twisted until I had to double over, clutching it, praying the pain would pass. At night, I'd find patches of grass near the roadside and try to sleep, pulling my backpack over me like it could fend off the cold. But the noises…" He shook his head, his voice trailing off for a moment before picking up again. "Coyotes howling in the distance. The crackle of leaves. Every little sound sent my heart racing. By the third night, I couldn't tell the difference anymore between what was fear, hunger, or just plain exhaustion."

"And then?" I whispered, barely audible. I wasn't sure I wanted to hear what came next, but I couldn't stop myself from asking.

Steven sighed, pressing his lips into a thin line before speaking again. "Luck… came in the form of an old black station wagon. Its headlights cut through the dust and gravel. When it stopped, a man leaned over the passenger seat and looked at me. A priest." His brow furrowed, a small, faintly amused smile flickering at the corners of his mouth. "Father Raul. He didn't ask too many questions. Just patted the seat next to him and said, 'You look like you need a ride, son.'"

"Thank God," I murmured, relief washing over me.

Steven chuckled softly, though the sound carried a rough edge. "It wasn't exactly simple," he said. "I lied. Told him my name was Chris. Just Chris. I didn't want to risk him figuring out who I really was. For years after that, I stayed with him in Huntington Beach. It was far enough away from New York to feel like another lifetime."

"And he didn't turn you in? Never told anyone who you were?"

"I begged him not to," Steven said, his tone softening. "And he didn't. The only condition he gave me was school. No arguments. That was the deal. I helped out around the church and did odd jobs for the parishioners. Collected hymnals, cleaned pews, anything they needed. For a while, life... settled. But school?" He barked out a laugh, one devoid of real humor. "That was hell. Kids don't change, no matter where you are. I was still the outsider. Always the target when someone needed one. It didn't matter that I'd gotten bigger, taller. Bullies always come in packs."

His hand moved to the back of his neck, rubbing it slowly. His voice thickened with unspoken emotion as he went on. "Father Raul tried his best. He gave me something to hold on to. One night, after service, he found me in the choir loft, staring at this dusty old guitar. It reminded me of my mom... the way she used to play. She was amazing." His brow furrowed, and for a moment, I thought he might get lost in the memory. Still, he continued, "Father Raul asked if I knew how to play."

I leaned forward slightly, captivated by the faint light softening his face as he spoke. "Did you?" I asked.

Steven shook his head, a faint, bittersweet smile crossing his lips. "No. And I told him so. But he didn't seem to care. He handed it to me and said, 'It's yours. Sometimes, music can say what words can't. Use it well.'" His voice wavered just slightly now, cracking under the weight of his words as his fingers tightened against the edge of the bed.

Tears slipped silently down my cheeks. "And did you?" I asked gently.

"Did you use it well?"

Steven's shrug was small, almost imperceptible. But his smile lingered, half-hidden beneath his furrowed brow. "That guitar became a part of me."

"Is he still alive?" I asked, hesitant, almost afraid of the answer.

His smile fell, his gaze turning downward. "I don't know," he admitted quietly, his tone heavy and full of something unspoken I couldn't name. "I didn't… I didn't look back when I left."

The weight of his words hung thick in the room, unspoken grief filling every empty corner. I could see it in his face, painted in the slump of his shoulders, etched into the lines around his eyes.

"You must've cared for him," I murmured, leaning forward slightly, my hands clasped tightly in my lap.

Steven hesitated, his shrug carrying an odd mix of acceptance and regret. "I did," he said simply. "Father Raul gave me the kind of stability I hadn't known since…" He trailed off but caught himself, his voice softening as he continued. "Someone at the parish taught me the basics, how to play a few chords. The rest… the rest was me. Hours alone, just me and that guitar in the quiet of an empty chapel. It was the only thing that still felt solid. Like it tethered me to the world. And for a while… that was enough."

His voice drifted off again, leaving the room filled with the quiet rhythm of hospital machines. The faint hum seemed to echo the pulse of a memory neither of us could touch.

I met his gaze then, and for the first time, a faint flicker of pride cut through the sorrow. "That guitar became everything to me," he admitted. "An extension of who I was. Of what I couldn't say out loud. It carried me. Before I knew it, I was performing solo. First at the church, then in this little seaside pub. Just me, the guitar, and whoever happened to be listening."

"You must've been good," I said softly.

Steven huffed a small laugh, though it didn't carry much humor. "After a while, staying there... it felt too safe, you know? I'd walked so far to get away from New York, from Hector, from all of it. But there I was, stuck again. Stuck in something small, something simple. Stable." He paused, his voice catching on the last word as if it left a bitter taste behind.

"And you left," I murmured, understanding the implicit truth in his words.

He moved to the foot of the bed, his gaze fixed on the bare floor as he nodded. "Yeah," he said quietly. "Downtown L.A. was waiting for me, with its chaos, its sharp edges, its everything. The lights never turned off, Sara. The noise never stopped. That's what drew me in, I think. Huntington Beach was too quiet for a kid with too many ghosts."

He paused, his mouth curving into something that wasn't quite a smile. "That's how I met Danny. He was a trainwreck. Older than me, twice over, with a thousand stories he'd tell a little too well after a drink or three. But the guy had this way... of turning a bad day into something almost bearable. Something we could laugh about later." Steven's tone softened, losing some of its earlier edge.

"Was he a musician too?" I asked, piecing together the life Steven described.

Steven nodded, leaning against the footboard now. "He was. And a damn good one, even if he was rough around the edges. Danny got me gigs. Nothing special. Bars that smelled like old cigarettes and spilled whiskey, where the crowd didn't give a damn who was playing as long as the jukebox worked. But it was something. Enough to pay for the next meal, the next rent check, the next drink. Enough to keep going."

He hesitated, drawing a slow breath. "Life with Danny wasn't like anything I'd known before. There were no rules. No curfews. Just this reckless kind of... freedom. Or at least, it looked like freedom back then."

"Did you feel free?" I asked, my voice barely breaking the quiet between us.

Steven gave me a long, hard look, shaking his head slowly. "No," he said simply. "It felt like running. Running from one thing toward another and never stopping long enough to see the wreckage I was leaving behind."

The silence that followed was almost unbearable. I waited, sensing there was more.

"Anything was fair game," he said finally, his voice dropping. "Drugs, girls, the booze… it all came easy. Too easy. Danny showed me how to flirt with the edge, how to dance along it without falling. And for a while, it worked. The high filled the empty corners. Numbed the ache. But it doesn't last, Sara. It never lasts. Eventually? The high fades, and the emptiness comes back louder than before." He exhaled sharply, his voice tightening. "That's when I knew I had to go."

"You walked away?" I asked cautiously, watching his face for any sign of what that decision had cost him.

"I didn't just walk away, Sara," he said, his tone sharp. "I ripped everything to pieces. Chris, Danny, the life we'd built together—I burned it all down. Stopped answering calls, stopped showing up to gigs. By the time Danny got the message, I was long gone. And for the first time in years, I used my real name. Steven. I left Chris behind with everything else."

I closed my eyes briefly, picturing the boy he described, always at a crossroads, always leaving. "And Archibald?" I asked after a beat.

Steven laughed bitterly. "That name?" He shook his head. "I stripped it off like a second skin. Left it somewhere I can't even remember. But of course…" His voice dropped, colder now. "Hector found me anyway."

"What?" I leaned forward, disbelief tightening in my chest.

He laughed again, the sound hollow. "Hector had his own net. Father Raul? Danny?" He turned suddenly, his dark gaze locking onto mine. "They were under his payroll the whole time. I thought they were my

225

safety nets. My lifelines. But no, Sara. They were his."

My stomach dropped as realization crashed around me. "No..." I whispered, shaking my head as though denying it would somehow make it less true.

Steven smirked faintly, though his eyes betrayed none of the humor. "Hector's always five steps ahead, Sara. Always. The gigs, the church, the people I thought cared about me? Hector Archibald III ran the whole show. No one slips through his fingers, not even me."

"That can't be right," I said, my voice breaking under the weight of his words. The betrayal I could hear in them felt like it had somehow become mine.

Steven nodded, his expression unreadable. "Control, Sara. That's all it's ever been about. No matter how far I ran, how hard I fought it, that leash was always there. Loose enough to keep me moving—but never enough to really set me free."

I sat back, the ache of his story settling under my ribs. "And yet, you're here," I said softly. "You're still standing, Steven."

He looked at me, his eyes dark and unreadable. "Am I?" he asked, the words so quiet yet weighted with pain and questions I couldn't answer.

"Yes," I said firmly, holding his gaze. "You are. And that's something Hector can't control."

For a long moment, he didn't move. And when he did, a faint, broken smile appeared. "Maybe," he murmured, his voice barely louder than the breath he drew after. "Maybe."

29

I perched on the edge of the couch that had replaced the uncomfortable chair beside the bed. The worn book lay open on my lap. My fingers trembled as I held the fragile pages, aged and familiar from years of reading and rereading. The room felt sterile, the harsh brightness clashing with the intimacy of the moment. Machines hummed steadily around us, their cold, mechanical rhythm a constant reminder of how precarious his life was. Wires crisscrossed Heck's still body, disappearing beneath the thin hospital gown. The hiss of the respirator filled the silence, sharp and unyielding. I hated that sound. Hated the wires. Hated how they seemed to hold him more than I could.

Heck's face was calm, almost serene, untouched by the violence that had pushed him here. The faintest flush of color brushed his cheeks today, and I longed to take it as a sign, a promise that he was coming back to me. But the machines, the tubes taped to his battered skin, whispered how wrong I might be. He was still fighting for every breath, every heartbeat.

Carefully, I reached for his hand, the one free of wires. My fingertips brushed his before I gently clasped it, cradling it as though he might break. I didn't want to hurt him, but I couldn't bear not to hold him.

"'I'll be looking at the moon, but I'll be seeing you,'" I read softly, my voice breaking the monotony of the machines. I glanced up at the skylight, where the moon hung faint and distant, its glow casting weak shadows across the room. "Pender," I whispered, his nickname tightening something in my chest. "This line... it reminds me so much of you. That's how we've always looked at the moon, haven't we?"

My voice shook as I closed Michael Ondaatje's *The English Patient* and rested it on my lap. "Do you hear me, Heck?" I asked quietly, leaning forward to rest my forehead against his hand. "That's your favorite line." It was barely a whisper now. Desperation twisted itself into my words, tightening around each syllable until I wasn't even sure I could get them out. "Do you know I'm here?"

There was no answer. No flicker of his eyelids. No twitch of his fingers in mine. Just the quiet beep of the heart monitor and that awful, relentless hiss of the respirator. It felt impossible that this was my Heck. That this unmoving body, so battered and fragile, was the same man who read me poetry under the stars, who laughed so hard he hiccupped when I told a joke, who faced the world's cruelties and still burned with defiance. His body looked whole, perfect even, but the truth of what they'd done to him was written in the bruises hidden beneath the thin cotton. The bullet wounds. The hands that left him scarred inside. The monsters who tried to break him.

"They can't hurt you anymore," I said suddenly, too loudly, my voice hoarse from holding back the scream that lived in my throat. That burst of anger startled me, but I didn't stop. "They're done, Heck. Peter Sullivan is behind bars. Sophie's being tried for what she did. They'll rot in prison for the rest of their lives. They'll pay for every moment you spent in their hands!"

The heat drained from me as quickly as it came, leaving me hollow. My chest ached as I gripped his hand tighter, my thumbs brushing over the stillness of his skin. Tears slipped down my cheeks quietly, unchecked. They broke him in every way they could—tearing at his body, shattering his mind. The physical torment had been relentless, but the psychological wounds ran even deeper. And when they were done, when they'd stripped him of everything but his defiance, they sent him staggering toward escape, only to shoot him in the stomach, as if to snuff out any remaining hope. Silent tears coursed down my face, the weight of his suffering too much to bear.

"No one can touch you now," I whispered. The words felt more like a promise than a fact, one I needed to believe as much as I needed him to hear it. "No one. Not while I'm here."

My love, my protection, couldn't undo what they'd done to him. They broke his body. Scarred him in ways I couldn't see but felt in every aching moment. They didn't stop until he was left bleeding and alone. But even then, Heck held on. He didn't give them what they wanted. He didn't break. I lifted his hand to my lips, shutting my eyes tightly against the relentless tears. They couldn't take him from me—not now, not ever.

"They'll pay. More than this," I whispered, my voice catching as anger and grief twisted together inside me. "Life in prison isn't enough." The words hung in the air, bitter and hollow. Justice felt meaningless. What justice could undo the pain they'd carved into him? What justice could bring him back to me, breathing and whole again?

My free hand moved to my belly, fingers brushing gently over its curve. "Heck, I wanted so much for you to see him... our boy. This little life we made. He's a fighter, reckless and strong, just like you."

I looked at his face, still so motionless, his lashes faint shadows against his pale skin. The words came quieter now, barely more than a prayer. "I need you, Heck. I need you to come back to me. To us. He needs you, too. To tell him those stories only you can tell. To show him your favorite books and teach him how to be brave. I need you to tell me that we can do this together."

My heart felt wide open, torn and raw, but no sound came from him. No sign. I pressed my forehead against his hand, my tears falling harder now, racking my body until I could barely hold myself upright. Still, I stayed there, letting his cold skin anchor me in the silence. Hours passed, the moonlight creeping across the room, wrapping us both in its faint glow.

"I'll wait," I whispered at last, my voice trembling but steady with resolve. "No matter how long it takes, Pender... I'll wait for you."

———

I wasn't sure how long I stayed like that—clutching the book to my chest, tears spilling silently as I tried to block out the memories of what they'd done to Heck. The images were too vivid, too raw. No matter how hard I tried to push them away, they always came back with a vengeance, torturing me relentlessly. A soft knock at the door pulled me back to the present. I dragged the heel of my hand across my cheeks, trying to collect myself before speaking.

"Yeah?" My voice came out rough, strained from crying.

The door creaked open, and Steven stepped inside. I glanced up, forcing a faint smile to my lips. It felt brittle, barely there.

Steven looked like a character casually walking out of a magazine spread. His long, curly hair framed his shoulders, wild and unruly. Gone was the bland hospital gown; he now wore his signature look—a snug black T-shirt that hugged his lean frame and well-worn jeans that fit like they'd been made just for him. His battered leather boots, scuffed and nicked, completed the ensemble. Heck's style had always been cleaner—sneakers, neat polos, effortless but intentional. Steven, on the other hand, looked like he'd stepped out of a gritty music video. Yet there was something disarming about him. His week-old stubble was trimmed just enough to suggest he cared, but not enough to imply he'd spent any real time on it.

"Hey," I greeted softly. "Feeling better?"

"Much better. They just took off the IV, so I'm wireless now," he said, leaning slightly into the doorway as if testing the mood of the room. A half-smile tugged at his mouth, steady and inviting. "Mind if I come in?"

I motioned toward a chair, my tone dry. "Please. I'm in desperate need of some halfway decent company."

Steven chuckled under his breath and stepped in, easing the door shut behind him with a finality that felt strangely comforting. The air in the room shifted, settling in a way that made breathing easier. He had that way about him—his presence filled the space without demanding attention. He crossed the room in a few long strides, his boots making soft taps against the floor, and paused by the bed, leaning over Heck.

"How's he doing today?" he asked, his voice quieter now, tinged with something like hope and fear colliding.

I pressed the book against my lap, my fingers curling over the edges of its cover. "His color's better," I replied softly. "But we're still waiting. Still hoping."

Steven nodded, his jaw tightening for just a second before he eased into the chair across from me. "He's going to be fine." His voice dropped, weighted with quiet determination. "He has to be."

I leaned forward, reclaiming Heck's hand, the wires brushing against my wrist. "That's what I keep telling him," I murmured, tracing tiny circles over his still fingers. "If anyone can fight through this, it's him."

Steven nodded again, brushing a stray lock of hair from Heck's forehead.

"So, you're officially on the mend," I said, breaking the silence.

"Seems that way." Steven leaned back in the chair, his long legs stretched out casually, though his fingers tapped an anxious rhythm on the armrest. "And look at me now—a picture of health." His smirk was sharp, but it softened with his next words. "I'm just waiting for the doctors to clear me."

I raised an eyebrow, letting a light laugh escape. "Do you have any patience for anything? Or are you planning a dramatic escape through the nearest window?"

"Don't. Tempt. Me." His lips curved into the kind of smile that made you believe he was seriously considering it. "I've got half a mind to walk out of here right now."

I laughed again, a little louder this time, the sound breaking through the tension in my chest. "Can't say I'd blame you. They don't exactly make hospitals inviting." My eyes flicked down to his boots—those scruffy, timeworn relics that seemed absurdly out of place in a sterile white-and-gray room. "But I have to say, you've really nailed the whole mysterious rock star in recovery vibe. Very on-brand."

He chuckled, low and unhurried. "You think this is part of the brand? I'll have to put 'mysterious rock star in recovery vibe' in my next album's liner notes."

A grin tugged at my lips. "Please do. I'll expect credit for the idea."

He ran a hand through his curls, his laughter softening. "What can I say? Gotta stay true to the persona, even when I'm laid up." But then his smile faltered, just enough for me to catch it. The weight of reality crept back in. His gaze flicked to Heck, lingering there, and his fingers stilled. When he looked back at me, the laughter in his voice was gone, replaced with quiet sincerity. "He's gonna get through this." The words carried a firmness, an unwavering belief I wasn't sure I could summon in myself just then.

I nodded, gripping Heck's hand tighter. The silence between us grew heavier, but it wasn't unwelcome. "Yeah. He will." My voice was steadier, though my heart still felt shaken. For now, hoping and believing had to be enough. It just had to be.

We sat there for a moment, the quiet between us natural and unpressured. His gaze drifted toward the window, soft and distant. I studied him then—the way his presence felt so different from Heck's, yet somehow familiar. Steven carried his calm like armor, his stillness a kind of quiet resilience.

"You're a lot like him, you know," I said, breaking the silence. The words slipped out before I could stop myself.

He turned to me, his brows lifting slightly. "Like Heck?"

"Not in the obvious ways," I clarified. "Heck's all... sharp edges and quick words. You're quieter. More..." I paused, searching for the right term. "Measured."

A faint smile tugged at the corner of his mouth. "Measured," he echoed, as if testing the word. "I don't hear that often."

"It's a good thing," I said quickly. "You make it easy to talk. With Heck, it's exciting but... different. You always feel like you're running to keep up with him."

Steven leaned forward slightly, resting his elbows on his knees. "Heck's good at making people chase him, isn't he?"

I nodded, biting my lip at the truth of it. "Always just out of reach. But I think that's why people love him. He's magnetic."

Steven's gaze softened, his smile tinged with something I couldn't quite decipher. "He is," he said simply. "Always has been."

It struck me then—how much Steven understood about Heck, even from a distance. Their lives were intertwined despite the gaps and silences that had divided them for years.

"You're not so far off, though," I said softly. "From Heck, I mean. I think you're... familiar, in a way."

He tilted his head slightly, his curls shifting as his expression grew thoughtful. "Familiar how?"

I hesitated. "It's hard to explain. But being around you feels like..." I trailed off, trying to find the words. "Like learning the things about him he doesn't say out loud."

Steven's gaze lingered on me, his expression unreadable for a long moment. Then he nodded, almost as if he understood.

"You're good for him, Sara," he said quietly.

The words landed somewhere deep in my chest, and I looked away, caught off guard by the unexpected weight of them. "I hope so," I murmured. "I want to be."

The silence that followed wasn't heavy—it was laced with something unspoken but understood. Talking to Steven in his quiet, steady way, I felt like I'd stepped just a little closer to a part of Heck I hadn't known existed. Somehow, Steven made me feel like I was treading closer to understanding Heck—like he was a bridge to parts of Heck I couldn't always reach. Of course, they were different in more ways than they were alike. Heck had a sharpness to him, all quick wit and charm, while Steven carried a quiet stillness that spoke volumes without saying anything at all.

"Your life seems... exciting," I said, choosing my words carefully as I fiddled with the edge of my sleeve. "I mean, playing for all those people, the way they cheer for you. Adoration at that level must feel... surreal."

Steven tilted his head, his lips quirking into a half-smile. "I don't really see it that way," he said after a moment. "Honestly? Most of the time, I'm just trying to keep myself together up there."

I blinked, surprised. "Really? You don't seem like the 'falling apart' type. You look—I don't know—so natural when you're performing." I bit my tongue when Steven raised an eyebrow. "I mean, I Googled you and saw an old video of you on YouTube with your band," I explained.

"Ah, I see." He gave a dry chuckle and leaned forward, resting his elbows on his knees. "That's the trick, isn't it? Make it look natural. Truth is, I'm pretty much a mess before every show." He hesitated, then added, "Sometimes, when there's no audience—just me, the strings, and silence—that's when I play my best stuff. No eyes on me, no pressure. But when the crowd's rowdy, up in your face? It's like..." He paused, looking thoughtful. "It's like, even when the noise is deafening, I find the farthest corner of the room, anchor myself there, and avoid eye contact like my life depends on it."

"You?" I shook my head, incredulous. "You're telling me Mr. Rockstar up here avoids eye contact? That's hard to believe."

He grinned sheepishly. "I'm usually sweating bullets up there, Sara. I promise you."

"Wow," I said, sitting back. "I thought performers were just born fearless. You know, grinning through nerves and glowing charisma and all of that."

Steven's laughter was soft but genuine. "Fearless? Far from it. Every time I think about stepping out into that light, my chest gets tight enough to snap."

"You have no idea how much I get that," I said, shaking my head with a bemused laugh. "You couldn't pay me to stand on a stage. Sing? Dance? Literally anything with an audience? Forget it. I'm so tone-deaf I'd clear the room."

His eyes sparkled as he smirked. "I don't believe that for a second. Bet you've got some hidden talent you're not telling me about."

I waved my hand dramatically, dismissing him. "Trust me. You'd run for the hills."

Steven chuckled, and for a moment, a comfortable silence settled between us. The kind of silence that wasn't demanding or expectant but just... there. I stole a glance at him—his relaxed posture, his gaze focused somewhere far, far away. He struck me as the kind of guy who carried his struggles quietly, locked away where only he could reach them. It tugged at something in me.

"So..." I ventured, breaking the quiet, "groupies. Are they real? Or is that just some overdone Hollywood trope?"

The question caught him off guard, and a crooked smile spread across his face. "Oh, they're real," he admitted. "But not as wild as you'd think. It's not all booze-drenched brawls and orgies in the back of a van, if that's what you're picturing."

"Wait, hold on." I gasped, my mouth falling open in mock horror. "Are you trying to tell me my rock-and-roll fantasy is a lie? No chaos, no scandals? What's next? No wild guitar solos in the rain?"

That did it. He laughed—a big, unfiltered laugh that lit up his face and pulled me in like gravity. "I hate to disappoint you, but most nights, I'm lucky if I get thirty minutes of peace to eat a burger backstage before we pack up."

"Wow," I said dryly. "Living the dream."

"Hey, don't throw shade," he teased, still chuckling. "Some of us just prefer quieter nights, okay?"

"Quieter nights? Don't tell me you're the guy who'd rather curl up with your guitar than, you know…" I wagged my eyebrows teasingly.

His shoulders shook with laughter as he leaned back, running a hand through his hair. "What can I say? Guitars don't talk back."

His witty response sent a laugh spilling out of me before I could stop it. It caught me off guard; I wasn't used to how easy this felt, how humor flowed naturally between us. That was one of the things I loved about being with Steven. No matter how heavy things started, we always found our way to laughter—the kind that left us gasping for air, tears in our eyes, until everything else—the worry, the chaos—faded into the background.

I glanced at him then, this time unguarded. And he caught me. For a split second, our gazes locked, and there was something unspoken there—a thread neither of us was quite ready to pull. But instead of breaking it, we both burst into laughter for no reason at all, the weight of things unsaid melting away for the briefest of moments.

30

In the days that followed, the adjoining hospital rooms no longer felt like hospital rooms. They had transformed into something else entirely —a strange mix of office and holding cell. A sleek, circular table now sat by the window, its metallic legs gleaming against the dull floor tiles. Four black office chairs were clustered around it, looking awkwardly out of place next to the harsh lines of medical equipment and the impersonal warmth of the cream walls. Papers were scattered across the table in organized chaos—contracts, financial reports, investment portfolios—all tiny fragments of normalcy invading this otherwise sterile space.

Helen sat beside me, her head bowed, brow furrowed in concentration as she flipped through another stack of documents. She was always here now, pen in hand, sorting through the endless flood of paperwork while Jeffrey kept us stocked. He had pivoted effortlessly from his usual work at the bank's headquarters to running errands for us inside the hospital. Every morning, a fresh batch of folders and files greeted us, brought in by Jeffrey with that quiet efficiency that never faltered, no matter the weight of the work.

I tried to focus on my share of it—the campaigns my team at Milliford still oversaw, the marketing plans I was supposed to keep tabs on—but the words on the pages blurred together into nothing. Gold Standard Bank's acquisition of Milliford had been so cleanly wrapped and secretive that most people didn't even know it had happened. It should have been easy and straightforward. It wasn't. Not in this room. Not with Heck lying just a few feet away.

My eyes drifted to the bed without meaning to, drawn as if the weight of my heart demanded it. Heck was motionless, too still—a sight that was at once familiar and unbearable. Tubes snaked across his pale skin, disappearing into the machines that kept him breathing, kept his heart beating. The ventilator released its cold, rhythmic hiss, a sound that drilled into me in the quiet moments when I least expected it. Wires trailed from his chest and hands, recording vital signs like some relentless scribe cataloging his fragility. The once-vivid bruises had begun to fade now, leaving behind a patchwork of pale yellow and sickly green marks that told the story of his suffering even when he couldn't.

His face, untouched by the violence that had ravaged his body, was the hardest to look at. There he was—so peaceful, so perfectly undisturbed, like he might open his eyes at any moment and flash me one of those soft, knowing smiles. But when I stared long enough, I could see the truth. I could see the pallor of his cheeks, the way his lips were just a touch too dry, his lashes too still.

The ache in my chest grew sharper, and I folded my arms tightly across myself in a futile attempt to hold it all in. My mind wandered, even as Helen's pen scratched against the paper beside me, her focus unbroken. I thought about everything—Steven's words, the lawyers' updates on the Sullivans, the endless documents that seemed more like a barrier to avoid the reality of this room. I thought about the man I fell in love with, who now lay trapped in a maze of machines, alive but locked away.

"I'll update Raul on this once I finalize the draft," Helen said, her voice practical and measured, cutting through the heavy silence. Her words didn't demand a response, and I gave none, nodding absently as I kept my gaze on Heck. Her efficiency hadn't wavered since this nightmare began. She had seamlessly slipped into her usual role, her ability to compartmentalize an unspoken lifeline for the rest of us.

I, on the other hand, was unraveling—slowly, quietly. The hospital lights above cast a harsh, unforgiving glow over everything, sharpening the edges of my every thought. The air felt dense and stale, despite the hum of the heater cycling through. I leaned back in the chair, my arms instinctively wrapping around the dull ache radiating through my ribs. I was past my due date now. Dr. Michaels had reassured me it was normal for a first pregnancy, but still, we were bracing for it to happen any moment.

For weeks, this room had been a hub of activity—lawyers coming and going, updates about the case tumbling into the fragile silence like breaking glass. Papers and laptops cluttered the newly designated "workspace" by the window, while Heck's bed never moved, never changed. My attention was torn between two worlds—the one where files needed signing and marketing strategies required my approval, and the one where Heck lay silent, where my love for him felt like a tide threatening to drown me.

Focusing was impossible. My gaze returned to him again and again, like the pull of gravity, until everything around me faded into static. There were moments when my hope flickered, fragile and fleeting, like the promise of light through storm clouds. Then, there were moments like this, when the weight of waiting became unbearable, and the quiet hum of machines tethering him to life grew deafening.

I swallowed hard and closed my eyes for a moment, pressing my palms against my forehead. "I'll look over the marketing figures by tonight," I mumbled to Helen, needing to say something to break the spiral in my chest.

When I opened my eyes, they landed on Heck again. I couldn't help it. I walked toward his bed, sat in the chair, and took his hand in mine gently, trying to avoid the tubes and needles that stuck with it. He was my anchor, even now, even like this. My throat tightened as I whispered so low that the words barely escaped. "Come back to me." My voice wavered for no one but him to hear.

Helen didn't acknowledge the crack in my tone. She continued to sort the papers methodically, her focus unshaken—but I knew she heard it. It didn't matter. Nothing mattered except the faint, fragile sound of the ventilator and the tiny hope it carried on its mechanical breath.

I thought of Steven's story. It wasn't just heavy—it was suffocating. His words lingered in the space we'd shared, heavy and unrelenting, like the stale air clinging after a storm. We hadn't spoken since his last visit. Not a word. I was too overwhelmed by his bare wreckage, and I suspected he was too drained to offer more. Each fragment of his past felt like a blunt instrument, bludgeoning its way into my understanding bit by painful bit. For the first time, I understood why Heck had spent his life so guarded, so distant from the glittering Archibald façade that, from a distance, dazzled but beneath the shimmer left jagged, broken edges too raw to touch.

I understood why he ran so hot and cold with Hector. One breath close to reconciliation, the next a burst of fire setting everything between them back to ash. And now this truth—why he'd never once mentioned Steven. A brother.

I looked down at Heck's hand, now warm against my palm. Helen had abandoned her work and sat across from me, her usually perfect posture slackened and weary. We were both waiting, silently willing him to wake up. I had so many questions.

Helen caught my eye and offered a small smile. It was soft and tentative, but underneath it, I could see the fractures. She looked kind, and once, I would've said she was one of the kindest souls I'd met. But now? Now I knew—her words, her anger, her inability to look beyond the infidelity had driven Steven away. My chest tightened despite myself. Maybe she'd been deeply hurt—perhaps the pain had clouded her judgment. I didn't know. I wasn't even sure how I'd feel if I were in her place. But knowing was different from excusing, and the weight of my sympathy for Steven outweighed my desire to justify her failings.

I now saw the void for all the months I'd spent with Heck—building a life, sharing whispered dreams and secrets under moonlit ceilings. A chasm I never knew existed. A brother buried somewhere in his past, left in the shadow of every scar Hector and Helen had quietly etched into him.

My mind refused to settle. Who was Steven to him now? Not a protector, not anymore, but... a ghost? Was this memory too raw and painful to resurrect?

I squeezed Heck's hand, my chest tightening as I exhaled slowly through my nose, trying to calm the storm building inside me. I glanced at Helen again. She shifted slightly in her chair, her shoulders slumped in a way that made her look older, as though decades had pressed down on her all at once. Like Steven, she carried more than she ought to. Her strength was frayed now, barely holding her upright beneath a weight too heavy for anyone to bear alone.

For the first time, the pieces fell into place with an almost painful clarity. Heck's fury at his parents wasn't just about rules or expectations. It was about the twisted world they'd built, the family fracturing beneath its veneer of wealth, and the people they'd warped with their expectations and games.

I thought of Steven walking away years ago—a teenage boy, weathered and unyielding, packing his few belongings and stripping his name from the Archibald legacy like a skin that no longer fit. Abandoning the only family he'd known, leaving Heck behind. Had Heck felt it as a betrayal? Or abandonment? Was there even a difference?

I clasped Heck's hand tighter, leaning forward until my elbows rested on my knees. I pictured him as a boy, young and impossibly alone. The image clutched at my chest with icy fingers. Steven had been his shield once, the place where he could find refuge. Until one day, that protection simply… vanished.

"When you wake up…" My voice cracked the quiet, surprising even myself. Helen turned to me, her eyes questioning. I hadn't meant to say the words aloud, but they were already spilling out. "When you wake up," I repeated firmly, stronger this time, "you and Steven have a lot to make up for."

Helen tilted her head slightly, her lips parting as though to offer some response. But instead, her gaze softened, and she gave a small, nearly imperceptible nod. "I know," she said quietly, her voice barely breaking over the hum of the machines around us.

The quiet that followed wasn't lighter—not by much. But it was… manageable. Like the aftermath of an earthquake—its weight still pressing in from all sides, but at least the tremors had stopped. For now.

I shifted in my chair, glancing at Heck. What would he say when he saw Steven again? Would he even want to see him, unearth those memories he'd buried so deeply? Would he understand why Steven left? Or would the pain of it crash over them all over again?

And Hector. God, Hector. His fingerprints marred every broken piece of this family, didn't they? From Steven on the subway to his years in California's shadows, to the L.A. alleys that swallowed him whole. Hector's leash wrapped tight around Steven's life, yet around Heck, it manifested not in control but in quiet rebellion. There were no chains for Heck, just burning resentment and the slow isolation it brought.

I thought of how Heck's jaw would tighten every time Hector entered a room, the way his words sharpened like weapons forged in silence. Hector had taught him that—the man who constantly watched, controlled, and measured him. The oppressive games Hector played hadn't started or ended with Steven; they had only morphed into something even more destructive.

They'd both been running. Steven with his bruised fists and broken chords, Heck with his guarded heart and a silence heavy enough to drown in. Running blindly toward something new, never looking back.

But now... now they had a chance. If Heck woke up—and I refused even to consider the alternative—they could face it together, the disaster of it all. They needed each other, even if they didn't know it yet, even if they couldn't feel it past years of resentment and loss.

I slipped my hand from Heck's grasp, leaving Helen behind, and drifted to the window, pressing shaky fingertips against the cold glass. The world outside was a blur of motion—skyscrapers stretching endlessly into the sky, honking taxis weaving through restless traffic, and people surging forward as if time couldn't keep up. New York City pulsed with life, unapologetic and unstoppable.

But here, inside these walls, the air was different. The silence pressed down, not peaceful but hollow, weighed by the kind of stillness where dreams seemed to fade unnoticed. My lungs filled with a breath that seemed to go nowhere, heavy and stagnant.

I placed a hand on my swollen stomach, feeling the weight of a life that hadn't yet begun. Turning away from the window, I faced the room's stillness once more—the hospital bed, the steady beeping of machines, and the fragile grasp of hope I wasn't ready to give up.

Heck looked peaceful. Too peaceful. Maybe this was a beginning for him and Steven, for the Archibald sword and shield. Or perhaps it was just the next chapter in an endless book of hurt and healing.

But then, a shift I hadn't expected. A pressure low in my abdomen, faint but undeniable. I froze as warmth trickled down the inside of my thigh, stealing the breath from my lungs. My hand pressed to my belly instinctively as my other reached for Helen.

"Helen," I whispered, panicked, almost trembling.

Her eyes widened as she reached for me, concern spilling from every inch of her face. The room tilted slightly, just faint enough to know that, once again, everything was about to change.

The door creaked open, and Christine appeared, her cheerful demeanor immediately melting into sharp focus as her eyes darted between me and the small puddle forming beneath me. She was calm, her voice measured as she stepped closer. "Sara," she said, her tone gentle but direct. "Your water just broke."

Everything stopped for a heartbeat—the room, the air around me, even my frantic thoughts. I turned to Helen, wide-eyed, and found her face mirroring my emotions. Together, we glanced down, following Christine's gaze to the telltale trail of water trickling down my legs.

"Oh," I breathed, barely above a whisper, my hands instinctively cradling my belly. "Oh no."

"Sara, breathe," Helen said quickly but reassuringly, her hands grasping my shoulders. Her calm was unraveling just slightly at the edges. "We'll handle this."

Christine was already moving, her small frame zipping past me to buzz for immediate assistance. "Sara, we're going to get you into labor and delivery now," she said over her shoulder, summoning reinforcements with calm efficiency. A wheelchair appeared in what felt like seconds, materializing as though the hospital itself were alive and anticipating this moment.

"No—no, Helen, I can't—" My voice cracked, panic swelling inside me. "What about Heck? I can't—"

Tears blurred my vision as Helen cupped my face, her steady, tear-filled eyes locking with mine. "Sara, listen to me," she said firmly. "Heck is in the best hands possible. Right now, that baby needs you. Heck needs you to be strong—for both of them."

I swallowed hard, my chest heaving as I searched her face for reassurance. Her strength and composure willed me to steady my shaking terror, even as the situation began to spin faster than I could control.

Helen didn't pause, helping me into the chair while Christine rattled off instructions to another nurse who had appeared by her side. My fingers tightened around Helen's arm as they moved me toward the door. Every step we took away from Heck's still form felt like another thread unraveling, pulling at the connection I clung to.

But in the pit of my panic, something deeper rose—resolve. For him. For the tiny life squirming restlessly in my womb now, as if urging me forward. I exhaled shakily, forcing myself to hold onto the flicker of hope. Heck had to wake up. He just had to—before our son drew his first breath, before those tiny eyes opened to a world where his father was there, waiting to hold him.

"It's too soon," I whispered softly, the words slipping out as Christine wheeled me into the hall.

Helen crouched slightly, her hand gripping mine tightly as she matched my pace. "It's not too soon," she said, her voice soft but sure. "It's the right time, Sara. Trust it."

I Love You, Sunday Sunset.

31

The blinding light of the hospital room felt harsher now, unrelenting. Each clinical white wall seemed to draw closer, carrying the weight of every fear and fleeting hope crowding my mind. The rhythmic beeping of the monitors wasn't a comfort—it was cruel, merciless, measuring the fragility of my world. For ten brutal hours, I had fought against my body, against time itself, but every contraction seemed to strip me of more than just physical strength. It felt as though the universe was slowly pulling my heart apart.

I was exhausted, drained in ways that went far beyond the labor. My knees had given out long ago, yet I couldn't stay in bed. I knelt against the cold floor, my forehead pressed to the mattress, my fingers gripping its edge desperately. The hardness of the tiles bit into my skin, but that pain was nothing compared to the gaping hollow inside me. My body screamed for relief, but my soul screamed louder. Heck. God, Heck... you were supposed to be here.

He was supposed to stand by my side—my anchor, my light in this storm. Instead, he was trapped just a hallway away, on life support, surrounded by machines that kept him breathing but robbed him of everything else. I could still feel the cold press of his hand in mine, lifeless and unmoving. The memory carved itself into my mind, a cruel, unrelenting weight. I had clung to his hand and begged, sobs tearing through me, my voice cracking under the force of my pleas. *Please hold on. Please wake up. Please come back to me.*

But he hadn't answered. He didn't squeeze my hand. He didn't open his eyes. The machines stayed silent but for the static hum of their indifference. And now, here I was, powerless once more. No amount of pleading could place him here, with me, where he had every reason to be.

Another contraction ripped through me, stealing my breath, and I gasped, gripping the bed harder as if the solidity of it was the only thing keeping me tethered to this moment. My son wasn't ready; I wasn't ready. Nothing about this moment was what it should have been. "God, this isn't fair," I whispered hoarsely, the words scraping and cracking against my dry throat. This wasn't just pain. This was devastation.

The memories blurred and twisted in my mind, spiraling into one another until I couldn't tell where one began and another ended. I remembered yelling for Steven, my voice breaking as I begged him to give everything he had left to save Heck. I remembered the surge of anger, the way I cursed Heck for not waking up, for not being here when I needed him most. My cries turned desperate as I pleaded for my mother, aching for her comfort as my body betrayed me, dragging me into a battle I wasn't ready to fight. I remembered the nurses gathering around me, their hands urgent but steady, pulling me into this sterile battlefield hours ago as nature took control. And I remembered Helen's sharp, commanding voice calling for Hector the second I was wheeled into the delivery room. I knew they were all out there right now—Hector, Steven, even Jeffrey—pacing in the hallway, their anxious energy filling the space where Heck's calm should have been.

They were trying—in their way, they were trying to fill the unbearable void Heck left behind. But it wasn't enough. Hector's sharp commands, Steven's unspoken worry, even their shared presence waiting for my son's arrival—they couldn't be him. None of them could lean in close, whisper soft encouragements in my ear. None of them could take my trembling hand in their steady one as I faced this impossible moment. None of them was Heck.

My chest tightened again, this time not from pain but from the clawing desperation that had wrapped itself around my heart. I wanted to trade everything—every ounce of my strength, every sharp pang my body endured—for just a moment with him here. Just one second where he could sweep his hand over my damp hair and tell me we'd get through this—together, as we always had.

Instead, my words fell to the quiet, unheard and unanswered. "Heck," I whispered, my voice fractured and raw. The tears came next, slipping silently down my face, and I didn't have the strength to wipe them away. "I need you." The plea hung in the air, fragile and breaking like glass.

The weight of the moment consumed me, every sound in the room drowned by the rhythmic cries of my soul. My boy was coming into the world, a piece of us brought to life, and yet the only thing I could feel was the emptiness left behind by the one person I needed most.

"Another deep breath, sweetheart," Helen coaxed gently, her voice trembling despite her calm tone. She hadn't left my side since my water broke. She held my hand in both of hers, her fingers digging into my skin with a quiet desperation she didn't voice. I clung to her like she was all I had left. And maybe she was. My mother couldn't be here, but Helen was. It felt right, in a way—like having a piece of Heck in the room with me.

"You're doing so good," she said quietly, her tears visibly brimming. I leaned heavily against her, my back pressing into her small frame as a guttural cry escaped my lips. Her arms wrapped firmly around mine, anchoring me as wave after wave of pain tore through me. Her breath was steady, brushing against my ear as she whispered soft words of encouragement, her grip unwavering. At that moment, she was my anchor, holding me together as my body worked to bring new life into the world.

"I know it hurts. I know it's terrifying. But you're strong, Sara. You're going to bring him into this world, and he's going to be... perfect." She tried to smile with those soothing words. I knew it wasn't easy for her, not with her son in another room, surrounded by tubes and life-saving devices.

I shook my head, biting back the scream building in my chest. My breaths came out ragged, words barely audible between the pain. "I c-can't, Helen. Not without him. He promised. He... he promised he'd be here. He'd cut the cord, he—oh God, I can't..."

Her face crumpled for a brief, unguarded moment. But instead of breaking, she leaned into me, pressing her forehead to mine. Her voice wavered, heavy with emotion, but her hands stayed steady. "You can do this," she said, fierce and unyielding. Her tears mixed with mine as she whispered, "I know it's unfair, I know it hurts, but we will get through this. Together. You're not alone." She glanced toward the door, her eyes filled with quiet determination. "Hector and Steven are just outside, waiting for you to fight through this."

And somehow, that was enough to hold me together—for now.

The room buzzed with chaos around me. Dr. Michaels stood at the center, guiding the nurses with a calm, measured voice that felt so distant from the storm raging inside me. They laid me back on the bed and strapped my legs open. The fluorescent lights above drained all color from the room, leaving everything washed out and stark. The antiseptic smell clung to the air, sharp and stifling. Nearby, a young pediatrician in pastel pink scrubs stood ready, her face calm but watchful.

I barely noticed the nurse's cool hand wiping my forehead until Dr. Michaels bent over me, his voice cutting through the noise like a lifeline. "Sara, you're doing great," he said, as steady as the ground beneath my feet. "He's crowning. I need you to focus now. It's time to push."

His words entered my ears like an eerie echo through water. I wanted to push. God, I did. But the fear paralyzed me. What if something went wrong? What if I failed him before he even got a chance to live? Tears stung my eyes as I shut them tight. And then, in an explosion of memory, I saw Heck. His crooked grin that first day at Shakespeare & Co. in Paris. That perfect afternoon when he showed up. The way his gaze locked on me was like I was the only thing that mattered.

Another contraction ripped through my body like fire. There was no escaping it now. "Heck!" I screamed, my voice cracking under the weight of the pain.

Time stilled as a whimper trapped itself in my throat. The pain was excruciating, but the fear was worse. What if something happened? What if I couldn't do it? What if the world was about to take him away from me, too? My cries filled the air as I fought against the terror clawing at my chest... and then I bore down with everything I had left.

"You've got this," Helen murmured, kissing my clammy forehead between sobs. "He's waiting, Sara. That beautiful boy is waiting to meet his Mama."

Her words spun something loose in my chest. With one final push—one final act of defiance, of love—I bore down with all I had.

The world seemed to shatter for a split second—into pain, release, and emptiness. A silence hung too long, a vacuum that drained every ounce of life from my body. I couldn't breathe; even the frantic pace of the doctors blurred into nothingness.

And then, suddenly, it came. That sound. A shrill, piercing cry that yanked me back to life.

"Oh my God," Helen whispered, a hand flying to her mouth. Tears spilled freely down her face as laughter broke through her sobs. "You did it. You did it, Sara! He's here!"

Dr. Michaels leaned down, a gentle smile on his face as he held up my son. His fragile cries tore through the chaos. "Meet your boy, Sara."

A nurse handed me his tiny, wriggling frame, warm and impossibly small in my trembling hands. My breath caught as I cradled him against my chest. Helen hovered next to me, her hands shaking as Dr. Michaels held out the scissors. I met Helen's gaze and nodded. If Heck couldn't do this, she was the only person I'd trust.

"I've got him," Helen whispered tightly, her voice cracking as she cut the cord. Tears blurred her sharp, elegant features into something deeply human.

The pediatrician took him for the briefest of exams, her gentle voice cooing as she assured me, "He's perfect, Mama. We'll bring him back in just a moment."

The moments stretched like lifetimes until the nurse returned, placing him in my arms again. "Okay, young man," she said softly. "Back to Mama, you go."

Wrapped in a pale blue blanket, his cries softened into gentle hiccups. And then—like the world paused just for him—his eyes flickered open, blinking against the light. Cerulean. Heck's eyes.

"Oh," I gasped, the tears streaming down my face before I could stop them. "He looks like..." My throat closed, but Helen finished for me, her hand brushing over his inky curls.

"Like Heck," she said, choking back her own tears.

I met her gaze, my voice brittle and shaking. "He's not here to see him, Helen. How can he not be here for this—or for him?" I sobbed harder, clutching the tiny miracle against me.

Helen's face crumbled, pure anguish filling her. "I know. God, I know," she said, her voice breaking. She sank into the chair beside me, holding my free hand. "He would've given anything to be here. He never wanted to miss this."

My cries deepened, the ferocity of love and loss colliding in a way that threatened to unmake me. Helen moved close, folding her arms around us both, murmuring quiet reassurances, even as her tears drenched my hair. For that brief window, the pain and the joy mingled in the most devastatingly beautiful contradiction. We stayed like that for what felt like hours, crying over the little boy who had his father's eyes, his father's hair, and—just maybe—his father's stubbornness.

The sheer contradiction of life itself was devastating and joyous all at once.

We were grieving one life while celebrating another. And the world felt impossibly heavy and achingly beautiful all at the same time.

32

When I woke up, the soft warmth of sunlight bathed the room in hues of gold and amber. My eyes blinked against the brightness, adjusting slowly as the light filtered through sheer curtains drawn back from the expansive windows. Outside, I could hear the faint hum of life—distant chatter, the steady rhythm of footsteps in the hallway. The sterile walls of the hospital room didn't seem so lifeless anymore; the light had softened them, warmed them.

Ah, because of the flowers—vases of them—roses, lilies, and daisies bursting with vibrant colors. They stood proudly on the windowsill and tables, transforming the room into something that resembled a floral shop. The petals seemed to stretch toward the sun, as if they, too, were waking up to a new day. Another bouquet had found its place on the small table near my bed, a mix of sunflowers and carnations that made everything feel a little less cold, less clinical. They had brought life into this room, and for the first time in what felt like forever, I felt a fleeting sense of peace as I took it all in.

"Good morning," came Steven's voice, breaking through my half-asleep haze. I turned my head slowly to find him sprawled on the couch across the room, one leg crossed over the other, a faint grin playing on his lips. "Finally, Sleeping Beauty awakens. I was about to call in reinforcements."

I smiled weakly, still heavy with exhaustion but oddly comforted by the familiarity of his teasing tone. "Good morning... I feel like I was run over by a train. Twice." My voice was scratchy, but the humor in his eyes helped ease the grogginess.

Steven chuckled, standing and stretching with an exaggerated yawn. "Well, considering what you've been through, I'd say you earned the extra shut-eye." Today, he wasn't clad in his usual black tee. Instead, he wore a green, blue, and gray plaid button-up over a dark gray shirt and well-worn jeans. Something about him looked almost... relaxed.

Looking around the room, my heart raced for a second. "Where's my baby?" I asked, sitting up a little too quickly before my body protested the movement.

Steven's hands shot up in a calming gesture as he stepped toward me. "Easy there, Mama. He's fine. They wheeled him off to the nursery a little while ago for his check-up... or whatever they call it." His voice was warm, reassuring. "Don't worry. He hasn't been alone. Helen's keeping a hawk-eye on him, and when she needs a break, I'm on baby duty."

"Oh no," I groaned in mock despair. "He's a day old and already becoming the most spoiled baby alive."

Steven laughed, the sound soft but genuine, as if it had been far too long since he'd found something to really laugh about. "You might as well get used to it. That kid's entire existence is going to be full of adoration, and you know it."

I smiled, shaking my head at his words as warmth settled in my chest. Then, a thought struck me, and I frowned. "What are you doing here, though? I thought you'd be back at home by now." My voice wavered at the end as another question surfaced. "How's Heck?"

Steven hesitated, but only for a beat before his features softened further. "His vitals are improving. Slowly, but they're trending upward. You just have to be patient, Sara. He's strong. He's going to wake up." He moved closer and perched at the foot of the bed, his voice steady but kind. "Right now, you've got someone else who needs you just as much. Take care of yourself and your little man first."

I nodded, the lump in my throat easing slightly. "Thanks for sticking around. I mean it. It's meant everything."

Steven tilted his head, his lips curling into an almost boyish grin. "Wouldn't have missed it. The second Helen called, Dad and I broke records getting here. We were pacing outside the delivery room, trading bets on when the little guy would make his entry." He leaned back with a laugh, spreading his hands in mock surrender. "I lost, by the way. My timing was way off."

I couldn't help but laugh softly, catching the mischievous glint in his eyes. Steven had casually called Hector 'Dad' today, like it wasn't a big deal. And the idea of him bantering with his father? That was newsworthy. "Yeah? What were the stakes?" I asked, raising a curious brow.

"Bragging rights," he said with exaggerated seriousness, leaning forward just enough to punctuate the words. "Still stings to lose, though." His grin widened as he settled his elbows on his knees, tilting his head slightly. "Speaking of big decisions, have you picked a name yet? Or are you sticking with Hector Junior Jr.?" His brow lifted, and that familiar mischievous grin lit up his face.

"Oh, Heck would have loved that," I said, my lips twitching into a brief smile before softening into something more wistful. "But no. To me, he'll always be my Little Hemingway."

Steven leaned back, nodding in approval. "Good choice. A literary name for a kid who's bound to be extraordinary. I like it. Just... don't make him use it in school or when he starts dating."

I shifted carefully, trying to sit up, but my body resisted, the dull ache a sharp reminder of the twelve hours of labor I had just battled through. Steven noticed and immediately moved to help, adjusting the bed's controls until I was sitting upright.

"Better?" he asked, stepping back once I was settled.

"A little," I replied softly. "Thank you."

"Good, because you've got to eat something. After what you've been through, you've earned a feast." He moved toward the intercom by the door. "What'll it be? Pancakes? Syrup? Bacon?"

I smiled at the familiarity of it all. "Pancakes with strawberry syrup and bacon," I said, feeling a soft pang in my chest. It wasn't just my favorite—it was mine and Heck's. "But... I want to visit Heck first."

Steven turned back to me, his expression gentle but firm. "Sara, you've got to take care of yourself first. Eat, get your strength up. Heck isn't going anywhere. I promise I'll take you to him as soon as you're done."

I hesitated, but the determination in his eyes had me nodding. "Okay. You win," I said softly. "Thank you... for everything. For being here. It makes all of this a little easier."

Steven's grin softened as he gave my hand a gentle pat before turning to the intercom to page the nurse. The room settled into a hush, the kind that carries a quiet reassurance, a fragile peace. No, things weren't perfect. Heck wasn't by my side when our son came into the world, and that ache was still there, heavy and constant. But for the first time, I could see past it, even if just a little. I was surrounded by love—solid, unwavering, like the sunlight now filling the room. It wasn't the way I'd imagined it, but it was enough to remind me that I wasn't alone, that I was still moving forward, step by step, toward a world where Heck would wake up and join us again.

33

Two weeks had passed, and the days had dissolved into one endless, surreal haze. I sat beside Heck's hospital bed, clutching his hand as though sheer stubbornness alone could tether him to this world. His chest rose and fell in delicate, uneven motions, the machines beside him doing most of the work, prolonging the little time we had left.

I had been there every day, whispering to him about our son—about Fifth. Helen had insisted that "Hector Archibald V" was his birthright, but to me, he would always be Fifth. Something simple. Something ours. Heck's and mine.

The room was quiet except for the soft beeping of the monitors and the muffled rumbles of hospital activity beyond the door. Thanks to the influence of the Archibald name, the adjoining suite had remained available even after I gave birth and was more than ready to go home. I stayed close, unwilling to leave his side. Besides, I was too scared to bathe Fifth, and it was a relief to have nurses on rotation to help me care for him. Fifth napped peacefully in the other room, his tiny chest rising and falling as he slept, blissfully unaware of the storm unfolding around him. I had panicked countless times over every hiccup or cry he made, and the nurses' reassurances were the only thing keeping me somewhat grounded.

Setting Ernest Hemingway's *The Sun Also Rises* on my lap, I studied the man I loved—my Heck. His face had grown more frail, yet he still looked like himself somehow. He was still my Heck. I leaned forward, brushing my lips against his temple.

"It's almost sunset," I whispered softly into the silence. "Your favorite time." My voice cracked, and I swallowed hard. "Hey, do you remember? We argued about Gertrude Stein once. You said she was just name-dropping when she called Hemingway's friends a lost generation." I gave a soft, strained laugh, forcing myself to hold onto something trivial, something simple. "She really said, *'You are all a lost generation.'* Isn't that one of her lines in *Midnight in Paris?*" This was our dance, our usual spot in the café. We talked about our favorite songs and movies. *Midnight in Paris* was our thing.

I opened the book where I'd left off, clutching it tightly in trembling hands. "When you wake up, and when you're well enough, I'll take you to Tribeca Trickle, and Lily will have brinner waiting for us. Like always."

My voice broke entirely on the last word. But then, miraculously, his lashes fluttered.

I froze. My heart clenched tight in my chest. "Heck," I whispered, leaning closer, searching his face. "Heck, it's me. It's Sara. Open your eyes for me."

And then he did. His cerulean eyes—fainter, weaker, but unmistakable —met mine, filled with a quiet resolution that nearly shattered me.

"Oh my God," I choked, tears spilling down my cheeks. I pressed the buzzer with frantic movements, signaling the nurses. "You're awake, Heck. Stay with me, please—please stay with me..."

He tried to say something, but his voice was blocked by the tube in his mouth—only a faint, raspy breath escaped before the nurses swarmed into the room. They urged me to step aside as they surrounded his bedside, checking his vitals. A deep stab of panic threatened to consume me, but I couldn't tear my gaze away from him.

"Don't leave," I whispered, covering my mouth with trembling fingers as sobs threatened to take over. And for a horrifying second, his eyes closed again. "No! Heck, please," I begged, my knees giving out beneath me.

"Sara," Dr. Arnold said gently, steadying me with a firm hand. His face was solemn, lined with quiet grief. "We need just a moment."

I nodded, numb, letting them work as the room blurred around me. My gaze stayed fixed on Heck's bed. His eyes had closed again. Desperation clawed at me as I fumbled for my phone and speed-dialed Helen. She answered on the second ring.

"Sara—what's happened? Is everything okay?"

I barely got the words out. "Helen, he's awake—he woke up."

Her gasp was audible. "Thank God. Oh, thank God. I'm coming now." The line went dead.

I turned my attention back to Heck as soon as I put my phone down. He drifted in and out of consciousness, his moments of lucidity fleeting and fragile. The adjacent hospital suites had been converted into a critical care unit for weeks, but now, the quiet intensity of the room was disrupted. Doctors stepped in with brisk, purposeful movements. I was asked to leave the room momentarily. Their faces wore unreadable expressions, but I knew from their urgency that he was not out of the woods yet.

———

When I stepped back into the room, after the swirl of doctors and nurses checking on him, Heck was fully awake. The sight stopped me in my tracks, my breath catching in my chest. He was still tethered to the ventilator, the steady hiss and hum of the machine filling the otherwise quiet space. His chest rose and fell in time with the pulse of the machine, but his eyes—those impossibly blue eyes—were on me. They were brighter, clearer than I remembered, and full of an emotion I couldn't quite name. Relief, maybe. Love.

Or something even deeper, something no words could encapsulate.

When his fingers twitched, I moved closer, sitting beside him. His hand lifted just enough to brush against mine, and I quickly took it, entwining our fingers. He squeezed gently, his touch weak but deliberate.

"Heck," I whispered, my voice breaking. "Oh, God, Heck." I kissed the back of his hand before resting it against my cheek, closing my eyes for a moment to soak in the reality that he was here. Awake. Alive.

He tried to speak, but the ventilator forced him into silence. His mouth moved, forming shapes I couldn't quite catch, but I pressed my other hand over his, shaking my head. "Hey, take it easy," I said softly, my voice trembling but steady. "We've got forever to talk. Just get better, okay? Build your strength." I kissed our joined hands, the tears I'd been holding back spilling over.

He smiled then, a fleeting curve of his lips, but it was enough. His eyes, deeper and more vibrant than the sky, said everything he couldn't. I saw the apology in them, the sadness, but mostly, I saw love. A love so powerful it filled the room, pushing out all the fear and uncertainty that had weighed me down for weeks.

The door opened, and Hector and Helen entered quietly. Their expressions softened when they saw Heck awake, but a nurse followed behind them before they could say much. "The doctors need to see you both for a moment," the nurse said to Hector and Helen. They hesitated, but I nodded, giving them permission with my eyes. They shared a brief moment with Heck before stepping away, leaving us alone again.

It killed me that I couldn't bring Fifth to him—not yet. His pediatrician and Heck's doctors had to approve first; until then, I had to wait. "Soon," I promised myself. "Soon." For now, it was just him and me, together again.

While I spoke softly about everything and nothing, Heck listened, his eyes never leaving mine. He smiled at the right moment, his hand still holding mine. Seeing him like this—not just alive, but here—gave me a hope I hadn't dared to feel in weeks. "You scared the hell out of me," I said after a long pause, my voice trembling as tears welled up again. "I thought I was going to lose you. Again. And Heck, I can't—I can't take it a third time." The sob broke free this time, its weight too heavy to contain.

His hand moved slowly to my face, brushing away the tears rolling down my cheeks. That simple touch unraveled me, his love solid and steady despite his weakness. His eyes drifted to my stomach, and I saw the question there.

I chuckled, wiping my eyes with my free hand. "You'll meet him soon," I said, my smile softening. "Oh, he looks just like you." Gently, I touched his face, tracing the lines I'd committed to memory but feared I might never see again. "I know you have so much to say," I whispered, leaning closer, "but patience, my love. We'll have all the time in the world." I kissed his forehead, closing my eyes, savoring the moment. I couldn't wait to feel his lips on mine again, to hear him say my name.

A soft knock at the door broke the spell. I turned to see Steven poking his head inside, his eyes searching the room quickly before landing on Heck. "Hey," I whispered, smiling through the tears. "Come in."

Steven entered cautiously, his usual confidence tempered by something raw and unguarded. His eyes glistened as he approached the bed, a small, unsure smile tugging at his lips. Heck's gaze shifted to Steven, and I saw the flicker of recognition, the softer lines of his expression as his brother stepped closer.

I stood, giving Steven the space he needed, and Heck turned his eyes to me briefly, as if asking what was happening. "It's okay," I murmured. "It's Steven."

Heck's eyebrows lifted, almost imperceptibly, and Steven stopped at the edge of the bed, his hands shoved into his pockets. "Hey, little bro," Steven said, his voice thicker than usual. "You gave us all a scare, you know that?"

Heck's fingers twitched, motioning toward the ventilator tube, but Steven leaned forward, shaking his head. "Don't. Not yet." His tone was gentle but firm, the kind of authority only older siblings could pull off without effort.

I hesitated. "I'll leave you two," I said, stepping back toward the door. "I need to check with Fifth's doctor anyway—that way, I can bring him here soon."

Steven turned his head, protesting softly, "You don't have to go—"

"It's fine," I said, brushing past him gently as I leaned down to kiss Heck's forehead again. "I'll be back soon, Pender." For the first time in forever, I saw some light return to Heck's eyes.

Before leaving, I glanced back. Steven had sat on the bed now, his forehead resting lightly against Heck's. Heck's hands trembled as they found their way to the sides of Steven's face, holding him there in an unspoken bond. My heart clenched at the sight, tears stinging my eyes once more.

I closed the door quietly behind me, leaving them to repair the years they'd lost, alone in a room where love could finally breathe again.

34

The room felt smaller than it was, the weight of the conversation bearing down on us like a storm cloud. We were all crowded around a conference table that didn't seem built for this kind of devastation. The medical director's office, clinical and detached, was an unfit stage for what felt like the unraveling of hope. My hands trembled as I clutched the edge of the table, my palms clammy against the smooth wood. The air felt too thin to breathe, as though the room had been drained of oxygen the moment I realized what they were truly saying.

"I... I don't understand," I stammered, my voice barely above a whisper. My hands wouldn't stop shaking, and I gripped them together as though they could steady me. "He woke up. He's weak, I know, but he'll recover. He got his new kidney and liver. I thought everything was going to be okay."

All eyes turned toward me—Dr. Kevin, Dr. Arnolds, and two others from the medical team stood silently in the background. Hector, Steven, and Helen were also there. But no one spoke to confirm or deny my desperate hope. Instead, there was silence, heavy and suffocating. The kind of silence that follows a declaration no one knows how to address. Moments ago, I'd stayed quiet while Hector and Helen argued and Steven demanded answers, but now that I'd spoken, their faces betrayed everything I didn't want to know.

Dr. Kevin shifted in his chair, clearing his throat as he adjusted the papers before him. "Sometimes a patient wakes up from a coma briefly... but it isn't always a sign of recovery." His voice was low and measured, as though he were trying to soften words that were inherently cruel. "There's a phenomenon we call a 'last rally.' It's not uncommon before death. The body rallies, briefly restoring brain function, but it's—" He hesitated, searching for a less brutal way to say it. Finally, he simply said it. "It's temporary."

Death. He said it like it was inevitable, like we all just had to sit back and accept it as fact. For a moment, I could only stare at him, trying to process the incongruity of the word in the context of Heck waking just hours ago. Alive, smiling, squeezing my hand. The image clashed violently with the cold, clinical explanation Dr. Kevin offered, making my head spin.

"He's awake now," I countered, my voice trembling as the tears I'd tried to hold back flooded my eyes. "He's fighting! He's always been a fighter."

Helen's chair scraped against the floor as she leaned forward, her chin trembling but her voice firm. "Is there really nothing else?" she asked, her gaze darting between the doctors. "He's a young man. He's healthy, apart from… apart from this. Surely there's something—some treatment, a surgery, anything." Her voice cracked slightly, but she powered through, her hands trembling as badly as mine.

Dr. Arnolds studied the table momentarily, gathering his thoughts before speaking. "The damage to Heck's heart is extensive. The blunt force trauma caused myocardial contusion—essentially, bruising of the heart muscle—and over time, that damage has impaired the heart's ability to pump blood effectively." He paused, his tone becoming even graver. "We've been monitoring for heart failure, and unfortunately, it's progressing. At this stage, the damage is irreparable." He hesitated, his voice heavy. "They… whoever did this to him… worked him over pretty badly."

Steven, who'd been sitting silently, his head bowed like a storm on the verge of breaking, suddenly shoved his chair back with a harsh scrape. "Those fucking bastards!" he exploded, his voice a low, dangerous growl barely masking the raw fury beneath. His fists clenched, knuckles white, trembling as he struggled to harness the volcanic anger threatening to spill over.

Chaos erupted in the room. Hector slammed his fist on the table with a force that made the water glasses jump, his booming voice clashing against Steven's heated tirade. Steven began pacing, his movements sharp, muttering curses under his breath as if the anger had nowhere else to go. I sat frozen, detached, unable to follow the torrent of words flying between them. My thoughts fractured. Were they arguing? Or agreeing? My head pulsed with the effort of trying to process it all, but the din of rising voices only pushed me further under the suffocating weight of it all. I took a deep breath and spoke the words we all failed to ask.

"Irreparable? He's been through hell, and you're telling me there's no way to fix this?" Hector's voice cut through the noise, sharp and commanding.

"To be blunt," Dr. Arnolds said, as calm as before, "we'd need a heart transplant to save him. But even then, his condition makes him a poor candidate. And to be clear, he's not at the top of the donor list. Time... isn't on our side." He looked at Hector now. "I'm sorry."

Helen sobbed quietly into her hands, her shoulders shaking. But I couldn't move, couldn't speak, couldn't even cry. I was frozen, paralyzed by the reality crashing down around me. The words "time isn't on our side" echoed in my mind like a broken refrain.

"I can pay whatever it takes to move him up that list," Hector finally said, his voice steely and commanding. "Use my connections, anything. My son needs to survive."

"That's not how it works," Dr. Arnolds replied evenly. "Organ allocation is based on medical urgency, compatibility, and other criteria. Even if money weren't an ethical issue, there's no guarantee we'd find a donor in time."

Steven stopped pacing, his back to us as he stared out the window. The rising sun cast long shadows across the room, cutting sharply against his tense frame. His voice was low when he spoke, calm, almost eerily so. "Then take mine."

The words shattered the air, drawing every pair of eyes to him. "No," Hector snapped immediately, the authority in his tone leaving no room for discussion. "That is not happening."

Steven turned slowly, his expression unreadable except for the spark of determination blazing in his eyes. "I don't care what you say. He's my brother—I'd give anything for him."

"You've already given enough, Steven," I said through my tears. My voice cracked as the weight of those words hit me. "You've sacrificed so much for everyone. Don't do this."

Steven's gaze softened when it landed on me, but his resolve didn't waver. "Fifth needs his father. I know what it feels like not to have a father on your side," he said quietly, looking now at Hector. "Heck is the future. He's your legacy, the next Archibald who will carry the family name and the business. Don't tell me you'd sit back and do nothing."

"I won't lose another son!" Hector barked, his voice booming, and at that moment, his mask fell away. He was no longer the stoic patriarch but a father clinging desperately to his family. "I won't allow it."

Silence fell again, thick and unbearable, until Helen broke it with a wavering question. "How much time?" Her face was pale, her eyes red-rimmed, but her voice had a surprising steadiness.

"Three days," Dr. Arnolds replied. The words hit like a knife to the chest, final and unforgiving.

Helen nodded, standing as she wiped her tears and squared her shoulders. "Then we make the most of it," she said quietly. "Every minute, every second."

Her strength in that moment broke me. She tried to smile through the pain, but it was the smile of someone barely holding on. I watched her gather her bag and leave, my tears finally spilling over as the realization settled in. Three days. That was all we had left. That was all he had left.

I Love You, Sunday Sunset.

35

Three days. Seventy-two hours. Four thousand three hundred twenty minutes. Two hundred fifty-nine thousand two hundred seconds.

When you're handed a clock with someone's life ticking against it, every second matters. Each breath, each moment—they cling to you, burn into you—like they're the last you'll ever get.

I couldn't leave him—not for water, not for food, not even for air. Anything beyond love, beyond laughter or simply being there, no longer mattered. After meeting with the doctors, we rushed back to Heck's room. His face lit up when he saw us walk in. Despite everything, he seemed... alive in a way I hadn't seen in so long. The ventilator was gone, and he was breathing on his own again. His impossibly blue eyes scanned us before stopping on the crib beside him, where Fifth stirred quietly in his sleep.

"Shhh," Heck whispered, holding a trembling finger to his lips, his voice a raspy hush.

I couldn't stop the tears. They blurred my vision as I hurried across the room and leaned over him. Pressing my lips to his, I poured every ounce of love and longing into that kiss. His attempt to kiss me back was slow and fragile, but I could feel it—that pull, that quiet passion that didn't need words. It was there, radiating from him.

"You really missed me," he teased, his voice weak but warm, a faint smile touching his lips. His unsteady hand brushed a strand of hair from my face.

"And you missed me," I whispered back, squeezing his hand gently.

His eyes moved to the crib, softening. "He's beautiful, Sara. The instant he came here, he just... took my breath away."

"He looks like you, Heck. He's all you," I said, my voice breaking as tears slipped down my cheeks despite my effort to hold them back.

"I asked them to keep him here a little longer so he could meet me." His voice lowered, apologetic. "I couldn't wait for you to introduce us."

"It's okay," I murmured, shaking my head. "I'm glad you had this time together... just you and Fifth."

His faint smile returned. "Another Hector in the family," he said with a flicker of pride as he looked at his father.

Helen and Hector stepped closer to the bed. "The long line of Hector Archibalds," Hector said, his voice steady and full of warmth. "I'm sure your great-grandfather is smiling down on you right now. How are you holding up, kid?"

Heck chuckled softly, a spark of his old self lighting up his pale features. "It's good to be back."

Then, his eyes shifted to the woman standing beside his father. His voice softened. "Mom..."

"I've waited for this moment, my darling," Sylvia said, her voice trembling as she reached for his other hand. She leaned down, kissing his forehead with gentle care. Heck closed his eyes, his face softening as though soaking in the love she poured into that quiet gesture.

It was a moment I wanted to last forever, to stretch beyond the boundaries of time. But time is so fragile, a fleeting thread that always pulls you forward.

He leaned his head back onto the pillow, his weakening body betrayed only by the brightness in his gaze. But his warm expression faltered as he glanced at the others standing behind me—the tension in their faces still fresh from moments ago. "What's with the long faces?" he asked, chuckling feebly. "Who died?"

As composed as the storm spinning inside her would allow, Helen kissed his forehead again, lingering a little longer than needed. "I've been knocking down walls for hours," she said, her voice light but firm. She turned to face me, then looked lovingly back at her son. "Darling, would you like to get married today?"

All I could do was gape at her. Heck tilted his head, staring at her in bewilderment before turning to me, his lips curling into a small smile that reached his eyes.

Before either of us could respond, Fifth's loud, protesting wail shattered the moment. Helen opened her mouth to move, but Steven was already there, scooping my son out of the crib with surprising ease.

"Now, now, I've got it." Steven cradled Fifth carefully, bouncing him softly in his arms. And just like that, Fifth's cries quieted, his teary face nuzzling into Steven's chest.

"My nephew wants to be part of this," Steven said dramatically, grinning as he glanced at Heck. Then, with mock seriousness, he bent his ear toward Fifth. "Ahhh... I see. He said he wants to be the ring bearer."

The room filled with laughter, soft but genuine, even as tears glimmered in Helen's eyes. For a brief second, it felt normal—timeless even.

Heck chuckled. His laugh was a little strained but full of love. His gaze settled back on me. "Sara," he started, his voice tender, more serious now. "Do you want to marry me?"

I blinked at him, unsure if the tears were happiness, heartbreak, or something tangled between the two. A smile broke through, trembling but resolute. "I didn't say yes before, not because I didn't want to, but because I was waiting for the perfect time. But you know it's always a yes, and I will say yes. Anytime. Anywhere." I kissed his fingertips gently, one by one, letting my tears fall against his skin.

"That settles it," Helen declared, jumping back into the conversation with purpose. "We've already set the wheels in motion. Sara, I took the liberty of picking out a white dress for you—and, of course, a tuxedo for Heck. The jewelry store will deliver the rings within an hour. Jeffrey spoke to the hospital chaplain earlier. Everything else we need will be in place." Her voice brimmed with determination, her energy unstoppable. She glanced over at Hector and Steven next, wagging her finger at them like a teacher scolding rowdy students. "And you two—your tuxedos are clean and waiting. Don't embarrass me."

Steven mock-saluted her, earning a laugh, and Hector raised his hands in faux surrender as Helen turned back to her son, her expression softening again.

Heck reached out weakly toward her, and Helen stepped closer, leaning over the bed so that he could cup her face in his hands. His fingers trembled, but his voice was steady as he spoke.

"If there's one thing I'm grateful for in this lifetime," he whispered, "it's you, Mom. You take everything ugly and make it beautiful. You find the good when there's none left to see. Thank you. For all of it. I'm so grateful."

Helen smiled through wet eyes but didn't shed a tear in front of him, her strength unyielding. "No, my darling," she whispered in return, her fingers brushing his stubbled cheek. "You're the best thing that's ever happened to me."

And in that moment, I marveled at them both—the fragility of his body matched only by the unyielding strength of his love and the resilience in her that no circumstance could overcome.

Heck knew. We all did. His time was slipping through our fingers like grains of sand we couldn't catch or hold. But he didn't complain. He didn't cry. He simply accepted it, welcoming each moment with the people he loved most.

Somehow, against all odds, we had something to hold onto—
something fleeting but pure. Love. Family. And now, the promise of a
wedding. Something beautiful amid the chaos. Something to remind
us that life still shines under the shadow of the clock.

36

The hospital room had transformed completely. What was once a stark space of white walls and humming machines now felt alive, a vibrant garden bursting with color. Every surface overflowed with flowers— roses, lilies, daisies, even wildflowers—spilling from glass vases and woven baskets. Their sweet, delicate scents dulled the harsh antiseptic smell, pushing back against the quiet, looming shadow of time. These blooms weren't just decorations; they were symbols of love, vivid bursts of life in a place so often defined by loss.

I stood at the door, unable to step inside just yet. My Vivienne Westwood wedding gown was beautiful, crafted from ivory silk satin that clung to me with the lightness of a whisper. Its draped neckline skimmed just below my collarbones, the folds of fabric hugging my frame in soft, sculpted elegance. Refined yet understated, it didn't need to scream for attention. At the back, a single pearl button fastened the asymmetrical bodice, and from there, the train spilled down like a quiet stream, pooling at my feet in delicate ripples.

"Thank you for this dress, Helen. It's… it's so beautiful," I murmured, my voice fragile, trembling with the weight of everything I wasn't saying. I looked at her, standing there with her quiet grace, and the words pressed against my chest, desperate to break free.

There was so much I needed to tell her. How deeply thankful I was— not just for the dress, but for the way she had shared Heck with me. For giving me a part of him, no matter how brief our time together had been. For letting me love him without reservation, for trusting me with the piece of him that was hers first.

I swallowed hard, my throat tightening. "I don't think I've told you this enough, Helen, but... thank you. For letting me have him. For trusting me to love him."

Helen's eyes softened, her expression holding both grief and love as she stepped closer. "It suits you perfectly," she said, her hands gentle as they brushed my arms. She leaned in and kissed both my cheeks, the warmth of her lips grounding me. "You'll take Heck's breath away." She closed her eyes briefly, as if gathering her thoughts. "I should be the one to thank you for loving my son the way he deserved to be loved. For showing him what love is and letting him feel that."

Her words lingered, fragile yet unshakable, as I looked down at the gown, my fingers brushing the silk at my sides. Its timelessness had drawn me in—its simplicity, its quiet dignity that refused to demand attention. I never imagined wearing it here. It should have been for a walk down the aisle of some sunlit chapel, the fabric rustling against cobblestones as we burst out to scatterings of rice and cheers. But here it was, pristine and perfect, though it carried the weight of a thousand memories never made.

I clenched the silk tighter in my hands, aching for what should have been but wasn't, for all the joy it was meant to hold but couldn't. Somehow, the contrast only made it more beautiful, more poignant— for everything it was and everything it could never be.

Helen stood beside me in the absence of my family, gracefully adjusting the bouquet in my trembling hands. The late-day sun filtered through the blinds, its warm orange glow catching on the delicate petals in her pale pink Carolina Herrera suit. Her eyes sparkled with unshed tears, yet her smile was steady and reassuring. "You're beautiful," she whispered, a softness in her voice that made me blink away my own tears.

"I don't want anyone else to walk me down the aisle," I told her, clasping her free hand. "It has to be you."

Helen's composure wavered, and for a moment, her lips trembled. But then her smile returned—strong, determined. "Then it would be my honor," she said, her voice steady. "He's waiting for you. Are you ready?"

I nodded, although my heart was pounding so hard it silenced every thought. "I think so."

"Then let's go meet him." She took my arm, her strength grounding me when I felt like I might float away under the weight of the emotions coursing through me.

The door opened, and the first notes of a guitar floated through the air. Steven was perched on a barstool near Heck's bedside, a sight that was somehow as surprising as it was perfectly fitting. The man, so often gruff and guarded, looked serene in his dark suit, his hair tied back in a neat ponytail. He cradled his guitar with familiar ease, his fingers coaxing a melody that wasn't the traditional bridal march but held something infinitely more poignant. It was Nolan Taylor's *Driving Me Home*.

And then he sang.

His voice wove through the room, low and rich, wrapping around us like silk. Every note felt like a message, every word filled with a depth that made my chest ache. Steven sang as though the song had been written just for this moment—for his brother, for us. His voice rose and fell, his guitar vibrating with emotion too layered to name. I felt it in my bones—sorrow, hope, love—all intertwined in his performance.

When I saw Heck, everything else faded. My eyes locked onto him, unable to look away. He was propped up in the hospital bed, dressed in a tuxedo that Helen must have moved mountains to arrange. The usual hospital gown was gone, though a blanket still draped over his frail body. Despite the weight he had lost, the paleness of his skin, and the sharpness of his cheekbones, he was just as handsome as the man I fell in love with. His deep cerulean eyes still burned with the same fiery passion that had captivated me all those years ago.

The rest of the world disappeared for a moment, leaving only the two of us in the room. His eyes met my hazel ones, and time stopped. The universe seemed to hold its breath, pouring all its energy into us, wrapping us in a love so extraordinary it felt like magic. It was like stepping into the final chapter of a story, the one that ends with, *And they lived happily ever after.*

I finally got my happy ending. That was all I allowed myself to cling to. Tomorrow could wait and take care of itself. What mattered was this moment, this day, with him.

His gaze never left mine as I walked slowly toward him. Each step felt surreal, like floating in some dream that could shatter if I moved too quickly. Behind Heck, Hector stood with Fifth cradled in his arms. My son slept soundly, unaware of the extraordinary world swirling around him. Helen smiled as she accepted the bouquet back from me, stepping aside to join Hector and our baby.

The flowers enveloped the room in a kaleidoscope of colors, but my focus never wavered from Heck.

"You're breathtaking," he whispered hoarsely when I reached the bed, his voice like smoke drifting through the air. He managed to lift his hand, brushing his knuckles against my cheek. Despite the tubes and monitors surrounding him, his touch was everything—steady, loving, and warm.

Tears blurred my vision, but I held them back. "You're the one taking my breath away," I whispered, pressing my lips gently to his fingers.

Steven finished the last note on his guitar, his voice lingering in the air for just a moment before silence fell like a benediction. He set the guitar down carefully, flashing us a quick smile as he joined the others.

The priest stepped forward, his presence unassuming but full of warmth. He began the ceremony with a short blessing, his words soft yet anchoring. It wasn't elaborate; there were no grand vows or long speeches. But it didn't need to be. The love in that room was so tangible it filled every word spoken, every pause that stretched in reverence.

When it came time for personal words, I reached into my heart and found them waiting, as if they'd been there all along. "I've loved you since the first sunset we shared," I said, holding his hand tightly. "Your soul is my home, Heck. And every moment I've had with you, every second, has been a gift I'll cherish until my very last breath."

Heck smiled, though tears had begun streaming down his face. His voice was raspy and strained, yet strong in its sincerity. "You've been my light in every darkness, Sara. Every moment with you has been worth more than a thousand lifetimes anywhere else."

The priest nodded, guiding us as we exchanged rings, the simple bands catching the evening sunlight filtering through the window.

When it was over, Helen approached me first. Her steps were slow, hesitant, as though each one was weighted with everything she couldn't bear to say. When she reached me, she cupped my face in her trembling hands and kissed my cheeks, her lips warm but unsteady. Then, without a word, she pulled me into an embrace so tight it felt as if she were pouring the very essence of her strength into me, anchoring me in the storm of our shared grief. Her breath hitched against my shoulder, but she didn't cry. Not yet.

She turned to her son, and there was something raw in her expression, something that made my chest ache. She reached up, her fingers brushing his hair as though memorizing the feel of it, and kissed his forehead as gently as she had when he was a boy. "Oh, my darling," she murmured, her voice shattering under the weight of her sorrow. "You've given us everything. Do you know that? Every ounce of your love... it'll carry me through a thousand lifetimes. But I—I would trade it all. Everything. My life, my soul, my world, just to have more time with you." Her voice broke completely, and the last words tumbled out as a whispered plea, desperate and raw. "Just a little more time."

Her son's lips quivered, his composure faltering. "Mom," he said so softly it was almost inaudible. "Don't... don't say that. Please. I love you. I love you more than anything. I'm sorry... I'm sorry I couldn't love you the way you deserved. I should have done better. I should have been better."

Hearing them, my heart splintered, and tears that I had tried so hard to hold back spilled freely down my face. Helen's shoulders began shaking now, her strength unraveling thread by thread, though she tried to keep herself together.

Heck turned to me, his eyes glistening, his gaze steady and unshaken despite the pain that must have been tearing through him. He looked at me for a long, unspoken moment, then shifted his attention to his mother. His voice was quiet but firm, carrying a weight that seemed to press into the room.

"When the time comes, Mom... please, stay with Sara," he said, his words catching slightly as he drew a shaky breath. "Be the strength I couldn't give her. She'll need you. She can't do this on her own. You'll be all she has... you and our son."

Helen gave a shaky nod, her entire body trembling as though it was holding too much grief to contain. "I will," she whispered, the words a quiet promise, though it sounded like it might shatter her to keep it.

And then they embraced, a mother and her son, neither willing to fully break free, holding on as though the moment could stretch across eternity. There was something unbearable in the way they clung to one another, as if willing time itself to slow, to stop, to give them even one more heartbeat together.

It was the kind of hug that wasn't just goodbye. It was everything they had left to say, everything they had already said, and everything they never would. And I stood there, watching, helpless against the overwhelming grief of knowing it would be the last time they would ever hold each other.

Hector was close behind, his gruff demeanor melting as he leaned down to speak quietly to Heck. I didn't catch the words, but the emotion was clear in his glistening eyes and the way he gripped his son's hand as if he could impart years of love in a single touch.

Steven swooped in next, his steps slow but purposeful, his gaze locked on his brother. When he reached Heck, he pressed their foreheads together. There were no words at first, just a heavy silence that carried the weight of twenty years apart. I knew they'd already said their goodbyes before the wedding, but part of me still burned with anger at how little time fate had given them to mend everything fully. Yet, as I watched them now, I realized they didn't need any more time. Somehow, in the quiet way they held each other, a lifetime of absence had already been healed.

"Stevie," Heck rasped, his voice thin yet warm. "Teach Fifth how to make the chocolate turbo plane."

Steven paused, his lips tugging into a wry smile at the memory. "That disastrous thing?" he said, chuckling, his voice thick with nostalgia. "Fifth and I? We have more cars to decorate, Heck." His laugh softened the room, lightening the unbearable weight of the moment.

Helen caught the shared memory, too, and for just an instant, her tears gave way to a quiet laugh of her own. It was a sound we all clung to, a fleeting burst of levity amidst the ache. The laughter rippled like a fragile thread stitching us together one last time.

Steven pulled back, shaking his head, his grin rueful. "Only you would bring up that insane contraption now." Then, without hesitation, he reached for Heck's hand, squeezing it tightly, his humor slipping into something deeper. "I'll take care of it. You know I'll take care of all of it. Don't worry."

Heck nodded, his lips curving faintly, his strength ebbing but his spirit stubbornly unyielding. "I know," he whispered, his voice soft yet resolute.

Steven took a deep breath, as if bracing himself, before turning to me. His crooked smile returned, though it was laced with something gentler now, bittersweet. "Well," he said, his voice lighter as he leaned down to kiss my cheeks, "you're officially my sister now. Welcome to this beautiful disaster of a family."

I laughed even as I cried, hugging him tightly. "Thank you," I murmured, my voice thick with gratitude.

Jeffrey, who had slipped in quietly at some point, clapped his hands gently. "Before we all scatter, I think there's only one thing left—a family photo." He held up his phone, angling it perfectly.

We gathered around Heck, Helen sitting beside him while Hector held Fifth close. Steven stood beside me, his arm around my shoulder. And in that instant, as the camera clicked, I felt the bittersweet ache of wanting to freeze time forever.

The moment was fleeting, like the last glow of twilight before night took over. One by one, they hugged me tightly—Helen pressing a kiss to my cheek, Hector gripping my hand with quiet strength, and Steven pulling me into a firm but tender embrace. They each lingered for a heartbeat longer at Heck's side, whispering their goodnights before leaving us in the sanctuary of ourselves. Their gift—the rest of the evening alone—just me and Heck.

The room shrank in their absence, the quiet amplifying the sound of Heck's gentle breaths and the steady rhythm of the monitor. It should have felt empty, but it didn't. Not with him still here. Gathering the folds of my dress in trembling hands, I moved toward him with care. I didn't stop to think about changing out of it; there wasn't time. Every second felt precious, too precious to waste. I eased myself onto the narrow bed, the satin whispering softly against the sheets as I curled close to him.

Our faces were so near that I could feel the faint caress of his breath against my skin, warm and shallow, the only thing keeping the silence at bay. Slowly, his hand lifted, frail but impossibly warm, and when our fingers met, they intertwined effortlessly, as if they'd always known this was where they were meant to be.

I held on, my grip tender but firm, my thumb tracing slow circles against his skin. That small contact spoke volumes, saying everything I couldn't put into words. Time seemed to still in the cocoon of our closeness. It was just us now, and though the weight of what was coming pressed heavy on my chest, at this moment, with his hand in mine and his breath mingling with mine, nothing else mattered but him.

"You're officially Mrs. Hector Archibald IV," he murmured, the mischief in his voice drawing a faint smile across his lips. His blue eyes, though tired, sparkled like they could still hold galaxies.

He reached up with shaky fingers, tucking a loose strand of my hair behind my ear. "You're beautiful, Sara," he breathed, his voice a soft caress. Then, surprising me with his resolve, he leaned in and kissed me deeply, passionately, pouring all the love he couldn't put into words into that single gesture.

The kiss wasn't like before—it wasn't fiery or desperate. It held no urgency, no frenzied passion. Instead, it unfolded slowly, tenderly, heavy with the weight of all the words left unspoken. His lips, soft and trembling, pressed against mine with a quiet purpose, as though he was pouring what remained of himself into this moment. I could feel the fragility in his touch, the way his fingers just barely brushed my cheek before falling away, spent.

I wanted to cling to him, to bridge the distance time and fate had carved between us, but I couldn't. Not this time. This kiss wasn't just an expression of love—it was a letting go, a final thread unraveled as he gave me all he had left to give. I memorized the feel of his faint breath against my skin, the flutter of his pulse like a fading echo beneath my palms.

Despite his weakness, he willed himself into that kiss as if trying to make it last long enough to carry me through a lifetime. I ached to feel more of him, to pull him closer, but I knew. I knew his body wouldn't allow him to love me the way we once did. And that was okay because this—just this—was everything. Feeling his warmth, his presence, his heart still beating beneath my touch. It was enough.

When he pulled away, his eyes met mine, tired but full of something eternal. And though my heart shattered under the weight of what I knew, I found a strange, quiet peace in the way he held me with his gaze. This was our goodbye. Painful and bittersweet, but beautiful in its fragility. For just a fleeting moment, it felt like forever.

"I'm sorry," he whispered, the words fragile and so unlike him. "I'm sorry I can't stay with you longer."

I pressed a finger to his lips, silencing the thought before it could break either of us further. "Shh… tonight isn't about how long we have," I said softly, my lips brushing against his forehead. "It's about this moment. Just you and me."

"Just us, Pender," he replied, his weak smile lighting up his face like the memory of sunlight.

I held his gaze, memorizing every unspoken word in those ocean-blue eyes. We didn't need to say it, but it was there, aching like a heartbeat between us—I love you, I love you, I love you.

Outside, the sun had long slipped beneath the horizon, casting the world into shadows. But here, wrapped in the fragile light of Heck's love, the darkness never reached us. His warmth tethered me, filling a void I couldn't bear to name. This was more than a moment. This was our eternity, fleeting but infinite—our promise. Even in the face of goodbye, we held onto the beauty we could grasp, the love we could still share. And there would always be enough light to chase the shadows away in that beauty.

Something beautiful to cling to.

37

For the first time in weeks, a fragile peace settled over me. Heck's arms cradled me, their strength fragile but alive, keeping the world's shadows at bay. I didn't want the night to end, didn't want to think of the clock ticking down, but he was already too exhausted. The activity of the day had drained him, and so, reluctantly, I nestled close and surrendered to sleep.

His breathing grew softer and steadier, pulling me into its quiet rhythm. I nestled closer, feeling his heartbeat beneath my cheek—faint but steadfast—and allowed myself to surrender. Sleep claimed me slowly, wrapping around us like a shield.

That night, there were no dreams, no nightmares, no restless intrusions. It was as though time itself had stopped, granting us one brief, merciful reprieve. The world paused, holding its breath, letting us rest against the storm waiting on the other side.

When I woke, the first rays of morning light were slipping through the gaps in the vertical blinds, weaving gold threads across the room's sea of flowers. The room was quiet, still, but something felt... off. I turned toward Heck, my heart instinctively tightening. His eyes fluttered briefly open before his lids fell shut again. His breaths came short, shallow, barely there, like his body was caught in a silent struggle.

"Heck?" My voice wavered, laced with dread. I leaned closer, placing a trembling hand on his shoulder. "Heck, can you hear me?"

There was no response. Panic shot through me as I scrambled out of the bed, my feet tangling in the sheets. My hand found the emergency button, pressing it with clumsy desperation. "Please, someone... please —he needs help!" My voice cracked with every syllable.

Within moments, the door burst open, and the room was flooded with urgency. The nurse led the charge, swiftly checking the monitors as alarms began to blare, piercing the stillness. Two doctors followed, steady and focused, their faces unreadable. I stepped back instinctively, the corner of the room swallowing me whole as I watched the medics descend upon Heck.

"We've got oxygen desaturation—SpO2 is dipping below 80 percent," the nurse called out, her professional tone betraying a hint of tension.

"Bag him. Start manual ventilation," the attending physician instructed, his hands moving with precision as he checked Heck's pulse. "Cardiac monitoring—they've already flatlined once overnight," he muttered to the other doctor, then louder, "Get the crash cart ready, just in case."

The words hit like ice water. *Flatlined? Crash cart?* I pressed a hand to my mouth, trying to keep the rising scream from escaping. My world narrowed to the controlled chaos around Heck's bed—hands moving wires, pressing syringes, placing oxygen masks—every second an eternity.

The faint rustle of movement from behind pulled me out of the storm of alarms and controlled medical urgency. A man in a gray suit stepped into the room, his silhouette crisp against the soft morning light. His phone was pressed to his ear, his posture stiff, his face hard to read. His presence was dissonant, out of place in this intimate fight for life. He turned and locked eyes with me, his voice low and firm as he finished the call.

"His father would like to speak with you," he said quietly, holding the phone out to me. His words, though calm, seemed heavy, final—like they carried the verdict of some cruel trial.

Trembling, I took the phone from his outstretched hand, bringing it to my ear as my knees nearly buckled beneath me. "Hello?" I whispered, though my voice broke under the weight of my fear.

"Sara." Hector's voice came through the line, calm but laced with restrained emotion, each word slow and deliberate. "The doctors are trying to stabilize him, but it's cardiac arrest. He went into arrhythmia earlier. They're preparing to wake him now—just enough to speak. Sara, this may be…" He paused, his breath faltering. "This may be the last time."

"No," I breathed, shaking my head though he couldn't see me. "No… we have time. Hector, they said there were hours… twenty-four hours, at least!" My voice rose, unsteady and cracking. "You're telling me he —he's too weak already? He promised me, Hector! He promised me he wouldn't leave. He can't—he can't…"

Hector's silence on the other end only amplified the scream building in my chest. When he spoke again, his voice was quiet but firm, threaded with pain. "Sara, I know. Believe me, I know. But things… things are changing faster than we hoped. They've told me what little energy he has left is being used for this, to speak with you. To see his son. Just one last time."

Tears streamed down my face as his words pierced through my chest like jagged shards. "No… no, Hector…" My hand gripped the phone like it was my only tether to reality. "This can't—Helen, she—"

"We're on our way, but there's no way we'll make it there in time. Helen…" His voice cracked, breaking through his composure. "She wanted me to tell you. Be there, Sara. For her. For all of us."

A sob tore through me, catching in my throat as I pressed my back against the wall. "I don't know if I can do this, Hector," I whispered, the raw vulnerability in my voice cutting through the chaos of the room.

"You can," he said firmly, though his own voice wavered. "You must. Do it for Helen. For Heck to see his son. Give him this, Sara."

His plea shattered the last piece of my resistance. My chest heaved with a broken cry, but deep down, I knew Hector was right. I wiped my tears hastily, though they kept falling, and nodded against the phone. "I'll do it," I choked. "I promise."

When the call ended, the phone slipped from my hand, clattering to the floor. I picked it up as I returned to the scene before me. The nurse adjusted the oxygen mask over Heck's face, and one doctor carefully injected something into the IV line, feeding it into his arm. The monitors beeped steadily now, their rhythm no longer a frenetic scream.

I inched closer, forcing myself to breathe as I approached the edge of the bed. One of the doctors glanced at me briefly and quietly said, "He'll be conscious soon. His vitals are extremely unstable. Please make it brief."

The heartbreak in his tone made my lungs collapse, but I nodded resolutely, swallowing the lump in my throat as I reached for Heck's hand.

I closed my eyes against the torrent of tears that blurred my vision. "I will," I murmured, my voice almost inaudible as I forced the words out. I wiped my face with trembling hands and handed the phone back to the gray-suited man.

Dr. Arnold approached me with the careful patience of someone delivering the impossible. He took my hand and met my eyes, searching for a sliver of understanding amidst my heartbreak. "Sara," he said gently, his voice a lifeline, trying to steady me. "We only have a few minutes. I'll explain everything, but you need to prepare yourself."

I nodded automatically, though the words barely registered. Everything felt distant, as if the world was being filtered through the static. A nurse appeared, cradling Fifth in her arms, his tiny form still bundled and warm from his nap. She handed him to me, and the feel of his weight against my chest briefly tethered me to the moment.

I turned toward Heck, my legs barely carrying me over to him, each step painfully deliberate. He was free of the tubes and wires that had tethered him to life—looking more like the man I loved, yet still so heartbreakingly frail. The warnings from Dr. Arnold haunted me, each one slicing through my threadbare hope. *Critical cardiac damage. Expect a collapse.* I had tried to deny it, screaming and pleading against it. But now, as I looked into his tired, knowing gaze, the truth was unbearable. He had woken up to say goodbye.

A faint smile tugged at his lips, the kind that always undid me, even now. I tried not to break as I sat beside him, my hands trembling as I fought to hold myself together, trying to keep from shattering completely. My voice broke as I whispered, "Hi… someone's here to see you." I glanced down at our son, my lip quivering, the sobs swelling and teetering on the edge.

He blinked slowly, his once-vivid eyes now dulled with exhaustion, yet a spark of warmth broke through as he looked at me. "Sara," he rasped, his voice barely a thread, "you're beautiful. You've always been so… beautiful." He blinked again, the effort looking like it might overwhelm him, but when his gaze shifted down to our son cradled in my arms, something changed. A light fought its way through that haze of pain.

"And… hello there," Heck breathed, his smile trembling and wider now, his voice nearly breaking with wonder. "My little man." His hand, so frail it felt like it might splinter, lifted from the bed, reaching out. I guided Fifth closer, his tiny hands curling awkwardly around his father's finger. A shiver passed through Heck, his breath catching like a sob might tumble out, but he held it, letting his thumb trace tiny circles on our baby's impossibly small knuckles.

"You're perfect," he whispered, his voice shaking, a tear tracing the curve of his face. His eyes flickered back to mine, that fleeting smile trembling with both joy and grief. "You've given me more than I could've… than I could've dreamed."

My chest caved as the weight of it all crushed down on me. His words, his gaze, the bittersweet love in his touch. Tears spilled freely down my cheeks as I fought to stay with him, to match the strength he somehow still found in himself.

I fell apart right there—breaking into pieces I could never hope to put back together. Clutching his other hand, I pressed it against my lips through the storm of my sobs. "Heck... don't. Don't say goodbye. You promised—you promised me."

His fingers, frail and unsteady, brushed against mine, his touch desperate to reassure even now. "Hey, listen... to me," he whispered, his voice so faint it almost wasn't there. He was holding on by threads, unraveling with every breath. "I know I promised. To grow old with you. To have gray hair, wrinkles... all of it."

"Gray hair, wrinkles, and all that," I choked, forcing the words past the terrible ache in my chest.

His smile faltered, then grew, weak yet stubborn, laced with a fragile sweetness. "I bought that cottage in Guernsey," he murmured, his voice breaking on each syllable, like every word might steal his last breath. "It was... going to be my wedding gift. For you. For you and Fifth. Summers there... not so cold."

His words cut through me like something sharp and unforgiving, and for a moment, we weren't in this sterile room filled with beeping machines. I saw us on that island again, where he'd once led me to the edge of everything he loved and dared me to dream with him. He'd traced the stories of his great-grandfather's love for a local girl in that painting, which he kept like a treasure in his gallery. Back then, I'd learned things about Heck that stunned me—that he was rich in a way that made me laugh out loud. That he was serious about chasing eternity with me.

"I'll show him, Heck," I begged, clutching his hand even harder. "I'll show him where the sea meets the rocks. But not without you. Please, not without you."

He blinked slowly, his entire body trembling from the strain. "Wish... I could," he whispered, his voice raw and broken, a single tear sliding down the curve of his cheek. Pain etched every word, yet his gaze stayed locked on mine. "But you will. You'll show him. Promise me, Sara."

His breath shuddered as he continued, his voice barely audible but filled with desperation. "Promise me you'll show Fifth. Take him to the places where our love grew. Show him the gallery. Don't... don't let me fade into just a memory. I want him to know me as he grows. Tell him to chase what he loves. That being an Archibald doesn't mean being trapped in something he doesn't want to be."

His eyes searched mine, pleading. "Show him what love is... what life should be. Promise me."

How can I? I wanted to scream. *When my entire world is you. When everything good, everything beautiful, when my whole world is you. How can I go on?* But the words stayed locked in my throat because he knew. He always knew.

He smiled again, so soft it broke me. His voice cracked, yet it was filled with something endless and unshakable. His thumb brushed my knuckles even as each breath pulled further and further from him. "Because you can," he whispered, his words slipping through the air like they might dissolve if I didn't catch them. "Because you've made my whole life... worth it. You gave me everything."

His eyes dropped then to Fifth, who began to stir in my arms as if the weight of the moment had reached even him. Heck's hand floated toward him, weak and trembling, and I guided his fingertips to graze our son's cheek, tiny yet perfect against his. Fifth scrunched his nose, letting out loud protests, and cried—annoyed at the interruption.

Heck laughed then, or something close enough that it split me apart again. "There he is," he murmured, his voice breaking into so many pieces, shards I wanted to gather up and keep. "That's my boy. Already got his mother's temper."

I laughed, too, but it was broken, soaked in the tears streaming endlessly down my face. "He's got your eyes," I said, clutching Fifth closer. "Your hair. Your warmth. Heck, he's so beautiful. He's you."

"And he'll always remind you of me," he whispered, his breathing shallow, his strength waning with every passing second. Heck's hand lingered on Fifth a moment longer, his smile softening, his eyes growing heavier. "Take care of our boy. Make sure he knows... how loved he is," he whispered, his voice now just a ghost of itself.

I held his hand like it was my only lifeline. Desperate. Afraid that letting go would erase him entirely. My heart broke against the loud, quiet nothing slowly swallowing us. "He needs you. I need you." My voice broke, colliding with my grief.

He smiled faintly, lifting his gaze to mine, filled with a softness I'd never forget. "Give him my Sundays, Sara. Every sunset. Tell him... tell him I'm watching."

I pressed my forehead to his hand, sobbing into his palm as his thumb, with the last of its strength, brushed along my cheek one final time. His breathing, shallow and strained, wavered as he looked at me with a gaze full of love, regret, and something painfully eternal.

"I love you, Pender," he whispered, his voice barely audible. His lips twitched, faint and familiar. "Always." Those tired, stormy eyes found mine one last time. We were there in the quiet connection we'd always had for an agonizing heartbeat. No words were needed between us, only the silence and our love.

And then his fingers slipped from mine, his hand falling limp, his eyes slowly closing while that softness stayed locked in his expression, painted there forever. For a single breathless second, we were still connected, as though the world itself knew what it was losing and dared not take him from me.

And then, the silence arrived. It clawed at me, suffocating, endless, only broken by the shrill, flat beep of the monitor next to him. It swallowed the air, the light, the world. I stared at him, waiting for something to change, something to pull him back.

And then, he was gone.

Just like that.

My everything. My heart. Gone.

I sat there, paralyzed, as the world crumbled beneath my feet. A scream clawed at the back of my throat, but my voice betrayed me, lost in the weight of what was happening. My body gave out, and someone gently pried Fifth from my trembling arms. I collapsed onto the edge of the bed, clawing for him. For what was left of him.

I buried my face in his chest, gripping his hospital gown as though I could anchor myself to him, as though I could keep him here. His warmth was still there—it lingered, fading with each second, slipping through my fingers like sand no matter how tightly I tried to hold on. His scent, so familiar, so him, was already turning into a memory I wasn't ready to keep. My sobs came like a flood, one after another, shaking my entire body until I thought I might break apart.

No one pulled me away. No one said a word. They just stood there, silent witnesses to my unraveling, letting me stay tangled in the last pieces of him. I didn't count the minutes or hours. Time dissolved into fragments because the only thing that mattered was what I couldn't hold onto.

I pressed my ear to his chest, praying for a sound—a heartbeat, a miracle. But there was nothing. Only the echo of my cries and the void his absence left behind. I whispered his name, again and again, as if it might call him back. But he didn't answer, and the emptiness filled the room until I could barely breathe.

They didn't move me. No one dared. They just let us stay, me clutching his lifeless form as though my desperation could bring him back. But even as I held him, I knew. He was already gone. And so was a part of me.

Helen burst into the room moments later, her face a mirror of my pain, and without hesitation, she pulled me into her arms. We folded into each other, collapsing under the unbearable weight of our grief. Our cries rose into the silence, raw and unrelenting, filling the hollow room with the sound of everything that had been taken from us. Her hands clutched at my back, desperate, as though holding me was the only thing keeping her from shattering completely.

Helen's breath hitched against my shoulder, her sorrow reverberating through my bones, and I realized then that we weren't just mourning —no, we were breaking. Together, we came undone, our sobs tangling as one, pouring into the emptiness he left behind. I clung to her, shaking, and somewhere within the darkness, I felt her press her forehead to mine, the simplest touch anchoring us as we drowned in an ocean of loss.

38

They wheeled Heck's bed out of the room, the squeak of the wheels grating against the heavy silence, cutting through the shattered pieces of my world. I couldn't watch it. My back was turned, my gaze fixed on nothing, my mind clinging desperately to his last smile, his last breath. They were taking him somewhere I couldn't follow now, somewhere cold and unfeeling, where they would prepare him for the funeral. I couldn't see him there. I wouldn't. I needed to preserve what little pieces I had left of him—the way he looked when he whispered his last words, when his hand fell still in mine. That was the memory I'd keep, the one I'd etch into my soul.

It was also my way of giving Hector and Helen their chance to grieve, their time to say goodbye to their son alone. Part of me wanted to go with them, to hold them and share in their loss, but I couldn't summon the strength. I couldn't move.

I stayed in the room, still in my wedding dress, anchored to the chair by the window—the one that had cradled me for weeks on end. My legs felt like they didn't belong to me anymore, and my arms hung limp at my sides. The world outside the window carried on, oblivious, the sun shining with cruel indifference. How could it shine when he was gone?

The door creaked open behind me, but I didn't stir. I barely heard the soft shuffle of footsteps.

"You need to eat. Or at least drink something," came Steven's voice, low and hesitant, like he wasn't sure if speaking would shatter me completely.

I didn't look at him. I didn't acknowledge him. My body felt like a shell, hollowed out and lifeless. My hands rested in my lap, numb and useless, as the weight of the water bottle he handed me pressed into them. I took it, but I couldn't bring myself to unscrew the cap, to lift it to my lips. I just held it there, my fingers gripping it like it was the last solid thing anchoring me to this world.

"I'm so sorry," Steven whispered, his voice breaking, each word heavy and raw, as if he carried his own unbearable grief. I heard it, but it didn't touch me. I was too far away, spiraling deeper into the void Heck had left behind.

Steven knelt before me, the sound soft, almost imperceptible, like he didn't want to disturb the storm enveloping me. I felt his hand brush my hair back, tucking a stray strand behind my ear with care I hadn't expected. His fingers moved to my face, tender and shaking, trying to wipe away the tears streaming endlessly down my cheeks. But they wouldn't stop. They couldn't.

"I'm sorry," he said again, his voice cracking open. The sheer weight of his sorrow pulled at me, but I couldn't respond. I couldn't move. Something warm pressed against my forehead, and for a fleeting moment, I realized it was his lips. A kiss, soft and broken, an offering of solace I didn't have the strength to take.

I felt his tears as they hit my skin, warm and mingling with mine. Steven's grief was wrapped in his touch, woven into every word he didn't say. And then, just as quietly as he'd entered, he rose and left. He didn't ask anything more of me. He didn't try to fill the silence. He just gave me the space to break, to fall apart completely in the wake of all I'd lost.

The silence swallowed me again. And I stayed there, clutching that unopened bottle of water, tethered to my chair by a sorrow so vast, so consuming, that I couldn't see the edges of it. I couldn't fathom a way out. All that existed now was the empty space where Heck had been, and I knew, in my heart, that nothing would ever fill it.

———

I didn't know how long I stayed there, lost in the stillness that had swallowed the room. Then, like a whisper through the fog, I remembered my son. He needed me as much as I now needed him. Dragging myself to the next room, I lifted him from his crib, his tiny body warm and steady in my unsteady hands. I returned to the chair by the hospital window, sinking back into that familiar place, cradling Fifth against my trembling chest. It was just the two of us now, held together by the fragile string of a Sunday sunset.

His small weight anchored me, a soft warmth pressing against the hollow cold that was slowly consuming me. Outside, the world seemed to mirror the ache within me. The horizon burned with fiery oranges and tender pinks, the colors spilling over one another like tears, as if the sun itself wept for what had been lost. It poured every ounce of its light into the sky, a final act before slipping away. I clung to that sight, to its fleeting beauty, as if it might somehow fill the vast emptiness Heck had left behind. But as the colors faded and the sun sank, I could feel that same quiet, inevitable departure. The way the light disappeared was like the way he'd gone, leaving me with nothing but shadows and the faint memory of warmth.

My thighs quaked under the crushing weight of my grief, but I held on. I held on to my son, his small, perfect hand wrapped so tightly around my finger, as if, even in his dreams, he knew he had to keep me here. My tears came steadily now, a ceaseless stream falling onto the soft crown of his hair.

"You should be here," I choked out, the words trembling like glass between my lips. Heck should have been here to see this. To hold him. To teach him how to tie his shoes, how to cast a fishing line, how to be brave—things I didn't know how to do without him. Grief twisted in my chest, sharp and merciless, as the enormity of what he wouldn't get to share with us settled in.

We stayed like that until the sunlight outside filtered weakly through the window, its golden rays casting a soft glow on the walls. The sunset spilled across the horizon, streaks of orange and pink fading into the endless blue, like a wound slowly closing. It was achingly beautiful and so cruel—a world still spinning, still serene in its indifference, as mine fell apart. Each passing second of that dying light felt like another piece of him slipping farther away until the horizon swallowed the last trace of the sun, leaving us in shadow.

Fifth stirred in his sleep, his tiny fist tightening around my finger as though he could feel the ache in my heart. The gesture shattered me entirely, sending another wave of tears cascading down my cheeks. But as the sun dipped lower and the world cooled under the encroaching night, I felt it—him—Heck. Not in the room, not in the flesh, but somewhere out there, beyond the colors of the dying sun.

He was out there, I told myself. Watching. Listening. His love stitched into every fiber of the fading sky, into the beating of our son's tiny heart. I closed my eyes, letting the warmth of that thought battle against the vast, cold absence around me. I didn't know how I'd live without him—how we'd exist in a world he was no longer a part of. But in the depths of this pain, as I clung to our son, I realized one thing.

He would always find me.

Just like in Shakespeare & Company in Paris.

Our little corner in New York City's Tribeca Trickle.

Fifth's eyes fluttered open, those clear, cerulean depths locking onto mine. They were his father's eyes—calm, endless, carrying the weight of a love that refused to be extinguished. My breath hitched as more tears spilled down my cheeks, blending sorrow and wonder into something I couldn't name. It was as if Heck was looking back at me, anchoring me to this moment, promising I wouldn't face this alone.

"But how could I love Sunday sunsets without you in it, Heck?" I whispered through the ache in my chest, the words trembling but full, carrying everything I couldn't say. Fifth's tiny fingers curled tighter around mine, the smallest, most fragile reassurance. And yet, it was enough.

The room filled with the quiet hum of fading light, the touch of warmth that lingered from the setting sun. Somehow, I knew Heck was there—not in some distant, unreachable place, but in the spaces between us. Above. Beneath. Within the light in Fifth's eyes, the beat of his heart, the love we'd never stop carrying.

Heck would always find me. Somewhere between the colors of the sky, in the stillness of the night, in the pieces of him that would live on, unyielding and eternal. And as the sun dipped entirely below the horizon, painting the earth in its parting glow, I knew—Heck would never leave us. He was everywhere, always. And he always would be.

EPILOGUE

Sunday.

The sun hung low in the sky, casting golden-hour hues over the neatly manicured cemetery. The sycamore tree swayed softly in the tender embrace of the late summer breeze, its outstretched branches curling like a guardian's arms over the small gray stone nestled in the lush, emerald grass. Hector and Steven had moved heaven and earth to plant that tree there—a living monument to Heck's memory. A simple wooden swing now hung from its sturdy limb, swaying faintly in the wind, a quiet echo of the life that once was, and always would be.

The inscription was simple and understated, just like him: *Hector Archibald IV – Beloved Son, Father, Brother, and Friend.* Beneath it, the words I had chosen were etched in smaller letters: *Forever our Sunday Sunset.*

I didn't use "Husband" because, in truth, he was forevermore a friend above all else. He was my greatest relationship—my greatest love of all. I knelt in front of the stone, brushing away a stray leaf that had landed near the base. My fingers lingered there, tracing the engraved letters as if my touch could somehow make them less cold.

"Heck," I whispered, my voice catching slightly. "I still miss you every single day. Five years… yet it still feels like yesterday. You were—and will always be—with me, my love."

The breeze picked up again, rustling through the sycamore leaves above, as if in reply. I smiled faintly, my tears refusing to hold back. "You'd love seeing him now, our Fifth. He has that same grin that drove me crazy the first time I met you. And your fire. God, he's so much like you, sometimes it scares me," I said, chuckling softly through my tears. "But he has my nose. Thank goodness for that."

Behind me, I heard the soft shuffle of footsteps across the grass. Turning slightly, I saw him—our son. Fifth stood there, his messy dark brown curls catching the evening light, his toy airplane clutched tightly in one hand. He was every bit his father's son, with those cerulean blue eyes and that mischievous energy. His smile was tentative, though. He knew why we were here, but even at five years old, he carried a kind of quiet strength beyond his years.

"Mommy?" Fifth said, walking up to me and slipping his small hand into mine. "Why are you crying?"

I wiped my face quickly and pulled him close. My voice trembled, but I softened it for him. "I'm not crying because I'm just sad, sweetheart. I mean, maybe a little..." I paused, my breath hitching, before I kissed his hair gently. "But mostly... mostly, I'm thinking about how much your daddy loved us. How he loved you. And how much I miss him. How I miss him so terribly it hurts—but we'll keep that love alive, won't we? We'll carry it with us, always."

Fifth tilted his head, studying me with a seriousness that felt so much like Heck, it made my heart ache. "Daddy loved you the most, right?" he asked.

I nodded, my throat tightening. "Yes, he did. And I loved him the most, too."

Fifth crouched next to me, his little finger reaching out to touch the stone. "Do you think Daddy can see us from heaven, Mommy?"

"I know he can," I said, my voice steady now. "Every Sunday, when the sun sets, that's his way of saying, 'I love you.' That's why we say it back, remember?"

Fifth nodded solemnly, looking out at the horizon, where the sun was beginning to dip further down. It painted the sky in shades of orange and pink, fiery and soft all at once, like a love letter from the heavens.

"I love you, Sunday sunset," he said quietly, almost to himself, but loud enough for me to hear.

I pulled him into my lap, kissing the top of his curly head. "That's right, sweetheart. Every Sunday sunset is Daddy's way of telling us he's still here with us, that he always will be."

Fifth turned to me, searching for something in my expression. "Do you miss him a lot, Mommy?"

"Every single day," I admitted, holding him tighter. "But having you here... it makes it a little easier. Daddy gave me you, and that's the best gift he could've left behind."

We stayed like that—just me and Fifth. The cemetery grew still as twilight set in, the fading sunlight spilling golden trails across the headstones. It seemed deliberate, as if the sky itself wanted to linger for just a moment longer. Heck's resting place glowed softly under the amber light, a quiet contrast to the chill seeping into the air.

I leaned forward one last time and reached out with trembling fingers. My touch found the stone, its surface unyielding, cold. My lips brushed against my fingertips before I held them above his name, etched so finely into the granite, and hovered there as though the space between us could carry the love I still held, infinite and undimmed.

The words came quietly, barely louder than a whisper, but heavy with everything I couldn't fit into the silence. "I'll keep loving you, Heck. Always. Even when it hurts."

My voice broke, trailing off into the hushed stillness around me. The evening air grew heavier, colder, but I stayed there for a moment longer, as though my presence could somehow fill the void that stretched endlessly now that he was gone. The golden light faded into dusk, leaving only shadows and my promise, etched as surely into my heart as his name was into the stone.

Fifth climbed off my lap then, tugging my hand as though sensing it was time to go. "Come on, Mommy. We don't want Daddy to miss the sunset," he said earnestly.

I smiled, letting him lead me toward the car. Every step away from that small stone felt heavy, but the little boy at my side softened the weight. Our love for Heck, carried in our hearts, in our whispers, and in every Sunday sunset, would never fade.

And as we walked off into the last light of the day, I whispered softly,

"'Night, Heck."

****

Friday.

I was late. The poster read, "8:30 P.M. / 11th Street Bar," but Raul and I had been trapped in a last-minute meeting that refused to end. Still, I couldn't place all the blame on work. Some of it belonged to the night itself—the restless pulse of a Friday in the East Village, energetic and chaotic, pulling at the city's seams. Ubers and cabs inched through gridlocked streets while laughter and music spilled from bars packed with revelers chasing infinite possibilities.

When Tony finally dropped me off, his usual calm presence felt like a thread tethering me to the frenzy. Tony wasn't just a driver—he'd been one of my anchors since my pregnancy, seamlessly balancing the roles of bodyguard, chauffeur, and steadfast protector for me and Fifth. I stepped out of the car and turned toward the bar. Its unassuming facade seemed alive in its own way, glowing faintly under the dim neon sign that buzzed in uneven flickers. The light pooled across the sidewalk, throwing restless shadows that danced to the rhythm of the city's ceaseless hum. For a moment, I stood there.

Then I hurried toward the entrance, my eagerness building as I stepped inside. The bar felt alive, wrapped in a strange, beguiling warmth mixed with the city's grit. The air hit me first, thick with a blend of music, cigarette smoke, the tang of spilled beer, and the savory notes of something sizzling nearby—burgers, maybe. Exposed brick walls held a quiet charm, covered in faded indie band posters clinging to the past, their edges curling with age, whispering stories of performances long gone.

String lights zigzagged across the low ceiling, casting golden pools of light that shifted and danced with the crowd below. The bar itself stretched proudly along one side of the room—a polished wooden counter worn smooth at its edges, evidence of the hands and elbows that had leaned on its surface over the years. Its mirrored backdrop gleamed with rows of bottles, their colorful reflections glinting like tiny promises. Bar tables filled the space in an artful disarray, lending an effortless, lived-in comfort.

Near the far corner, a pool table drew a cluster of beer-clutching players. Their laughter rang out in bursts, rippling through the hum of conversation, music, and clinking glasses. The atmosphere felt layered, textured—a tapestry woven of moments, of strangers converging in fleeting harmony. For a brief second, I stood there, taking it all in.

The stage, tucked in the center, was compact and intimate, its raised platform barely large enough to hold Steven's band. The drum kit gleamed under the soft glow of purple stage lights, flanked by a couple of amps and mic stands that seemed to lean in with expectation. Two large screens aired liquor ads and band lineups for the week. The audience pressed close to the stage, their faces lit with scattered reflections of the string lights as they swayed to the beat. It was the kind of space where you felt the music more than you heard it, where it thrummed through the floors and pulsed in your chest.

It had been years since I'd stepped into a place like this. Even longer since I'd allowed myself to surrender to the kind of night where music and life intertwined. Nightlife in New York City always reminded me of Heck—the electric unpredictability, the soul-baring rawness. Memories of him hovered on the edges of my mind, and I kept a tight grip on them, afraid that letting go would mean being swept completely under.

My life had reshaped itself around routines, each day folding neatly into the next. Workdays merged into a steady grind, marked by the demands of my new role. Taking over Heck's position in marketing and advertising had been intense, but I was known to clock out sharply at 6 P.M.—unless an extended meeting, like tonight's, kept me tied. Those evenings mattered. They were my solace, spent with Fifth, wrapped in the comforting ritual of bedtime stories and the quiet joy of watching him drift into sleep. Weekends carried a different rhythm, filled with his activities. Saturdays often saw Hector taking his grandson on yachting trips with Steven sometimes, while Helen folded him into the revival of Heck's old art studio, now under Zaldy's care—Heck's right-hand man. I hadn't set foot in the gallery for years. It was one of the many spaces I had left frozen, untouched, since Heck had gone.

Still, it had become Fifth's second home—a place alive again under his tiny, thoughtful touch. He had his own little corner there now, painting with Heck's old brushes, creating something new out of tools that once carried so much of his father's energy. Sundays, though, belonged to us—me, Fifth, and Heck. We began with brunch, maybe a walk through the park, or a small toy-shopping trip. But the heart of Sunday lay in the afternoons, when we'd visit Heck. Every week, without fail. It was sacred, our time, a tradition so deeply rooted it remained unbroken. Everyone knew not to interfere.

Dating? Entertaining suitors? They had no place in my world. Nights spent in places like this? Long behind me.

But tonight, Steven had convinced me—pulled me, really—out of my carefully preserved rhythm. For once, I'd stepped away from the predictable, letting the edges of my routine blur.

The music was already alive when I stepped into the dimly lit bar. From the back of the room, I scanned for Steven, only to find him center stage, commanding the room with ease. He was mid-song, belting out the Ramones' *I Wanna Be Sedated* against the driving rhythm of his bandmates—a drummer and two guitarists who thrashed with energy.

Steven was in his element. His black button-down shirt hung open at the neck, casually revealing a subtle chain and enough confidence to fill the room. His darker pants fit perfectly with his worn black boots, and his hair—shorter now than last time—encircled his head in soft curls, accented by the well-kept beard lining his jaw. A striking, mature presence compared to the free-spirited chaos I remembered, but still... Steven.

He gripped his guitar with a steady hand, playing fluidly, moving as one with the music. I noticed his left-handed precision, the way his fingers danced across the frets effortlessly, as though the guitar was part of him. At times, he held his guitar upside down with confidence. His eyes were mostly closed as he sang, his expression lost in the music, transcending the small stage and cozy crowd. Was he imagining another audience, another time? I wondered, my chest tightening. Music had always been his escape; tonight, Steven wasn't just performing. He was alive in a way most people only dreamed of being.

I found myself smiling despite the sadness I felt—bars and cafes always reminded me of the past I wanted to bury, if it wasn't already buried. Steven wasn't just good—he was brilliant. I finally understood why he had never quite been able to leave this part of himself behind, even now, juggling it alongside his new role at Gold Standard Bank. Music wasn't just what Steven did—it was who he was.

When he opened his eyes—those cerulean gems, so startlingly like Heck's—they scanned the crowd briefly before landing on me. Recognition sparked immediately, and he smiled—a boyish grin that crinkled the edges of his eyes, so familiar and yet so uniquely his. I raised a hand in a small wave, and his gaze lingered just a beat longer before he turned back to the mic, finishing the final notes of the song with a flourish.

Watching him under the soft haze of the stage lights, a quiet pride swelled within me. Steven had always been talented, but tonight, something felt different. His presence radiated a thrill that rippled through the room, threading itself into every note, electrifying the air. For the first time in what felt like forever, I found myself enjoying the music, the pulse of nightlife—a piece of the world I'd shared with Heck and thought I had long buried. But it hadn't disappeared. That part of my life had only dimmed, burning quietly until tonight, when it flickered back to life.

Here, with Steven, it was alive again—within the songs pouring from the stage, seeping into the walls of this unassuming bar. A place that could have been just another venue took on new meaning, transforming into something more—a reminder of the beauty I'd once embraced and what still remained. And for the first time, being here didn't feel like a truce with my grief. It felt like reclaiming something fragile but beautiful—a spark of a life I once loved, with Heck, letting it guide me again.

I waited through two more songs, letting the music wash over me, before the first set drew to a close, signaling a much-needed thirty-minute break for the band.

When the last notes of the set hung briefly in the air and applause erupted, Steven hopped off the stage. He zigzagged through the pressing crowd, mostly women vying for his attention, until finally, he reached me. Without a word, he looped his arm around mine and led me toward a quieter corner.

"It's the first time I've seen you play with this setup," I said softly, nodding toward the stage that still seemed to hum with the echo of their performance.

"I hope I didn't disappoint," he replied with a lopsided grin, though his eyes tracked how my fingers fidgeted with the condensation on my beer bottle.

"Not at all," I said, smiling. "But why are you so far from the other guitarists? Is it because you do vocals, too?"

"Partly," he said, leaning back in his chair. "But mostly because I'm a lefty. If I stand too close to the others, their headstocks end up clashing with mine when they move. Trust me, it's happened too many times." He laughed, shaking his head.

"That actually makes sense," I said, grinning. "I've noticed before—guys like Kurt Cobain or Paul McCartney. Iconic lefties."

"Yep. Though McCartney's mostly known for bass, he's a pretty amazing left-handed guitarist too," Steven added, his tone easy and confident. "And then there's Tony Iommi," he said, his eyes lighting up like he'd just uncovered the holy grail. "The guitarist from Black Sabbath. The godfather of hard rock and heavy metal! The riffs, the power—he basically invented it all. Total legend." He leaned in, gesturing wildly before flashing me the devil horns. "Seriously, he's so underrated. But the people who know—oh, they KNOW. He's absolutely one of my favorites. No contest."

"Looks like you're in the right company," I teased with a laugh.

"I like to think so," he said, flashing a playful smile. "Though being a lefty can feel like a bit of a handicap sometimes. But hey, I've been at it long enough that I've learned to make it work."

"Well, it definitely sets you apart, and it does make for great conversation," I said, leaning in. "And, for the record, you look great up there on stage."

"That's a bonus," he replied, grinning again. "I just have to make sure I'm always on the 'right' side of the stage—literally and figuratively." He laughed, and the sound was infectious. That kind of laugh tugged at the corners of your mouth until you couldn't help but join in.

His beer arrived, and he gently tapped the bottle against mine. "Enjoy the night, Sara. The day doesn't end with the sunset. That's just the curtain call—the stars take the stage, and the moon watches quietly from the wings." His words were light, almost playful, yet there was a weight beneath them, something unspoken but understood.

I looked at Steven, his cerulean eyes catching the dim light, so heartbreakingly like Heck's, yet unmistakably his own. They held a softness, a quiet strength, as if they carried the weight of the same ghosts I did. For five years after Heck left us, Steven stayed. Not to step into Heck's place—that was never his intent. No one could. But this runaway prince, once lost in his self-imposed exile, had returned. Not to mend what was irreparable, but to stand at the edges of the void Heck left behind, unflinching. He stood among the wreckage of our lives, amidst the broken pieces of me, of Fifth, of Hector and Helen, not to fix what was shattered, but to walk through it with us. And in that quiet, unassuming way of his, he reminded me that we could still find strength, even in ruins.

We sat together in the cozy shadows of a dimly lit bar, the hum of life around us blurred into the faint echo of a melody. The music lingered in the air, fragile and tender, like the remnants of something beautiful that refused to fade completely. And in that fleeting stillness, I felt it— that thread, delicate yet unyielding, tying us together. Two people carrying different griefs, stitching them into the fragile beginnings of something new.

These moments, the ones we often overlook, weren't placeholders for what had been lost. They were the quiet seams holding the fabric of our lives together, binding pain with hope, memory with movement. They weren't perfect, but they didn't need to be. They were real.

Steven's hand brushed mine, tentative, like asking permission. I didn't pull away. Maybe healing wasn't about patching the holes left behind but learning to live with them, to build something softer around their edges. And even with the shadows of what we'd lost still lingering, I realized we were both still choosing to stay. To try. To be here.

In that soft, dim light, I allowed myself to exhale. Not everything could be repaired. Not everything had to be. But maybe, just maybe, life could still be whole, even with its cracks. And maybe, if we were lucky, we'd find something beautiful in what remained.

****

I Love You, Sunday Sunset

Oh, sweet Sunday sunset, love of mine,
A gentle whisper in the twilight's chime.
Your amber hues kiss the day goodbye,
As we bid adieu with a contented sigh.

You are the pause before the week's new song,
The quiet moment when shadows grow long.
A soft surrender to the night's embrace,
As Monday's promise begins its chase.

No more the echo of familial laughter,
Now anticipations of what comes after.
The nights, the days that are wholly ours,
Unseen, untouched by the sun's final hours.

We yearn for the freedom that darkness brings,
Underneath the moon and its silver wings.
For when Sunday's sun dips low and bows,
Begins a tale that the silent night allows.

Gone are the elders' watchful eyes,
In the cloak of night, our secret lies.
A world that spins for us alone,
A love as wild as the wind has blown.

So here we stand at the edge of light,
Hand in hand, ready for the night.
With every Sunday sunset, my heart takes flight,
To the promise of days bathed in our own delight.

So, I love you, Sunday sunset, end of the week,
You're the prelude to the adventure we seek
With you, the mundane quietly recedes,
And in its place, our own story proceeds.

Excerpts from **GNIGHT, SARA / 'NIGHT, HECK**
Copyright © 2024 Justine Castellon and Mike Dee

ACKNOWLEDGMENT

Writing this sequel was never part of the original plan. When Mike Dee and I created Gnight, Sara / 'Night, Heck, we envisioned it as a single, self-contained story. But as time passed, I realized that Sara's world still had so much more to offer—so many untold stories waiting to be shared. Unfortunately, Mike couldn't co-write this time, and without him, I couldn't tell Heck's story the way it truly deserved to be told. Heck was as much Mike's creation as he was mine, and no one could have done him greater justice. In this novel, you'll see a different Heck —not in Mike's voice, but through Sara's perspective. Thank you, Mike, for dreaming up Sara and Heck with me and for creating one of the most unforgettable characters I've ever had the privilege to write— and to read. Co-writing their story with you was an honor, and this book simply wouldn't exist without you.

My deepest gratitude goes to Frances Amper-Sales. You were my compass, my challenger, and my advocate, shaping every scene to resonate in the most meaningful way. I'll never forget your advice: "If you're going to write Heck out of this story, the next male lead has to be equally, if not more, compelling." That thought became my guiding light, pushing me to aim for something more than ordinary.

When the idea of creating a musician character emerged, I quickly realized how little I truly knew about their world. Authenticity has always been at the heart of my storytelling: I wanted this character to feel real. That was how Mike and I brought Sara and Heck to life, and I wanted to stay true to that approach. That's when fate introduced me to Kowboy Santos—a musician who grew up surrounded by music, raised by parents who were both legendary artists in the very city where my new character, Steven, lived. Kowboy is no ordinary musician; he's an exceptionally talented artist who not only writes music but also crafts dialogue and envisions story scenes. He even contributed some of Steven's dialogue and words, breathing life into the character.

Together, Kowboy and I brought Steven to life. He gave Steven a soul, a voice, mannerisms, and rhythm. More than that, Kowboy shattered my assumptions about musicians, revealing the depth and truth of their world. With patience and generosity, he shared his experiences, allowing me to observe his performances, feel the energy of his craft, and witness the raw beauty of music in motion. I watched stage lights illuminate his face as his guitar became an extension of his soul. He even fact-checked my research, ensuring that my portrayal was grounded in authenticity. Without Kowboy, there would be no Steven. This sequel simply wouldn't exist without his insight and support, and for that, I am forever grateful.

To my husband, Carlos Castellon—my partner in every way—thank you for standing by me through the countless hours I spent immersed in Sara's world. Your love and patience allowed me to pour my heart into this story. You remind me every day why I believe in love stories —because ours is one worth writing about.

And finally, to you, the readers—thank you for opening your hearts to this book and these characters. I hope this story made you laugh, cry, and believe in the power of love and resilience. Life has a way of moving forward, even in the darkest times. My greatest hope is that this book serves as a reminder of that. This story is for you.

With love and gratitude,

Justine

ABOUT THE AUTHOR:

Justine Castellon
A brand strategist and corporate spindoctor with an inherent talent for crafting captivating narratives. Her professional insights blend seamlessly with her passion for literature. She authored and published three novels: **Four Seasons**, **The Last Snowfall**, and **Gnight, Sara / 'Night, Heck**.

Fall in love with these 3 charming romance stories from Justine Castellon

❧ FOUR SEASONS
A struggling New York writer's dreams come true when a chance encounter with a Hollywood star shoots her into a glittering world of romance and fame. But, as love and illusions shatter, she must rebuild her life and rediscover her own voice in the aftermath of heartbreak.

❄ THE LAST SNOWFALL
A writer-turned-heiress marries a British Hollywood star, only to be swept into a high-stakes world of love, betrayal, and buried secrets. As ghosts from the past threaten her marriage and power struggles consume her father's empire, she must confront the ultimate question: how far will she go to protect the life she's built, and at what cost?

☾ GNIGHT SARA/'NIGHT HECK
In a bustling New York City café, amidst the noise and chaos, two souls, a young copywriter and a reluctant heir, find a unique sanctuary. This romantic drama delves deep into the complexities of friendship, self-discovery, and the choices that define our lives.

www.justcastellon.com